about the author

Ann S. Epstein writes novels, short stories, and memoir. She is the author of *A Brain. A Heart. The Nerve.* and her stories appear in *Sewanee Review, PRISM International, The Long Story, Passages North, Red Rock Review, William and Mary Review, Tahoma Literary Review, The Copperfield Review, The Normal School, Carbon Culture, The Offbeat*, and other journals. She also has a Ph.D. in developmental psychology and M.F.A. in textiles. Her historical works often mix fact and fiction, and she is gratified to have forgotten what is and is not real by the time a story is finished.

To learn more about her work, visit her website:
asewovenwords.com

On the Shore
Copyright © 2017 Ann S. Epstein
All rights reserved.

Print Edition
ISBN: 978-1-925417-32-6
Published by Vine Leaves Press 2017
Melbourne, Victoria, Australia

This is a work of fiction. Any similarity between the characters and situations within its pages and places or persons, living or dead, is unintentional and coincidental.

Cover design by Jessica Bell
Interior design by Amie McCracken

National Library of Australia Cataloguing-in-Publication entry (pbk)
Author: Epstein, Ann S., author
Title: On the shore / Ann S. Epstein.
ISBN: 9781925417326 (paperback)
Subjects: Historical fiction.
Immigrants-Fiction.
Jewish families-Fiction.
War and families-Fiction.
Dewey Number: 823.92

On the Shore

Ann S. Epstein

Vine Leaves Press
Melbourne, Vic, Australia

To the courageous immigrants of every generation who cross land and sea to begin a new life for themselves and their children. I am indebted to all my grandparents and my father for making the arduous journey from Eastern Europe to America over a century ago.

part one

Shmuel, 1917

chapter 1

In the bright sky above the sooty bricks of the Navy recruiting station, Shmuel Levinson sought God's forgiveness for violating the commandment against lying. Falsifying his age would mean giving a fake name too. There would be no way to notify his parents if he were hurt, captured, or killed. So be it. He'd take that risk to win the Great War for America, which had welcomed his poor family to its shores fourteen years ago. Gratitude to this country, along with a desire to prove his manhood, drove Shmuel's decision. Also, if he let himself admit it, a desperate need to escape his father.

No celestial message of absolution appeared overhead however, only wispy clouds as insubstantial as Shmuel himself. The knish he'd eaten an hour ago to boost his weight churned in his guts like a spinning torpedo. Every man entering the grimy doors ahead of him looked twice his size, half again his age. He willed his stomach to be quiet and followed them inside.

The recruiter's name badge, on a chest wide enough to strain his starched regulation shirt, identified him as Lt. Giordano. "Name," he barked.

"Sam Lew... Lord. Sam Lord."

"Age?"

"Eighteen." Shmuel expanded his chest to make his voice sound as deep as the cantor's at the Eldridge Street Synagogue, but it cracked on the second syllable.

The lieutenant looked up at Shmuel's curly side locks, making him conscious of the pale orange fuzz dotting his chin too. His Adam's apple bobbed with every swallow.

"You gotta be twenty-one to enlist," Giordano said.

Shmuel pointed to the slogan on the poster above their heads. "Join the Navy. The Service for Training and Travel. Ages 17 to 35." The first time he'd seen it, in the window of United Drugs, he fretted he'd have to wait a year and the war might be over. That's when he got the idea of lying about his age. After all, the Babylonian Talmud permitted lying in the cause of peace, and this war was being fought to secure a peaceful world. He decided to add an extra year to his age to be safe. Eighteen, the word "chai" in Hebrew, also meant "life," and he wanted to show he was ready to give his in this noble fight.

"It's older for Jew boys. Their mamas won't let 'em enlist until they're twenty-one."

Sam forced a scowl. "Then I'm twenty-one."

Giordano turned to the red-headed recruiter, Cdr. Kelly, at the next table. "Hey Mick, Mr. Samson Lou Lord Almighty here says he's full grown."

"What do you care, Dago Wop? Jew boy wants to die for America, sign him up."

The lieutenant swivelled back to Shmuel. "You know how to change your own diaper?"

Shmuel tried to match his sneer. The best he could manage was a twitch in his left cheek.

Giordano handed him the completed form. "Follow the blue line down the hall so a doc can check your balls."

Shmuel had planned to call himself "Sam Lewis." Lewis was the last name his mother wanted to take when she and his father arrived at Ellis Island carrying him and two suitcases held together with twine. His father refused, telling the immigration official it was Levinson, and so their family name from Lemberg, Austria followed them across the ocean.

Shmuel hoped calling himself "Lord" didn't desecrate God, but it gave him a twinge of triumph to defy his father, an unhappy man who wanted to live through his son. Avram was a frustrated scholar, limited by poverty and his own rigidity. America would give his child a chance to become what he couldn't. Shmuel didn't know what he wanted for himself, but he knew that he didn't want to become his father. America was his land of opportunity now, and Shmuel would join the fight to safeguard that it stayed that way until his own dreams took shape.

Shmuel proceeded to a cavernous white-tiled room where men stood naked, clothes tied in makeshift bundles, waiting for the next medical examiner. Briefly, he envied their uncircumcised penises, wishing he had a foreskin to lengthen his. The sacrilegious thought mortified him. It was not worthy of someone versed in Talmud, of someone whose father dreamed his son would become a rabbi. Ashamed, he tucked the fringes of his prayer shawl, together with his undergarments, inside his rolled-up clothes. The knotted tzitzit from his tallit still protruded but there was no time to shove in the telltale fringes before a weary doctor ran a cold stethoscope over his narrow, hairless chest. Shmuel coughed to suppress a giggle. The doctor frowned and listened to his lungs again.

"I'm ticklish," he said, humiliated, but not wanting the doctor to think his cough was a sign of tuberculosis, which would disqualify him from serving.

The doctor snickered, then tapped the box where Shmuel's age was written on the form. "Sure you know what you're doing Sam? Rotting in the trenches isn't like being tickled."

Shmuel nodded. He'd heard that the water- and mud-soaked trenches were worse than the filthiest tenements on the Lower East Side, where he lived. His thigh muscles clenched when his testicles were palpated and he prayed not to have an erection. Those around him squirmed in pain. Shmuel wondered if the doctor was going easy on him, thinking he was still a child. Relief and resentment mixed. How could he show he was a man if those in authority underestimated him?

"Not many Jews in the Navy." The doctor shone a light in Shmuel's eyes. "Your people join the merchant marine where you can make a profit shipping supplies to the troops overseas."

Shmuel bit his tongue. He didn't want to challenge the doctor, but why did people assume that all Jews cared about was making money? Calmly he said, "I aim to be a gunner or fireman on a destroyer. Someone has to protect the merchant convoys from German subs."

The doctor shook his head. "I can't picture Jews on battleships. You're a land people."

Shmuel knew, to the contrary, that Ancient Hebrews were seafarers. In Genesis, when Jacob blessed his sons, he said, "Zebulun shall dwell on the shore of the sea." Once more, he resisted the temptation to correct the doctor, as his father would have done. It was foolish to act arrogant toward a man deciding his fate. Instead he quoted the Navy poster that had first lured him with the idea of replacing Torah study with adventure: "Don't read about history. Make it."

"Open your mouth. Good. Now close. Do you go around the city memorizing posters?"

Shmuel stared with dismay at the blush spreading down his body. New posters appeared weekly in the window at United Drugs, where the Shipping Board had deputized store managers to recruit half a million men. Shmuel and his friends, Yaakov and Bernie, went there for root beer on Wednesday afternoons after religious school. His father disapproved of any time that Shmuel didn't spend studying at cheder, but his mother said he deserved a break, and snuck him pennies she saved from the grocery money.

"Oh, you'll travel," the doctor sneered, "seeing the ocean before you're cut in half by a torpedo. You know twenty-five Allied vessels are sunk for every German U-boat we take down?"

"Our ships have depth chargers now," Shmuel said. "We'll destroy their subs before they can fire a shot at us."

"I've heard that kind of bravado before. You smart kids think you're invulnerable. It's the ignorant ones who have the good sense to be afraid of dying." The doctor peered inside Shmuel's ears. "Unlike us, Germans give their submarines numbers, not names. Keeps things impersonal. You're going up against the most efficient and brutal fighting machine in the world."

Shmuel remained quiet, but testing himself against a formidable enemy was precisely what appealed to him. He was tired of using his brains to please his father, and being tormented for them by his classmates. The Italian and Irish boys who planned to join up after graduation called him a Hymie coward. "Kosher chicken, turkey, quail. Kraut just sneezes, kike turns tail," they taunted, doubtful he'd betray his birth land to fight for America. His mother was right to want to change their last name. They should have taken English first names too, but in their cramped third-floor walk-up on Mott Street, they remained Avram and his wife Rivka, and Shmuel and his younger sister Dev, short for Devorah, the only Levinson born in this country. As American as she strove to be, she nevertheless liked her Hebrew name. Two months ago, when she turned twelve, she'd happily confided in Shmuel that her nickname made her sound, "like a little devil."

Shmuel could have Americanized his name to Samuel when he started school, but at age five he was too young to think of going against his father, a man he both admired and feared for his unyielding beliefs. By the time he regretted missing his chance, it was too late. Being called Sam, a plain English name, might have squelched the teasing and made him less self-conscious of the strawberry birthmark that ran from behind his right ear to just below his hairline. When he was old enough to grow payess, he wore the side locks to cover it, despite their being an Orthodox tradition even his father didn't follow. That thin red welt was why he'd enlisted in the Navy rather than the Army. Sailors could wear their hair as long as civilians; soldiers had to shave their heads.

The doctor checked Shmuel's scalp for lice. He traced the birthmark but said nothing. "You might have to cut these off." He twisted the silky blond payess around his fingers.

At sea, with his hair grown coarse and below his earlobes, Shmuel wouldn't need them.

"Last chance to change your mind." The doctor put down his examining tools and picked up the form. "I can't prove you lied about your age, but I don't need proof other than my say-so to reject you for a medical reason. All I have to do is check one of the disqualification boxes."

Shmuel hesitated. He looked at the hairy arms and muscular thighs of the men around him who were putting their clothes back on. He got dressed too, tucking the fringes of his tallit into his waistband instead of letting them hang visibly below his coat. "I'm ready," he said.

The doctor shrugged and signed the application. "I hope your God is a better saviour than mine. Report for duty Friday. The buses will take you to the Training School in East Boston."

Shmuel went back outside, trembling in the chilly November air. Perhaps he should have taken the name Zebulun, Zeb for short. Like his forebears, he was now one of the seafaring members of his tribe.

chapter 2

Shmuel was still shivering when he climbed the warped stairs and opened the unpainted door to his family's apartment. He told himself it was the nasty weather, not fear or a change of heart, causing him to shake like an unprepared student who sees the rabbi turn toward him with the next question. Rivka, saying he didn't look well, put her hand on his forehead, but Shmuel brushed it off. "I'm not a baby anymore."

"To a mother, her children are always her babies." Rivka smiled and walked back across the cracked linoleum floor to the stove.

"It's cold out, that's all." To prove it in the only way she'd believe, Shmuel said he was hungry and peeked under the lid of the pot simmering on the back burner. Inside was their typical Tuesday leftover supper, the carcass from the Shabbas chicken, picked clean and boiled with egg noodles, potatoes, and onions. It seemed the smell of onions emanated from every apartment, seeping into and out of the building's stained walls. He sighed, wondering if sailors ate better. The Navy's food budget must be a million times bigger than the Levinsons'.

Dev sat at the scarred pine table doing homework. Shmuel looked over her shoulder, ready to admire his sister's diagram of the digestive system. "Mama's right," Dev said, covering the page with a dishrag. "You look ready to upchuck your kishkas and you better not do it on my drawing!"

"What if I did? It's not up to your usual standards. The intestines are wound too tight."

Dev snapped back. "Flibberty, jibberty. What's eating you?"

"Nothing, but I need something to eat and Papa won't be home for another half hour."

"I can make you a bowl of borsht," Rivka offered, reaching out her hand again before pulling it back and tucking it into her apron pocket.

"How about fried wasps? Crispy snake skin? Pickled pigs ears?" His sister grinned.

"Don't be disgusting." The very thought made Shmuel feel like throwing up for real.

Rivka wore a look of horror on her face. "Shush, Dev. People don't eat those things."

"Yes they do. I saw them in a store window on Pell Street."

"What were you doing in Chinatown?" Shmuel said.

Dev giggled. "I tricked Leah into going there after school today." Shmuel raised his eyebrows. His sister's best friend was her exact opposite. Dev loved going where she didn't belong; Leah never stepped out of line, unless lured there by Dev.

"I told her I needed to copy Chinese characters for my art class. We're practicing with ink pens." She lifted the dishrag. "See, I'm using one for my biology illustration."

"I can't believe Leah went along. She's doesn't even like to look at pictures of trayf!"

"Well, to be on the up and up," Dev admitted, "she dusted out after a minute, before I even pretended to copy the letters. She said just standing outside the store was too malodorous."

"Leah actually used that word?" Rivka asked.

"No, but it's a good one, don't you think? It means stinky. Or you could say something smells noxious, odious to the olfactory system, fetid, or frowsty. That last one is British."

Shmuel smiled. Dev's obsession with words drove most people crazy. He found it lovable, except when she showed off. Then she was irritating in the way only a younger sister could be. Rivka went out of her way to ask Dev questions. Shmuel suspected she did it to encourage his sister to use her brains. Avram, on the other hand, pointedly ignored her, which only made Dev work harder for his attention, even if it entailed using doubtful slang expressions she'd picked up from the racier kids at school. Half the time Shmuel suspected Dev didn't know what they meant, and occasionally neither did he. If Avram sniffed even a hint of impropriety, he ordered Dev to be quiet and help Rivka in the kitchen. Then their mother would play peacemaker and ask Dev to teach her the new word while they washed the dishes. Avram would grunt and wait impatiently for the women to clear the table so he and Shmuel could talk Torah, man to man.

As if beckoned by Shmuel's thoughts, Avram walked in. Despite the chill, he looked like he'd stepped out of a steam bath. In a sense he had, after bending over a pressing machine at the dress factory for twelve hours. The heat had untwisted the fringes of his tallit, rendering them as wilted and lifeless as his thinning hair. The sight made Shmuel wonder how he would hide his strawberry mark when he got older and lost his hair too. Maybe he wouldn't live that long.

Side by side, Shmuel and Avram washed their hands in the enamelled basin and Avram said the blessings as Rivka and Dev dished out the food. Shmuel barely had time to slurp a spoonful before his father began the nightly ritual of quizzing him on what he'd studied at cheder that day. Since Shmuel had skipped religious school to go to the recruiting station, he had to think quickly to fake it. Fortunately, the class was reading Genesis, whose familiar stories were less fraught to discuss with his father than later books of the Torah with their nitpicking laws. "We read the passage where Laban, Rebecca's older brother, tries to dissuade her from leaving home to marry Isaac. The rebbe asked us why Laban wanted his sister to wait ten days before deciding whether to go." Too late, Shmuel realized that biblical conflict was uncomfortably close to the ongoing rivalry between Gershon, his mother's big brother, and his father. Onkel Gershon hadn't wanted Shmuel's mother to marry his father either.

"And what did you say?" Avram looked directly at Shmuel, sitting on his right, but Shmuel glanced at his mother, sitting on his left, before returning his father's piercing gaze.

"I said one interpretation is that Laban was being protective. Rebecca was young. She was being asked to travel to a strange land, far away, and to marry a man she'd never seen before. In all likelihood, she would never see her own family again."

Avram objected. "The servant who came to fetch Rebecca brought jewels and other presents. Laban was simply trying to extort more gifts before letting his sister go." At last he began to eat in earnest, spooning soup with a steady hand, as though the matter were settled.

"You could see it that way." Shmuel spoke hesitantly.

"Could?" Avram put down his spoon. "No. Torah makes it clear in later chapters that Laban is deceitful. He cheats Jacob again and again, tricking him into marrying Leah, making him work an extra seven years to marry Rachel, and then stealing Jacob's livestock."

Shmuel bowed his head to his own bowl. He was no longer hungry, but let his father take it as a gesture of acquiescence. An hour ago, he'd have welcomed the hot soup to get rid of his chills. Now, the argument with Avram had inflamed his desire to leave. Joining the Navy was not only a means of fleeing his father's expectations, but also a way to trade the petty squabbles at home for the real war overseas. He chafed at Avram's assumption that he'd take his side against Gershon. His father and uncle fought more than he and Dev had as children. Shmuel knew Rivka tried not to put him in the middle, but he feared their lifelong rivalry would shorten hers.

The Navy should make a new poster, he thought. "Join a family united in its mission." It sounded good, although surely even military families fought. Suppose the Navy fuelled rivalries more intense than Avram's and Gershon's, ones that risked men's lives? His decision was made, but when supper ended, Shmuel's intestines felt as tight as those he'd accused Dev of drawing.

part two

Dev, 1917

chapter 3

When I showed her the stain on my underpants, my mother slapped me hard across the cheek. "To make the blood flow," she said, before hugging me and exclaiming, "Mazel tov!"

I was ready to mash her mush, or mush her mash. I'd have to ask my big brother Shmuel what the expression was. He didn't use slang, but he corrected mine so I wouldn't make a ninny of myself, which I did a lot. Or embarrass him in front of his loud-mouth friend Yaakov or Bernie, the quiet, cute one. It was wrong to think nasty thoughts about Mama, but I didn't ask to get my period. I cringed when she and Tante Yetta whispered about their monthlies like it was some cabalistic mystery. Besides, her excuse for hitting me was applesauce, a minhag, a silly old Jewish custom. Mama knew better. She was a hip lady who marched for women's suffrage.

I tried to look aggrieved so she'd feel bad about hitting me. Aggrieved was my newest adjective. Mrs. O'Brien, my English teacher, gave the ten smartest kids in our class a hard word to learn every week. I lapped them up like a well-behaved puppy gobbling treats. When Mama just ignored my sorrowful expression, however, I followed her to the laundry hamper by the back door leading down to the stinky, wet basement and out to the alleyway with the clotheslines we shared with our neighbours. Tante Yetta washed out cloth pads because she and Onkel Gershon had a private bathroom to hang them, but my mother kept a box of disposable Lister's Towels at the bottom of the dirty clothes hamper, where my father and brother wouldn't see them. She showed me how to tuck the towel inside my underpants and fold the used ones before dropping them down the incinerator. Now I understood why women put money in a special box on the counter at United's. The druggist knew what the women wanted so neither he nor they were embarrassed by their asking aloud, and he gave them a parcel covered in plain brown paper, which they slipped into their shopping bags unobtrusively. That was another Mrs. O'Brien word.

If I were pale and slender, like Mama, I could be unobtrusive too. My brother took after her. Sometimes I snuck a peek at her red-blonde curls, which were chopped off after she married back in Lemberg, in accordance with Jewish tradition. There she'd wrapped them in a linen cloth and worn a simple brown wig. After they got to America though, she let her hair grow out again. It's not as shiny as when she was younger, but the colour still makes you think of the country, not the shtetl. My father gently pulls her head onto his shoulder and strokes it when he thinks Shmuel and I aren't watching. Wearing a wig is the only old-world practice he's happy she gave up.

I did get my mother's curls, but otherwise I'm dark and solid like Papa. Not fat and jiggly like my best friend Leah's bubbe, but muscular. I can hit a baseball as good as any boy and I hide my broomstick bat behind the Pesach dishes in the basement storage bin. I'd be mortified if Papa found out. Mama wouldn't mind, but I want the satisfaction of having my own secret.

Despite my mother's thrill over my becoming a woman, the slap made me feel as if I'd done something bad. It nagged at me, like last year when I asked to help light the Shabbas candles and my father said it was a sacrilege for a little girl to play at such a holy task. I'd tried to sound sincere, but it was like he saw through me and knew I was trying to ingratiate myself with him instead of honouring God. Mama let me strike matches to light the stove, but I wanted the power to make the candles flare, drawing Papa's eyes to my hands and his ears to my prayers.

I wondered if Onkel Gershon let my cousins bench licht. Zipporah was six years older than me, and Ruchel four, same as Shmuel. They'd been having periods a long time and could no longer visit the men's side of the synagogue, a line I'd now be forbidden from crossing too. That wouldn't be so bad, if it meant I could sit with Ruchel more often. I liked watching her roll her eyes when Reb Stern told women to leave services early and prepare their homes to receive the men. "You're like Miriam," the rabbi once said, "first to cross the Red Sea and preserver of the rituals that will continue to bind our people together." To which Ruchel had muttered, "Miriam dies unmourned in the desert and Moses gets all the credit for leading us to the Promised Land." Tante

Yetta had whispered "Shah, Ruchel!" but Mama barely nudged me when I giggled.

The girls at school were expected to keep the boys in line too. None of them had begun to menstruate yet, even those with breasts. I wished I hadn't started so I wouldn't have to act like a grown up. Perhaps the true meaning behind Mama's slap was a warning not to disgrace our family, like those skatey Catholic girls who got pregnant and had to get married. My cheek burned. Mama didn't know me if she thought I'd commit such a shanda. Or maybe she did.

"Hurry and set the table," my mother said, "we're running late." It was less than an hour before sundown, and my father and brother would soon be home from shul for Shabbas dinner. I spread out the linen cloth my mother had cross-stitched before her wedding, back in the old country. The cloth hid the ugly pine boards and made our table look as beautiful as the mahogany one in Tante Yetta's dining room. I put Papa's kiddush cup in front of his chair, at the head of the table. The silver goblet was the only orchid in our house. Orchid is the perfect slang word for something expensive.

Onkel Gershon and Tante Yetta's apartment was full of orchids, because when my uncle arrived in America, he studied at night to become an accountant. He made enough money to sponsor my parents to come here too. Shmuel was just a baby then. My uncle is a big macher in the synagogue and even among the Jews who don't belong to our congregation. People respect him and ask him for help, but I'm not sure they like him. He can be bossy. I don't know if you have to be that kind of person to become a macher, or if having power makes you act that way. My father tries to order my mother around, but not as much as Onkel Gershon tells Tante Yetta and my cousins what to do. I wish I were rich like them, but I wouldn't want to be in their family.

Actually there is one other orchid in our house, but I'm not supposed to know about it. It's a pair of silver candlesticks in a velvet-lined box. I discovered them hidden beneath my mother's braids when I was snooping in the bedroom closet. I wanted to ask about them but for once I kept my mouth shut. My mother didn't mind my seeing her old hair, but my precocious woman's intuition told me she wouldn't want to reveal the story behind those candlesticks.

My mother's seat at the table was opposite my father's, close to the stove. I sat on my father's left, near the sink, so I could clear the dishes while my mother served the next course. Shmuel's chair was on Papa's right, where he could put his hand on my brother's head to give him the traditional Shabbas blessing before we began the meal. Leah's father blessed all his children. My friend Leah deserved it because she was good, or maybe she was good because he blessed her. I wanted my father's blessing too, but he saved the special Hebrew words for his son. I had to be satisfied with the English words Mrs. O'Brien gave me and nine other kids.

"Slice the mandelbrot before it cools down," my mother said. She'd taken the dough out of the oven just before I showed her my under-pants and it was already getting too hard to cut into the diagonal cookies we dipped in our tea. Mama didn't mind baking her heav-enly honey-nut cake, and she agreed with Papa that homemade babka tasted better than bakery bought, but I saw her annoyed scowl when he insisted she bake her own cookies too. There were perfectly good ones at the grocery store. She didn't go against him, though. My father's sole concession was allowing her to buy sandwich crèmes for Shmuel and me to pack in our lunch boxes. Of course, they had to be Hydrox, not Oreos, which were made with lard.

I ate an Oreo once, three years ago, in fourth grade, when I traded a Hydrox for Bridget Mahoney's Oreo. The chocolate part was softer and it got quaggy if you dunked it in milk too long, but the filling was sweeter. I pronounced the Oreo too utterly too too.

"Gottenyu! You're eating trayf!" Leah worried God would strike me down. She wanted to grab the forbidden cookie out of my hand, but she was too afraid to even touch it.

"I'm fine, Little Miss Goody Two Shoes." I turned three pirouettes to prove it. Then I made a deal with Bridget to swap a cookie a day. A couple of hours later though, my stomach was queasy. I never knew if it was the lard or fear of God's punishment that made me sick, but I cancelled the deal. Leah was too nice to give me an I-told-you-so look.

My curiosity about forbidden foods wasn't dampened, however. Not long ago, Leah and I looked in a store window on Doyers Street, in Chinatown, filled with crabs and snakes and tiny birds on skewers with pearly eyes. When I told her, "Chinese people don't die from eating those things," she said, "They're not Jewish." I couldn't dispute her reasoning, and I admitted they looked disgusting. Still, I thought it might be okay to taste one as long as I didn't swallow it.

There are other American foods I would fully ingest in a heartbeat, like Jell-O. It's even kosher, because the meat gets boiled out of the gelatin. Too bad Papa doesn't trust it. Even Mama gags at anything that merely looks like it's trayf. So, if I want permission to be adventurous, I have to do it in ways that don't involve food. That's why a year ago I began campaigning to bob my hair. I picked up the argument with my mother that night while I set the table. "Even you said my hair looks like a rat's nest. If it was short, the curls wouldn't get as tangled."

"You forgot the knife for the challah." Mama took the braided loaf out of the oven and set it beside my father's kiddush cup.

"Ersatz." I pointed at the knife's pearl handle. Mama looked blank. "It's not a real orchid."

Her pale skin reddened and she slammed the knife on the table. "You have real, beautiful hair. Dark and thick like Papa's mother's, may she rest in peace."

"Irene Castle wears her hair in a bob."

"She's one of us?" My mother, like other Jews, had to identify our people. It was partly to take pride if someone had done well, and partly to prepare for the backlash if they'd done wrong.

"She's an actress and a dancer. She doesn't want her hair in her face when she spins."

"You're going to be a biologist, not an entertainer. You'll wind your hair in a neat bun when it's time to look under a microscope."

I was sorry I'd told Mama about my dream to be a scientist, and hoped she hadn't spilled the beans to Papa. She was excited about my having a career, but all he wanted was for me to get married and have children. "For your information," I announced, "Irene Castle was born in this country. May I remind you that I was too!"

"Nu?" Mama's hands rested on her hips.

"You always tell Papa we should be more American. Yet whenever I try, you stop me."

She sighed. "I went against tradition to grow my hair. Now you want to cut yours off. You can do what you want when you're old enough, but until then you'll listen to your parents."

"I could cut it off right now with a pair of scissors. Or a knife with a fake handle." I stopped, afraid I'd gone too far.

Instead of getting angry, Mama pointed to the clock and smiled. "Sorry, mamele. It's past sundown and there's no cutting allowed on Shabbas."

"Then I'll cut it on Sunday. And throw away the curls. I won't save mine like you did."

My mother ran a hand down her freshly washed hair. Leah's bubbe said it was a mitzvah for husbands and wives to make love on Friday night. My mother turned off the stove, leaving a low flame under the cholent. The sweet potato and vegetable stew would bubble until sundown the next evening, giving us something hot to eat when Shabbas ended. "Your father and brother will be home any minute. Let's have sholem bayess, peace in the house, on this day of rest."

chapter 4

"Is Shmuel here?" Papa, his beard still matted from sweating over a pressing machine at the dress factory, didn't say hello to me or give my mother the customary Shabbas kiss.

My mother held the lid of the soup pot in mid-air. "He wasn't with you in shul?"

My father brushed past her to the sink and turned on the rusty faucets full force. He performed the evening's ceremonial hand-washing, only instead of gently pouring the water over his palms, he hurriedly splashed them and snatched the towel out of my mother's hands. Still agitated, he swiped the black kippot from his head and took from her the white one, embroidered in blue silk. Through the bedroom door, I saw him change from the tzitzit he wore under his shirt to the matching white and blue tallit, which he wore over it in honour of Shabbas. Unlike Shmuel, Papa didn't wear payess, but he was meticulous about his ritual garments. Mama washed and ironed them on Thursday night. I think she enjoyed the peace that enveloped Papa when he put them on as much as he did.

Tonight, however, he twisted and churned beneath them. "It's a shanda! The only reason a future rabbi is permitted to miss services is on account of a grave medical emergency."

"Were Yaakov and Bernie there? Dev, run and ask if they know where Shmuel is."

"No! It's after sundown," my father said. "We don't interrupt another family's Shabbas meal to ask after a boy who's too forgetful or sinful, God forbid, to honour the commandments."

A flush spread across Mama's cheeks. "He could be hurt or lying sick somewhere. I knew he didn't look well earlier this week." Knowing my mother, I figured she was imagining the worst.

"Maybe he got locked inside cheder," I said. My brother was studying to go to yeshiva and sometimes stayed late at religious school. "You know how addlebrained Reb Stern can be."

"This matter is not your concern, Dev." My father sat down at the table. "Addlebrained? Where does she get these words?" He frowned at my mother, who remained standing.

"Can't we wait a minute? Maybe Shmuel's on his way, God willing, all in one piece and with a good reason." My mother wrung the towel she'd given my father to dry his hands.

Papa jabbed his finger at her chair, then mine. I sat down right away but she went into the bedroom. When he followed and closed the door behind them, I ran to the window, hoping to see Shmuel hurrying down the block. All I saw was Mr. Geary stumbling out of Paddy's, where the electric sign flashed "Pure lager, beer, ales, and porter." Every Friday, while Jews celebrated the arrival of the Shabbas bride, our Catholic neighbours sat in the saloon drinking.

I wondered if Shmuel really could be sick someplace. He'd been acting strange lately. We used to whisper well into the night after our parents went to bed. I slept on the foldout couch and he spread a pallet next to the stove, which he fed during the winter to keep the apartment warm. He never failed to ask about Mrs. O'Brien's special words, but a few days ago he just crawled under his blankets and turned away from me. I had to start the conversation myself.

"How's tricks?" I asked, showing off my latest lingo.

Shmuel pretended to snore.

"Guess what today's word was."

"I'm sure I'll hear you use it eventually."

"Contrarian. Do you know what it means?"

"Yes."

"Why are you being it?"

"I'm tired, Dev. We did two study sessions on the Mishnah today and my brain has no room for English vocabulary."

"You're being chiselly!" That was another new slang word. A fast eighth-grade boy had said it to Bridget when she refused to smile at him. I was betting that my brother hadn't heard it before. "It means unpleasant or disagreeable."

Shmuel sat up and flicked his right payess over his shoulder, a gesture that meant I was annoying him. Now we were getting somewhere.

"Want to know what I did today? I made Leah hide with me behind St. Anne's until a nun brought out the garbage. Then I scooped out a wad of bacon grease. I heard that if you smear it on roller skates, they go faster."

"If Papa ever found out ..."

"I didn't eat it, ignoramus. It was a justifiable experiment in search of a scientific truth." Again my brother didn't ask. So I told him. "You should have seen me flying down Delancey. I almost knocked over the potatoes outside Kestlebaum's produce stand. It was out of sight!"

"Stop acting like a lunachick, Dev. Don't you know there's a war going on?" My brother lay back down, rolled over, and soon he was snoring for real.

After staring at the empty street for a couple of minutes, I tiptoed across the kitchen and put my ear against the bedroom door. My father had stopped ranting about Shmuel and my mother was murmuring. I couldn't hear what she was saying, but Papa chuckled and then they were quiet. I pictured my father giving my mother the kiss he'd failed to deliver when he got home.

Before they came out, I laid a patch to the stove and pretended I'd been stirring the soup the whole time. Papa looked at me funny. Quizzically was a good word to describe it. The three of us took our places at the table. My mother, preparing to light the candles, draped a scarf over her head, then took it off, looked to my father for approval, and offered it to me. I put it on, lit the candles, circled my hands three times over the flames, and covered my eyes before reciting the brucha. My father nodded at me, raised his cup of wine to make kiddush and then said motzie over the challah.

It was time for the blessing. Shmuel's empty chair sat there like a child's missing tooth. My father stretched his right hand across his chest and placed it on the dark curls I inherited from his family. I bowed my head, but the words he said, while ancient, were not those given to Shmuel each week. He was told he would have strength of character and be a leader highly regarded by our people. I was told, "Now you are a woman like Sarah, Rivka, Ruchel, and Leah. Marry well and may your children be as numerous as the stars in the heavens and the sands on the shore."

So that's what my mother had said to divert his rage from my brother. I was embarrassed and angry, yet my father's words were sweeter than wine. I wondered if getting my period would have been enough to earn his attention, or if he'd blessed me only because Shmuel wasn't there. Maybe becoming a woman wasn't so bad. For a moment, I was glad my brother was missing.

"Dear God," I silently prayed, "forgive me for not worrying about Shmuel, but is it sinful to want the same blessing our ancient forefather, the first Avram, passed down from You?"

I swallowed a spoonful of the steaming chicken soup as though tasting something new and strange. The golden liquid satisfied a multitude of hungers. How could I ever think I needed more?

chapter 5

All night I lay on the couch listening for Shmuel. I went to the bathroom six times to check my pad, but there wasn't much blood. My mother had warned me that if any got on my underpants I should wash them right away before the stain set. I forgot to ask her where to hang them. If they were on the line with the rest of the laundry, they wouldn't draw attention, but one pair flapping in the wind would be an utter mortification. My mother never had to hang a lone pair of drawers for all to see. I'd have to be vigilant about changing my pad too, but I couldn't be wasteful either. I never thought of us as poor, but I was willing to bet Tante Yetta's cloth pads were made of silk.

The sun still wasn't up when my parents came into the kitchen. I closed my eyes.

My mother's voice dropped to a whisper. "If not the police, let's at least go to one of his friends."

"We do nothing until Shabbas is over," Papa said.

"Not so loud, Avram. Dev is still asleep."

"We should be too. And Shmuel as well, next to the stove." My father threw in a piece of wood, although the room was already too warm, then groaned when he realized what he'd done. It was Shmuel's job to load in a big pile before sundown on Friday because you're not allowed to lift, only stir, on Shabbas. The laws about what the rabbis consider work can sound silly, but Papa is scrupulous about obeying them. He sank into a chair and buried his head in his hands.

"God will forgive you." My mother touched his shoulder gently. "It's an emergency. At such times, we're permitted to make exceptions."

"This is an emergency of Shmuel's own making, not an act of God."

"You don't know that. Please, Avram, let's ask for help. Or at least for information."

"I will not commit another sin on account of our son's transgression."

"Then say something to my brother at shul this morning. Gershon knows people who can help find out where Shmuel is." I hated the pleading in my mother's voice. If it weren't for the rule about men and women sitting separately, she could have asked Onkel Gershon herself.

"Today is for talking to God, not to relatives and friends." Papa didn't need Shabbas as an excuse not to talk to his brother-in-law. He was ashamed that Gershon was more successful than him. Shame made my father envious, envy made him feel guilty, guilt made him angry. At least, that was my theory. When I shared it with Shmuel, he said I was very sophisticated for my age. It made me proud. Later, when I learned the word "astute," I decided I was that too. I wished I knew the words to say to make my father and uncle get along, but I wasn't astute enough for that.

"As long as I'm up, I'll go to shul early and start praying. Maybe God will tell me where our son is. I'll see you and Dev after services." My father spread honey on a slice of cold challah and shrugged into his coat. "And Rivka, don't wear that skirt again this week. It's immodest."

My mother stared at the door after he left. For a radical thinker, she was a conservative dresser. She wouldn't even show a bit of ankle like other women. Recently, however, she'd bought a skirt with a zippered waist, claiming it was easier to put on, but Papa said opening and closing zippers was work and thus verboten on Shabbas. I doubt the ancient rabbis decreed that. There weren't any zippers three thousand years ago. If I were her, I'd have worn the skirt to defy him. When I grew breasts, I vowed, I wouldn't even wear a corset. That showdown might happen soon, now that I'd become a woman. I hoped I'd be braver than my mother. She was more likely to go behind my father's back than stand up to him face to face.

I decided to start with a small act that would upset my father—if he noticed. "I can't go to shul," I told my mother. "I have bad cramps." I bent over and grimaced for effect.

She smiled and massaged my stomach. "God makes exceptions in matters of health." She showed me how to make cramp bark tea and put the kettle on a back burner next to the cholent. "Sometimes God demands more of women than men, but He also allows us greater latitude."

That was a new word and it came from Mama, not Mrs. O'Brien. I wouldn't give her the satisfaction of hearing me use it, but I was eager to try it with Shmuel, whenever he showed up.

I hadn't counted on being bored at home. There's nothing to do on Shabbas except read and walk. Even jigsaw puzzles are considered work. I was tempted to pull out my 500-piece picture of the Rocky Mountains from under the couch. It was a Chanukah present from my aunt and uncle. Fear of Papa, not God, stopped me. It galled him that Gershon gave me and my brother presents he couldn't afford. He might also notice I'd finished another snowy peak and I didn't want to get him angry after finally getting his blessing last night. I half-hoped he'd be annoyed about my missing services, but he'd been too distraught about Shmuel to make much ado about it. That's from Shakespeare. Besides, going to synagogue was less important for women. Our duty was at home, keeping the family together. To rile Papa, I'd have to do something more obvious.

I wished that Leah were here and was a little sorry I hadn't gone to shul so I could share my big news with her. I wondered if she'd be excited for me or jealous. I was ambivalent about getting my period, but I'd still be upset if she'd gotten hers first. She'd never use cramps, even real ones, as an excuse to stay home. Leah actually listens during Reb Stern's D'var Torah and shushes me when I whisper to her about Bernie. She gives Ruchel an impatient look when my cousin disapproves of the rabbi's old-fashioned ideas. I tease Leah that she'll be a rabbi's wife, maybe even marry Shmuel, when she grows up. I think she likes the idea of being a rebbetzin, but I'm not sure how she feels about Shmuel. Sometimes I think she has a crush on Bernie, like me.

The water in the kettle was barely warm. I turned up the heat so the tea would brew more quickly. I didn't much care for it, but it was a new taste and I drank it down before lowering the flame. As long as I'd broken one rule, I gave myself permission to break another. I went into the bedroom, my parents' private sanctuary, and stood on the bed so I could see my whole body in the dresser mirror. I wondered if I looked different now that I was a woman.

First I studied myself straight on. Same sturdy body, not any frailer, but no new curves either. Then I turned sideways, peering over my shoulder and batting my eyelashes to mimic Theda Bara's vamping pose on the poster outside the Sunshine Cinema. I licked my lips and half-opened my mouth. I'd tried to talk my father into letting me see *Rose of Blood* but he refused, even when I argued that Theda Bara was Jewish. The ads called her the Egyptian-born daughter of a French actress and an Italian sculptor, but she was born in Cincinnati and her real name was Theodosia Burr Goodman. Not even Jewish pride was enough to persuade Papa, however.

I was filled with angst at the thought I'd have to stop being a tomboy, but it might not be a tragedy if I could be the next Theda Bara. I'd shorten my name to Dev Lev or something sexy, like Violet Lace. My dresses would be more stylish than my cousins' hand-me-downs, and I'd buy my parents a ten-bedroom house bigger than my uncle's apartment. I'd be rich enough to hire a detective, and he wouldn't have to be Jewish, so he could search for Shmuel on Shabbas.

When my parents came home, my mother went through the Havdalah ritual that marks the end of the Sabbath. I hoped she or my father would let me light the wicks on the braided candle or douse the flames in the kiddush cup, but neither looked toward me. Papa dipped his fingers in the wine and touched them to his eyelids as a final blessing while my mother's hands stayed in her lap. We didn't pass around the besamim. No one was in the mood to smell the cinnamon, cloves, and myrtle in the spice box, the sweet, tangy aroma meant to fortify us until next Friday night.

After picking at our food, my mother and I washed the dishes, including those soaking from last night. Cleaning was another type of work prohibited on the Sabbath, one of the few that gave women a rest. I was surprised the rabbis had included it.

My mother scrubbed at the baked-on cholent in the cast iron pot. "I don't understand your objection to Pyrex," she told Papa, repeating her regular Saturday night complaint. Usually it irritated me, but tonight its predictability was comforting. "It would be much easier to wash."

"Please, Rivka, not again. That pot's been in the family for generations."

"Gershon bought Pyrex dishes for Yetta. It takes her half as long to clean up now. And since they're made of glass, we wouldn't need separate ones for milk and meat." She eyed the chipped and mismatched china crammed into the paint-peeled cupboard. I don't know what she planned to fill the shelves with instead. My aunt had four sets of dishes, everyday milk and meat, and a fancier set of patterns for holidays and company. Like us, the Mendels also kept dishes just for Passover, but they were displayed in a big hutch, not packed away in cartons in the basement.

"If we were meant to keep one set of cookware, Moses would have

brought down Pyrex from Mt. Sinai along with the stone tablets."
Sometimes Papa could be funny.

"Then let me buy that new S.O.S. steel wool with the soap already
in it." She flung the Brillo pad into the sink, splashing greasy water in
her eyes and making them tear.

My father sighed. "You can't, Rivka. The soap is made with beef
tallow."

My mother knew this. Every Jew who kept kosher did. She handed
me the garbage.

Taking the trash to the bin in the alleyway behind the building
was my brother's nightly job, except on Saturday. Then it fell to me
because he and my father sat together at the table to begin studying the
next week's Torah portion. My mother hadn't cleared away his unused
setting.

"She can't do that anymore." My father snatched the bag out of my
hand. "It's not proper for her to be alone outside after dark."

"I'll do it." My mother grabbed the garbage from my father.

"You don't belong out there either." They faced off, each holding one
side of the wet, smelly bag.

"Who's to know?" I asked. "Do I look any different than last week?"
My father relented. "But come right back."

"Lickety split," I promised. "Faster than a gassed-up hayburner."

The street was as deserted as the night before, but the saloon's raucous
laughter rushed down the alley, echoing danger rather than glee. If
being a vamp meant that men like those at Paddy's would snort and
leer at me, I was no longer sure that I wanted to emulate Theda Bara.

I lifted the lid of the trash bin, eager to throw my bundle inside and
flee back upstairs. Hanging over the edge of the can was a familiar-
looking fringe. In the glow of the street lamp, I unrolled Shmuel's tzitzit.
Two pale locks of hair, his payess, fell onto the cracked pavement, where
they shone like the feathers of a fledgling fallen from the nest.

part three

Gershon, 1917

chapter 6

"Shmuel wasn't at evening services either." Gershon Mendel handed his wife Yetta his coat and studied her from behind. She was much wider than when they'd stood under the wedding canopy in Lemberg twenty years ago, proof he'd fulfilled his promise to his wealthy father-in-law to become a good provider in America. "Did Rivka say anything to you at shul this morning?"

"When I asked her if Shmuel was home sick, Rivka frowned, so I thought maybe yes, but she didn't really tell me. Did Avram talk to you?" Yetta draped her husband's large tweed coat on a padded silk hanger, stroked the ermine lining, and hung it in the hallway's double closet.

Gershon snorted. "My brother-in-law wouldn't tell me the time of day, even if the poor shmendrik could afford a watch." He and Avram had been rivals since childhood. Avram hated Gershon for marrying up into Yetta's family, while Gershon never forgave Avram for marrying his sister out from under his nose and keeping her in poverty, despite Gershon's attempts to help.

He gave his new Homburg to his younger daughter Ruchel, who threw it on the marble shelf, knocking the other hats askew. She was becoming increasingly disrespectful toward him. Gershon opened his mouth, but Yetta quickly straightened the hats before he could say anything. He decided to let it go; there were bigger things on his mind today. Gershon entrusted his worn sidur, the prayer book passed down by his father on the eve of his departure, to his older daughter Zipporah. As she set it carefully in the drawer of the inlaid table, he made a mental note to call the shadchen to see if the matchmaker had found her a suitable husband. Yetta still held out for a love match like theirs, but Gershon was adamant that his daughter not end up with some poor shlemiel. He'd never take a chance on his child's welfare like Yetta's father had with him. Gershon had paid the shadchen handsomely to find a future son-in-law who met his exacting qualifications, both financial and scholarly.

"I'm home a bissel late," Gershon said, settling his girth into the embroidered chair at the head of the dining room table. "So many people asking me for help." Unlike Avram, the other congregants at the Eldridge Street Synagogue, of which Gershon was president, couldn't thank him enough for helping them make their way in this country. He joked that if they were Catholic and he were the Pope, his ring would be so covered in shmutz from their kisses, he'd have to hire an assistant just to polish it. "I need a good meal after dispensing all those favours."

"Dinner will be a bissel late too." Yetta poked the meat with a fork to see if it was done, and closed the oven door. "I sent Margaret home early, she should take care of her poor mother who's not well. Then I had to wait until after sundown to put the roast in the oven myself."

"Yetta, we've been over this a hundred times. You can't cook on Saturday because it's Shabbas, so we pay Margaret to do it. Sunday is her Sabbath. She gets the morning off for church and she can take care of Mrs. Fitzgerald then too."

"Why not give her Saturday afternoon and Sunday morning both? According to Torah, even slaves should be allowed to observe a complete day of rest."

"Since when are you a Torah expert?" Gershon's talent for scholarship, evident since he was a small boy, was his ticket out of poverty. He saw no reason for his wife, or any woman, to be concerned with matters beyond the household. Yetta was from one of Lemberg's esteemed families, the baalei h'batim, so unlike most girls, she'd been educated by a private tutor until age twelve. After that, however, she wasn't allowed to read the Talmud, and that suited him fine.

"Mama's right." Ruchel tossed a linen napkin alongside each hand-painted china plate. "It says so in Exodus and again in Deuteronomy. A learned man like you should know that."

Gershon grabbed his daughter's wrist as she set his place with the silverware he'd given Yetta on their tenth anniversary. "One more word young lady, and I'll pull you out of the girls' cheder class." He'd resisted sending either daughter to religious school until Yetta convinced him it would make them better wives and mothers. Zipporah had in fact been content to learn the scriptural reasons behind the rituals performed at home, but Ruchel showed off her knowledge of sacred texts by questioning their meaning. She was sixteen, the same age as her cousin Shmuel, but in this only, his brother-in-law Avram had been luckier than him. Shmuel was a good son, who, like Zipporah, didn't disobey his parents. Ruchel both aggravated Gershon and set a bad example for her young cousin Dev. Worse, the more she defied him, the more Gershon found himself craving her approval and respect. He wanted them as the final proof that he'd succeeded in this new land, but she challenged his authority as readily as she did ancient Jewish laws.

"Shah!" Yetta shooed Ruchel away. "Your father's right. What do women know of God's intentions?" She turned to Gershon, "Next time, I'll tell Margaret to start the roast, on low heat, it shouldn't get overdone, *then* she can leave early." Gershon started to protest, but she put a plump hand on his arm. "Sholem bayess," she reminded him. "Always you make life easier for those at shul, you should stop arguing in your own home." To reestablish peace between them, she gave Gershon double portions of gefilte fish and chopped liver while the meat finished cooking.

"You think I should go to Rivka's after dinner? Maybe something really is wrong with Shmuel." Yetta continued setting the table. "They don't got money what to pay a doctor, but we could give ..."

Gershon cut her off. "It will be too dark by then. Besides, if the Levinsons need our help, let Avram come and ask us himself." He hoped his nephew wasn't sick, but he gloated at the thought of Avram being upset that his son had missed services last night and again today. Seeing Yetta's reproving look, he hastened to say, "Even if Shmuel is under the weather, I'm sure by now he's eating a slice of Rivka's honey-nut cake and reading next week's Torah portion."

Yetta smiled. "Nu, nothing stops your nephew from studying. He's like you."

It was Avram who pushed the boy, but Yetta was right that Shmuel's quick mind was more like Gershon's than like his own father's. Gershon had been the star pupil at cheder, besting not only Avram, but the older boys as well. When he was eight, his teacher made him recite a passage of Talmud in front of his parents and the curious customers who stood in the doorway separating the family's living quarters from their store. Gershon was nervous, but he performed flawlessly. Old men pinched his cheek. His mother made him a glass of tea with condensed milk. It was a grown-up treat that his parents rarely made for themselves .

"Your son has the makings of a Talmudic scholar," the rebbe told them. Minding the store was honourable labour, he said, but the Mendels should let their son use the talent God gave him. His parents turned over all but his heaviest chores to Rivka so Gershon could spend extra hours studying. His sister never complained; she was proud of him. And how had he paid her back? Four years later, he'd almost let her die. The only thing that kept him from giving up on Avram entirely was repaying a debt to his sister that he was too guilty to ever admit to her.

When the roast was finally ready, and Yetta had summoned the girls to the table, Gershon made a big ceremony of carving it. His wife had seasoned it with a heavenly blend of minced garlic, onions, and freshly ground paprika. Even though Yetta had grown up with servants, her mother insisted that she learn to cook and sew. Gershon could afford to pay others to do these things, but he accepted his wife's need to take charge of feeding and clothing the family herself.

He served the others, saving for himself the end pieces dense with spices and the juiciest middle slice. Ruchel started eating right after the blessing, but the others waited until he'd taken the first bite and began the conversation. "Morris Shumansky pleaded with me to find him a job. He said he'd eaten everything but the shirt on his back. Just to think of Morris eating his own filth can kill a man's appetite." Gershon demolished his noodle kugel in two forkfuls.

"He lost yet another job?" Yetta cut her husband a second square of the savoury pudding.

"He's got a tuchus for brains."

"Still, you can do something for the poor man? He shouldn't starve to death." Yetta put smaller portions of kugel on the other plates.

"I told him to go to the Crisis Conference tomorrow to get food. He kissed my hands so hard, I thought he was going to eat them too. Meanwhile I'll call Arnie Haber after supper and convince him that he needs to hire Morris as an errand boy."

Ruchel slid the roast closer and cut herself another slice. "How do you intend to do that?"

Gershon moved the platter back toward himself. "My business methods are not your concern."

Yetta fiddled with her silverware. "Nu, anyone else? Mrs. Meltzer?"

"They can't keep the old woman at home any more. She wets the bed. The daughter flung her arms around me and wept when I said I'd find a place at Hadassah House. Her husband had given her an ultimatum, either your mother goes or I do."

"Imagine saying such a heartless thing!" Yetta scrunched her napkin. Zipporah smoothed it out again and patted her mother's hand.

Gershon couldn't imagine threatening to leave his wife, his biggest prize, for any reason, but he was glad he'd never been faced with caring for an elderly, incontinent parent. He and Yetta had left when theirs were in good health. His mother and father died while he was still in night school, but Yetta's lived long enough for him to write them about his success. It mattered more to him that his rich in-laws knew he'd made it in America than that his own parents did. He hoped they'd kvelled about it to the rest of the shtetl, rich and poor alike, before they passed on.

"The girls and I will help move her when a bed frees up." Yetta smiled at Zipporah, who smiled back. Ruchel sighed and shrugged, earning a stern look from her mother.

"I'll look in now and then to make sure Mrs. Meltzer is treated well. After all, she's a landsman from Lemberg." Gershon pushed away his plate, which Yetta quickly cleared and replaced with a glass of tea sweetened with raspberry jam and a thick slice of marble cake.

"Anyone else whose salvation you'll engineer?" Ruchel lingered over her dinner plate, daring her father to wait until she was finished with her meal before he started his dessert.

Gershon scooped a large bite of cake into his mouth and chewed noisily. "In fact, Hymie Rosenthal sought me out after everyone else had left."

The women, including Ruchel, caught their breaths. Hymie had married a gentile, a pretty Catholic girl who bought onions and peppers from his horse-drawn cart instead of shopping at the Italian produce store around the corner. Their marriage had been the biggest shanda of the shul last year. Even Yetta, that most tolerant of souls, had clucked her tongue.

"He's unhappy," Gershon continued. The faces around him looked satisfied, as if to say, "We told you so!" He was more sympathetic. Marrying a non-Jew was to some a sign of leaving behind the old country and being accepted in America. He didn't approve, but he understood.

"Nu, what can the man do? He can't make her not his wife. Catholics don't believe in divorce."

"Hymie doesn't want a divorce. He still loves her." Or perhaps, thought Gershon, he refused to admit defeat. "But it bothers him that she badmouths his Jewish friends."

"He still has friends among our people?" Ruchel asked in the cynical voice she'd cultivated lately. It made Gershon want to plug his fingers in his ears.

"He just wants her to be as nice to the Jews as he is to her Catholic friends. He asked me for advice, he's too ashamed to talk to anyone else."

Yetta's curiosity got the better of her disapproval. "So what did you tell him?"

Gershon spoke haltingly. "I told him to move into a building that has Jewish and Catholic families. You hang your laundry on the same line and put your garbage in the same cans, you act nicer to each other." That's how he was able to trade favours with the gentile aldermen. Some Jews didn't approve, but no one complained when they benefitted. "Did I say the right thing?"

Yetta told him she supposed he knew best, and Zipporah silently deferred to her mother. Ruchel, however, rewarded him with a genuine smile. "Advice worthy of a King Solomon."

Gershon suppressed a smile of triumph and nudged the cake platter toward Ruchel. He stood. "Ruven Kleinschmidt's building has a vacancy. I'll call him now."

chapter 7

The roll-top mahogany desk shone with a fresh coat of fragrant O-Cedar polish. They owned so much furniture that the maid rotated which pieces she cleaned each week. Knowing how proud Gershon was to have a separate room called a study, Yetta made sure that the only thing Margaret polished more often than his desk was the sideboard from which she served their meals.

His hand vacillated between the Torah and the telephone. He should start next week's reading about the friction between Jacob and his brother-in-law, Laban. Every year he tried, in vain, to learn a lesson from it. But Laban wasn't likeable and neither was Avram. Besides, helping others was a mitzvah. Surely God would understand if he kept his promises to his fellow congregants tonight and waited until tomorrow to study. He dialled Ruven Kleinschmidt.

"With all due respect Mr. Mendel, but if I rent to Mr. Rosenthal and his shiksa wife, half the Jewish families in my building will move out. Who wants to live next door to a scandal?"

"I'll tell you who. Mrs. Appelbaum, Mrs. Schwartz, and every other yenta. You should charge extra for furnishing them with gossip to spread."

"You'll make good on the broken leases if they flee like rats from a sinking ship?"

"If you cut me an extra five percent when they don't." Gershon wanted the Jewish tenants to stay. Yet if they remained merely to say bad things, it would mean his advice was wrong. Did people ever spread good gossip? Yetta would say yes, but she thought well of everyone. He could ask Ruchel, but having just gotten her approval, he dared not risk getting her pitying look. What was that expression Dev used, "Quit while you're ahead?" He'd keep quiet and hope for the best.

Next Gershon called Arnie Haber about a job for Morris. Two years ago, Arnie, who sold yard goods, was caught shorting clients by wrapping fabric around thicker pieces of cardboard to boost the weight of the bolts. With bribes in district court, plus a share for himself,

Gershon had helped him avoid prosecution, but he suspected Arnie of padding bolts again. By pledging not to blow the whistle and foregoing half his share, Gershon persuaded Arnie to give Morris a job.

After that call, Gershon's energy flagged. Solving tonight's problems had been too easy. He preferred harder challenges that involved more creative arm twisting, like finding a place in a nursing home for a destitute woman who wet herself. He'd tackle that tomorrow, when his mind was fresher. Ditto the Torah. Enough doing good for one evening. He deserved a reward. Even if he wasn't hungry, another glass of tea and a second slice of Yetta's marble cake seemed only fair.

Zipporah and Ruchel were quiet behind the closed doors of their rooms. Gershon owned the building and his family occupied the entire first floor. He'd knocked down the walls between the four apartments to make eight spacious rooms for them, while he rented the smaller apartments on the two upper floors to professionals and merchants. He didn't allow sweatshops here, although he permitted them in his other buildings where families lived in the back room and toiled alongside as many as a dozen garment workers in the front room. The heat of steamed wool and the sickening smell of shvitzing bodies mingled in their airless apartments. He didn't know how they stood it, yet their prayers of thanks for the opportunities of this Promised Land were as fervent and loud as his. Who was he to deny them this chance? If he didn't rent to them, someone else would. And another landlord would probably charge more. Gershon slept well at night.

He'd also dug up the back alley to create a garden. Yetta planted a few vegetables, but mostly she grew flowers. Neighbours considered this frivolous and wasteful, which to Gershon only confirmed his status, but the flowers also served a purpose. When he needed a favour from an Irish alderman, he presented the man with a rose for his wife. Or his mistress. Gershon enjoyed the perks of power, be it a choice cut of lox or a bottle of peppermint schnapps, but he'd never been tempted by the flesh of any woman other than Yetta. He grew impatient for the Shabbas bride to arrive every Friday night so he could make love to his own bride. After two decades, he hadn't lost his ardour, nor had she. Tonight, coming upon her alone in the kitchen, he wondered if they might make love again, even though the Shabbas bride would not return for six long days.

Yetta was wrapping left-over roast beef when Gershon approached her from behind and nuzzled her neck. She hastily put the package in the ice box, as though trying to hide it from him. "Remember when we put food on the fire escape, it should keep cold?" she asked, facing him.

Many tenement families, unable to afford an ice box, still did. Now he promised to buy her a new invention, called a refrigerator, that chilled food with chemicals. No one else he knew had one. "Then you wouldn't have to wrap the food in so many layers," he told her.

"I'm wrapping because ..." Yetta hesitated when Gershon raised his eyebrows. "It's for Margaret to take home tomorrow. God willing, the meat will give her poor mother strength."

"They have their own church for that." Gershon knew his wife was raised to share her wealth, but he resented it whenever she acted with more generosity than him. "Better I should take the leftovers to Morris Shumansky."

"Tzedakah isn't just giving charity to Jews," Yetta said. "All immigrants are strangers in a strange land. Torah says to be good to them because we were once strangers in Egypt."

"Again with the commentary on scripture? Stop getting ideas from Ruchel. Your job is to take care of your own family. Let me worry about the widows and orphans."

"Shmuel is part of our family. You think maybe something is really wrong with him?"

Gershon sighed with exasperation. He wished there was a way for his wife to be nice to Rivka and the children without benefitting Avram, but he didn't see how.

Yetta rested her head against his chest, a familiar gesture to calm him. "Nu, how can I not do for others when we're so comfortable ourselves? You've done well for us, Gershon."

"I have, haven't I?"

"Better than my parents and everyone else in Lemberg dreamed." She tugged him toward the bedroom. "Of course, God helped a bissel. Even Moses needed the Almighty's intervention."

Gershon let his wife lead him down the hall. "God only allowed Moses to take our people to the edge of the Promised Land. I'm helping them move in."

part four
Shmuel, 1917

chapter 8

Shmuel stood stripped, wet and shivering with hundreds of other men on the deck of the Calvin Austin, a floating boot camp for those with no sailing experience. Everything around him was gray: the sky, the deck, the faces of the men who didn't have their sea legs yet. When the recruits, now called boots, were ordered to box up their clothes and ship them home, he'd made up an address in Brooklyn, figuring the East Boston post office wouldn't bother to track the returned package. His hair had been cut short but not shaved, leaving the strawberry mark still partly hidden. Aboard ship, there wouldn't be time for haircuts. He'd grow his hair long, like the sailors in the posters.

The supply clerk tossed him a uniform. Shmuel, eager to cover his body, was dismayed to find that the pants sagged and the shirt hung on him half empty.

"I need a smaller size, please."

"If you're man enough to be in the Navy, you're man enough to fill out whatever damned size I give you." The clerk chose a uniform, seemingly at random, for the boot behind him.

"Please, sir, I need a size wee wee." The dark-headed man ahead of Shmuel batted his eyes and drew wolf whistles, mincing down the line.

"A blue skirt, sir," said a burly Irishman, "short enough to show off my dainty ankles."

Shmuel's strawberry mark throbbed. He'd have to hold up his pants with an extra notch in his belt or tie a piece of rope around his waist, assuming one of those fixes passed inspection. At the next station, the supply officer issued him a hammock, pillow, blanket, and thin mattress. Handing him a mattress cover, the sailor grinned, "This, kid, is your fart sack."

"Fair ladies don't fart." A wiry Italian grabbed Shmuel's mattress cover and tossed it in a game of Monkey in the Middle. Shmuel spun around and chased after it, dizzy with shame.

"Drop it!" barked Lieutenant Junior Grade Mikovski. The fart sack, mid-flight, fell to the floor. "In the next eight weeks, you'll learn self-discipline. Horsing around is for Army jokers, not Navy men." The boots lowered their heads like chastened schoolboys. Mikovski turned to Shmuel. "As for you, girlie, your job is to protect and defend, beginning with your gear. If you can't guard a goddam fart sack, how the hell do you expect to safeguard a fucking ocean?"

Shmuel picked up the mattress cover. Shaming was part of training, but he'd hoped that in the Navy he wouldn't get picked on more than anyone else. Now he stood out as a target.

The supply clerk called out the names stenciled on a teetering pile of drawstring canvas bags. "Nick Ryan." "Joey Tomasio." "Sam Lord." Feeling like a fraud, Shmuel claimed his bag. The dark blue ink of the "S" in Sam ran at the head and tail, like the pink edges of his strawberry mark. Mikovski said that they'd spend the afternoon learning how to sling a hammock and stow it with their uniforms, oilskins, weapons, and other gear in these sea bags. It seemed impossible that the sacks, a skimpy two feet by three feet, could contain everything the Navy gave them.

"Who are you, miss?" Mikovski, blonde and blue-eyed, yet solid as a stevedore, peered at the block letters on Shmuel's bag. "Lord? Hah! Titles don't count for shit here. Bluebloods need extra toughening. I'll see to your training. Personally." Now Shmuel knew for sure the lieutenant had singled him out for abuse. The pitying looks of the others confirmed his conclusion.

On day two, unsteady as babies learning to walk, the boots began negotiating decks, ladders, and passageways. When Mikovski wasn't prodding Shmuel, Nick Ryan and Joey Tomasio took over the hazing. They pressed their bodies into Shmuel in the narrow openings, reminding him of the passage in Genesis when the men of Sodom push up against Lot in a sexual frenzy. His instinct was to shrink away until he recalled a saying from the Mishnah that "to destroy a single human soul is to destroy an entire world." He'd enlisted in the Navy to save the world, and refused to let his soul be destroyed before he'd even set sail.

Shmuel shoved himself hard back against the two men. "Something I can do for you fellas?" He leered the way he imagined the men of Sodom had. Ryan, his pale skin reddening, backed off immediately.

Tomasio just grinned and ground his hips, but when Shmuel held his ground, he too retreated. Then both men clapped Shmuel on the shoulder to let him know he was one of the gang now. Shmuel scaled the next ladder with a confidence he'd never felt in school, until he caught Mikovski's curt nod and sinister smile. He wouldn't let Shmuel off so easily.

The rest of that week, spent memorizing the Navy's arcane language, restored some of Shmuel's fleeting confidence. Studying was second nature to him. He mastered Navy jargon by imagining he was teaching new words to Dev, and soon referred to the kitchen as the galley and the eating area as the mess. Harder to get his tongue around was the ship's food, much of it made with pork. Shmuel tried to abstain from meat, but after long drills in the salty air, his hunger exacted a compromise. He passed on sliced bacon and ham, but asked forgiveness to remove pieces of pork and just eat the baked beans. Afraid of being branded a picky eater, he avoided attention by sitting with different men at each meal, but Tomasio and Ryan began to join him.

"What's the matter, Lord? Not as tasty as mom's home cooking?" Tomasio stabbed a piece of ham off Shmuel's plate and shoved it in his mouth.

"Nah. Eyes bigger than my stomach. I already had three slices. I shouldn't have taken seconds." Shmuel patted his gut and puffed out his cheeks.

"Growing boy needs as much food as he can stuff in," said Ryan, sitting on the other side. He transferred two slices from his plate onto Shmuel's.

Shmuel laughed and tossed them back to Ryan, but he felt compelled to finish his beans. Under his friend's watchful eyes, he couldn't pick out the pieces of pork. Anxious he'd gag when the trayf hit his throat, he wolfed them down. Then he realized that made him look hungry after all, so he ate more slowly. He chewed each mouthful. Smothered in tangy sauce, the pork tasted fine. The next morning, he tried a slice of bacon. That was good too. A slab of ham at lunch was even more satisfying. A couple of days later, it no longer mattered what or with whom Shmuel ate.

chapter 9

The more at home he felt in boot camp, the more Shmuel allowed himself to think of the home he'd left behind. He hoped his family wouldn't come after him, yet he wanted them to miss him even as he warned himself not to miss them. What could they be thinking? Had Dev seen him staring at the recruiting posters? She'd be hurt that he hadn't confided in her, and envious that he, a boy, had the freedom to take off. His mother would worry herself sick and try to understand why he'd left. Rivka would want to find him and bring him back. His father wouldn't care why he'd gone, only be furious that he had. If Avram wanted Shmuel home, it wouldn't be out of concern for his safety.

Shmuel reassured himself that tracing him would he hard. Tens of thousands enlisted every week and he could be at any of the forty training sites from Portland, Maine to Portland, Oregon. Still, Avram could be relentless in pursuing what he wanted, whether working his way up from pinner to presser at the dress factory, or insisting on his son becoming a rabbi.

"What if I'm not cut out for it?" Shmuel had dared to ask when he turned fifteen. He and Avram were at the kitchen table studying commentaries on the golden calf. That morning, the rabbi had given a D'var Torah on the transgression, saying the Jews had to learn how *not* to act like slaves after four hundred and thirty years of bondage in Egypt. His sermon had likened the biblical story to his immigrant congregation learning to live like free people after escaping the bonds of the countries they'd left behind. "But," he warned them, "God redeemed us from slavery with an outstretched hand in order that we could freely worship Him, not that we might do as we pleased."

"Not be a rabbi? What else would you do?" Avram had asked Shmuel, genuinely puzzled.

"I don't know," he confessed. Like the Jews wandering in the desert, Shmuel had no idea where he was headed.

"Has Gershon been telling you to study accounting?" Now his father sounded suspicious.

"No, I'm not interested in numbers, but I'm not a leader like Reb Stern. When he speaks, his words inspire people." Shmuel smiled. "Dev is the word person in our family, not me."

"Half the things she comes out with she learns from you and your friends. The rest, from the worst students at school. But you don't have to head a congregation. A rabbi can lead the people with written words. And they outlast those that are spoken." Avram nodded at the books arrayed before them, as if nothing more needed to be said on the subject of his son's future.

Shmuel didn't voice his doubts a second time. He tried telling himself he was suited to the life of a rabbi, where scholarship, not manliness, was all that mattered. If only he'd succeeded in convincing himself, he wouldn't be here. Instead, deep into the second week of training, he was subjecting himself to intense physical conditioning: swimming in frigid waters, performing numbing calisthenics, running tortuous obstacle courses, and climbing up towering masts on swaying ropes. Shmuel suffered leg cramps and rope burns. Even the toughest boots complained.

He might have given up if his brains hadn't rescued him again, for at the same time the men's bodies were being put through their paces, they had to learn Navy ranks and ratings, visual signalling, and steering annotation. Although far from Avram's intention, studying Talmud had prepared Shmuel for just such mental exercise. The others, some barely literate, sought his help and he found that he enjoyed teaching them. It was the same with knots. At night they leaned over his hammock as he demonstrated the magnus and tautline more slowly than Mikovski had. Their thick hands got tangled in the twine, while Shmuel's slender fingers were flexible from years spent tying the tzitzit on his tallit.

"Hey, Lord. How come you're so good at these fucking knots?"

Shmuel couldn't tell them that compared to the ritual knots he'd grown up with, hitches, marlins, and constrictors were easier than a game of cat's cradle. If anyone had asked if he were Jewish, he wouldn't have denied it, but except for Ryan and Tomasio, he'd rather they not know. His fair colouring let him pass as someone other than he was, and he wanted to keep it that way.

"I worked at a newspaper plant," he lied. Again. "Rag paper is really heavy. If you didn't lash the bundles tight, they split open. Do it once, the boss smeared your face with ink. Twice, he fired you." Shmuel's fib drew sympathy. Former factory labourers and dock workers them-selves, the other boots said they knew what it was like to be humiliated. They still got plenty of that in the Navy, especially from Mikovski, but they seemed grateful that Shmuel was taking the brunt of it. He in turn was grateful to belong, but he often wondered if he was paying too high a price. He'd gone to war to discover what he was made of, not to lose so many parts of himself.

Once Mikovski realized that Shmuel's brains and hands had made him something of a leader, he found other ways to shame him, begin-ning with Shmuel's underdeveloped body. The lieutenant made him do one hundred and fifty push-ups instead of a hundred, and run the obstacle course forward and in reverse. He put spikes around the metal drums, leaving Shmuel half an inch of clearance. If Mikovski decided Shmuel ran too slowly, he assigned him ship-painting duty. Others given this punishment emerged as splattered as kindergarten children, but Shmuel's fastidious brushwork further enraged Mikovski. He hurled a can of paint on the deck and made Shmuel scrub it off. As resentful and exhausted as the extra work made Shmuel feel, he also knew it was toughening him up. Mikovski saw it too, making him drive Shmuel even harder in his anger and frustration.

For a big man, the lieutenant was unusually agile. His bulk was pure muscle. Men stood in awe as he shinnied up a mast and swooped down faster than a hawk snatching a peanut off a train platform. They copied his ascent, swaying and praying at the top, then closed their eyes coming down while grabbing a handful of rope every few inches. None attempted his smooth free fall.

"Eyes open, boys. Like this!" Mikovski scampered up again. A quarter of the way down, he slashed the outermost strand of rope with his pocketknife, tugging twice for good measure. He was too high up to hear, but it was easy to imagine the plies popping under his weight. Once he'd landed lightly back on the deck, Mikovski bowed to Shmuel. "Your turn, your lordship." He snapped the knife closed and slipped it in his pocket.

If Shmuel refused, he'd be sent to the brig. If he accepted, he might end up with broken limbs, or worse. He decided lock-up wasn't an option and started up the rope. Ryan and Tomasio moved to the base of the mast to break his fall with their bodies, but Mikovski told them to back off. On his way up, Shmuel passed the place where three of the seven plies had unravelled. He squeezed both hands above the frayed spot to lessen the strain as he shinnied past. Descending, his feet felt for that same weak spot, but the thick rubber soles of his regulation sneakers blocked all sensation. Mikovski yelled up to him. "Look at *me*, sweetheart, not at the sky or the inside of your eyelids. I want to see your beautiful blue peepers gazing into mine every inch of the way down." Shmuel felt dizzy enough to throw up on the lieutenant's head, but he didn't dare stop or close his eyes. He stared unblinking at Mikovski, looking up only once when he slid past the shredded section. Two more strands had uncoiled, leaving just two plies intact. He quickened his pace and the rope held until he hit the deck. For once Shmuel was thankful his muscles hadn't fully bulked up yet. Another week of boot camp, and the rope would have broken under his weight. His friends pulled him into formation and thumped him on the back. He began a silent prayer of thanks, then stifled the instinct. It wasn't God who'd delivered him, but his own guts.

Mikovski barrelled between them and yanked at the rope like a lion tearing off the limb of its prey. The splayed end crashed down and whipped around his feet. After ordering the supply clerk to get a new rope, he dismissed the men and told them to report back at 1400 hours.

Shmuel saluted. "Permission to remain on deck and do calisthenics, sir," he said. Tomasio stood behind him. "Request same, sir." The others lined up too, a devoted congregation.

Mikovski glared, pivoted, and followed the clerk below deck. "One, and two, and three," Shmuel chanted loudly after him, like a cantor giving voice to the prayers of the faithful. Unlike true believers, however, his limbs were shaking. In their eyes Shmuel had won, but he'd forever after have to inspect every rope before trusting it to hold him. Mikovski had frayed his nerves.

chapter 10

The third week of training again tested the boots' brains as they learned the chain of command and courtesies accorded each rank. It meant as little to these working class men as knowing which utensil to use at a formal dinner, but at any hour a superior could quiz them and mete out punishment if they didn't bark out the correct answer. Tomasio complained that his head ached from trying to keep the five grades of admiral straight. Meanwhile, Ryan searched in the middle of the book for the lieutenant rankings. Shmuel told him to turn back to the beginning. "It's right after ensign, which is what we'll be when we graduate. See if you can find Mikovski's ranking."

"Damn. He's just a notch above us." Ryan slammed his book shut.

"So why should we be afraid of him?" Tomasio asked Ryan.

"Because he has the power to decide whether we pass or flunk out," someone answered.

"And either way he can make our lives miserable while we're here," said another.

They looked at Shmuel. "Lieutenant Junior Grade doesn't scare me," he bluffed. But he knew that being one rank up from the bottom made you mean. The Navy was like the Lower East Side that way. Immigrants who'd been there a year felt superior to greenhorns. Catholics beat out Jews because they had Jesus in common with Protestants, and German Jews assumed they were better than those from the Austro-Hungarian Empire, especially poor Galicians like his family.

Day and night, the tired men also took turns at watchstanding, recording sunrise and sunset and keeping a log of drills, inspections, salutes, and flag displays. Entries had to be made in pen, not pencil, and errors crossed out but not erased, in case the log was used as evidence in legal proceedings. The uneducated boots cursed in frustration at their indelible mistakes, and offered to pay Shmuel in cigarettes if he forged their entries. He shook his head, but not because he didn't smoke. Despite the lies he'd told to get into the Navy, and the identity he kept secret from them, Shmuel knew that the men had to trust his honesty if he wanted to keep their respect.

His self-respect at risk too, Shmuel told himself he was done with lying and betraying his faith from this point on. He kept his resolve all week, until he was assigned Saturday watch duty. Keeping the log book meant writing on the Sabbath. Having already hauled ropes on Shabbas, not to mention eating trayf, it seemed hypocritical to worry about violating another stricture. Yet it troubled him. Last year, he'd joined Saturday afternoon sessions at shul where two men could argue three interpretations of Torah, but were forbidden from writing down their ideas, often embellished, until the following day. Unlike Jews, the Navy did not permit ambiguity or revision. Recording had to be exact and contemporaneous, a word Dev would have loved.

Ryan volunteered to cover for him. "Bandage your hand and tell Mikovski you got a bad rope burn and can't write." Shmuel was sceptical but it was better than admitting the real reason.

"What's the matter, Lord?" Mikovski squeezed Shmuel's bandage hand. "Ain't you got calluses by now?" He grinned. "Unless you're one of those Jew boys who won't write on Saturday? Had me one of them, once. Pissed himself learning to fire a gun and slunk home to his mama."

"No, sir. I just have a sore hand from sliding down a busted rope."

"But it'll be all better by Saturday, right?" Mikovski pulled off the bandage.

"Yes, sir!" Shmuel saluted. Navy regulations, and Mikovski, had overruled God.

Finally, at the end of week four, the boots had their first break from training. They were given a month's pay and a free day to walk around East Boston. They moved awkwardly on land, braced for the ocean swells that were miles from the city's broad streets and narrow alleyways.

Shmuel went with Ryan and Tomasio to the gedunk stand, the sailors' name for the base commissary. They stood in front of the candy counter. After a month of mess trays with food in controlled portions, choice bewildered them. Ryan said he thought sailors were supposed to buy life savers. Tomasio took a bag of Amalkaka, chocolate-covered animal crackers. Ryan grabbed a package too. Shmuel hesitated, afraid they were made with lard. It was silly to care after eating pork, but for some reason, the idea of lard nauseated him. Also, "kaka" was

Yiddish slang for shit, something he wouldn't tell his friends for fear of spoiling their pleasure too. In the end, he bought Mary Jane's, whose taste reminded him of Rivka's honey-nut cake, and joked that it was a good workout for his jaws, the only part of him that the Navy wasn't exercising.

"As long as you keep your mouth shut in front of Mikovski," Tomasio said, and he and Ryan bought a bar of the taffy candy too. They savoured it slowly after gobbling the cookies.

"You ready for some companionship, boot boy?" Tomasio nudged Shmuel in the ribs.

Shmuel blushed and imagined his strawberry mark reddening too. Tomasio turned to Ryan.

"Sorry, I'm a do-it-at-night man." The young Irishman looked as uncomfortable as Shmuel felt. It was mid-day and they had to be back on the ship at 1600 hours, long before dark.

Tomasio cajoled them, saying any obliging whore would turn out the lights and drape a scarf over the window, but when Shmuel and Ryan fussed with their candy wrappers, he didn't push it. He said he was off to find something sweeter and would meet them back at the gedunk stand at 1545. Too embarrassed to look at each other, Ryan and Shmuel walked downtown in search of a dark movie theatre, where, for the next two hours, they and a theatre full of recruits watched Fatty Arbuckle and Buster Keaton shorts. Happy to blot out the indignities of camp and avoid thoughts of what lay ahead, they laughed more loudly than the movies' antics deserved.

Then, with over an hour of leave remaining, Shmuel suggested visiting the stalls along the wharf that catered to sailors. They still had most of their pay left, and while many men sent their unspent wages home, Shmuel didn't know what to do with his. Both men bought socks, and Ryan bought stationery to write his girlfriend. Shmuel pretended to believe Ryan had one. Then Shmuel picked up a snow globe with an ivory carving of a twin-masted ship. It would have made a nice Chanukah present for Dev, a paperweight to hold down her word lists. But when he turned it upside down, the masts became the legs of a naked woman, while the prow and stern became huge breasts glistening under the swirling flakes.

"Should I buy this for Tomasio?" he asked Ryan uncertainly. "I think he'd appreciate it."

"Liar!" Two stalls down, a group of sailors hounded a small greying man in a black jacket with frayed tzitzit hanging below the hem. "Not German," the frightened man insisted. "Sephardic."

"Huh? Never heard of it." A sailor, whose rolled-up sleeves revealed lurid tattoos from wrist to elbow, spit in the face of the cowering Jew. "It means he's from southern Europe, not the north where the enemy is from." Shmuel walked towards the angry crowd without hesitation. Ryan pulled Shmuel in the opposite direction. "It's not our fight. Save it for the real war."

Shmuel shook him off. "Sephardic Jews came to America in 1492, same as Columbus. Been here longer than most of our families." He rolled up his sleeves too and clenched his fists. Without tattoos, his sunburned muscles shone as brightly as the ivory breasts in the snow globe.

"You sure about that?" a sceptical sailor asked.

Shmuel, relieved he hadn't been recognized as a Jew, searched his mind to say something believable. "Our neighbours in Brooklyn were from Spain. Sephardim are very loyal to America."

"What about them other kind of Jews?"

"Ashkenazy. They're loyal too." Shmuel wished he could point to himself as living proof.

The tattooed sailor pumped Shmuel's hand. "As my Irish grand-mother says, 'I'm glad I didn't die yesterday or I wouldn't have known that.'" He eyed the snow globe, adding "You're okay, Mick." In Ryan's company, Shmuel had passed as a fellow Irishman. Others were creating an identity for him. Was this any better than his father deciding who and what he should be?

Back at the gedunk stand, Tomasio guffawed at the bawdy trinket, before muttering his thanks. It wasn't the lewdness, Shmuel realized, but the gesture of friendship that made him uneasy. To cover his embarrassment, Tomasio bragged about taking on two at once at the whorehouse.

"Shmuel took on a whole crowd," Ryan said, "and with his mouth, not his fists."

Shmuel let Ryan tell Tomasio the story, not out of modesty but because he was too tired to talk any more. Freedom was messy; he craved the orderliness of the ship. The other men seemed relieved to be back on board too. The Calvin Austin had become their home, albeit a temporary one. In four weeks, they'd be leaving home for the second time in two months.

Emptying his pockets that night, Shmuel discovered that he still had nearly twenty-five dollars left. He stashed the bills in his sea bag. One month ago, he would have saved the money to pay tuition at the seminary, fulfilling Avram's wishes. What did he want for himself now? He thought about how naturally he'd fallen into the role of teacher at boot camp, and how earlier today, he'd turned around an ugly incident by explaining geography and history to an immigrant as raw as those he'd grown up with. An idea began to take shape. Suppose he attended yeshiva after all, but with the goal of opening his own cheder, a school for curious young boys, instead of training to be a rabbi. Having discovered the power of his voice, he could use that same pedagogy to help Jewish boys learn not only Talmud, but also how to live like Americans in a world more complex than the shtetl where their parents had grown up.

Pedagogy, another word Dev would relish. If they were having one of their bedtime conversations, he could teach it to her. But his sister was on her own now. And so was he.

part five

Dev, 1917

chapter 11

Sunday breakfast was silent and cold. My father had won the argument that lasted until dawn. He was adamant that if his son was in trouble, God would send word to us. We would not look for him. In the meantime, we were to assume his disappearance was voluntary. My body, lying rigid on the couch, had finally succumbed to exhaustion and the desire to blot out my parents' voices. I fell into such a deep sleep that I didn't wake up during the night to feed the stove. It was another reminder, as we shivered around the table, that Shmuel, who never failed in this task, was gone.

My father went to work but my mother didn't want to leave the apartment in case there was news of my brother, so she sent me to United's for a package of Lister's Towels. Before Shmuel started acting weird, he used to take me there once a month for a cola. Soda was another thing Papa didn't allow in the house, even though it wasn't trayf. He gave the usual excuse, that you couldn't be sure what was in the bottles or on the hands of the people who delivered them, but I think it was the cost. Onkel Gershon bought Hires by the case and he was as kosher as Papa.

The druggist raised his eyebrows when I put the money in the special box on the counter.

"My mother sent me." I should have stopped there, but I added, "She's not feeling well," which implied there was more I wasn't telling. The druggist waited, but when I simply stared at him, he handed me the package. I slipped it under my arm, regretting I hadn't brought a satchel.

It was still early in the morning, so my chances of getting home unobserved were good. The Catholics in the neighbourhood wouldn't be going to church for an hour, and Jews were at work or catching up on the errands they were forbidden to do yesterday. I took a chance that the street would remain deserted and lingered outside to look at the Navy poster in the window.

The last time we got sodas, Shmuel stopped to read the poster too. I'd been impatient, hoping to get in a game of potsy with Leah before it got dark, but today I looked more closely. Against an image of a sailor and a flag were the words: "Be Ready! A U.S. Party will visit the Navy Recruiting Station to examine and enlist men for the Naval Service on these dates." The last two dates on the list were coming up; the one before had taken place Tuesday of this week.

"Thinking of disguising yourself as a boy and enlisting? Or just looking at the cute sailor in the picture?"

I knew before I saw his reflection in the window that it was Yaakov. My brother's friend thinks he's an egg, a big person destined for a big life, but the only thing big in his future is his mouth. I knew Bernie would be right behind him. He was cuter than the sailor on the poster, but he wasn't stuck on himself. He was self-conscious about his skin, which was a little blemished.

"Just having perturbations about our brave men fighting overseas. There's a war going on, if you hadn't noticed." I tried to brush past them, but the package knocked against Yaakov's jutting elbow and fell to the pavement. When I blushed and bent to retrieve it, he snatched it up.

"What's in here?" He held the parcel to his ear and shook it.

"Give it back. It's for my mother." Once more I'd said too much. Yaakov tossed the pads to Bernie. I was ready to run home without them, but Bernie held the plainly-wrapped box out to me. "Here, Dev. Whatever it is, I'm sure Mrs. Levinson needs it."

"Thank you, Bernie." The skin on his lightly-pimpled cheeks turned red when I said his name. He looked like he wanted to run home too.

"Shmuel wasn't in shul," said Yaakov. "You hiding him in another mystery package?"

Wisdom told me to keep my mouth shut and escape, but again I opened it. "Maybe you're the one hiding Shmuel." I tried to sound flippant, but my voice cracked at my brother's name.

"What do you mean?" Bernie stepped closer to me.

"He's been missing since Friday morning." I'd sassed Yaakov just for fun, but suddenly the words of my taunt rang true. My mother's first instinct had been right. If anyone had a clue about where Shmuel was, it would be his two best friends.

The boys looked at each other and then back at the recruiting poster. "We thought it was just a lot of talk," Yaakov said. "It never occurred to us that he'd go through with it."

Bernie paled, making his pimples more prominent. "If I'd known he was serious, I would have spoken to your parents."

"He's only been gone two days. I'm sure Papa can find him and make him come home."

"That might be hard, Dev. Your brother's smart, like you. He knew he'd have to lie about his age to enlist. I'm guessing he lied about his name too, so the Navy couldn't check up on him."

Now I did run home. When I became a star, I promised myself, I wouldn't pull a Theda Bara. I'd keep my real name.

chapter 12

My mother sent me to fetch my father. I was almost never alone with him, but now that I had a chance to command his full attention, he was too upset or angry to talk.

"I think Shmuel ran off to the Navy," I said, waiting for Papa to ask how I knew. He didn't even look at me, just ploughed ahead toward home. "The poster says you have to be seventeen to join up. Do you think he lied?"

"I think you should leave this to me and your mother," he said.

When we got back to the house, Onkel Gershon was waiting with Mama, sitting in Papa's chair. Shmuel's place setting had finally been cleared away. I wondered which of them had done it.

"You didn't need to pull your brother away from his work," my father said to my mother as soon as we walked in. The apartment was still chilly but sweat poured from his brow.

"I'm an accountant," my uncle said. "Unlike you, I don't have to work on Sunday." He leaned back and pointed my father toward Shmuel's empty chair. My father remained standing.

"He hasn't shipped out to sea yet. Gershon says they need to train them first." My mother, hand on her throat, swallowed twice. "All we have to do is find out where they sent him to boot camp and tell the Navy our son is only sixteen. Then they'll have to let him go."

"Or lock him up for lying to the government." My father's hands had burn marks from the pressing machine that I could have sworn weren't there when he blessed me two nights ago.

My uncle, seeing the alarm on Mama's face, patted her wrist. "No one's going to arrest the boy for wanting to serve his country, Avram."

My father crossed his arms. "You're going to stop them, big shot?"

"I have connections."

"No one cares about a Jewish boy or his patriotism. This country can manage fine without our fighting skills. Better we should study, keep to ourselves, and stay out of trouble."

"Sometimes we have to make noise outside the community to help ourselves back inside it. Obviously, studying Torah and living in peace with his own kind wasn't enough for Shmuel."

"It's not enough for you Gershon, but it was fine for Shmuel. He would have made a good rabbi."

"He'll still make one. We just have to bring him home." My mother gripped my father's powerful forearm. "Please, Avram. My brother is a friend of Alderman Samuel Dickstein. If the authorities refuse to look for Shmuel, he'll slip him a bribe. Gershon says that's how it's done."

My father gritted his teeth. "We don't have the money to bribe an alderman."

"I do." My uncle beckoned my mother back to the table. She stepped halfway there.

"Shmuel is dead," my father declared. "There's no one to look for."

Mama gasped, but Papa commenced to sit shiva, the seven days of mourning. He ripped the lapel on his jacket, took off his shoes, and set them outside the door. Next he went into the bedroom and hung a cloth over the mirror. Mama followed to stop him, but when he told her to leave it, she retreated to the kitchen and stared at the stove. I heard Papa rummaging in the closet, toppling boxes and ripping the butcher paper he and Mama used to wrap precious possessions. When he emerged, he was swathed in a large tallit I'd never before seen. The blue embroidery on the yellowed silk was faded, but the fragile cloth was shot through with pure gold thread.

"Your grandfather's prayer shawl! I didn't know you brought it here." Mama reached out to touch the tightly-wound fringes.

"I was saving it to give to Shmuel on his ordination," Papa said, brushing past her as he drew the old tallit around him. He sat on a stool, not a chair, to signify that his son's death had brought him low, and prayed silently. If I'd been permitted to join him, I would have prayed for Shmuel's safe return, but Papa considered his son dead. The Catholic kids at school talked about their souls in the afterlife, but Jews didn't believe in that. So what was my father asking of God?

"You need ten men to make a minyan," my uncle reminded Papa. "You can't pray alone."

"God allows exceptions in case of emergencies." My father turned toward the wall.

"Then you'll sit shiva alone too. I won't organize the shul's chevra kadisha to bring you meals. A burial society serves families of the dead,

not the living. Yetta and I won't visit either until this nonsense stops."
Onkel Gershon looked at my mother. "Meanwhile, you'll carry on as
usual." Last he stared at me, buttoned his fur-lined coat, and shut the
door firmly behind him.

My mother watched him go, her usually busy hands hanging powerless at her sides. I felt powerless too, caught between my parents,
my father and my uncle, the changes in my body and the loss of my
brother. For the first time since my period began, I felt a gush of blood
between my legs. If this was the power of womanhood, I didn't see
what good it could possibly serve.

part six

Gershon, 1917

chapter 13

Gershon hadn't told Yetta earlier that morning that it was Rivka who'd called and urged him to come over right away. He'd said it was Ruven Kleinshmidt asking him to see if the apartment he was cleaning out for Hymie and his shiksa wife was satisfactory. Gershon wanted to focus on comforting his sister, and confronting Avram, without using his energies to reassure his wife. He also needed more information, and wanted to make a plan, before letting Yetta and the girls know Shmuel had run off to join the Navy. Not until he felt in charge would Gershon share the news and tell his family that he'd handle everything. Otherwise Yetta would insist on stepping in, Zipporah would fret, and Ruchel would give him advice that he didn't need or want. Solving a problem as serious as this on his own would give Gershon another chance to prove to his younger daughter that his influence could be used to help the powerless, not just for personal gain.

"Sit Rivka," he'd said, when he found her pacing around the table. He was used to the eight large rooms in the Mendels' apartment, and the Levinsons' front room, barely half the size of his study, was as crowded as the tiny stockroom of their parents' grocery store in Lemberg. Gershon had taken a seat himself, hoping his sister would follow his example. She didn't.

"Calm yourself. Shmuel's been gone only two days. I'll find him and bring him home. Trust me. I know my way around these things. The people who can track him down owe me."

"What about Avram? He won't accept your help." Rivka, more than anyone, knew the history of their rivalry. As children, he and Avram not only competed in their studies, but also in games of skill. Each spring in the shtetl, boys dug holes in the earth, filled them with last fall's rancid walnuts, and pitched a stone at the holes. Whoever got closest took the nuts inside, and at the end of the game, the person with the most nuts was the winner. When they were ten, Gershon swore he'd beat Avram, the cobbler's son and reigning champion, once and for all. He practiced pitching all winter, and won the first game come spring. Avram never regained the title that year.

"I promise you, this time Avram will accept my help." Gershon had sought the words to reassure his sister. "This isn't a competition over nuts in the hole, it's about rescuing his son."

Rivka's sigh had echoed in the air and Gershon shivered at the sound of her despair. The house was colder than usual and he'd wondered if the Levinsons had been forced to cut back on fuel for the stove. Looking around the kitchen for more wood, he'd noticed for the first time that Shmuel's place was still set for Shabbas dinner and rose to clear away his nephew's wine glass and dishes. He'd felt awkward in the kitchen, the domain of Yetta, the girls, and Margaret at home, but it wasn't as if Rivka's apartment had lots of storage space. There was one cupboard with one obvious shelf for him to add Shmuel's kiddish cup and chipped plate to the others.

"You're right," Rivka said, still not sitting but finally no longer pacing. "Avram has to be reasonable." Gershon was glad he'd convinced her, even though he didn't believe it himself. If only the powers of persuasion he'd used with Yetta's father to win her hand could for once work with Avram. Not because Gershon wanted to score another victory over his brother-in-law, but because by saving Shmuel's life he could finally make up for nearly causing Rivka's death.

chapter 14

Sitting in Rivka's kitchen, facing this crisis amid the signs of her poverty, Gershon thought back to another crisis caused by their meagre beginnings. The winter that Gershon was twelve was unusually cold and the peasants who farmed in the countryside made fewer trips into town to shop at the Mendels' grocery store. To help out, Gershon got a job assisting the baker. The work was heavy, but as his muscles got stronger, he was allowed to carry sacks of flour from the grain merchant's delivery van into the baker's shop. Sometimes the merchant himself, Yetta's father, showed up to negotiate a big sale.

Two weeks before Chanukah, Yetta accompanied him. Gershon, covered in flour and red-faced with embarrassment, had tried to keep his back to her, but was forced to turn around to set down a tray of steaming loaves fresh from the oven. He wiped his brow with his sleeve.

Yetta opened the mother-of-pearl clasps on her coat. "It's hot in here. I'm sweating too." She dabbed the tip of her nose with a linen handkerchief and handed it to Gershon.

He held it at arm's length, intimidated by its heavenly lightness and delicate embroidery.

"My mother taught me to sew last year. Now that I'm eleven, I'm learning how to bake."

Gershon eyed the coarse brown loaves cooling on the counter. Yetta would bake with the white flour her father sold his wealthy customers, using Viennese honey from bees who dined on lavender and roses, not the honey Gershon and his friends collected in the nearby clover fields.

"I'll bring you a piece of nut cake the next time we come here," Yetta promised.

Her father was speaking to the baker. "My porter will make the delivery next week, then I'll come in to settle up." He looked around the shop and said, "I see you've found an industrious young man to help you out." Turning to Gershon, he asked if he were a bar mitzvah.

"Next year, sir, I'll turn thirteen and be called up to the Torah."

"Industrious yes, but not quite a man," he said and smiled. While he shook hands with the baker, Yetta took her handkerchief from Gershon's paralyzed fingers and slipped it into his shirt pocket. Striding to the door, her father caught them exchanging a shy smile. His expression grew puzzled, then alarmed. Gershon heard a whip crack as their carriage sped down the icy street.

A few days later, the baker promised Gershon a Chanukah bonus. Gershon's father, Julius, wanted to use the money to repair the wooden bins where he stored matches, which got ruined when damp seeped through the rotten boards. Feigel, his mother, hoped to make his sister a new coat. Rivka was two years too big for her old one, and when she came in from hauling water or wood, her exposed skin was chafed. She'd developed a cough that was getting louder and deeper.

Gershon had other plans. He told his parents that rats had raided the flour and the baker, rather than giving him a bonus, was sending him to the city for more. Then he asked the baker if he could borrow the cart to buy lumber for his father. The baker handed him the reins and gave him the afternoon off. Gershon drove to the city where he bought a hand mirror for Yetta. It was made in Germany and the enamelled back was as blue and yellow as a summer sky.

The following week, Yetta's father held her arm tightly as he escorted her into the bakery. Gershon had to find a way to give her the mirror. Unloading a tray of rugelach, he suggested to the baker that they give some of the cinnamon-raisin cookies popular at this time of year to their esteemed guests. The baker readily agreed and when he handed over the money for the flour, Yetta's father reluctantly released his grip on his daughter to count it. Gershon beckoned her toward the oven and walked in front of the counter to hide Yetta from view. With his right hand, he gave her a cookie; with his left, the mirror. "Happy Chanukah," he whispered.

She held the glass so that both their faces were reflected in it, his glistening with hope, hers radiating delight. They smiled at their image and then, briefly, directly at each other, before Yetta slipped the mirror into her coat pocket. She skipped back to her father. "Papa, these are better than Mama's. Do you think she'd be upset if we brought some home?"

He suggested it would be kinder to disguise the baker's cookies by mixing them in with his wife's. The baker told Gershon to wrap them up as a gift. Gershon was clumsy tying the string around the box, but Yetta's deft fingers made a neat bow. Their hands touched as he handed over the package. Her father grabbed it and swept his daughter out into the cold.

Rivka lay in bed the first night of Chanukah, too sick to eat potato latkes. As she alternately shook with chills and sweated with fever, her breath came in rapid bursts between dry, hacking coughs. Feigel used scarce wood to keep water boiling on the stove in hopes that the warm, moist air would sooth her daughter's lungs. Still, over the next four days, her condition worsened. Rivka vomited back even a sip of tea, and his mother was terrified when her lips and nails turned blue from lack of oxygen.

"Send Gershon for the doctor," Feigel told her husband.

"We can't afford him."

"Then get the feldsher. He's cheaper."

"We can't afford him either." Julius threw another stick of wood in the stove, but relented as pain spread from Rivka's chest to her abdomen. The feldsher confirmed she had pneumonia. He said to apply clay poultices every hour, and wrote a prescription for a serum to take to the apothecary. Julius nodded, but put the slip of paper in his pocket. In lieu of payment, he agreed to give the feldsher kerosene and matches for the rest of the winter. "The matches better be dry," the feldsher said, wrapping a scarf around his neck. "Not like the last batch you sold me."

Two days later, Rivka coughed up phlegm streaked with blood. Feigel thrust out her hand and Julius turned over the prescription. Gershon raced to the drug store, paying for the serum with his mother's promise to sew a new coat for the apothecary's wife. Feigel hoped to use any leftover scraps of wool to lengthen Rivka's coat if—no, when—she got better. But the wife was so fat that the coat used up every bit of material.

As Rivka drifted in and out of consciousness, each member of the family held a private conversation with God. Gershon imagined Julius venting his anger at being too poor for a real doctor, and Feigel asking for a miracle like the one being celebrated at this season. He listened to Rivka, in fevered dreams, ask to race through summer fields, picking fruit. But guilt made any attempt at prayer stick in Gershon's throat. His chest ached as though he too had been stricken with pneumonia.

At last, the words came to him. "Dear God, let Rivka live and I will forget Yetta and devote myself to study."

On the eighth and last day of Chanukah, Rivka's fever broke, answering Feigel's prayers. The harsh winter ended as early as it had begun, followed by a mild spring. God softened toward Julius. Cheered by the warm weather, peasants came into town more often and bought extra supplies at the store. Berries ripened ahead of schedule. Eager to help Rivka regain her strength, everyone in the family poured fruit, cream, *and* condensed milk into her bowl.

Gershon left his job with the baker and ceded the championship of nuts-in-the-hole back to Avram. He took advantage of the lengthening days to sit in the rebbe's study and pore over the ancient texts. Being inside also lessened the likelihood that he'd have a chance encounter with Yetta. He willed his mind, heart, and spirit to think only of the sacred Torah scrolls.

Alas, banishing thoughts of Yetta was impossible. After his bar mitzvah, Gershon had been admitted into the Hevra Sha-as, the town's Talmudist society, of which her father was a member. Debating minute points of law with him was a weekly reminder that the rules of wealth and poverty kept Gershon from his daughter. Nevertheless, for six years after Rivka's recovery, he made no attempt to contact her. The honour he brought his family through his studies continued to keep Rivka and his parents healthy. Even if he regretted the Mendels' lack of money, they didn't.

chapter 15

The memory of Rivka's near death was as fresh as yesterday as Gershon walked home from her house a quarter of a century later. He was glad to leave her neighbourhood, stinking of overflowing garbage and horse droppings, and get back to the well-kept area of the Lower East Side where he lived. Thinking about the challenge of finding Shmuel gradually improved his mood too. Not only would he repay Rivka, he'd have the satisfaction of demolishing Avram's mule-headed claim that Shmuel was dead. The only downside to finding his nephew was that Avram could once again brag about his son, the future rabbi. A lesser man than himself, Gershon thought, might wish the boy had run away and disappeared for good.

Yetta was bent over the oven when he walked in, checking the brisket to see if the meat was tender enough to pull away with a fork. "Feathers flying off bones," she called it. "Twelve minutes, it should be ready," she said. Now that Gershon no longer worked on Sundays, his wife cooked a big midday meal like the gentiles. "So, the apartment will make Hymie's wife act nice to Jews and Jews will learn a shiksa's garbage stinks no worse than theirs?" she asked.

Gershon unwound the heavy woollen scarf from his mouth and nose and breathed in the welcome aroma of his own house. No matter how rich his neighbours, the hallways still stank of the foods they cooked in the countries they emigrated from. "As long as she cooks with vegetables from Hymie's cart, the garbage will smell the same," Gershon said.

After wrapping his arms around her ample waist, he went into the dining room. Yetta followed. She moved a cut-glass bowl of nuts from the sideboard to the table and watched to make sure he took a fistful of cashews, his favourite, before she settled down next to him. Now that he had her full attention, Gershon announced, "Shmuel has run off and joined the Navy."

Yetta put her hand to her throat. "What are you saying? He's sixteen, the same age as our Ruchel. Since when does this country send children to be killed?"

"Shmuel is like his father, headstrong and stubborn. Only smarter, like me. He must have convinced the recruiter he was old enough to enlist."

"The Navy allows Jews?" Yetta groaned, remembering her severe nausea on the boat to America. She said she couldn't picture someone choosing to spend months at sea.

"For all I know, he lied about his religion too."

Yetta dabbed her eyes with her apron. "They know where he was sent?"

"They don't even know for sure it was the Navy. Dev says his friends saw him looking at a poster outside United's." Gershon patted Yetta's hand. "Don't get yourself in a tsimmes. We can't do anything until tomorrow when the recruitment office opens."

"You can help find him?"

"Rivka wants me to. Avram is already sitting shiva."

"Just like that, the man declares his son dead?" Yetta inhaled sharply. "How is Rivka?"

"Like you'd expect."

Yetta called the girls into the dining room and told them what had happened. "Our food can wait," she said. "I'm going to see Rivka now."

"No!" Gershon thrust away the bowl of nuts. "I said that as long as Avram persists in his nonsense, you and the girls won't visit and the chevra kadisha won't bring meals."

"For shame Gershon. She's your sister. Suppose Zipporah or Ruchel disappeared."

"Yetta, I forbid it." Gershon's eyes warned his daughters too. "Get washed for dinner."

Tears staining her cheeks, Yetta returned to the kitchen. Moments later a platter clattered to the floor. "It's all right," she called in a quivering voice. "The meat wasn't on the plate yet."

Zipporah went into the kitchen to help her mother clean up.

"I'm going to see Tante Rivka and Dev." Ruchel thrust her arms into her coat and rushed out the door, knocking Gershon's hat from the shelf to the floor as she swept past.

Gershon ate a hearty meal. He refused to discuss Shmuel, afraid Yetta would try to dissuade him from banning her visits to Rivka, but underneath his small talk he was busy calculating who to call and who would need to be paid in order to rescue his nephew. Frustrated that he had to wait until Monday to begin his search, Gershon directed his energy toward finding a place for Mrs. Meltzer. He retreated to his study and seized the phone.

It was answered on the first ring. "Hadassah House for the Elderly and Infirm, Joseph Cohen, proprietor, speaking." The home served three Lower East Side congregations. Gershon persuaded local businessmen to donate goods and services; in exchange he threw contracts their way. Many, who like him had left elderly parents behind, relieved their guilt through these acts of tzedakah. Mr. Cohen was not one of them. He claimed it was charity enough that he ran the place cheaply and efficiently. Gershon suspected the man skimmed food, linens, and light bulbs for his own family.

"Joe, I need a place for Mrs. Meltzer."

"Her daughter and son-in-law can give me something for the bed?"

"You got openings, Joe. Two residents died last week. I'll move her in on Monday."

"I got three on the waiting list who can pay full price. Subsidies and donations alone can't keep the place going. You knew when you made me proprietor that I'm a businessman, like you."

"I know the sinks leak and the old people's bones rattle from the cold." It galled Gershon that Mr. Cohen let the residents live that way. Avram was worse, forcing his own family to stay in that small, stinking apartment when they could live better with Gershon's help.

"You're telling me to fix the sinks and the boiler? These things take money, Gershon."

"I'm telling you to stop skimming the coal Moishe Friedman delivers in order to heat your own house, and to admit Mrs. Meltzer. I'm also warning you I got two gentleman with business smarts *plus* hearts of gold, just arrived from Galicia, who can take over your job."

Mr. Cohen cleared his throat. "Give me until Monday afternoon. Anything else I can do?"

"The shul needs a new roof. The classrooms in the attic get wet when it rains."

"I'll drop off a donation tomorrow." Mr. Cohen sighed and said goodbye.

Gershon stroked the polished surface of his desk and smiled to himself. "One more thing before you go, Joe. Mrs. Meltzer likes her kreplach seasoned with extra pepper but no salt."

At last, Gershon was ready to resume his weekly Torah studies. Perhaps the text would reveal a message from God about how to search for Shmuel, just as the forefathers sought signs (an angel, a dove, a girl at the well) that they were on the right path. You had to be astute to recognize them, however. He'd learned growing up in Lemberg that his own brains, while admittedly a gift from the divine, were what ultimately got him what he wanted in life, especially his beloved Yetta.

chapter 16

The shtetl where Gershon and Yetta were born was actually five kilometres south of Lemberg, but Jews took the name of the city because it sounded more cultured. The Catholic peasants who farmed the surrounding countryside didn't care, as long as their fields and animals were fertile. Market day was the big event each week. Peasants sold cartloads of produce and spent their money in the Jewish shops, including the Mendels' small grocery store. The farmers spoke Austrian-German, the Jews Yiddish, so they gestured to exchange vegetables and livestock for kerosene, matches, and dry goods. Gershon, on his way to cheder, hung around the marketplace, where he quickly picked up the foreign language. Soon he was called out of school to translate complex deals, and earned a reputation as a "smart" boy. His parents protested that God gave him brains to study Jewish law, not to trade gentile goods, but the rich gvirs overrode their objections.

One October day, fire broke out on the edge of town where hay had just been harvested. The peasants' barns and houses were attached, forming a continuous ring to keep the Jews out, but that also made the fire spread quickly. Farmers loaded whatever they could fit into their carts and drove into town. Jews took them in and raided their own meagre stores of food to feed them. When space and rations ran out, Yetta's father bought lumber to build the peasants huts and donated barrels of flour for bread. As winter settled in, tempers frayed. The poor Jews kvetched that while they ate simple meals—radishes and herring for breakfast; soup and a bit of chicken for dinner—the Christians in their heated huts dined on meat provided by their rich host.

Gershon was listening to just such complaints the day Yetta, a girl of Rivka's age, walked into the Mendels' store and bought all the lump sugar. To him she seemed a foreign figure newly arrived from Vienna, or even London. Dark, curly braids, escaping from a fur hood, framed her wide and friendly smile. She spoke to him as an equal, prefacing her order with, "Please."

"So much sugar? You must drink your tea sweeter than Empress

Elisabeth." Gershon tried to mask shyness with bravado, but his arms shook lifting the ten-kilo bags onto the counter.

"It's not for me. Papa says the farmers, no less than we, should have sugar in their tea."

"No amount of sugar will sweeten them!"

"Don't judge them so harshly. Think of all they've lost. Surely it's a mitzvah to share whatever we can with them, especially the little children."

Gershon felt chastened. "With such sweet thoughts, you don't need any sugar yourself." He offered to load the sugar in a wheelbarrow and walk her back home, but she pointed to her pony cart out front and helped him carry and stow the bags herself. Gershon didn't know whether he was more surprised by her strength or the fact that her father let her do such menial work.

"Papa says manual labour, especially on behalf of those less fortunate, keeps us humble."

Gershon didn't feel humble watching her drive away. He felt exalted. Just standing next to her made him feel rich. Yetta's father next bought kerosene and matches for all the peasants, and so for a short time his parents grew rich too. The fire had been good for business.

In spring, the peasants were back on their farms, taking the lumber with them. Gershon and his friends had the streets of the shtetl to themselves once again. Late one evening, after the game of Nuts-in-the-Hole in which Gershon beat Avram, he saw Yetta again. Rivka had just come to call him home to study, when Yetta marched past arm-in-arm with a group of rich girlfriends, laughing and singing as though the glow of twilight had been created for them. She smiled at him and Rivka with a brightness that outdid the setting sun. Her companions made nasty comments about unwashed riffraff. Yetta scolded her friends, but their locked arms trapped and pulled her away.

As Yetta looked back at him, Gershon smiled and waved at her until Rivka elbowed him in the ribs. "I thought you were smart," his sister said. "You should know better than to get ideas in your head about the daughter of a baalei h'bata." For the next two years, the difference in their status had drawn a line between them, until the day Yetta came to the bakery with her father. Soon after, Gershon's guilty promise to devote himself to study had separated them another six years.

When he was eighteen, and Yetta seventeen, Gershon could stand the frustration no longer. He went to the shadchen and asked the matchmaker to arrange their marriage with her father.

"Are you meshugga?" she asked. "Her father will choose a husband from the city, not the shtetl." To Gershon's protest that a rich man's son was no match for a brilliant scholar, however poor, she laughed and said, "He can't match your chutzpah either." Only after failing to persuade the shadchen to speak on his behalf did Gershon, desperate, go to Yetta's father himself.

Ready to mount a defence against similar ridicule, he was instead met with a practical question. "How do you propose to take care of my daughter? She was not raised to be conceited, but she is accustomed to certain luxuries."

Gershon thought quickly. "I'll tutor the sons of the wealthy preparing for bar mitzvah."

Yetta's father raised his eyebrows. "Every other scholar hires himself out to do the same. Lemberg is neither that big nor that rich to support all of you."

Gershon tapped his forehead. "Seykhl. Wits. I'll use mine to compete for business."

"This I would relish seeing, were it not for the fact that Yetta's well being is at stake."

"I would do anything for your daughter."

"That is what both reassures—and scares—me." Yetta's father stroked his beard. "The Talmud teaches us to be careful not to make a woman cry because God counts her tears. Woman came out of man's rib. Not from his feet to be walked on, not from his head to be superior, but from his side, to be equal. From under the arm to be protected, and next to the heart to be loved."

Gershon too quoted the ancient rabbis. "A man should love his wife as much as he loves himself, and honour her more. He who honours his wife will be rewarded with wealth. As much as I love and honour your daughter, I'll be the wealthiest man in all of Lemberg, in the entire Empire!"

"Testimonials are touching but you must physically honour the obligations set forth in the ketubah, the marriage contract." Yetta's father listed them: conjugal rights, shelter, a garment for each season, sufficient oil and wood for cooking, enough bread for two meals a day, wine if the wife was accustomed to drinking, and a silver coin— ma'ah—as pocket money every week.

"The wife must fulfil her duties too." Gershon, growing impatient, enumerated on his fingers. A wife was expected to act modestly, even if her husband was the only person present. It was her role to maintain sholem bayess, peace in the home, and to cook and clean. If her dowry was sufficient to hire someone, as Yetta's would be, she was obligated to perform only "tasks of affection," that is, making the bed and serving her husband food. "I would not ask more of her."

"The Talmud states that if a man cannot provide his wife with the basics, he must hire out as a day labourer to earn enough to pay for them."

"I would live by the sweat of my brow, instead of the wisdom of my brains, if necessary."

"Rashi says that a man must also provide his wife with perfume and jewellery."

Gershon was momentarily crestfallen, then defiant. "Her very breath is to me sweeter than perfume, her radiant smile is the finest of jewels. So shall I consider her bedecked with finery."

The older man frowned. "These are the gifts she gives to you. Rashi says that you must give them to her."

Gershon wondered if Yetta had kept the mirror he'd given her six years ago. "I will hold a mirror before her eyes and give back to her, magnified, the perfume and jewels of her soul."

Yetta's father clasped his hands in thought, then summoned his wife, a devout woman who was known for her charitable deeds. She was aghast. "Farshtendlekhkeyt, intelligence, does not put food on the table!"

"And when you married me, what did I have?"

"A small business only in those days, but still more than one can say for Mr. Mendel."

"And who, if not you, gave me the foundation to turn a small business into a big one?"

"God," she answered.

Yetta's father smiled at his wife's firm tone. "The rabbis teach that God's presence dwells in a pure and loving home. We raised Yetta pure. They love each other. With God's help, they too will manage." He bowed slightly. "Of course, if you object, the marriage will not take place."

Yetta's mother closed her eyes in prayer, then looked Gershon up and down. At last, she nodded. "He is a highly regarded scholar. His father is an honest man. May God bless them."

The wedding was a lavish affair. Not only were relatives and business associates from the city invited, but everyone in the shtetl was welcomed to partake of the five course meal and bottles of imported wine. Gershon and Yetta stood under the same wedding canopy as her parents had, and when Gershon crushed the wineglass beneath his feet, it was from her family's finest crystal.

The newlyweds were twirled in chairs above the guests' heads. Gershon looked down on his parents and his sister Rivka, standing uneasily beside his in-laws. People filed past them, two mismatched families united by this gossiped-about marriage, to offer congratulations. Avram and his parents were among the well wishers. It seemed to Gershon that Avram lingered in front of Rivka longer than it would take to say a simple "Mazel Tov!" His sister appeared to blush, but when Gershon tried to look at them more closely, he was lifted and spun around. By the time he was set down, Avram was drinking with their old cheder classmates and Rivka was in a tight circle with her girlfriends. Dizzy with joy and wine, Gershon decided it had been his imagination.

When the last of the company left, Gershon's mother began to collect plates and glasses. Yetta's mother gently laid a hand on her arm, telling her to leave it to the servants. Everyone was tired, she said, and they were giving the young couple a carriage to spend the night at a hotel in Lemberg. They'd have the Mendels over for Shabbas dinner next week. The women embraced, stiffly, and Yetta's mother went to fetch a small trunk with her daughter's overnight clothes.

Gershon stood alone in the quiet market square with his parents.

"You've done well for yourself." His father wiped the gravy-stained lapel of his only suit.

His mother straightened her wig, knocked askew by the awkward hug from his new mother-in-law. "I never dreamed a child of mine would become part of such an eminent family."

Gershon pictured them eating at a fancy table in the home of Yetta's parents, dressed in the same clothes they'd worn to the wedding, watching nervously to choose the proper utensil. They looked tiny and shop-worn. He enveloped them in arms grown sturdy from carrying heavy Torah scrolls. "Opruen zikh, don't worry," he told them. "I will never forget where I came from."

Remembering where he came from was what drove Gershon to help impoverished immigrants after he'd become a rich man in America. It's what fuelled his commitment to find Shmuel and bring him home to his poor sister. He was sure his money, accompanied by a little arm-twisting, would let him succeed. Some might see his belief in himself as arrogance, but to Gershon he was just using the brains God gave him to do good. Let women worry about sholem bayess, peace in the home. Men were obligated to perform tikkun olam, healing the whole wide world.

part seven

Shmuel, 1917

chapter 17

It was not until the fifth week of boot camp that the recruits first touched a weapon. To Shmuel, the smallest gun felt heavier than the densest Talmud tome. Mikovski, on the other hand, wielded a pistol with the same easy aggressiveness he deployed when shinnying up a rope. After shredding the bull's eye, he called on men at random to step up to the firing line. Not knowing who was next kept them off balance and they shot wide the mark. Thelieutenant clucked at them like Tante Yetta trying to keep him, Dev, and their cousins in line at Seward Park. Only his aunt was good natured about it.

Shmuel fixed his eyes on the target, not Mikovski's face, while waiting his turn. He recalled long Shabbas afternoons of staring at scripture, afraid to blink lest his father scold him for not paying attention. He remembered holding up the Torah scroll during services, willing his muscles not to tremble under its weight. Firing a gun required the same unwavering gaze and steady arm. If he could do it under Avram's eyes, he could stand up to Mikovski.

His first two rounds didn't even hit the outer ring. Mikovski ordered him to stand closer. The next four shots strayed too. The lieutenant sneered. "What's wrong, Lord? Too long since you been fox hunting?" Shmuel tried, and failed, again. In the Torah, his people marched to battle with swords and sling shots. Surely that applied to modern-day warriors carrying guns and rifles.

"You're not like that piss-pants Jew boy who went home crying to his mama, are you?" Mikovski aimed his pistol at Shmuel's genitals and snickered. "Practice good if you want to ship out and not flunk out." Shmuel did practice, first with small-bore arms and later with long-range railroad guns. His marksmanship wasn't great, but it was good enough to earn him a satisfactory grade. Nevertheless, it irked him that he passed as a non-Jew more easily than he passed target practice.

Mikovski goaded him and the other boots further. "It's a snap to stand still and take aim at 1400 hours, but a Gerry in a U-boat don't know day from night. You gotta do it without sleep." He woke them at 0300 hours, made them lift weights until their arms ached, and put them through target practice again. Shmuel was dragged from his hammock more than the others, three or four times a night. The colder and rainier it was, the more often the toe of Mikovski's sneaker poked his rear end. It took all of Shmuel's self-control to keep his mouth shut and his arm steady.

Others bit their tongues too, except when writing home, when they let their misery pour out. After a month of suffering together, they trusted one another enough to read their letters aloud. The bravest admitted fear, but most bragged to bolster their morale. "I can make a flotation device with coveralls while I'm in the water and put it on in three seconds." They complained about studying. "I've read more books in the Navy than in high school." Shmuel smiled. A hundred and forty years of Navy rules were a footnote compared to three thousand years of Jewish law.

Railing against authority was common too. Shmuel invented people to write to so he could be one of the guys. "Dear Buddy," he read, "They asked a zillion questions and if you got one wrong, you had to do twenty push-ups. I got mine right. So they made me pick a number from one to twelve. You can never get that one right." He stowed the letters in his pocket, and when the men scurried to middle-of-the-night drills, eyes too bleary to focus, he threw them overboard.

Once he didn't see Tomasio standing behind him. "Said something you regretted?" the Italian asked. "I try not to write stuff that'll worry my mama. Like saying the food here stinks."

Shmuel improvised. "I had second thoughts about writing a girl I met just before joining up." It was easy enough to add a girlfriend to his assumed identity.

"You never mentioned her before. Holding out on us?"

Tomasio asked if he had a picture.

"Nah," said Shmuel. "Why keep her on the line when I don't know what will happen to me?" Tomasio grinned and said that since Shmuel was free, they could visit the ladies together on their next shore leave. Shmuel touched his strawberry mark, grateful for the moonless night.

It was harder to invent a good reason why he never got mail from home. When he said his parents couldn't read or write, someone suggested that the same neighbour who read Shmuel's letters to them should take dictation. That's what other illiterate parents did. Shmuel sidestepped the advice by saying, "Even if they answer the next one, we'll have shipped out before it gets here." At that, the men grew sombre. School would soon be over and the real war would begin.

With only three weeks of training left, the boots now looked as able-bodied as the sailors on the posters. Their hands grew a second layer of calluses from hauling ropes and they slid slick as their oilskin coveralls into the lifeboats they hoped would save them if a sub set the ship ablaze.

Mikovski cracked his knuckles as the men lined up for the next exercise. "If you thought drowning was a Navy man's biggest fear, you're dead wrong. Fire's your worst enemy." He led them off-ship to an area surrounded by high metal walls and reeking of lighter fluid. Mattresses on the other side of the wall substituted for life boats. "In five minutes, all this stuff will be put to the match." He pointed to the members of the fire unit. "They'll use the hoses at full force to knock it out, but you gotta run through the water and flames, get over the wall, and slide down the ropes to safety." The boots waited for Mikovski to demonstrate, but this time he whistled for another junior officer to take his place. He himself returned to the ship before a single match was struck.

Sweat poured down the men's faces. They were eager to go first, while the flames were still low. Nearly tripping over one another, they raced across the wooden planks, grabbed a rope, and hurtled over the wall. Shmuel was in the middle of the pack, waiting to be called. "Move to the back, Lord. You're going last." The substitute trainer held up the order from Mikovski.

By the time Shmuel's turn came, flames rose halfway up the fake masts. The floor was as slippery as the alley behind the Levinsons' building where women dumped their wash tubs out the window. The junior officer crouched beside a pile of sandbags at the opposite end of the deck. From behind the wall, the other boots shinnied up ropes to watch, while firemen stood poised to squirt Shmuel directly if he caught fire before reaching the other side. Instinct told him to recite the Sh'ma, the prayer Jews say before sleep and at the moment of death. But he was wide awake and determined not to waste his life on a training exercise. He studied the faces of the other men who seemed a mile, not a mere ten yards, away. Ryan and Tomasio hovered to the right of the free rope left for Shmuel to grab. To their left was Sandler, a fleshy, dark-haired man whose stubbornness reminded him of Avram. Seeing him was the final goad Shmuel needed.

"Get moving, Lord. It's only going to get worse." The trainer thumped the sandbags.

Shmuel spit into his hands, widened his eyes, and lunged across the deck toward Sandler. He gripped the rope and catapulted over the wall. The soles of his sneakers were melted but his body was unscathed. The row of mattresses vibrated with cheers. Shmuel shook with terror and relief. This test had better be the ultimate one; he wasn't sure he could pass any more.

Mikovski returned just as the boots, having vaulted back inside the training area, sloshed through knee-deep water carrying Shmuel on their shoulders and chanting, "Lord, Lord, Lord." The junior officer saluted, grinned, and handed him the forms. Mikovski crushed the papers and threw them in the water swirling at his feet. He watched the ink spread like a pool of blood as Shmuel, hoisted in the manner of a groom at an Orthodox wedding, was paraded past him.

Shmuel, however, wasn't in the mood to celebrate. Despite surviving the ordeal, he felt as defeated as Mikovski looked. What had he proven, that a boot as pig-headed as Avram could spur him to action? That the will to defy the lieutenant had made him run blindly into the flames? He was still letting himself be defined in opposition to others. When would he begin to define himself? Perhaps it would take the war, and facing a real enemy on his own terms, to discover who he was.

That evening, the local YMCA provided a jazz band to entertain the recruits. They played *Tiger Rag* and *Rock-A-Bye Your Baby With a Dixie Melody*, finishing with *Anchors Away*. Mikovski, who showed up near the end of the concert, scoffed that it wasn't an official Navy anthem.

Tomasio shot back. "Who cares, sir? It's our fight song." Shmuel, his thoughts lingering on warfare, said, "*The Star-Spangled Banner* was about a naval battle too." Even Ryan, emboldened by Shmuel's bravery that day, dared to speak up to Mikovski. Patting Shmuel on the back, he said, "Hear that, sir? The Army ain't got a song that famous, or a boy as smart and tough as our Sam."

Mikovski stormed off. At 0400 hours, he dragged Shmuel on deck, hosed him down, and assigned a hundred push-ups. He shoved him back in his hammock without letting him change into dry clothes. Shmuel lay awake all night, afraid of seeing Mikovski's sneer imprinted on his eyelids.

chapter 18

A week after they practiced escaping a fire, the boots learned to seal doors and stack sandbags to prevent one from spreading. The order seemed backwards, but as the clock ticked down to the hour of deployment, they had to trust that the Navy knew what it was doing. Maybe knowing you could escape if you had to made men more willing to tough things out before giving up. Shmuel wondered if he might have stayed at home if he'd believed he had options short of escape. Could he have found a way to seal Avram's mouth or sandbag his demands?

It was too late to think about what might have been. With less than two weeks before the men set sail, women from the Social Services Bureau arrived on base to set up a plan for them to stay connected to home after shipping out.

"Sam Lord," the tiny gray-haired lady read from her file. "Or should I use Samuel?"

"Sam is fine."

She verified his Brooklyn address. "Your parents?"

"John and Dorothy."

"Siblings?"

"None." Shmuel also answered in the negative to questions about aunts, uncles, cousins.

"A shame." The woman put her hand on his arm. "Families are so important."

"I had a lot of friends. I played sports."

She brightened. "My grandson Albert is wild about baseball. He's small but wiry, like you. Would you like Social Services to help you keep in touch with your teammates at home?"

"They're all in the service too."

She wrote an "X" on the form. "Religion?"

"We don't practice one." Shmuel looked at his hands.

The woman frowned. "Can you suggest another way for us to comfort your parents during this period of separation?" She spoke as if the sailors were going away to boarding school. There was no mention of the Bureau notifying families in the event of capture, injury, or death.

"Just tell them I've been well-trained and trust my pals to look out for me. That's what I write in my letters. They'll be reassured if you say the same thing."

She made a note in his file. Then she ran through the services the agency provided. First was a packet of stationery and stamps so he could continue writing home. Shmuel didn't want them taking up space in his sea bag, but neither could he risk throwing them overboard. When the woman took a break to get a glass of water, he slipped them back into her satchel.

"We deliver care packages. Families buy their boys cigarettes, candy and chewing gum, socks. Mail this postcard to your parents so they'll know to send them to us, and we'll ship them to you." She handed him a card with the instructions and address printed in several languages.

Shmuel said he didn't smoke or eat a lot of candy.

"Every fighting man needs dry socks, dear." The woman pressed the card on him. At least it didn't take up much space. Finally she asked if he had a memento from boot camp, or perhaps a keepsake he'd brought with him, that he wanted the Bureau to mail home for safe-keeping.

Shmuel handed her the rope he'd used to hold up his pants the first week of training. He no longer needed it. The regulation belt, not even tightened to the last notch, worked fine now.

"I don't understand." She held the stained and twisted twine at arm's length.

"My folks will. Just say the equipment has been de-acquisitioned." Shmuel imagined the sister, whom he'd just claimed not to have, reading the notice to his fictitious parents, all sitting on a couch in their nonexistent Brooklyn walk-up. Having spent eight weeks in a world wholly invented by the U.S. Navy, Shmuel saw the Lords as no more or less real than his true family.

Boot camp culminated with battle stations, a twelve-hour exercise that recapitulated two months of training. The men scaled ladders from the Calvin Austin's upper to lower decks in thirty seconds, ran a forty-obstacle course in a minute, did two hundred push-ups and sit-ups, swam a mile in frigid and oil-slicked waters, hit their mark with firearms, hauled ropes, and sealed the ship's compartments to contain the damages of war. Everyone graduated. They were no longer boots, but full-fledged sailors. Shmuel donned his Navy ball cap and passed in review before the chain of command.

Mikovski, at the bottom of the chain, was the first to salute him. "You wouldn't have made it if I hadn't pushed you," he whispered. "Just remember, Ensign Lord. Surviving boot camp ain't the same as getting out alive at sea."

"He's full of himself," Tomasio said as they worked their way up the line. Ryan agreed. "You got through on your own brains and guts." Shmuel wasn't so sure. He'd joined the Navy to get away from his classmates' taunts and his father's rigid expectations. Perhaps he'd needed Mikovski to stoke his defiance and guarantee that his attempted escape was successful.

The new ensigns mingled on deck, the day's heat and the pride in their chests warming the metal ID tags around their necks. Not until 2100 hours, while packing their bags, did the sweat of fear turn their aluminium disks cold. Come dawn, some would head to the Mediterranean, the rest to Scapa Flow in Scotland's Orkney Islands or to Queenstown, Ireland. For security reasons, they wouldn't be told their destination until they set sail. Shmuel and Tomasio were bound for the same place, Ryan another. Mikovski, returning to sea duty, was going wherever Shmuel was.

"How much you wanna bet I land in the fair Mediterranean?" Ryan teased.

"A plugged nickel," said Shmuel. "I'd rather bet that Tomasio and I are off to France to patrol the Atlantic."

"Ooh, lah, lah." Tomasio whistled. "In Paris, I'll teach you what your fancy books can't."

"Wherever they send us," Ryan said, "we gotta promise to meet in Boston in a couple of years. Maybe we'll even get Sam the Scholar here to eat a lobster."

They listened to the other men breathing raggedly or tossing in their hammocks.

"Ever wish you'd mailed the letter to that girl after all?" Tomasio asked Shmuel.

"Surer than ever that I was right to deep-six it," he answered. The real letter he regretted not writing was to his parents. He'd failed the fifth commandment, "Honour thy father and mother." And the "girl" to whom he owed a letter was Dev. There was no commandment to honour one's sister, but Shmuel had violated her trust. Dev was so open to the world. He hoped he hadn't added the word "disillusioned" to her vocabulary.

The rabbis taught that kindness superseded honesty, yet Shmuel had fretted more about not telling the truth than about hurting those he loved. In the end, lying had come easily. It had gotten him into the war. Getting out would be harder; falsehood had no place in combat. Aboard the Calvin Austin, Shmuel's chest rose and sank with the swell of the waves. For what he swore was the last time, he prayed to the God that he'd just told Social Services he didn't believe in, to keep him afloat.

chapter 19

Shmuel, Tomasio, and Mikovski were aboard the USS Leviathan, bound for Scapa Flow, the Bay of the Long Isthmus, where American troops would serve with the British Grand Fleet. The third night out, Shmuel relieved Tomasio on watch. They craned their necks at the cold, clear sky, marvelling at the sight of more stars than either thought possible growing up in the city.

"What's that line in your bible?" Tomasio laughed sheepishly. "My mom beaned me good when I had to repeat catechism class twice. I wish I'd taken that stuff more seriously now."

"God promises Abraham, the first Jew, to make his offspring as numerous as the stars in the heavens and the sands on the shore." Shmuel now understood the enormity of that pledge. He'd seen grains of sand on the beach, clumped together. There was something about seeing the stars, each emitting its own light in the firmament, that brought home the idea of multitudes.

"Either God doesn't keep His promises or He takes His own sweet time about it. Your people aren't too numerous." Tomasio glanced at Shmuel. "No offense meant, book boy."

"None taken." Shmuel smiled up into the dark. Tomasio's irreverence reminded him of Dev's recent defiance of their mother. He wondered if she'd ever have the nerve to challenge their father. "When you talk about my people ... I'd rather the others not know I'm Jewish."

"Not afraid, are you? You proved you can hold your own. Unless you're ashamed?"

"Neither." Shmuel swallowed, grateful for the dark. "It's easier, that's all. One less reason for someone to pick a fight. Allows me to focus on the real battle."

"Not self, but country?" Tomasio quoted the Navy's unofficial motto.

"That's it." Shmuel hoped Tomasio could see his smile of gratitude in the starlight. They saluted each other and Shmuel climbed up to the crow's nest, testing every inch of rope with his quaking hands. After the stillness on deck, he welcomed the stinging wind that whipped his hair, grown long again, into his eyes. It felt like a punishment he deserved, for sins too vague and abundant to enumerate. Two months of sun and sea had turned his hair nearly white, and made it thick and coarse. It hid his strawberry mark better than payess, yet tonight the stain pulsated as insistently as the stars above. The ugly flaw reminded him that he didn't control his fate. He could run away, but only the Almighty knew where, if ever, he would eventually settle.

By the time his watch ended near dawn, Shmuel was ready to leave the cold vastness of the heavens above for the warm galley below. He sought out the mess table where Hamble Weir, a British sailor assigned to help the American destroyer navigate the mined water of the Atlantic, was regaling the sailors with tales of the engagements he'd already survived. Though barely twenty-one, he'd been in the war for four years, almost from the beginning. He too had lied about his age to enlist, but unlike Shmuel, he'd done it with his family's knowledge and consent.

"I was at Jutland when the Gerries sank the Lutzow," Hamble was saying when Shmuel sat down with a breakfast tray of pancakes and ham. "The first tin fish struck direct on her prow. Blighty amazing hit, considering we were zigzagging and belching black smoke to protect the merchant ships." He described how the explosion made timbers splinter into matchsticks, glass shatter like icicles pelted by snowballs, and steel girders groan as they were wrenched apart.

Mikovski, across the table, said he'd heard that the boilers had withstood the blow.

"Righto. They were two decks below and the compartment was automatically sealed off when the water rushed in. The electricity stayed on too. Eerie how the lights lit up the men dying around us, but the twenty-seven down in the boiler room were spared."

Mikovski breathed a sigh of relief, as if he too were spared, until Hamble leaned forward.

"Except they were trapped inside. Eventually, the pressure got to be too much, the seals gave way, and the boilers exploded. I'll never forget the sickening hiss of steam escaping."

"They die of smoke inhalation?" a sailor asked.

Hamble shook his head. "Burned to death. No remains left to identify."

The scrape of forks ceased; men gulped air, not coffee. Mikovski looked ready to lose his flapjacks. Shmuel, still puzzling over why the lieutenant had left the fire drill rather than staying to gloat over making him run last, now understood. For Mikovski, drowning was like dying at home. Fire was alien turf. It terrified him.

Hamble continued. "The ship convulsed and settled on her port side, submerging the gun turret. Anything not tied down slithered down the boards into the sea. Radio wires curled up like ringlets in the flames and shredded flags fluttered from the mast." He painted a ghastly scene of the Lutzow's deck littered with bodies, some in uniform, others naked as the day they were born.

The galley clock said 0800 hours. Mikovksi rose and ordered the men to the next rotation, but the Lieutenant Commander overrode him and said they could wait until Hamble was finished. Most looked like they would have preferred to leave. Mikovski remained standing.

"How did you survive?" Shmuel asked Hamble.

"Kicked off my boots and put on a life belt. The two lifeboats that cleared the explosion were full, so I fastened a rope to the sturdiest timber at hand and shinnied down the ship's side."

"Wasn't the water cold?" Tomasio hugged himself. Others clutched their balls.

"Warmer than I expected, heated by the fire. The dark was worse than the cold. After the boilers exploded, the only light came from enemy fire. I'm not much of a swimmer ..."

"How did you pass Navy boot camp?" someone asked, "or whatever you Brits call it."

"Same as you," Tomasio teased. "Doing the breast stroke and floating like a dead man between laps when the instructor wasn't looking."

Laughter broke the tension. Hamble joined in until Mikovski's cough silenced everyone.

Hamble resumed. "When I couldn't get away, I was afraid the ship would topple over on me. Either that or I'd be sucked down the tunnel created when water rushed into the hold. That's what happened to the chaplain after the boilers exploded. A minute later, he was vomited back out, minus his oilskin, but otherwise none the worse for wear."

"Better to drown than be burned alive, right?" said the galley chief, looking to Mikovski to agree. The lieutenant blinked once, saying nothing, but Shmuel could have answered for him.

"I held my breath a long time, but when I got desperate for air, I swallowed a mouthful of the North Sea. It was like drinking the last tears of the dead men bobbing around me."

The sailors squirmed. Tomasio asked Hamble how he'd finally been rescued.

He'd been picked up on a raft barely big enough for three, but holding six. Around them, floating men sang *Nearer My God to Thee*. "Drifting away from the flames, the water got chilly," Hamble recalled. "A white light appeared in the distance. One man had a torch, what you call a flashlight. It was waterlogged, but it worked. He signalled in Morse code and the searchlight from a rescue ship answered that they'd pick us up. After a long wait, it pulled alongside and dropped a rope ladder. Two men came down and heaved us onboard."

There was a loud exhalation of air. Only Mikovski was silent. Hamble's rescue seemed of little interest to him. He was lost with the men incinerated in the boiler room.

"They wiped us down with rough towels, gave us each a bowl of soup and a basin of whiskey, and after we thawed out, they directed us to a wide berth with plenty of blankets."

"How long did you sleep?"

"I didn't at first."

"Afraid of nightmares?"

"Afraid of the silence."

"After the awful noise of battle, I'd expect a man to welcome the quiet of sleep."

"During the battle, you get used to the loud guns, the ship's throbbing engines, and the swish of water. Otherwise, it's eerily still. I needed to hear the men around me breathing."

The sailors held their own breath until, at last, they were dismissed. Hamble stood slowly with them. "I'll tell you, mates, if humans want to see hell on earth, all they need to do is board a destroyer being blown to pieces and taking brave young men down to Davey Jones's locker."

Shmuel lingered after the others left. Coming off night watch, his next rotation was inside his hammock. "Is it easier to sleep now?" he asked Hamble.

"Swimming's gotten easier. Sleep always comes hard."

The Brit's words proved prophetic. That night, even the gentle rocking of his hammock failed to quiet Shmuel's mind. Rescued from a life adrift, he had no sense of who he was now. His body wasn't that of a boy from the Lower East Side, his mind was full of learning absent in books, and his spirit had abandoned the faith of his youth. Like the shaken survivors of the Lutzow, Shmuel was afraid, only his fear wasn't rooted in the past, but streaming toward an unknown future.

His fingers slid inside his shirt and traced the letters on his ID tag. "S-A-M L-O-R-D." At last he began nodding off to the lullaby of the ship's engines. He knew that when he awoke, Sam Lord would no longer be a made-up name. It would henceforth be his real one.

part eight

Gershon, 1917

chapter 20

On Monday, three days after his nephew's disappearance, Gershon was first in line at the Navy recruiting station, wrapped in his best coat, when the heavy metal doors opened at eight.

"There's no record of a Shmuel Levinson enlisting last week." The clerk, standing behind a gritty counter that Gershon disdained to touch, slid his narrow finger down the columns of the wide ledger, each bearing hundreds of names.

Gershon wasn't surprised, but he also knew from helping immigrants that those who changed their names often kept the same initials. He asked for all the S.L.'s.

"Do you know how long it would take ...?" the clerk began.

Gershon smoothed out a ten dollar bill and thirty minutes later had his answer: four hundred and fifty-eight names. Ruling out those too foreign for Shmuel to have gotten away with still left over three hundred. He asked for phone numbers, planning to call their parents until he came to someone who didn't exist.

"I'm not permitted to release that information, sir."

"My nephew falsified his age. His mother is frantic. Under the circumstances, you can break the rules." Gershon reached into his wallet again.

The clerk stiffened. "If the boy lied about his age, it's a legal matter out of my control. The Community Board will have to approve your request before this office can proceed." He slammed the ledger shut and called for the next person in line.

Gershon went to see Rivka, expecting Avram to be at work, but he was home, sitting shiva. His brother-in-law davened, swaying and mumbling, in a corner of the darkened room. The two men ignored each other. Gershon told his sister how he planned to overcome this temporary setback.

"I spoke to Alderman Dickstein and got permission to address the Board tomorrow night. They'll petition the Borough President, who'll pressure the district court to give its approval to release the information." Gershon was sure he could penetrate all five layers of bureaucracy by spreading around enough money. He thought he heard a snort interrupt Avram's prayers.

Rivka too expressed scepticism. The borough and the district court were well beyond the Lower East Side territory where her brother held power. "Suppose we're wrong and Shmuel didn't even join the Navy? We should put a missing persons notice in *The Jewish Forward*."

Gershon rejected the idea outright. "Those ads are for women whose husbands run off and disappear, not for sons who go off to fight for their country."

"Then write a letter to Bintel Briefs for advice on how to trace him. We can't be the only family whose boy has done this." Rivka rummaged in Dev's school things for paper and pencil.

Gershon stayed his sister's hand. "I know you're trying to be helpful, but Bintel Briefs is a column for greenhorns and riffraff, not for settled immigrants and respectable people like us."

Avram rose and pulled away the black cloth covering the window. The afternoon sun lit up the stained walls of the apartment. Turning his back to the glare, Avram stared at his blinking brother-in-law. "You forget, Gershon. We Levinsons, unlike you Mendels, *are* the riffraff of America." He jerked the cloth back over the window. "Now go!"

chapter 21

"Well, well. It seems I have the privilege of once again addressing Mr. Mendel." The man whom Gershon had known in Lemberg as Sergeant Stepanic leaned back and crossed his arms. In the nearly twenty years since he'd tormented Gershon, the sergeant had also emigrated and gained a degree of clout. He sat just to the left of the chairman of the Community Board.

Gershon's stomach sank, remembering the power the sadistic Stepanic once held over him. Two weeks after he and Yetta were married, Gershon, Avram, and Lemberg's other young men had been conscripted by the Austro-Hungarian army to suppress a growing tide of national unrest. Government wagons came to the market square to collect the draftees. Jews huddled on one side, Catholic peasants on the other, noses running with fear and bone-breaking cold. Gershon stood alone, grateful for the fur overcoat and warm boots Yetta had bought him on their honeymoon.

"You, Jew! Over there with the others!" From an angular face, Staff Sergeant Stepanic's lips popped out as pink and swollen as two rain-bloated worms. He ripped Gershon's sleeve with his bayonet and used his rifle butt to shove Gershon toward the group. The others pulled away and turned their backs on him, making it clear they resented him for having moved up in the world. Yet a fortnight ago, they'd been happy to drink the wine and eat the food at his lavish wedding.

After bouncing over rutted roads all night, they reached camp in a misty dawn. The men were fed hunks of stale bread, mouldy carrots, and weak tea, and sent to unheated barracks to sleep on cots without blankets. Three hours later, as a light snow fell, Sergeant Stepanic marched them onto the field for their first drill. "Jews up front. Catholics in the rear."

"Since when are Jews put ahead of Catholics?" someone whispered.

Avram snickered. "When they want us to be killed first."

"By rights, I shouldn't even be here," Gershon muttered.

Stepanic overheard. Gusts of steam spewed from his fat lips as his gloved hands yanked Gershon out of line. "You think you're better than everyone else?"

"No, sir, but married men are not eligible for conscription."

The sergeant's hot spittle sprayed Gershon's face, but Gershon refused to wipe it off. He asked if Gershon was a God-fearing man, and when he replied that he was, Stepanic threatened, "You'll fear me more than God by the end of training," before butting him back in line.

The next morning, as the men were marched around the frozen field, the sergeant again pulled Gershon out of formation and dragged him to camp headquarters. Expecting the worst, Gershon instead heard the commanding officer telling his father-in-law, "The marriage wasn't registered when the conscription order was issued. I can't do anything about it."

Yetta's father held out five hundred kronen. "There's always something one can do."

The officer rubbed the bills between his fingers. Stepanic rubbed his own fingers, awaiting his share. The officer frowned, but Stepanic stood his ground until Gershon was ordered to pay the sergeant with his new boots. Stepanic strode around the room, admiring the smooth leather, before thrusting his old cracked boots at Gershon. He stood over him as he bent to slip them on. Not until Gershon stood up did Stepanic's face register disappointment that his scapegoat was leaving.

"I'm not done with you, Jew boy. Soon married men without children will be called up." Stepanic's fleshy lips smiled once again. "And next time you won't be able to buy your way out."

Gershon was relieved to be free, but he didn't like being dependent on someone else for favours. "I appreciate your help," he told Mr. Rubin, "but I don't want special treatment."

"I'm not doing this for you," Yetta's father had replied. "I'm doing it for my daughter."

A few months later, faced with the threat of being drafted again, Gershon and Yetta left for America. The night before, they attended Avram and Rivka's wedding. It was arranged so quickly that Gershon had no time to protest. He hadn't even been aware of the betrothal before the date was set. He'd heard Avram had been shot in the knee, a minor wound, but bad enough for the army to release him. Beyond that, their lives had diverged so much that Gershon had erased Avram from his mind. Now their paths would cross not merely as school-mates, but as family.

The wedding party was simple, limited to close friends and relatives, including Yetta's parents. Yetta went to the city to buy a gift, and after all but a few guests had left, insisted Rivka open it right then. Rivka, already alarmed by the weight of the package, opened her eyes wider when she saw the silver candlesticks nestled in a wooden box lined with dark blue velvet..

Yetta hugged her. "I wish Gershon and I were staying in Lemberg so you and I could be like sisters. Think of us in America when you light the Shabbas candles."

Rivka drew back. "My mother gave me her candlesticks. Perhaps you can return these to the jeweller? They're beautiful, but I'm afraid someone will steal them."

Yetta's face fell, but she recovered quickly and smiled. "God willing, you'll be blessed with two daughters, real sisters. To one you'll give your mother's candlesticks, to the other, these."

"Come Yetta." Gershon, protective, led his wife toward the door. She was oblivious to the resentment her wealth caused, but he couldn't be angry at his sister either. He'd once felt alienated from the town's rich families too. On the way out, he extended a cool hand to his new brother-in-law. "I trust you'll provide well for my sister without me here to goad you."

Avram's hands stayed in his pockets. "I'll take good care of Rivka because I want to. And because I can."

"As soon as I'm settled in America, I'll sponsor you to come over too."

"I don't need your help. I'll make it there on my own, if and when I choose to go."

Rivka put a hand on each of their arms. "Enough. Childhood is over. Let's make peace." Wiping her eyes, she hugged Gershon hard. She and their parents might never see him again.

chapter 22

But a few years later, he and Rivka did see each other, and here in this new country, Gershon had a chance to make amends for the sin he'd never brought himself to confess. Except that now, facing his old nemesis at the Board meeting, Gershon saw his opportunity threatened. Stepanic's angular face had grown mottled and fleshy, but his lips still writhed with evil. Disheartened, Gershon stared at the man's sheer ugliness until he felt confident by comparison. He stated his case methodically, as if reviewing an account with a client.

"How do we know your nephew isn't of age? Maybe you're just trying to track down a deserter who's shirking his duty." Stepanic silently mouthed the words, "Like you, coward."

"I assure you, gentlemen, my nephew is only sixteen." Gershon looked each man in the eye. Heads nodded, but the chairman and several others were sceptical. They wanted proof.

"I'm afraid Jews born in Lemberg weren't issued birth certificates," he said, "but this may suffice." He flourished a parchment attesting to Shmuel's bar mitzvah, dated three years earlier and signed by the rabbi and other dignitaries from the synagogue, including himself. For those unfamiliar with Jewish customs, he explained the ritual whereby boys became men at thirteen.

"So if a Jewish boy is a man at thirteen, surely after another three years he's old enough to fight for his country?" Stepanic smirked and stared pointedly around the table, but the Board members were busy studying the document. When they looked up, Gershon opened his custom-tailored woollen coat and placed his polished wallet beside his leather gloves.

"I move we approve the request," the chairman said. All except Stepanic voted in favour.

part nine

Dev, 1917

chapter 23

It was strange to come home from school all week to find my father sitting shiva in the darkened front room. Disconcerting was a good word to describe the sight of him, wrapped in my great-grandfather's tallit, perched on a stool, and praying feverishly for what, I didn't know. Nor did I know what to do with myself. With the covered windows blocking the light, and my father's stool blocking the steamer trunk where I usually worked, I couldn't do my homework. What excuse could I give my teachers? My brother is missing but my father acts like he's already dead?

By Wednesday, when my assignments were piling up, I waited for Papa to take a breath and bent down to ask if I could do my lessons. "My biology teacher throws an ing-bing if we turn in our assignments late," I said, holding out my textbook. There was a microscope on the cover, but to my father I was invisible. He simply readjusted his prayer shawl and davened back and forth faster. Mama motioned me to the kitchen and cleared a space at the table. Perhaps my father didn't consider what I was doing studying, reserving that term for what he and Shmuel did—used to do—when they read and discussed Torah.

I wondered if Papa missed those sessions as much as I missed talking to my brother about what I was learning in biology. After the gloom and silence in the apartment, I would even have welcomed Shmuel teasing me that my diagram of the digestive system was "all balled up." In the last few days, I'd also heard a passel of new slang words I was dying to ask him about. What did it mean when Bridget told Frankie, "Sorry, buster, the bank is closed." I thought it had something to do with her not wanting to kiss him, but Frankie often mooched money so maybe she meant just what she said. Jews always looked for deeper meanings instead of taking things at face value, unlike Bridget and her Catholic friends. I envied their less complicated lives.

At first, Mama tried to convince Papa to stop sitting shiva. "Our son is still alive," she insisted. "Acting like he's dead is tempting the evil eye."

"You're a modern woman," my father said. "Since when do you believe in spirits?"

My mother tried a different tack. "At least wait while Gershon tries to find him."

Hearing Gershon's name only fuelled Papa's resistance. He acted like he didn't even want Shmuel back if my uncle was the one who delivered him, and mentioning Gershon's efforts made him pray and daven harder. I thought my father would rock himself off the stool, but this was real life, not a slapstick movie. In our house, the shortest word or smallest gesture was deadly serious.

The only time Papa left his stool was for supper. In our religion, not even death interferes with eating. People bring food by the armload to families sitting shiva. Because of my uncle's ban, however, no one came to our house. Well, Ruchel came once, but since my cousin can't cook, she arrived empty handed. Mama ended up feeding her.

Then late on Friday afternoon, as I climbed up the stoop, Tante Yetta walked out of our building. She was holding a big bag and I could feel waves of heat and smell heavenly aromas emanating from it as she leaned over to plant a wet kiss on my cheek. My aunt sighed. "Your father won't let me in the door, so you take this to your mother." She gave me the bag and another kiss.

My father didn't look up when I walked in but the smell must have given me away. "Take the food back."

"It'll be dark by the time she gets there," my mother said. "You don't have to eat it, but why can't Dev? She's a woman now; she has to grow up strong and healthy."

It was a good thing Papa couldn't see me blush. I wanted to make my mother shush, but I also wanted to eat Tante Yetta's food. If my changed biology was the excuse, Amen.

"There's nothing wrong with the food my money buys, Rivka. Throw Yetta's food out!" My father shot up, tore the bag from my hands, and thrust it at my mother. She froze, holding it in front of her, then walked mechanically toward the trash can.

I intercepted and snatched the bag. I drew out a tin of cookies and put it next to the sink, followed by a large pan covered in a dish towel.

Not chicken, but roast beef. I got a serving platter and set it on the table. I was going for the noodle pudding when Papa grabbed the roast in his hand and dumped it back in the bag. Warm juice ran down my arm and leaked through the sack.

"Don't you know wasting food is a sin?" I screamed.

Papa folded his arms and glared. Sidestepping around him, I marched to the sink, yanked the lid off the tin, and crammed a handful of cookies into my mouth. Papa took me by the scruff of the neck and bent my head over the sink. He pried my mouth open and stuck his fingers inside, scooping out dough. I tried to hold onto the sweetness before my father could steal it from me, but I couldn't swallow with my head down. Instead I clenched my teeth. He tried to cram the slimy bar of kosher dish soap between them. I wanted to curse him and his stupid prayers. Papa, not the enemy, would kill Shmuel and life would never taste good again. The fear of gagging on the soap kept my lips closed, but all the swear words I heard on the playground raged in my head.

Mama yelled at Papa to stop and pulled us apart. Terror blazed in her eyes. My father and I faced each other, trembling and panting. Tears ran down my cheeks. His were dry. After rinsing his hands, he returned to his stool, closed his eyes, and resumed praying. My mother wiped my face and told me to go into their bedroom and lie down. She'd never done that before. The rare times I entered my parents' room, I'd snuck in when no one else was home. I would have preferred to run out of the house, but now it really was dark and I was afraid to walk past Paddy's saloon where a lounge lizard, blotto on hooch, might pop out the door and try to open my bank.

At first, lying on my parents' bed, I thought about Mama more than Papa. Had she sent me to the bedroom to protect me from my father, save him from himself, or restore sholem bayess in the house for her own sake? She was justified in wanting peace, given how distraught she was about Shmuel, but I wanted her to be thinking of me and taking my side. Admitting this was unlikely, I then nursed my grievance against Papa. I didn't care that it was wrong to defy him. Acting like Shmuel was dead was defying God's right to make that decision, and that was worse.

An hour later, when my mother called that supper was ready, resignation about Mama and righteousness toward Papa had calmed me down. I was cocooned in self-pity. I'd decided to go to Leah's house the next morning, when my parents were at shul, so she could cluck and joke and do whatever else friends do to make each other feel better. Meanwhile, I'd enjoy a good wallow. When I walked into the kitchen, the Shabbas candles were burned halfway down. Mama must have kindled them right after sending me to the bedroom because you're not allowed to strike a match after dark. I remembered the joy I'd felt lighting and reciting the blessing over the candles a week ago. It seemed like a year. Would Papa ever give me permission to light them again? Would I have to apologize to him first? Or would he hand me the matches as a way of apologizing to me?

I took my seat on Papa's left, opposite my brother's empty seat. There'd been only three place settings at the table since Sunday, when Onkel Gershon came over. Sometimes, when I got home from school and my father's eyes were closed in prayer, I caught Mama sitting in Shmuel's chair. She never said anything when I looked at her, just stood and went back to chopping onions. Once I sat down after she got up, pretending the warmth of the seat came from my brother's body, not hers. She let me sit without saying anything either.

Mama dished out soup and chicken, the usual Shabbas meal. Papa ate; she and I picked. The bag with Tante Yetta's roast beef was nowhere in sight. Nor could I smell it. While I was in the bedroom, Papa or Mama had carried it to the trash bin in the alley, where seven days ago I'd found my brother's tallit and payess. Whichever of them did it had broken a rule by carrying on the Sabbath, but I sensed Papa wouldn't care. Tomorrow in shul he'd say Kaddish for Shmuel, alone, in front of the whole congregation. That too, as Onkel Gershon had said, violated Jewish law, which required at least ten men. It would be another rare instance of my father not observing community rules, but since my brother's disappearance, Papa had lived in a world of his own.

chapter 24

The next day, escaping the gloom of our apartment, I basked like a cat in the sun that streamed through Leah's front window. She sometimes stayed home on Saturday mornings to take care of her bubbe, who had trouble walking, while her parents went to shul. While her grandmother slept in the back room, I poured out my heart. Well, not all of it. I couldn't tell her about Papa scraping the food out of my mouth. A few things are too embarrassing to reveal, even to your best friend.

"It's driving me bonkers to see my father sitting shiva. Like Shmuel was only alive as long as he was obeying Papa, but now that he wants to fight instead of study, he's dead."

"Nothing mattered more to your father than Shmuel's ordination," Leah said. "Admit it," she nudged my shoulder and smiled, "You were jealous."

"I confess." I held up my hands. If anyone other than Leah had stated such a bald truth about me, I would have been mortified. "But I'd become a nun if it would bring Shmuel home."

"God forbid." Leah lowered my hands. "You don't have to go to that extreme."

"My father is going to ridiculous extremes. He's snapped a cap, lost his lid."

My friend didn't smile at the vivid expressions. "It's not as strange as you make it sound. Think how many parents sit shiva when their child marries a gentile. If a son or daughter leaves the faith, they might as well be dead." Leah tilted her head in that way she has when she sure she's right. It makes me want to disagree with her, even when I don't, but I wish I could be as certain about my beliefs as she is.

I defended myself by challenging her. "Think how many parents relent when the first grandchild is born."

Leah's mouth twitched but she wouldn't back down. "Torah places great value on honouring one's parents. It's the fifth commandment, even before not committing murder."

"Or adultery," I added, just to see her blush, and maybe to forget my fight with Papa.

"In fact," Leah continued, ignoring my teasing, "Deuteronomy says that parents can have a disobedient child stoned to death. Shmuel spurning your father's wish might seem to him like the ultimate disobedience."

"I can think of worse." I wiggled my eyebrows and smirked until I made Leah laugh. The bright sound almost blotted out the dark memory of my father's hand in my mouth.

"I know you can." She wagged her finger. "Seriously, Dev. Be patient. Your father's heart is broken. When your uncle gets news of your brother, he'll soften."

"Hah! He'll harden."

Leah twirled the ends of my braids and stroked my cheeks with them. "Shiva is a week, just two more days to go. Your father will be back at work on Monday. Life will resume."

"Shiva ends, but the period of mourning is a full year. I'll be ready for the loony bin by then. Worse, I don't know how my mother will keep from going meshugga."

"She's stronger than you give her credit for, Dev. Her faith will sustain her." Now Leah tugged gently on my braids. "Meanwhile, until your brother comes home, she'll have more time to watch over you and keep you out of trouble."

I groaned. I hadn't thought of that. Mama was pretty lenient with me, but with Shmuel gone, she'd be worried about losing me too. "My mother is strong," I admitted, "but I don't think she's as solid in her faith as you. She questions things, like women not having the right to vote."

Leah frowned. "It's not the same. You can change laws in a democracy. They're made by men. You can't change the laws given to us by God. They're carved in stone."

"But even those laws are interpreted by rabbis."

"With divine inspiration," Leah insisted. "We trust them to tell us what to do."

"Judaism is all about what we *can't* do," I complained. "Torah has a hundred and ninety-four mitzvot that begin, 'Thou shalt not,' and only seventy-seven that say, 'Thou shalt.' Besides, most laws are written with men in mind. Women might as well be dead, the same as Shmuel is to Papa. What's the point?"

Leah opened her mouth, then closed it, on the verge of tears. She had no answer.

"The point of life for women is to have children and raise them to carry on our tradition." Leah's bubbe, whose voice was often tremulous, spoke with confidence from the back room.

Leah's body relaxed. She gave me that triumphant tilt of her head, as if to say, "See?"

I shook mine in response. If that was true, did it mean half of Mama's life would be wasted if Shmuel didn't return? Leah read my mind. After all, we'd been best friends our whole lives. "Shmuel will come home," she murmured, echoing what Mama and I had insisted all week. A cloud blocked the sunlight from coming in the window. Suddenly I wasn't so sure.

"I'll have children and so will you," Leah said firmly. "We'll bring them up like brothers and sisters and become fat old bubbes together." She jiggled her cheeks, trying to cheer me up.

I knew that having children was what Leah wanted more than anything. It's not as if I didn't want them, but I wanted more. "You'll make a wonderful mother and bubbe," I said.

We hugged goodbye. I had to get a wiggle on if I wanted to get home before my parents. Halfway down the stairs, I realized that in all the tumult over Shmuel's disappearance, I'd forgotten to tell Leah my other big news. Now my body was ready for me to become a mother.

part ten

Gershon, 1917

chapter 25

It took two weeks and cost Gershon another two hundred dollars before the request approved by the board snaked its way up the line, but at last he received a stamped authorization to obtain the telephone numbers of the men recruited the same week as Shmuel. He looked forward to gloating when he handed it to the Navy clerk who'd snubbed him, but someone else was on duty the day he returned. That clerk gave him the information, indifferent as to why he needed it.

Calling the long list of names left little time for Gershon's clients or family. On the third Friday, Yetta resorted to the hand mirror. "You're obligation is to your wife too," she said, "as much as to your sister." If she only knew how he'd once forfeited his sister in favour of his wife.

One by one, Gershon crossed off names: Shepherd Landry, Scott Lattimer, Stuart Leach. Parents told him their sons had gone to boot camp as close as Cape May, New Jersey, and as far away as San Diego, California. Some thought he was calling with bad news—a boy killed in a training accident before he'd even shipped out to sea—and were so relieved not to be told their sons were dead, that they turned talkative. Simon Lundgren's mother, for example, complained to Gershon that her son had never so much as set foot in a rowboat. "They had to send him to a special boot camp for know-nothings. He writes that his stomach's too empty and his brain's too full for him to sleep at night. How they expect to make a sailor of that boy is anybody's guess."

A boot camp for those ignorant of boats. At last, a clue. When Simon's mother told him it was in East Boston, Gershon hung up and boarded a train. By then, seven weeks had passed since Shmuel's disappearance. Boot camp ended after eight. Standing in the Main Concourse of Grand Central Terminal, Gershon gazed up at the astronomical design on the ceiling and asked God to bless him on his journey. He hoped it would be smoother than the one he'd taken two decades earlier, but equally as successful in the end.

If he'd been a pessimist, Gershon would have seen that long-ago voyage across the Atlantic as a bad omen. The hold stank of human waste and seasickness. Yetta clung to him. She'd tried to be brave but she lost heart along with stomach lining. Carrying all they owned in four satchels, they boarded barges to Ellis Island where they walked single file under the sharp gaze of two public health officials, who had six seconds to determine whether they would be admitted to their new country. Thankfully, they reached the end of the line without any chalk marks to indicate the physical or mental defects that would send them to the infirmary or worse, back home.

Five hours after getting off the boat, they were issued landing cards and took a ferry and an elevated train to the Lower East Side. The streets were covered in horse manure, the same as in Lemberg. Gershon reached into Yetta's valise for the silk scarf with which she covered her head when lighting candles. He tied it around her nose and mouth and led her to their two-room apartment on the top floor of a three-story walk-up. The hallway reeked of the spices of their new neighbours. He leaned against a grease-stained wall, overcome with exhaustion and disappointment. "The smell of America."

Yetta recovered more quickly than he did. Removing the scarf and breathing deeply, she took a stew pot from her bag, plunked it on the stove, and reminded him that good news in the Torah was always preceded by a good meal. Then she went downstairs to get acquainted with the food peddlers they'd passed on their way, returning half an hour later with a chicken, onions, and some vegetables Gershon had never seen before. Without hesitation, she began to prepare dinner. Meanwhile, Gershon unpacked their few belongings. He placed his prayer book on the window sill. The Torah commentaries from his student days he left at the bottom of the satchel, which he shoved under the bed. Yetta called. Their first meal in America was ready.

Gershon kept his pledge to his father-in-law to do menial work if that's what it took to support his wife. Every day except Saturday he trudged to a sweatshop where he swept floors for twelve or more hours, bringing home six dollars a week. When Shabbas came, he was too tired and sore to make love to Yetta, until one Friday evening he came home to find her reclining on a pile of pillows. She beckoned him beside her and pulled from the folds of her skirt the enamelled hand mirror he'd given her as a boy. "You remember the midrash from Exodus?" she'd asked.

Gershon smiled. The story went that when Pharaoh asked how Jewish slaves could be so prolific after days at heavy labour, he was told, "When women carry food and water to the men in the field, they bring a mirror for them to gaze at together. The women tell the men, 'You are the most beautiful.' 'No, it is you who are the most beautiful,' the men reply. They play this teasing game until the men are aroused. Then the women place bits of bread on their husbands' tongues, wet their lips with water, and draw them into lovemaking."

Yetta looked at Gershon's tired eyes in the mirror. "You are the most beautiful."

He gazed at the reflection of his wife's dark, glittering eyes and protested that it was she.

Yetta lit the Shabbas candles. She held the cup of wine while Gershon said kiddush and lifted it to his mouth. When he finished the blessing over the challah, she pinched off a piece and put it between his moist lips. Together they carried the pillows back to the iron bedstead.

At first, Yetta, more than Gershon, turned the Mendels into Americans. On July Fourth, when he got a day off in the middle of the week, it was she who insisted they take the elevated line to Coney Island and ride on the carousel. "How did you hear of such wonders?"

"You listen instead of talk all the time, you learn," she said. They snuggled in the tiny sleigh and gaped at the painted horses that reminded them of her father's carriage in Lemberg.

That night, in the oven-like heat, it was also Yetta who insisted they sleep on the fire escape like their neighbours. Gershon was embarrassed, but she fashioned curtains from the silk scarves she'd bought, convinced that someday they'd own a piano to drape them over. When Gershon had succumbed and stripped to his undershirt, his wife surprised him one more time.

He stared suspiciously at the big half-circle of strange-looking fruit. "What's this?"

"Watermelon." Yetta turned as pink as its flesh as the juice dribbled down her chin.

Gershon did the same. America's streets weren't paved with gold, but its fruits were the colours of jewels, and promised riches just as sweet.

Yetta continued to accept poverty more easily than Gershon. To her it was an adventure leading to the future; to him, a source of shame evoking the past. Gradually, however, lulled by the rhythm of the broom by day, and Yetta's contented breathing at night, he began to dream of the future again too. So, when he saw a handbill for free classes at the College of the City of New York, he enrolled. Instead of immersing himself in words as he'd done all his life, he decided to give numbers a chance and studied accounting at night. It took him five years to get his degree. In the meantime, he wrote to his sister about life in America, and she wrote back about the shtetl.

Dearest Rivka: We've taken in a roomer who sleeps next to the stove, and four borders who take meals with us because they have no one to cook for them. I wanted to charge extra for Shabbas dinner but Yetta said feeding them on Friday night was an act of tzedakah and sat them at our table for free. I'm humbled by her goodness. You and your friends in Lemberg misjudged her.

Dear Gershon: Life continues to get harder. The rest of the country is industrializing, but Galicia is kept rural to grow food for the cities. Peasants suffer and take it out on us Jews. Thank God we have had no pogroms, but last week when Avram tried to collect payment for a pair of boots he'd mended, the farmer ran him off with a pitchfork and accused him of being a gonif.

Dearest Rivka: We celebrated our first year in America with the birth of our daughter Zipporah, named for Yetta's aunt. With an infant in the house, we no longer have a roomer, but fees from the borders paid for a dresser and a baby carriage. I like my accounting classes, but I miss words, so I started a Torah study group at the synagogue. When the men discovered I'd been personally tutored by the rabbi, they asked me to lead the sessions. I'm also giving English lessons. You may remember how, even as a boy, I hung around the peasants and was quick to pick up another language. The old immigrants want the new ones to learn English and stop speaking Yiddish. It is a source of tension, but I side with the settled ones, a sign I'm becoming a true American.

Dear Gershon: After we buried Papa, Mama took ill and the feldsher said she would not make it to Chanukah. On a happier note, I am pregnant. The baby will be born in the new century. Avram is hoping for a boy. We will name him Shmuel, after my late father-in-law.

Dearest Rivka: We too have a new baby, another girl, named Ruchel. Yetta apologized for not giving me a son, but I prefer a house full of women. I won't have to scold them to study or worry about what they will become. Their mother will teach them to make a good home, and be patient and generous like her. I am done with my classes and have begun to advise clients. We moved to a bigger apartment and no longer have borders. There is a separate room for the children, and I bought Yetta a piano. Now that Avram's mother has passed on too, you should come to America. I can sponsor you and we have room for your family to stay with us until you get settled.

Dear Gershon: Thank you for your kind offer, but Avram refuses to accept it.

Dearest Rivka: Your husband is selfish. If he will not emigrate for his own sake, or to spite me, tell him to come for his son. Shmuel deserves a better life than you can give him in Lemberg.

By the time the Levinsons finally took his money to come to America, two years later, Gershon was president of the Eldridge Street Synagogue. He paid for the bar mitzvah of any boy whose family was too poor. Yetta was head of the Women's Charity. They brought meals to the elderly and sick, and donated household goods to engaged couples. Remembering Rivka's resentment over the silver candlesticks, the furnishings Yetta gave newlyweds weren't fancy, but they were clean and in good repair. She also bought each woman a hand mirror as a wedding gift.

Gershon gave his wife presents too, but they were expensive. On their fifth anniversary, he handed her a jewelled besamim, the spice box used in the Havdalah service marking the end of Shabbas. She inhaled the cinnamon, cloves, and orange peel and admired how the box's green and blue gems sparkled in the lamplight. "I almost feel too guilty to enjoy it. We have so much and others have so little."

"Don't feel guilty. Feel grateful. It's a sign of my love for you and God's goodness to us."

Each week Yetta made a new mixture for the besamim, blending Jewish spices with the oregano, curries, and pepper flakes used by their old neighbours. She brought the fragrant mixture and an occasional roast to the Levinsons. If Avram wasn't home to make her return them, Rivka accepted these gifts "for the sake of the children." Meanwhile Yetta surreptitiously looked for the candlesticks, but concluded they'd been left behind or sold in Lemberg when the Levinsons were destitute. Rivka would have hidden where the money came from, so Avram wouldn't refuse it.

For his part, Avram hid nothing. From the moment he landed in America, until Shmuel disappeared fourteen years later, he continued to resent his brother-in-law's help, even more than he envied his success. The one thing he could hold over Gershon was his son, named for Avram's father, and destined to become the scholar and rabbi that Gershon in the end had not. And now that Avram's sole advantage was gone, Gershon intended to wrest every benefit from this reversal of fortune. It was a long and lonely train ride from New York to Massachusetts, but Gershon expected that on the return trip, he would have his nephew's company and a swift passage home.

chapter 26

"No credentials, no admittance." A Navy guard blocked Gershon's access to the Calvin Austin's gangway with a rifle. Gershon explained his mission but the young man stood firm and repeated those four words. In his haste, Gershon had come without a plan or official piece of paper, only a wad of money in his pocket. This could be difficult. Boston was more Irish than Tammany Hall.

Looking for an edge, Gershon remembered that two years ago Morty Richter had married an Irish Catholic woman whose brother was a police detective in Boston. As with Hymie, the shul was scandalized, but in this case, when the woman converted, Gershon had intervened to allow the wedding to take place in the sanctuary. Calling in the debt, he phoned the man now, praying that he was on better terms with his brother-in-law than Gershon was with Avram.

"Morty, I need a favour to get past some red tape."

Morty was indeed friendly with his wife's brother, but hesitant to ask him for help.

Gershon sighed, hearing Morty's unspoken request for yet another favour from him. If the matter were less urgent, he would have hung up. "What would convince you?"

"Well, the wife is in the family way again ..."

"You need a bigger apartment?"

"With an icebox? A window in the bedroom would be nice too."

"I know just the place. I'll see to it as soon as I get back to New York. Meanwhile, you'll call your brother-in-law in Boston today? I'm running out of time."

It was almost a week before Mr. Richter reached his wife's brother and the detective met Gershon at the ship. He spent his days pacing the docks and sheltered overnight on empty fishing boats. By the time the Calvin Austin's captain led him down a series of ladders to a small office overflowing with maps and nautical gear, Gershon was seasick. His stomach lurched with every swell of the harbour. He was used to standing on solid ground, in command of his own territory.

The captain was brisk but discouraging. "The war's taken millions of lives. Even those wearing ID's with their real names are buried where they fall, in unmarked graves, or else they simply go down with their ships. How on earth do you expect me to trace your nephew?"

"He's been gone two months. I thought he might still be here at boot camp."

The captain relented. "When did you say he enlisted?" He checked the log of recruits who arrived the week Shmuel went missing. "Sorry," he said. "That batch shipped out at dawn today."

"Where?" Gershon would pay whatever it cost to hitch a ride on the merchant marine vessel that his nephew's destroyer was accompanying across the Atlantic.

"England, Scotland, Spain, Algiers." The captain shrugged and stood up. "Even if I knew, security doesn't allow me to tell you."

The train disgorged Gershon at Grand Central Station late that night. He stared at the terminal's four-sided clock, its opal faces surrounded by a marble and glass pagoda, and watched the hands rotate past midnight, to one o'clock, then four in the morning. Each chime rang dully in his head. At last, he descended to the IRT platform beneath the grand edifice to return to the grimy Lower East Side. Lulled by the rocking of the subway, he awoke with a jolt at his stop, but instead of getting off, he rode to the end of the line, exiting at Coney Island just as the sun was coming up.

He walked along the deserted boardwalk, past the carousel horses poised mid-gallop until spring. He recalled that long-ago summer night in the cocoon Yetta created on the fire escape, his mouth filled with the sweet memory of watermelon. Life tasted sour now. It was better when they were down yet hopeful, finding small pleasures while laughing at bigger indignities. Jews had been in that position for millennia. Gershon was wrong to think he could escape his people's fate.

His search for Shmuel had reached a dead end. Perhaps Avram was justified in sitting shiva for the boy after all, but that made his brother-in-law a loser. Gershon turned back and hurried to the subway. The day he arrived in America, his wife had reminded him that in the Torah, good news came after a good meal. Gershon was hungry. Yetta would feed him.

part eleven

Sam, 1918-1919

chapter 27

The voyage across the Atlantic was like boot camp, days filled with exercises and housekeeping, but in living quarters so cramped that the ensigns bumped into one another getting dressed. No one dared complain, though. They'd heard that other ships were so crowded, sailors were forced to sleep on deck. At least when Sam and his shipmates were off duty, they could crawl into racks stacked three across and four high, in a space the size of a laundry chute. Mikovski had assigned Sam a middle rack, knowing that when the sea turned rough, he'd have no wall to wedge his back against for support. His choices were to tie himself down or be thrown to the floor.

Alarms woke the men at 0600 hours for morning drill. After pushups and weight-lifting, they stood for first inspection, then raced to the mess hall for breakfast, where the pocked insides of the water tanks tinged their coffee red and flavoured it with rust. Mikovski supervised every exercise, his voice bellowing with sadistic glee while the men, blindfolded, practiced sealing pipe leaks. "You gotta be able to feel your way around a ship when the enemy shoots out the lights," he warned them. Eyes covered, the stumbling ensigns practiced extinguishing random fires too, but Mikovski let another officer lead the fire exercise, just as he had during training.

Twice a week, the equipment was dismantled, repaired, and reassembled, then repainted to prevent corrosion. This routine was Mikovski's favourite because he alone determined whether the work passed inspection. If not, he dictated the punishment. He often assigned Sam to clean the lockers where matches and ammunition were stored, then got on his knees to shine a flashlight underneath. "Tsk, tsk, Lord. I see mould and mildew. Wet ammo is ruined ammo." He made Sam scrub the lockers again with a toothbrush until the bristles were worn down, then apply two coats of paint. Massaging his raw knuckles at night, Sam wished the Navy had an appeals court. As a boy, it had irked him that Jews rarely agreed on a point of law. Now he craved a second opinion.

The area below deck was also checked regularly for leaks, bad wiring, and peeling paint. Mikovski claimed the floor should be clean enough to eat off. During one inspection, he asked Sam if it was suitable for serving the admiral a meal. When Sam said yes, Mikovski demanded proof. He spilled a stream of hot rusty water from the mess hall onto the floor, where it puddled around a pile of oily rags. When Tomasio bent to wipe a spot with his knee, Mikovski shoved him away and held Sam's face down. Sam gagged, but swallowed, refusing to lose his breakfast.

Mikovski grinned. "Next time, Tomasio, it'll be your turn to lap up the admiral's tea." He told the men to put away the paint cans and oily rags, but a minute after he'd left, they dumped everything back on the floor and climbed into their racks. Then they marched off to a dinner of the same mystery meat, limp vegetables, and gummy pudding they'd eaten since shipping out.

After this unsavoury meal, they had two hours to play cards and re-read magazines whose every word they'd memorized. To lift their spirits, Tomasio usually strummed his guitar and beat jungle rhythms on empty paint cans, but that night the men were too morose to join in. Frustrated, he turned his back, crouched down to scrounge in his locker, shoved his hand down the front of his pants, then stood and faced forward with what looked like an enormous erection.

Hamble made as if to grab Tomasio's crotch. "Mate's been holding out on us. He's got a bunch of girlie pictures rolled inside his gear."

Dancing out of Hamble's reach, Tomasio pulled out a huge cigar. He stroked and sniffed it. "Finest Cuban blend," he said. "I was saving it for after we tin fished our first sub, but what the hell. Might as well stoke up now." Tomasio continued waltzing around, pretending to smoke with one hand and swill liquor with the other. He grabbed a lit kerosene lamp used to illuminate the lower bunks and held it close, like a dance partner. "I'm a hoochie coochie man," he sang, twirling and stumbling as though inebriated. Everyone clapped, egging him on. High on laughter, Tomasio didn't pay attention to where his feet were going until he tripped over the paint cans and oily rags. His "dance partner" flew out of his arms and landed on the pile.

Tomasio barely had time to say, "Oops, sorry sweetie," to the lamp before the rags burst into flames. Mikovski rushed in just as a paint can exploded, as though he'd been lying in wait outside the doorway. The flames were dense but confined to the area where the men had shoved the supplies earlier. Even so, Mikovski blanched and fled to the stairwell, where he could be heard retching until the noise was muffled by the thump of blankets beating out the fire. Tomasio dumped wet sand bags over the smouldering mess and stomped on it, just to be sure.

Several men were trembling. Tomasio looked miserable, but no one said anything. Sam guessed they didn't want to make him feel worse. Sam took charge of the clean-up. When it was finished, there was only half an hour of break time left to shower and dress before the late afternoon drill. Navy showers were limited to thirty seconds—ten to soap and twenty to rinse off—so Sam, covered in soot and grease, washed quickly. When he emerged, Mikovski stood brandishing a stopwatch.

"Thirty-two seconds." Mikovski smirked at the circle of men in various degrees of undress. "Someone else will have to decrease his time accordingly. I'll let your majesty choose who."

Tomasio stepped forward. "I started the fire, sir. I'll take the shorter shower."

"I was the one who didn't put away the paint cans," another sailor said. "It should be me."

One by one, each man stepped forward to accuse himself of failing to clean up, saying he alone deserved to have his shower time docked. Sam pretended to dry his face to hide his grateful smile, but Mikovski threw the stopwatch at him, where the glass shattered around his bare feet. "No one else showers," the lieutenant ordered. "Get dressed and report on deck in two minutes."

This period before supper each day was reserved for competitive games of strength and speed, organized by the commanding officer who believed they kept sailors ready to fight. Hamble called them "Shit hot elitist nonsense," a holdover from the wealthy C.O.'s prep school days, but men of inferior rank were powerless to protest. Besides, Mikovski, born as poor as those he supervised, shared the officer's enthusiasm. The ensigns didn't give in to their superiors completely, however. Each night, they secretly decided who would win the next day and by how much. Sam took notes to make sure the victories were evenly distributed among them and wouldn't arouse suspicion.

Clouds began rolling in during weight lifting, and the seas were so choppy for the target shooting that Tomasio, whose turn it was to win, had trouble steadying his arm to aim accurately. The final contest was running laps on deck. It required agility as well as speed to navigate the narrow space around the equipment and weapons. If you forgot to duck under the guns, you'd be knocked out cold, a common event when you were sleep-deprived. With high waves rocking the ship, it would be even harder to move forward, duck, and maintain balance, all at the same time.

Sam was the last to run. Tomasio had raced early in the pack and the worsening weather made the lead he'd established plausible as well as real. Sam was relaxed, knowing he could finish his lap leisurely and then everyone could retreat below deck. Mikovski stood next to him, cradling a new stopwatch, and yelled over the roar of the wind. "Win this race, Lord, and I'll cancel the punishment. All the men can shower, for a full minute, after supper."

Mental and physical agility came easily to Sam, but speed had never been his forte. Starting down the port side, he knew halfway that winning was impossible. It was hard enough just to keep his balance. The gun turrets were on the starboard side. All he had to do was turn and make it back safely. Heavy rain pelted him. The men didn't need showers anymore, just the dry, warm air below.

Sam was puzzled to see Mikovski midway down the deck, instead of at the bow where the others waited. Behind him, out of Mikovski's view, Tomasio was frantically slapping his forehead. If Sam weren't so winded, he'd have smiled at his friend's antics. Not until he drew closer did Sam understand it was a warning. Mikovski had lowered the gun turret so Sam couldn't duck to avoid it. It would hit him in the groin unless he detoured or slithered underneath. Since Mikovski was blocking him from circumventing the gun, Sam had to stop running and crawl below it.

Mikovski hauled him up. "No one showers tonight," he cackled. "And for failure to finish the lap, Lord, twenty-second washes the rest of the month." He asked the C.O. what game was next, but with twenty-foot waves now crashing over their heads, the officer ordered the men below.

"Permission, sir, to keep them on deck." Mikovski, balancing easily on the shuddering planks, suggested it was an ideal time for them to practice refuelling the destroyer from the tanker while they were underway. Their only experience until now had been refuelling a stationery ship.

The C.O. looked sceptical. "Perhaps tomorrow after we've ridden out the storm."

"War is fought in all conditions, sir. Why waste this opportunity to prepare the men?"

Hamble, who'd been watching from the railing, pointed at the roiling black clouds to the north. "I reckon the winds are moderate gale force, or will be within the hour." There was no definitive reading from the ship's instruments yet, but Hamble had spent enough time at sea to judge accurately without them. "In my opinion, you'd be taking an unnecessary risk."

The officer wavered. Only when Mikovski added what a great morale builder the exercise would be, did he agree to let the refuelling go ahead. He put Mikovski in charge, requested a report by 1900 hours, and hurried down the hatch. The wind slammed the door shut behind him.

Tomasio mimicked the tanker crew's reaction at being radioed to pull up alongside the destroyer. "Read you, USS Leviathan. Order crazy as shit. Throw lieutenant overboard. Over and out." Mikovski was out of earshot, but the men were too scared by what lay ahead to laugh. Sam felt he'd survived one ordeal only to be thrust into a worse one. Maybe that's what war was like.

The tanker pitched from side to side as it ploughed toward them, prompting a new worry that the raging sea would smash the fuel-filled vessel into their ship, igniting both. Recalling Mikovski's ashen face when Hamble described the men on the Lutzow getting burned alive, Sam wondered if he'd considered that possibility, but the look on the man's face now was pure glee.

Playing it safe, the tanker's navigator left a wide channel between the ships. This lessened the chance of a collision, but it meant the fuel hose had to be thrown farther to reach the destroyer. The pitch was further complicated by erratic winds, which shifted direction every few seconds. Mikovski could barely be heard above the howling and crashing, but his sparkling eyes directed the action. "Lord, get your soaking ass into position to catch the hose."

Sam staggered to the railing. The first two throws fell short. The third cleared it, but the hose writhed on deck like an angry serpent. Sam fell on his knees and grasped it just as the wind pulled it back overboard. Blood welled and spilled from his abraded palms. Mikovski signalled the tanker crew to try again. Once more, Sam grabbed hold of the smooth, heavy rubber. At first he held on, but the wind changed direction and hauled the hose back. If he hadn't let go, his head would have smashed into the railing with ten times the force of running into the gun turret.

The lieutenant kicked Sam aside and raised his arm for the hose. The instant it landed on deck, his calloused hands trapped it and his powerful arms hauled it to the fuel cap. Securing the line with one hand, he unscrewed the lid with the other, inserted the nozzle, and signalled the tanker to let the gas flow. It didn't take long to top off the Leviathan, already half full.

For the second time in an hour, Mikovski yanked Sam to his feet, but instead of gripping his arm, he hauled him up by the hands. The salt water penetrated Sam's lesions and stung. For good measure, Mikovski's thick fingers squeezed and rubbed them. "Pampered rich boys' hands," he spat and turned Sam toward the others on deck. "If this had been a battle, we'd never have survived." Sam found no sympathy in their faces. They, and he, knew the lieutenant was right.

Hamble stepped forward. "Wind's over fifty knots an hour. Past time to go below." The C.O. had left Mikovski in charge, but he was relishing his victory enough to let the Brit call the shots. Hamble led the way to the hatch. Mikovski held Sam back until they were the only two left on deck. Sam didn't mind going last. It meant the others couldn't talk about him behind his back.

Then, just as Sam grabbed the hatch cover, the gale shifted direction again, hurling him back against Mikovski's chest. Coming from the port side, the wind blew Sam's hair up over his right ear, exposing his strawberry mark. He instinctively reached to cover it, losing his grip on the door. It clanged shut. Mikovski yanked it open and pushed Sam through, tumbling down the stairs after him. Sam picked himself up first and limped to his quarters. Mikovski followed.

The men, half-stripped, stopped drying themselves when they entered. Mikovski went into the lavatory and emerged with a rusty razor that Tomasio had dangled from a rope with a sign that read, "In case of emergency, slit enemy's throat." He lathered Sam's scalp and shaved his head, removing every trace of hair around his right ear and leaving coarse patches elsewhere. "Write a report of the refuelling, Lord, and have it in my hands by 1900 hours." That was in seventy-five minutes, during which time the others would be eating supper. Sam didn't care. He wasn't hungry.

His report meticulously reported Mikovski's justification for holding the drill, Hamble's reservations, the disbelief of the tanker crew, and Sam's own unsatisfactory performance. In the instrument room, he documented that the winds had reached whole gale force, averaging over 60 mph, while they were on deck. He saved this fact for last, hoping it would show Mikovski for the fool he was, but he doubted the lieutenant would actually file the report. His real intention was to isolate Sam from the talking and camaraderie at supper. The tactic worked. For the first time since his earliest days at boot camp, Sam felt like an outsider, a man who wasn't like the others, a Jew.

That night, the men themselves were still too shaky to talk. Tomasio strummed his guitar, but no one made requests or sang along. He played for himself, while they dealt hands of solitaire or lay on their backs, smoking. After lights out, their breathing was as ragged as the storm winds howling outside, perhaps considering the irony of being killed by Mother Nature, not the enemy.

At 0200 hours, Tomasio whispered from the rack next to Sam's. "The guys wanted to sneak food back to you, but Mikovski was watching us like a hawk."

Gratitude and relief flooded Sam. "Just as well you didn't. It would have attracted rats."

Tomasio made barfing noises. "Rats run away from the crap they feed us, not toward it." A comfortable silence settled for a while until he said, "I'd kill for a plate of my nonna's ziti right now. My mom's a good cook, but after nonna came over, true greatness came out of our kitchen."

"I was named for my dad's father, but I never knew my grandparents. They stayed behind."

"There were lots of Jewish families in the neighbourhood where I grew up," Tomasio said. "Good smells came out of their apartments too."

"There were lots of Italian Catholics at my school," Sam remarked, but didn't say how mean they were to him. "They're the only people I know who use more garlic than Jews."

Tomasio chuckled. "Jews and Catholics, both experts at dishing out food and guilt."

After his humiliation at the hands of Mikovski, Sam wasn't ready to laugh.

"I've been thinking." Tomasio's voice was hesitant. "Suppose you wore your birthmark as a badge of pride, kind of like Christ's stigmata. A reminder of who and what you are."

It was a kind thought, but Sam would never see it as anything other than a badge of shame. Before he grew too old to let Rivka to touch him, he'd allowed her to kiss it when she tucked him in at night. She wasn't superstitious, but retained a primitive belief that it protected him from the evil eye. Ancient priests sacrificed only unblemished animals; the mark meant Sam would be spared.

Avram ignored it, just as he refused to acknowledge any other imperfection in his son. Sam wondered whether, if his father had kissed the birthmark too, he'd still be at home tonight.

The storm worsened toward dawn, its 80-knot winds rolling the ship like tenement kids pitching marbles. Most sailors grew nauseated; even Hamble succumbed. Tomasio, assigned a middle rack like Sam, had no wall to brace against, so Sam lashed his fart sack to an overhead beam, which cut the swaying in half. Seeing how well it worked, he lashed the other hammocks with whatever spare line he could find. Finally, he put empty paint cans on the floor in lieu of barf buckets. Mikovski walked in as Sam emptied a can and scoffed that he was playing nanny to a bunch of babies. Sam looked toward Hamble to defend the crew, but the poor Brit was in no condition to speak.

Suddenly, Mikovski, looking green himself, lurched and grabbed one of the ropes Sam had tied overhead. "Seasickness can strike anyone, sir," Sam said, knowing he'd be punished for his smart tongue later. He didn't care, especially when Tomasio guffawed before throwing up again.

Mikovski glared. "It's not seasickness. The doctor thinks it's a virus."

The men stopped retching as if paralyzed by fear. They, like Sam, had heard of a deadly flu that was killing sailors in Spain. Sam wondered if a crew member had brought it aboard the Leviathan. Mikovski continued. "The sickest men need to be quarantined to stop the virus from spreading."

Sam surveyed the tiers of racks. Several men looked too limp to stand, let alone walk. "I don't think they can make it to the infirmary, sir."

"That's why you're going to carry them, Lord. I want to see just how strong you are."

Now Hamble raised his head. "He's the lone healthy man among us. It's insane to expose him to the worst of whatever this bug is."

Mikovski drowned him out. "And after your lordship transports them, you'll be the chief nursemaid." He removed a piece of paper from his pocket which Sam recognized as the front page of the report he'd written. Mikovski folded the paper into a nurse's cap and placed it on Sam's head, tilting it above his ear to expose the strawberry mark.

"Are you trying to get Sam killed?" Tomasio's voice was unexpectedly strong. Without answering, Mikovski grabbed a can and raced out. Sam heard him filling it just outside the door.

By afternoon, the gale had passed but sickbay couldn't hold everyone who was ill. The doctor concluded they were suffering from neither seasickness nor the flu, but food poisoning. Everyone who'd eaten last night's pudding was afflicted. Sam, who'd been forced to skip dinner, was spared. Those who had seconds, like Tomasio, were worst off. He lamented being sickened by something that tasted so bad. "At least when you get the clap, you get to enjoy yourself first."

Twenty-four hours after the illness began, a dehydrated Mikovski, known for his hearty appetite, came to the infirmary too. Sam donned his nurse's cap and took extra good care of him, holding his forehead and murmuring soothing words the way Rivka had comforted him as a boy. Reducing the lieutenant to a sick child returned an iota of power to Sam. He refrained, however, from thanking Mikovski for preventing him from eating dinner so that he could write the report whose cover he now wore on his head. The lieutenant would punish himself enough.

chapter 28

After nearly three weeks at sea, everyone grew tired of the endless expanse of gray water and gunmetal gray paint on deck. Even Hamble complained of the "bloomin' boredom." With many still in sickbay, the recovered crew members worked double shifts. Weak and underslept, they were jumpy. One gunner mistook the wake of a school of fish for a torpedo and rang the alarm. Another time, when a hydrophone picked up vibrations beneath them and the men prepared to fire a depth charge, they discovered at the last minute it was a rock and not a German U-boat. There was lots of teasing after these incidents, as the men, still in the middle of the ocean, were not ready to get serious until the ship approached land. So it was that when a sleeping ensign was awakened in the instrument room at 0400 hours by the signal of a nearby submarine, he at first discounted it. Scapa Flow now was within the ship's sight and he reasoned the electric waves were provoked by the thousands of land mines and sunken concrete barriers protecting the base. By the time the USS Leviathan's C.O. determined that the signal was real, the submarine was closing in.

There were a dozen mines nearby, each filled with three hundred pounds of TNT. The ship's wireless operator radioed to shore for the mine closest to the U-boat to be detonated, but the land operator radioed back that the submarine was approaching the Leviathan so quickly that triggering a mine could seriously damage the ship as well. Sam was sent to fetch Hamble out of sickbay. Only he knew these waters well enough to guide the U.S. destroyer safely into Scapa Flow's harbour.

"Either way, we'll go phut," Hamble said, "so trip the fucker before Gerry gets closer."

The underwater blast released waves so high that those on deck knotted ropes around their waists and lashed themselves to any fixed object to keep from being washed overboard. When the waves subsided, Sam peered through the railing, expecting to see submarine debris and body parts littering the sea's surface. There was nothing there, however, only the sickening realization that the U-boat and its men had sunk to the ocean floor. As the Leviathan continued to roll wildly, Sam remembered the heaving stomachs of the men still in the infirmary and hurried below deck.

He heard vomiting long before he reached the doorway. The medic, struggling to stay upright himself, raced from rack to rack, emptying buckets and mopping the floor. Pots of water boiled on the stove to sterilize the towels he'd used to wipe the men's mouths and butts. As a sudden aftershock sent the prow of the ship skyward, the flames on the burners leapt sideways, igniting a stack of dirty towels waiting to be washed. Sam quickly swept them into the steaming puddles on the floor and stomped out the fire. He'd barely extinguished the blaze, however, when a crazed Mikovski staggered out of his bed and raced past him, heading for the stairway up to the deck. The lieutenant would rather drown than burn, Sam realized, racing to stop him.

Mikovski's upper body was halfway over the rail when Sam got to him. If the pitching of the ship hadn't thrown the lieutenant backward, he would have hurled himself overboard. As the waves rolled the Leviathan upright once more, Mikovski was again poised to jump into the water. Sam crawled across the deck and grabbed his legs. The lieutenant tried to shake him off. He might have succeeded if his limbs weren't weak from his prolonged bout of food poisoning. Even flat on the floor, however, Mikovski continued to struggle. He clawed at Sam's arms and tried to knee him in the groin. When Sam pinned him down, the lieutenant spat in his face.

The other sailors froze. At first they thought Mikovski had come on deck to gloat over the sinking of the U-boat. Then they thought Sam was attacking the lieutenant and tried to pull him off. Only Hamble, who, like Sam, had seen Mikovski's ashen face when he heard of the men in the Lutzow's boiler room burning to death, sized up the situation. He flung off the sailors piling on top of Sam, and together they held the lieutenant down. Eventually Mikovski grew limp, threw up, and passed out. With Sam carrying his arms and Hamble his feet, they returned Mikovski to sickbay.

"I'm napoo," said Hamble, crawling back into his own rack. "Done, used up." Tomorrow he'd need all his strength and wits to help navigate them into port. Sam knew he should let Hamble sleep, but he had to ask whether the Brit had any idea what made some men so terrified of fire, especially one with the iron guts of Mikovski. Hamble closed his eyes. Sam thought he'd nodded off until he said, "It's the angry blokes who are obsessed with fire. Some are drawn to it, itching to strike the match themselves. Others run from it, afraid of what's burning up inside them."

They listened to Mikovski's staccato breathing for a minute before Sam left Hamble's bedside. The lieutenant returned to duty the next day, never saying a word about what happened.

It was evening when the Leviathan eased into port at Scapa Flow, the sailors amassed on deck for their first sight of land in twenty-one days. From dawn to near dusk, Hamble had slowly guided the ship past hundreds of mines and around concrete barriers that left no ripples on the water's surface. As they approached the pier, the men saw a French steamer wrecked after crashing into one of the barriers. Half of it was below the water, the rest grounded on the shore like a beached whale. Sam said a silent thanks to the able Brit who would soon board a merchant marine vessel bound for New York to guide the next American ship back through these waters of war.

British boats lining the harbour dipped their flags as the U.S. destroyer slid past. "Don't often see the Union Jack saluting a ship not its own," Hamble said, and was surprised when Sam asked why the exception. "You boys are risking your lives to save us. Or have you forgotten that's why you're here?" Sam hadn't forgotten, although his reason for enlisting was more to prove he was an American than to save Europe. Now he wasn't sure what had made him cross the Atlantic.

The closer they got to land, the more the wind picked up. The sailors' hats were blown overboard and floated on the water like a small flotilla of lifeboats. Tomasio, the colour back in his cheeks, stood at the railing as if defying the wind. His hat flew off his head, then stopped in mid-air. Tomasio reached for the string hidden inside his jersey, which he'd tied to the brim, and reeled it back in. The others, including Sam, roared with laughter. Those who hadn't already lost their hats tossed them into the sea. Tomasio was the now the only one left wearing a hat.

Sam stood bare-headed with the rest. His hair was growing back, but the strawberry mark was still quite visible. At this moment, it didn't matter. No one on the shore noticed. To them, he was another brave American who'd prevented an attack by a German U-boat. He was more of an American in Scapa Flow than he'd been in New York.

chapter 29

The sailors on the USS Leviathan didn't see any more action after their close call with the U-boat. Once arrived at Scapa Flow, they installed more mines, patrolled for subs, and unloaded artillery from American merchant ships. Often they were assisted by ten-and twelve-year-old boys, war having claimed all the island's men. Sam imagined Dev chafing that girls weren't allowed to pitch in too. The work would have been less tedious if she'd been working alongside them, although her slang might have driven some of his shipmates batty. Boredom notwithstanding, many sailors were grateful to have escaped battle. Others, Sam and Tomasio included, were disappointed. The entire crew followed the war's progress on the wireless, confident the Americans and Brits would win, but the C.O. hammered them to keep up their guard until it was over. The desperate Germans could still mount an attack at any time.

Safe aboard ship, and often lolling in port, the men had time to think of home and write letters. They had to be short, however, because stationery was scarce, and they couldn't include anything that might reveal their location or manoeuvres in case the mail was intercepted. To throw off the enemy, the sailors were given picture postcards from far-off places to write on.

"Why write home when you can't tell your folks where you've pulled into port?" one sailor said. "What does it matter?" a second asked, "when the Germans inflate how many destroyers they've sunk, so our families think we're dead anyway?" "That's why we write, to prove we're not," answered a third. "I write to remind my girl back there that I'm here, even if I can't tell her where 'here' is," said a fourth. Those with pictures of girls taped inside their lockers agreed.

"I want to remind the girls *here* that I'm here," Tomasio said to loud laughter. The third week in port, he'd gotten Sam to remind them too. It wasn't Paris, but Scapa Flow's lasses were happy to boost the morale of the American sailors. Now that he was no longer Shmuel, Sam found it easier to join the others for a pint at the pub or an hour with a barmaid. He'd thought losing his virginity would either visit a plague of guilt upon him or be another big step in shaking free of his father. It was neither. Instead, like many of his shipmates, a night on the town was just one more routine job in carrying out the war. Only Tomasio continued to take delight in each new conquest, and Sam often went along for the simple pleasure of seeing his friend's joy.

Sam didn't want to lie again about why he didn't write home, so he put pen to paper, then buried the letters and postcards in his duffle. At first he thought of writing to the parents he'd invented, then Dev or Bernie, both of whom were easy to talk to. He settled on his Onkel Gershon. They'd never been close, but from afar he felt a kinship that was missing in New York. Each had become a leader in a community far from home. Though his father and uncle were sworn enemies, Sam wondered if his own accomplishment would please his father. True, Avram had envisioned him heading a group of scholars, not a fighting force. But he was using his God-given talents, like Bazalel and Oholiab in Exodus, who applied the skills and knowledge invested in them by the Almight to build a portable tabernacle for the Jews in the desert.

"Dear Onkel Gershon," the first unsent letter began, "I bet you're surprised to hear from me. My whereabouts are secret, but I can say that I'm well and doing something more useful than reading Talmud. You also studied as a boy, but gave it up to become a businessman. Were you motivated by money or a higher purpose? Perhaps you simply wanted to fit in as an American. I too fit in, but to do so, I've given up more of my past. I don't know if this is a step forward or backward, or a sideways detour. Nor am I sure where I'm going, but I know I was right to leave. My father would disapprove. Perhaps this is one matter on which he and you would agree."

Later, Sam wrote: "People who seem different on the surface can be similar at heart. My friend Tomasio is Catholic, outgoing, and funny. He is eager to sin but easy to forgive. Dev, also my opposite, would find him a kindred spirit. Yet he and I also have much in common, both of us poor and shaped by faith and family, in my case a demanding father, in his case, a strict Father."

As the war wound down, Sam used the letters to ponder his future. "The ocean voyage here was disconcerting, yet being landlocked is equally unsettling. I remember the time you and Tante Yetta took Zipporah, Ruchel, Dev, and me to the beach at Coney Island. When you said I was the only one of us four children to have crossed that expanse of water, it opened up in me a sense of possibility. Where I am now, the snug harbour is the opposite of the open sea. How can I keep my life intimate and real, yet pursue that vague and enormous promise?"

The pace of life onshore picked up when British soldiers serving in France and southern Europe began coming home in 1918. Sam and his shipmates were rapt listening to the infantrymen's stories of sleeping with rats in flooded trenches and cowering beneath booming cannons, at once envious of their exploits and thankful to have been spared the horrors. Bragging soon turned to panic, however, as the transport ships ferrying the soldiers north also carried the Spanish flu.

The first wave, in winter, spread rapidly among the old and young, but a second wave, attacking that spring and summer, hit the soldiers themselves. The pandemic was more than the U.S. Navy could keep up with, confronting the medical corps with a choice between sending its limited team of doctors down the Atlantic coast, keeping them in Great Britain, or returning them to the overwhelmed bases back in America. Not that treatment could help many victims. Tens of thousands of troops, more than the number who died in battle, succumbed to the dreaded virus. They literally choked on their own bodily fluids as blood, thick as jelly, oozed into their lungs.

Sam was among the first to get sick. He felt a shivery twinge at breakfast, and his hand shook recording the medical supplies being unloaded that morning. By lunch, his skin had turned a vivid purple and the spots on his cheeks were the same mahogany colour as his aunt and uncle's dining room table. The hospital was filled with soldiers wounded in the war, so medics, wearing gas masks, carried Sam to the schoolhouse which had been converted into a makeshift clinic.

Tomasio started to follow the stretcher. The bigger of the two medics pushed him back.

"Sorry sailor. Your pal's going into quarantine. And you're going back to the ship to wash the inside of your nose with soap and water. Now, tonight, and again in the morning."

"My snot already passed inspection." Tomasio waited for a laugh, but when the medic just turned away, he swung him back around. "Nothing personal, but I'm going with my friend." The smaller medic shrugged and tossed him a flimsy muslin mask. "It's your funeral, sailor."

Sam was deposited on a cot. In less than half an hour, forty other beds were taken. Blood spurted from the nose of the soldier next to him and sprayed the opposite wall. The lone nurse on duty ducked. Not long after, the dead man's uniform was added to the pile of sputum-and blood-soaked clothes in the corner, waiting to be burned if and when there was a break. His body was loaded on a stretcher and whisked onto one of the lorries bound for mass graves. A minute later, stretcher bearers dumped a new soldier on the empty cot. There wasn't time to strip and change the bedding, but neither was there much point. He'd probably be dead by morning too.

Sam lay on his side staring at Tomasio's anxious eyes peering at him above the mask. He missed seeing his friend's smile. Sam felt a cough erupt from deep inside his chest. He tried to cover his mouth, but was too weak to move his arm. All he could do was look at his hand on the filthy sheet, its oxygen-deprived skin the same cyanide blue as a once-proud sailor's uniform.

The nurse gently wiped Sam's face and held out a glass of water. Sam lapped up a few drops, feeling like the scraggly cats Rivka occasionally brought home when their apartment was overrun with mice. Tomasio dipped a clean rag into the glass, squeezed water onto Sam's brow, and then dripped some between his trembling lips. The nurse nodded at him with gratitude.

Tomasio winked and asked her a question, but his words were muffled underneath the layers of muslin. He ripped off the mask. "Can I buy you a hot toddy after your shift is done?"

Her stunned looked was either because Tomasio had exposed himself to a torrent of germs or because an invitation to drink in a sea of death was horrific. Then the nurse touched his arm and admitted the distraction would be welcomed. She'd meet him at the chalkboard in an hour.

Sam managed a weak smile. He was heartened his friend hadn't lost his ability to charm.

"Not to tarnish my reputation," Tomasio said, covering Sam with his own jacket, "but nurses wouldn't look at the likes of us while there were officers and doctors around. It's just now when admirals are spitting up their innards and the only physicians around are old farts called out of retirement, that they'll give a lowly ensign a chance. Any healthy body looks good to them."

"You need to *stay* healthy," Sam rasped. He'd made up his mind to stay overseas while he figured out what to do next, but Tomasio was at the top of the list to ship home. "Take it from a scholar. It would be stupid of you to get sick now."

"I don't leave Scapa Flow until you leave the hospital, I mean this schoolhouse. A good scholar like you ought to graduate in no time." Tomasio wagged his finger. "That's an order!"

Sam tried to salute but he couldn't lift his hand higher than his chin. It fell back on the stained bedclothes as a stretcher unloaded another man into the cot next to him. It was Mikovski.

Tomasio put his mask back on. "Time for my date," he said, and left.

A thick stream of blood leaked from Mikovski's mouth onto his pillow. He turned away from the reddish-brown puddle, toward Sam, and croaked, "Lord?"

Sam braced himself for abuse, but Mikovski closed his eyes and shuddered. His skin was bluer than Sam's. The priestly words of Deuteronomy came to him. "Justice, justice shall you pursue." Sam waited to feel a sense of righteousness at Mikovski's sentence. All he felt was pity.

Early the next morning, a fit of wet coughing woke Mikovski out of a sleep so deep that Sam wondered if he'd died during the night. Sam was already awake, staring at the wet gray dawn backlighting the streaked windows. He rolled on his side and whispered, "You lived to see another day." Then he pointed toward the pile of dead men's uniforms, still waiting to be taken outside and burned. Mikovski wouldn't or couldn't turn to look. He stared at the ceiling. "You too, Sam." Startled at being called by his first name, Sam waited for Mikovski to say more, but the lieutenant had dropped off again.

Shortly after Mikovski awoke, Tomasio was brought in and given the cot on the other side of Sam. His cheeks were blotchy, but still faintly pink. Propping himself on an elbow to look past Sam, he said to the lieutenant, "Getting crowded here in the schoolhouse. We need someone to flunk out."

Mikovski looked ready to speak, but was short of breath. For the first time in two days, Sam wasn't, but he couldn't bring himself to laugh at his friend's joke. To make amends, he asked how his date had gone last night. To his surprise, Tomasio failed to brag about his conquest. "Greta's a good girl," he said.

Over the next few days, Sam's colour returned and his breathing grew easier. Tomasio, not as sick to begin with, also got stronger, although they both tired easily and slept most of the day. Mikovski drifted in and out of consciousness. Greta took his pulse every couple of hours and said a short prayer of thanks when it appeared she wouldn't lose another patient.

"Damn, he's still alive," Tomasio muttered each time she left, no longer expecting Sam to respond. Soon, however, even that snide remark turned into a claim of victory for them all. Their morale was boosted further when Greta brought news of the surrender and marvelled how lucky they were to survive the flu. "It's the darnedest thing," she said, "how it kills the youngest and strongest. Doctors say it's because people our age haven't built up immunity like older folks."

So why, Sam wondered, had he and Tomasio come through, while Mikovski was still touch and go. Tomasio said they'd grown up in more squalor and developed more resistance, but Sam sensed Mikovski had suffered worse and pushed harder to get out. The struggle had turned him mean. He might not be so bad one-on-one, but he had to prove himself in front of a crowd. At first he'd picked on Sam for his weakness, but later, when Sam became a leader, he had to take him down even more. Mikovski hated Tomasio simply because he made people laugh, a power the lieutenant would never have, no matter how far up in rank he climbed.

Greta, buoyed by their survival, slowly began to relax too, and let Tomasio cajole her into raiding the officers' food stores to double his rations. He coveted Oxo, a beefy drink supplement, said to fortify the immune system. Tomasio shared half the cubes with Sam, but once Mikovski slowly recovered his appetite, Sam slipped them to the lieutenant. Tomasio was flabbergasted.

"After what that S.O.B. did to you? I thought turning the other cheek was a Christian virtue. Is this some Jewish thing too?" Sam couldn't explain it. Mikovski hardly qualified as one of the widows or orphans Torah commanded Jews to look after. It was easier to say he himself wasn't hungry. Tomasio said that in that case, he'd keep the extra rations himself. Nevertheless, he continued leaving one Oxo cube per meal in Sam's cup, keeping silent when it disappeared.

On her own initiative, Greta also brought them treacle and vinegar, a foul concoction the Brits swore by. "Not even Hamble Weir would call this vile drink good for you," Tomasio said. Sam wondered if the seaman, shuttling U.S. destroyers and transports across the Atlantic, had managed to escape the Spanish flu. He hoped the royal sailor hadn't gone phut.

"Never could figure out why Weir was assigned to the Leviathan." Mikovski swung his legs over the side of his cot and stood up for the first time since arriving. "Guy didn't know his ass from his elbow. American discipline, not British intelligence, guided us through those mine fields." He kicked the bedpan out of his way and walked shakily to the bathroom. Tomasio raised his middle finger behind the lieutenant's back, but Sam smiled. Mikovski's rant was a sure sign he was getting better. Sam needed his nastiness to goad him on. The more Mikovski's natural animosity was restored, the more confident Sam felt that he himself would return to normal too.

Sam and Tomasio's own short trips to and from the john lengthened into walks around the schoolhouse. Tomasio visited those who had passed the crisis point, but Sam found himself drawn to the bedsides of those least likely to make it. Every day the pile of soiled uniforms grew higher, as delirious men were brought in and dead bodies borne out. Staff doused the clothes in alcohol to sterilize them until someone would have time to take the lot outside and burn them. It wouldn't take much to set the soaked blues and khakis aflame once they got around to it.

"Mary, Mother of God, help me." A red-haired soldier's head flopped from the edge of the bed back onto his pillow. For a second, Sam thought it Ryan, his and Tomasio's buddy from boot camp, but a mole on the boy's left cheek, barely darker than his eggplant mottled skin, told him it was a stranger. Sam took the young soldier's hand.

"Grant me absolution, Father."

Sam stammered. "I'm not ..."

"Tell me what I done wasn't so bad."

"You did what you had to, son. God understands and forgives you." Sam's words could have come from any religion, but they satisfied the boy. His narrow chest caved in with relief. Sam cradled him until he fell asleep. By dinnertime, another young soldier occupied the bed.

"How do you do it?" Tomasio asked. "I don't have the strength to look the dying in the eye, let alone hold them in my arms."

Sam had no answer to that question either. He didn't know if he believed the words he said but for the sake of those he comforted, he tried to speak them with conviction.

"Damned flu is worse than the Germans," Tomasio went on. "At least Fritz justifies what he does in the name of some cause. The flu doesn't take sides. It just kills whoever is in its path."

"My priest calls it a punishment from God," Greta said, "a rebuke for our sins." Tomasio snorted that such talk was claptrap, but Sam wasn't so sure. Who but the Almighty had that kind of power? The flu was like one of the plagues God visited on the Egyptians, not to free the Jews so much as to prove that He alone could whip any rival gods. When Sam seemed to side with Greta, Tomasio turned on the charm. Praising her earlier success with food rations, he begged her to sneak in cigarettes. "Drawing in the smoke will help to strengthen our lungs," he claimed.

"Hogwash!" the nurse declared, her good will restored after Tomasio's heresy, but she agreed to smuggle in a pack of fags if they didn't smoke them when the doctors did their rounds. Sam made a mental note to pass along the word "fag" to Dev. He'd stopped collecting words for her when he got sick. Doing so again was another sign that his body and mind were recovering, but Sam couldn't go home until his soul had healed too. He didn't know when, if ever, that would happen.

He asked Tomasio for a couple of cigarettes. Tomasio started to hand them over, before eyeing him suspiciously. "Wait. You don't smoke. You planning to give these to Mikovski too?"

Sam grabbed them before Tomasio could cram them back in the pack.

"Do you know how fucking precious these are?" Tomasio looked at Sam with disgust. "I bet he doesn't even thank you for them." Sam pocketed the cigarettes. He was counting on an ornery Mikovski to accept them as his due. The last thing he wanted from him was gratitude.

Later, when the doctors were gone and the men gathered near the disinfected clothes to smoke, Tomasio tried to take the cigarettes away from Mikovski. He glowered at the lieutenant. "I get them, I distribute them, and lower ranks get their fags first. You'll get yours *if* there are any left over."

"Like hell," said Mikovski. He blew out his match, tossed it over Tomasio's shoulder, and attempted to take a draw, but his lungs didn't have the strength. Nor apparently had they recovered enough to fully blow out the match. It flared up and landed on the alcohol-soaked uniforms, which exploded in a fiery ball. The force of the blast knocked Tomasio on his face.

After the explosion, the schoolhouse was eerily quiet. A second later, those whose lungs were strong enough shouted; those who were too weak banged on cots, trays, or anything else metallic in a call to be saved. A siren wailed outside as Greta rushed in. First she stomped on the fire, then she poured bedpans of water on it, but the flames were too high and spreading too fast.

Tomasio's face turn bluer than when he'd had the flu. Sam, afraid his friend would be overcome by smoke inhalation, stepped forward to drag him away, but someone on the floor behind him clawed his ankles and pulled him in the opposite direction. Sam wrenched his body around and saw that it was Mikovski, his grasp strong despite his weakened state. "Let go," Sam snarled, trying to shake him off. Fire had made Mikovski want to kill himself on the ship but on land it made him determined to survive. Why didn't he get up and run outside on his own steam?

As Sam stood immobilized, Greta began herding any men who could stand toward the door. The rush of bodies was what finally freed Sam's feet. He got swept up in the crowd, and Mikovski, his hold unwavering, was pulled along with him. Not until the lieutenant's body had been dragged several yards on the cold ground did he finally release his grip on Sam's ankles.

Sam panted with fear and rage. He pulled back his foot to kick Mikovski but almost lost his balance. Once he was steady again, he pivoted around toward the schoolhouse. The bedridden were being carried out on mattresses and stretchers. Sam looked at each face as he raced back to the burning building, but Tomasio wasn't among them. Sam was a yard from the door when the schoolhouse collapsed. Flames shot skyward the way blood had shot from the sick men's lungs.

He saw and heard more death that night than he had fighting the war, yet Sam could not bring himself to say Kaddish. It was a strange prayer, recited for the dead, yet the word death did not appear in it. Instead, the ancient Aramaic text exalted God's name and asked the Holy One to grant peace in our lifetime. How could Sam praise God for a life that was barely lived?

Two days later, Sam was discharged from one of the cottages that served as a temporary infirmary. The sun was white hot and thin pillars of smoke floated up from the ground where the school had stood. Everything was flat except for a black mound in a far corner of the yard. Sam walked slowly toward it. It was the molten mass of what had once been the school bell. He took off his ID tag and clanged it against the unyielding lump of metal, tolling the death of his friend.

part twelve

Gershon, 1919

chapter 30

Gershon paced while Yetta took in his trousers for the second time in six months. His appetite had disappeared along with Shmuel. Yetta tried to get him to eat by cooking roasts in the middle of the week and baking a different cake every day. She stood over him like a mother cajoling her sick child to eat. He felt guilty about disappointing her, but guiltier about not finding his nephew.

It was almost a year since the Armistice. Troops were coming home, but still there was no word of Shmuel. Gershon petitioned the War Department, only to receive a form letter saying the government appreciated every family's sacrifice, but with millions of deaths worldwide, they must accept that their unidentified sons were buried in mass graves or in the ocean. Money didn't help. Gershon's generous gifts to Senators Wadsworth and Calder were acknowledged with signed photos. He tore them up; he wanted information, not pictures.

He refused to believe that Shmuel was dead. The Armistice hadn't ended the fighting in the Russian and Ottoman Empires, so Gershon held out hope his nephew was stationed there. If only he could prove it. Then he read about an upcoming victory march down Fifth Avenue and knew what he had to do. Forget the military brass and politicians, he'd stop sailors in the parade and ask if they knew Shmuel. It was like looking for a needle in a haystack, a useful expression Dev had taught him, but he'd overcome impossible odds before.

Yetta called him meshugga; Ruchel said it was the most cockamamie idea she ever heard. Even Zipporah admitted it was crazy. Gershon didn't care what his wife and daughters thought. He'd promised his sister to find the boy before his brother-in-law's self-imposed year of mourning was up, and he'd failed. Gershon seethed when Avram gloated in bitter satisfaction.

As Yetta bit off the last thread, Gershon tried again to convince her he knew what he was doing. "Have I ever given you reason to doubt my judgment? I chose to marry you, didn't I?" His wife encircled him with her arms, something she hadn't been able to do since he was a skinny newlywed on the boat to America. Her touch reminded Gershon that he hadn't made love to her for three Sabbaths. He hugged her back, a tacit promise he'd make up for it when he got home.

Yetta relented, but remained worried. She told Ruchel to go with him.

"It's a fool's errand," Ruchel said. "Let him play the fool on his own."

"For shame!" Yetta, who rarely got mad, wouldn't tolerate any insolence that threatened peace in their home. She handed a bag of babka to Gershon. "Take, you shouldn't go hungry."

Gershon swatted it away, but changed his mind when he saw her hurt look and reached for the bag. Ruchel beat him. "I'll pass out cookies to all the hungry Jewish sailors marching down Fifth Avenue," she said, opening the door and walking ahead of her father to the subway stop.

They stood apart at the station and didn't sit together on the train. The rocking motion typically lulled Gershon to sleep, but today he imagined the marchers' boots pounding inside his skull. The subway car filled with passengers heading uptown. He worried that if they all exited at 107th Street, where the parade began, he'd be lost in the crush. Forgetting that Ruchel was with him, he bolted from the train at 59th Street, planning to catch the march at the halfway point.

"Wait!" his daughter called and tumbled onto the platform behind him, just before the doors closed. Gershon raced upstairs to the street. This time, he thought, let her keep up with him.

Crowds lined the curb, waving flags and tossing hats and handkerchiefs in the air. Others peered from windows draped with red, white, and blue bunting, or threw fistfuls of pennies and shredded paper over balcony railings. Craning his neck, Gershon saw troops a few blocks away, advancing quickly. He moved to a lamppost on the corner, where an effigy of the Kaiser hung. Wind knocked the dummy against his hat brim. "For goodness sakes, Father, stand over there." Ruchel tugged him toward a tree in the middle of the block, but he refused to budge. The broad intersection would give him more room to dash out and accost the sailors when they walked by.

"Mr. Mendel, I didn't know you were a patriot." It was Joseph

Cohen, the manager of the old-age home whom he'd bullied into admitting the incontinent Mrs. Meltzer the same week that Shmuel disappeared. Last year, the congregation recited Kaddish for Cohen's son, who'd served in the Army. Yetta had organized the chevra kadisha to bring food to the family while they sat shiva. Cohen tipped his hat to Ruchel. "I didn't expect a man with daughters to show up today."

Gershon searched for the perfect retort, but was distracted by the approaching marchers. Ruchel grimaced and answered herself. "We're sorry for your loss, Mr. Cohen. Coming here is our way to express gratitude to you and the rest of the country."

A man ran past waving a banner that read, "Liberty cannot die!" Behind him, a group of men, their faces painted black, slowly carried a coffin to symbolize the millions of anonymous war dead. One of the pall bearers wore a Navy uniform. Gershon fell in beside him and asked where the sailor had gone to boot camp and served afterwards. He was told Atlantic City, and in the Mediterranean.

"My nephew may have been there too. Perhaps you know him." Gershon described Shmuel, a fair-haired boy who would have worn a tallit beneath his uniform. He might have regrown his payess. The sailor looked puzzled. Gershon couldn't think of the English words.

"I believe the boy was sent to the Ottoman Empire to continue fighting."

"Your nephew wrote where he was stationed? I couldn't let my family know."

Gershon said he'd found out through other channels. The sailor sized up Gershon's fine wool coat, which hung on his thin body, and fancy leather shoes, scuffed by the surging crowd.

"So now you've fallen on hard times and can't pay channels to find him. Well, tough luck mister, but the families here today are suffering worse losses." The sailor snorted and shouted to his fellow pall bearers, "Let's pick up the pace before Pershing's troops overtake us."

Out of breath, Gershon turned back and faced the first wave of oncoming soldiers. They were dressed in trench helmets and full combat gear. Again, Ruchel tried to pull him elsewhere. "Can't you see they're from the Army, Father? Come stand with me back on the corner."

Gershon looked at the lamppost, where Cohen still stood, eying Gershon with the same sad superiority he'd seen on Avram's face when every lead dead-ended. Today he would not be defeated. He shook off Ruchel's arm and charged up the street as a deafening volley of rifle shots and cheers erupted for General Pershing. Gershon's shouted questions to the line of soldiers went unheard. He yelled louder, but they saluted at the crowds and marched past him without breaking formation. When had people stopped listening to him? He tripped and stumbled as a cannon rolled down Fifth Avenue, behind the first contingent of troops. Ruchel ran into the street to help him up, assisted by Cohen, who retrieved Gershon's trampled hat and held it out to him.

For the rest of the afternoon, Gershon followed the marchers downtown, falling further behind. He heard his voice ratchet up from commanding to pleading, but was powerless to control it. After Cohen peeled off, Ruchel continued to track him from the sidewalk. Women embraced the troops and once, when Ruchel caught Gershon's eye, she ran out to plant a kiss on a soldier's lips before darting back to safety. Gershon froze, debating how to punish her, when a sea of blue uniforms amid the hordes of green drew him in their wake. Most smiled reflexively, tired of the accolades and ready to go home. A few strained to listen before casting the pitying look they'd give a mad man. "I'm not meshugga!" Gershon said, the English word escaping him again.

The parade ended at Washington Square Park, near their apartment. The crowd dispersed, leaving a few stragglers sitting around the fountain beside pigeons pecking for peanuts. Gershon and Ruchel stood under the arch. "Mother will plotz if you walk in like a beat-up shtetl kid," she said. Gershon let her brush his lapels. As they started home, she pulled Yetta's cookies from her pocket, crammed one in her mouth, and snickered. "That was a day well spent." Crumbs spewed on his freshly groomed coat.

Gershon stopped walking. It was one thing for his daughter to talk like that to him in the privacy of their own home. Never before had she been sarcastic to him in public. Was this how American children spoke to their parents? Was her rudeness the backhanded proof of his ultimate assimilation?

"Sorry." Ruchel stopped too and held out the bag. "I should have shared."

"I'm not a child." Gershon grabbed the sack, stepped to the curb, and emptied the cookies through the sewer grate. Ruchel snatched the bag back, crushed it, and threw it down the hole atop the crumbs. She clapped her hands clean, sneered at him, and pivoted back toward the park.

Gershon had a sudden image of feeding babka to Ruchel as a baby. At the first taste of sweetness, she'd look up at him like he was a god delivering a miracle. Her rosebud lips had opened for more, but while she chewed, her eyes stayed locked on his. When had her adoration turned to scorn? Gershon watched her skip away in the fading light. He blinked and limped home. There were more ways than one to lose a child.

chapter 31

Soon thereafter, as the last men were coming back from the war, Gershon assumed concerns about national security had loosened and made one last attempt to find out where the Navy had shipped his nephew over two years ago. It surprised him that the information was still classified. He would have to return to the Community Board and petition them to intervene on his behalf.

Stepanic, reclining at the head of a long polished table, was now the board's chairman. Unlike Gershon, who'd continued to get thinner, his old nemesis had grown more substantial. He dressed in style, broad chest nearly popping the buttons on his silk vest, in contrast to Gershon's own flapping suit jacket and sagging trousers. Only Stepanic's worm-like lips looked the same as they had over twenty years ago, the first time he'd relished having power over Gershon's fate.

Those lips now smiled with confidence. "We meet again. Still trying to find your son?"

"My nephew."

"Ah, yes. You only had girls. I have four sons who served bravely and came home alive."

Gershon let the remark pass and explained his new petition to track down where Shmuel was first deployed and whether he was later transferred to the Eastern Front. He needed the board to approve his request before it could work its way through channels to the Navy's top command.

"I don't understand why the information can't be released at this point," one of the board members said, "but we don't make the rules. The petition seems reasonable to me."

Another disagreed. "We've reviewed a score of similar requests in the last month alone, and we can't grant them all without annoying the higher ups. We've got to debate each one on its merits. Some parents are searching for a second or third son after losing their other boys."

Gershon tried to maintain control in front of Stepanic, but his voice choked as he pleaded with the divided board. "If only you could see the boy's mother. She's aged thirty years in less than three." He described Rivka's worn face, all the while picturing Avram's gloating one. Stepanic had remained silent, but now he leaned forward. Gershon was sure he'd lost until Stepanic looked each board member in the eye and said, "The poor woman's been waiting a long time to find out what happened to her son. Let the other requests take their place in line."

Gershon stepped outside while they voted. Before he could decide whether to eavesdrop or pace up and down the hall, Stepanic called him back in to announce the board's unanimous approval. Moreover, Stepanic would urge that the matter be expedited and that the Navy write to him, instead of sending a form letter to the family. He intended to relay the news to Gershon in person. When all the men said they'd light votive candles for his nephew's safe return, Gershon didn't question whose God they would pray to. Stunned, he simply thanked them for their help.

Stepanic stepped out from behind the table to pump his hand. "Whatever the outcome, you'll be able to rest in peace." He licked his swollen lips like the serpent who tricked Eve in the Garden of Eden. Gershon wondered what Stepanic was plotting. Was he flaunting his power? Or was it just possible that, having grown fat and happy, he could embody the Talmudic ideal of generosity, giving with no expectation of reward? Gershon's head ached from debating with himself. He put on his hat to drown out the cacophony of inner voices.

Heading home, Gershon reflected that the Psalms exalted qavah, patience. We are told to be still and neither fret about those who prosper nor those who do evil, for the Lord holds all to account. At the same time, Judaism wasn't satisfied with mere belief; it also demanded action. Gershon had done all he could. Now he had to be still and wait.

chapter 32

Gershon wandered aimlessly through the rooms of the Mendels' apartment. He couldn't imagine how the Jews had held on for forty years in the desert, not knowing what was to become of them. Yetta urged him to take a walk, open a book, visit the synagogue, anything to make him less dershlogn. A few days later she announced that she'd gotten tickets to the Thalia for the following night.

"I'm in no mood for the theatre, especially the vaudeville schlock those greenhorns like." Gershon slumped at the dining room table, staring into a cup of cold tea.

"Since when did you get so fancy shmancy?" Yetta cocked an eyebrow, but promised him the plays would be good, an Isaac Dov Berkowitz original and two Sholem Aleichem translations.

Gershon frowned. "Who needs a reminder of shtetl life? I came here to escape that."

"A reminder is just what you need to see how good a life you made in this country. A bissel fun, like they say here, is what Mr. Doctor ordered." She plunked the tickets on the table.

He counted them. Five. That meant both girls were coming. Gershon squirmed, having barely spoken to Ruchel since the parade. But why was there an extra ticket? For a minute, he panicked that in her desire make peace in the family, his wife had asked Avram to join them. Unlikely as it was that Avram would have accepted, suppose he had just to annoy Gershon?

"Ruchel invited Dev," Yetta explained. "It's dark like a tomb at your sister's. A fourteen-year-old girl needs a bissel fun too. Besides, you know how star-struck our niece is." Gershon didn't, but he was so relieved Avram wasn't coming that he asked for a fresh cup of tea.

The next evening, he looked with satisfaction at the high class of people in the lobby. Dev ogled the six-foot chandeliers, which she pronounced the cat's meow. It was hard to maintain a sour mood in her presence. Gershon realized it was her first experience with live theatre. Avram insisted he couldn't afford it whenever Yetta suggested the Levinsons join them, and he wouldn't let the Mendels buy them tickets. Before Shmuel disappeared, Rivka would have been tempted, but her desire for entertainment vanished with her son. Ruchel was right to think her cousin needed a break from that depressed household. He hoped Avram knew he was paying for it.

Yetta herded everyone to the refreshment bar for coffee and Danish. While she talked to Zipporah about the shadchen's renewed efforts to find her a husband now that suitable men were home from the war, Gershon eavesdropped on Ruchel and Dev. "... highest grade in biology," his niece was saying, "but I'm afraid to tell Papa. He'll pitch an ing-bing if I mention college."

Ruchel snorted. "No grown-up will take your college plans seriously if you don't stop using childish slang. What about Aunt Rivka?"

"Mama used to be excited about my going to college to study science." Dev sipped the coffee, another first for her, Gershon guessed. She added three more teaspoons of sugar.

"And now?"

Dev's eyes teared. "She never talks about it anymore. She's too grummy, I mean depressed, over Shmuel."

"Your father should be proud that you want to do medical research." Ruchel spoke firmly. "Jews are commanded to do tikkun olam, world healing. You could fulfil that commandment by discovering a cure for some horrible disease, like the Spanish flu."

"If Papa thinks of me at all, it's to marry me off." Dev looked guiltily at Zipporah. So did Gershon, but his older daughter and wife were too busy with wedding plans to have heard her.

"Our parents came here to give us a better life," Ruchel told Dev. Gershon smiled to hear her give him that credit. "I know Uncle Avram's heartbroken about Shmuel, but he still has you."

Dev pressed her lips together. "Your father worships America as the land of opportunity, but mine would have been just as happy if my brother was a respected rabbi in Lemberg." She shrugged. "It doesn't matter anymore. He's given up on the future."

Gershon felt a rare pang of sympathy. Failing to find Shmuel had also robbed him of hope. He used to feel that the ner tamid, the eternal light inside the synagogue, burned within him too. No longer. Yet he swore he wouldn't turn into another Avram. He'd tell Dev not to give up either.

Ruchel squeezed Dev's shoulder. "Don't let your father hold you back." Though Ruchel's back was to him, Gershon sensed her remark was addressed to him as much as to her cousin. The pleasure he'd felt a moment ago when Ruchel acknowledged his good intentions evaporated.

"That's hotsy-totsy advice. Sorry." Dev smiled and gulped down the rest of her coffee.

Gershon set his uneaten pastry on the bar and sidled over to Yetta and Zipporah, who peppered him with questions about which prospective son-in-law he favoured. Their trust in him restored a glimmer of self-confidence, but he still felt shaky, even when Yetta handed him the tickets to lead the women into the auditorium. He sat on the aisle, listening to their chatter. Dev's excitement was again infectious. When the curtain rose, he willed himself to forget his troubles. Yetta was right. He needed distraction, not only from his nephew, but from his younger daughter.

Berkowitz's play *The Townsmen* began. The tenement scene resembled the Mendels' first apartment on the Lower East Side and could double for the two cramped rooms the Levinsons lived in today. Dev's sigh of disappointment was audible. No doubt she expected to see on the stage a world as fantastic as the one she'd swooned over in the lobby. The dismal sight, recalling the humiliations of his childhood poverty, shattered Gershon's resolve to enjoy himself too. Two characters, an older immigrant and a newcomer, took centre stage. The audience laughed as the greenhorn uttered familiar worries: people here talked too fast, walking on pavement made him stumble like a shikker, the roar of the subway was scarier than an army of drunken Cossacks descending on their village. Here was no better than there. The Christians still held all the power.

"Not to worry!" the old-timer said. "In America, we Jews run the show!" At that line, everyone guffawed. Even Dev squealed with delight. Gershon sat stone-faced. Two years ago, he'd have recognized himself and laughed too. He missed being the man who once helped people find jobs and housing. Now he couldn't find a missing boy. His eyes settled on the floor, where they remained for the rest of the performance. By not looking at the stage, he could blot out memories of the shtetl, but he couldn't shake the sting of failure today. Acid from the two sips of coffee he'd had in the lobby crept up Gershon's gullet and blistered his throat.

After the curtain fell, he ushered the women out quickly, eager to end the evening and escape into sleep. Dev slipped behind the others to walk beside him. "What's eating you Onkel Gershon? Ruchel called you a wet blanket tonight, but you're sad all the time, like my mother. You hardly visit us anymore." Gershon stiffened, but Dev, still exhilarated by the play, seemed to feel no inhibition about talking to him so frankly. "It's because of not finding Shmuel, isn't it?"

He stopped, rooted to the pavement. Yetta and the girls were half a block ahead, too far away to hear. Still, Gershon couldn't speak. He closed his eyes and nodded.

"Don't give up hope," Dev said. "Don't make my father right. You're still the big cheese. You run the show." She kissed his cheek and skipped to catch up with her aunt and cousins.

Gershon picked up his own pace. Some people said that as Catholics like Stepanic gained power, life would get better for the Jews too. He didn't agree. On the other hand, Stepanic might relish succeeding where Gershon had failed. And if his enemy did succeed in finding Shmuel, Gershon would win too. Maybe having Catholics in power wouldn't be so bad for the Jews after all.

Two weeks later, Gershon let himself feel optimistic when Stepanic invited him to his office. He accepted coffee and a china plate of bow knot chrusciki, although he was too excited to sit in the overstuffed chair he was offered. Stepanic's slimy lips were arranged in an almost-warm smile.

"I didn't expect you to call me so soon," Gershon admitted.

Stepanic leaned back and lit a cigar. He held out the box, but closed the lid with a loud thwack as Gershon reached to take one. "Shall I get right to the news?"

The cup and plate rattled in Gershon's hands. He set them on the edge of the desk.

Stepanic unfolded a sheet of embossed stationery and began reading. "With regard to your first inquiry, we regret to inform you that there is no record of the aforementioned Shmuel Levinson having enlisted in the service of the Navy in 1917, nor at any date prior or thereafter."

Gershon already knew that. He waved his hand impatiently.

"With regard to your second inquiry," Stepanic continued, "our files indicate that all the personnel trained at the Naval Militia School in East Boston were deployed in Great Britain or along the coast of France until the termination of hostilities on the Western Front. Those who did not perish have since been recalled to the United States. Only those shipped to the Mediterranean from other training facilities were reassigned to the Eastern Front pending a second armistice."

Although Stepanic read on, all Gershon heard was an occasional phrase — unidentified servicemen, buried at sea, condolences to the family on whose behalf this inquiry was made. Stepanic's lips curled in a gleeful grin, and he licked them repeatedly until they glistened with spittle. When he at last finished, he folded the letter and pointed again to the chair.

This time Gershon sat. "There must be some higher office you can write."

"The War Department is as high as it goes."

Gershon held out his hand for the letter.

"You don't believe me, Mr. Mendel?" Stepanic thrust the document in front of Gershon's face and poked a stubby finger at the raised seal. Unlike the form letters Gershon had received the last two years, this one, addressed to Stepanic, was signed by hand. "Your nephew's ship was attacked by a U-boat. He's lying on the bottom of the ocean. Face it. Your search is over."

The room was spinning. Gershon tried to steady himself by focusing on the toes of his shoes, which Yetta had polished last night. The reflection of his stunned face made him dizzier. Stepanic held out the cigar box again, this time leaving it open, and asked if there was anything else he could do to help. Gershon slammed down the lid and lurched outside into the fetid air.

In a daze, he walked to the Eldridge Street Synagogue and rested his palms on the ornate carved doors. Was this how Jacob felt after his sons reported that his beloved child, Joseph, had been killed by wild beasts? "Why does everything happen to *me*?" the Hebrew patriarch had cried. Gershon tore his lapel. It was a sign of mourning reserved for parents, children, and siblings of the deceased, but was he not as bereft as Avram, the boy's father? He walked through the doors and paused at the threshold of the sanctuary, raising his eyes to the ark where the silk-wrapped Torah scrolls sat behind the bima. Then he turned and left. There was no point in praying now. What could he say to God other than curses?

part thirteen

Dev, 1919

chapter 33

Papa refused when Mama begged him to sit shiva with us. "I already mourned Shmuel. Chasidim believe in reincarnation but for me, once dead is dead enough."

"That time didn't count," she said, hanging a black cloth over the window. "You can't say Kaddish until the rabbi pronounces someone dead." My mother appealed to his penchant for obeying rules, but my father was aggravated because it was Onkel Gershon who'd found the Talmudic tract that convinced Reb Stern to say Shmuel was gone. In Jewish law, the nostrils, not the heart, signify the passage from life to death. "We no longer hear his breath going in and out," my uncle reasoned, "so the lack of sound in our ears, more than Shmuel's disappearance from our sight, proves he's dead." The rabbi agreed and Shmuel was officially declared deceased.

Still Papa resisted Mama's plea. "I recited the prayer for the dead when my son abandoned his faith," he told her. "In God's eyes, that counts." But to my mother and me, Shmuel had not only been alive before, he hadn't stopped being a Jew. He'd only stopped studying to be a rabbi.

Mama kept trying. "You prayed alone, without the required minyan of ten men. It was an embarrassment then, it will look worse now if you're the only one who *doesn't* pray."

That made Papa give in, but not before he raised another objection. "No body, no coffin. Besides, we can't afford one and I won't take a pine box from charity." Mama had an answer for that too. My uncle had already bought a hardwood casket and cemetery plot, and he claimed we didn't need a body. According to the Talmud, Jews don't show the corpse because it gives your enemy a final invitation to mock you. Again, my father lost out to my uncle.

Since there was no body, I suggested we put a token of Shmuel inside the coffin instead. I was thinking of the recruiting poster rolled up under the couch. When the war ended, I'd asked the druggist for it and now, whenever I missed my brother, I took it out and talked to the sailor in the picture. Mama liked my idea, but before she could say what she'd put inside, Papa put the kibosh on the plan. I bet she was thinking of Shmuel's payess. I'd forgotten about his sidelocks after I found them in the garbage, but a year later I saw them in the closet, wrapped up with the braids Mama had cut off when she got married. I kept mum since I wasn't supposed to be poking around in there. Also, I'd been afraid Papa would make Mama throw the payess back in the trash.

Unfortunately, Papa had a reason to leave the casket empty that even Gershon accepted. My father said ancient Egyptians buried their dead with personal possessions, hence Jews, having been liberated from slavery in Egypt, were forbidden from copying them. My uncles's agreement almost made Papa reverse himself, but the coffin stayed bare. When we lowered it in the ground and threw handfuls of dirt on top, it sounded as hollow as our apartment without Shmuel.

During the week we sat shiva, there was a long-awaited sense of relief, but a new wave of sorrow overwhelmed us too. Except for Papa, who sulked like a sixteen-year-old, the same age my brother was when he left. It made me question all over again why Shmuel took off, whether he really cared about the war or used it as an excuse to run away from home. By the time I turned sixteen, well over a year from now, the period of mourning would be over. I was past ready.

My mother was comforted that so many people came to sit shiva with us. It was the first time since the disappearance that all the Mendels were at our house, although only Tante Yetta and my cousins spoke to my father. Neighbours stopped by, even Catholics, with cake from the Jewish bakery. Safer than making something themselves that might not be kosher. The rabbis who'd taught Shmuel shuffled in too. They addressed Papa, but grew silent when he scowled and pulled his tallit around his shoulders. It was his regular Shabbas prayer shawl, not the one he'd been saving to give Shmuel on his ordination. That special tallit disappeared after the first time he sat shiva. Rebuffed, the rabbis discussed Talmud with my uncle, unaware they were fuelling my father's rage and grief.

Shmuel's classmates, who'd graduated without him, also paid their respects, including his pals Yaakov and Bernie. Loud-mouthed Yaakov blubbered to Mama, "We could have stopped him." If he thought his acting guilty would make her feel better, he was all wet. Didn't he have the brains to know it would make her more splenetic that his friends hadn't said anything?

"We couldn't have stopped him," Bernie confided to me. He was taller and not as skinny as that day outside United Drugs. "Shmuel knew his own mind." I wasn't sure of that, but Bernie saying so helped me feel better. It made Shmuel the master of his own destiny, which is how I wanted to remember him. Otherwise I'd be flooded with remorse thinking my parents and I had let him down. I was fed up listening to Yaakov make a spectacle of himself. I was done with crying, period. Sometimes my eyes stung but tears no longer spilled out. I was afraid if I stayed in that hot, crowded apartment another mournful minute, I'd start to wail and flail like Yaakov.

"I have to extricate myself from this drama," I said. Bernie followed me out to the alley.

It was early evening and the laughter coming from Paddy's Saloon was as disconcerting as the sobs emanating from our house. As near as I could tell, Prohibition hadn't done much to change the drinking habits of our Catholic neighbours. They simply drank a larger quantity of watered-down beer to get as spifflicated as before, and stumbled outside to pay the water bill.

"Do you really think Shmuel was sure about what he was doing when he enlisted in the Navy?" I asked Bernie. Maybe he knew something I didn't. After all, friends confided things to each other that they wouldn't tell their families. I confessed nearly everything to Leah.

"No, but nothing me or Yaakov said would have made a difference." Bernie watched a man lurch out of Paddy's and weave down the street toward us. "Your brother was more certain about what he didn't want than what he wanted. Or, he was confused about both, and figured a destroyer would be as good a place as any to sort things out."

That made no sense to me, but maybe coming face-to-face with death helped you make up your mind lickety split about what to do with the rest of your life.

"One thing I'll say for Shmuel." Bernie's body tensed as the dipsomaniac came closer. "He was brave. He wasn't good at standing up for himself, but when the Micks and Wops picked on a Jewish kid smaller than us, your brother would step in and deflect the fight onto himself."

I wish I'd known how to deflect some of our father's pressure from Shmuel onto me, but Papa wasn't as easily dissuaded as the boys at my brother's high school. For them, any Jew would do. For my father, only Shmuel was a worthy target for his dreams. And disappointments.

"What do you think you're doing? Can't you see there's a lady present?" Bernie yanked me behind him as he shoved aside the drunk, who'd stopped to relieve himself a foot from where we stood. Urine ricocheted off the brick wall and splashed down the front of Bernie's coat. The man muttered a fuzzy apology and fumbled to button his fly. I peeked over Bernie's shoulder to watch and stared as the old boozer zigzagged back to Paddy's. I remembered being woozy last Pesach when my parents let me drink all four glasses of wine during the Seder. The giddy feeling had momentarily lifted our gloom, until the alcohol unstoppered Papa's anger and Mama's tears. I wondered what it would be like to get drunk without sorrow lurking in the background.

"I'm sorry you had to see that," Bernie said, his remaining pimples red with indignation. I was sorry I hadn't seen more. The last time I looked at a penis was ten years ago, when Shmuel and I were still young enough to stand together in the washtub on Friday afternoon while Mama heated water on the stove to pour over us. She was making us clean for the Sabbath. Of course, I couldn't reveal my dirty mind to Bernie. It was almost too shameful to admit to Leah.

At the same time I was disappointed, I was also flattered that Bernie wanted to defend my virtue. The weekend Shmuel disappeared, he'd protected me from Yaakov's teasing outside the drugstore. I wondered now what Shmuel would have done if he'd been here when the drunk pulled out his dingus to pee. I suppose acting manly was as important to Shmuel as it was to Bernie, or anyone their age. Maybe that was the real reason my brother joined the Navy. If so, nothing my mother or I said would have mattered. I doubted my father could have convinced him there were other ways to be a man either, but if Papa thought he could, he'd feel guiltier than us. Maybe it was the guilt that made him so angry. It wasn't Shmuel he couldn't forgive, but himself.

Thinking of Papa made me want to thank Bernie for acting like he cared about me. Mere words seemed lame, but when I reached toward him, Bernie pulled back. My face grew hot. He mumbled something about his urine-stained coat not being fit to touch. We stood apart in awkward silence until he asked if I'd do him the favour of going to the movies with him next weekend, when the family was done sitting shiva.

My jaw dropped. My gams wobbled.

"If your father will let you," he added, covering the blemish on his chin with his hand. His fingers were as long as he was tall.

I had no intention of asking. Mama had barely persuaded Papa to let me go to the theatre with Onkel Gershon. Suppose he refused on the grounds that I was too young, although I considered myself mature for my age. Worse, he might shrug and say it didn't matter one way or the other. "I'm sure my father will say yes," I told Bernie. "Of all Shmuel's friends, Papa liked you best."

Bernie's shy smile couldn't mask his pride. His lips quivered. "Sometimes I have to force myself to have fun. I miss Shmuel." My eyes filled. For the first time in months, I let the tears spill out.

I hung around the phone the rest of week so I could answer it before my parents. I worried they'd get hinky, suspecting I was up to something, but I think they were grateful. People kept calling to offer condolences and spout platitudes. After a while, kindness gets tiresome.

Bernie waited until Sunday morning to ring me up and ask if I could go to the movies that afternoon. I'd read in Bintel Briefs, the advice column, that a man should call by mid-week to ask a woman out, but maybe he was just waiting to give my parents more time to get over their grief.

"Did your father say it was okay?" Bernie's voice was hushed as though he were asking for something sacred. Maybe he spoke quietly because he was calling a house of mourning.

"Yes," I fibbed, crossing my fingers, then quickly uncrossing them, afraid the Christian gesture made the lying worse. "He thinks it's good for me to get out of the house." I don't know why I added that. Me and my big mouth. I still hadn't learned when to plug it. Bernie said he'd pick me up at 1:30, but I said we should meet at the theatre. "Seeing you will remind Mama of Shmuel and she'll start crying all over again." I silently asked God to forgive my whopper.

"I never thought of that. Girls know these things. They're closer to their mothers."

He was mistaken, although Mama considered us allies. She gave me more attention and freedom than Papa, but where was the victory in that?

Bernie suggested we see *The Lost Battalion*. It was about American soldiers trapped in a forest in France during the war, and many of the actors in the movie were survivors who played themselves. "Yaakov says the rescue scene is really exciting. It will be a good distraction."

"How? When Shmuel is lost forever?"

Bernie was embarrassed and apologized for not thinking of that too, but I was pitching baloney. It was a ruse to get him to see Theda Bara in *The Lure of Ambition*, a movie about a fallen woman who saves a duke from being murdered by his crazy wife and marries him after the wife dies of a heart attack. After his gaffe, Bernie would have agreed to anything I suggested.

I got to the theatre a teensy bit late, enough to let Bernie arrive first but not get nervous that I wasn't coming. Playing hard-to-get made no sense to me. Why not be on the level about what you wanted? If you pretended you weren't interested, you might never get the mazuma.

Bernie was ogling a poster of Theda Bara in a low-cut dress when I got there. He looked away and blushed, and when I said I could see why she was called a vamp, he turned twice as red. "You look nice. I mean not too nice," he said. "I know you're not supposed to get dressed up ..."

I'd agonized about what to wear. With shiva just over, I couldn't put on my glad rags. I told my parents Leah had invited me to her great aunt's house and I was getting a little dressed up out of respect. My mother pronounced my get-up fine, but my father, who was going back to work for the first time in a week, hurried out the door. Too bad I hadn't borrowed Mama's zippered skirt to snag his attention. He did tell me not to talk slang to Leah's relatives, and to be home in time to help Mama make dinner. I smiled because it meant he'd listened to where I was going, but I was annoyed that all he cared about was me buttoning my mouth and cooking.

Outside the theatre, smells from the food vendors' carts filled the air. I was tired of eating the limp briskets and soggy noodle kugels people had been bringing us all week. Biting into some crunchy popcorn would be absolutely divine. I suggested to Bernie that we buy a bag.

"Suppose it was popped with lard. You wouldn't buy food if you weren't sure that it was kosher, would you?" Bernie loosened his collar. I smiled coquettishly, like I'd been joking, but I was worried. What if Bernie were as strict about rules as Leah? I decided to sacrifice my taste for deviant food so I could taste something better, but again I was disappointed because Bernie put a lid on his desires while we watched the movie. He wrapped an arm around my shoulder but when it trembled, he put it back in his lap. I leaned toward him to let him know it was all right, but he didn't try again. I sighed and contented myself seeing Olga Dolan, the Theda Bara character, smooch with the ritzy English duke. That made me feel better. She was hotter than popcorn! Afterwards we went to the drug store for sodas, like Shmuel and I used to. Bernie was a polite conversationalist. Unlike boys my age, who only talked about themselves, he asked about me. "I'm different than other girls," I confided. "My friend Leah says I'm ambitious."

"Not like that Olga Dolan in the movie, I hope." A drop of root beer flew out of his mouth.

I ignored the sputtering to spare him embarrassment, took a demure sip on my straw, and murmured, "I'm no bearcat. I'll use my wits, not sex appeal." Bernie looked relieved and nodded for me to go on. I told him I was keen on biology and hoped to be a scientist. "A map of arteries and veins is prettier than a lace wedding gown." I sighed thinking of the diagram in my textbook. The very word "heart," with its breathy vowels and rounded "r," was a satisfying mouthful.

"Shmuel always said you were smart." Bernie took a long, manly draw on his straw.

I almost cried again, right there, to think that my brother bragged about me to his friends. His praise had to count double since I got none from Papa. I told Bernie what I'd never told anyone. "After Shmuel left, I imagined my heart grew a fifth chamber where he snuggles inside. If I need a shot of courage, I tap my chest and he pumps oxygenated blood all through my body."

"With an extra spurt to your brain." Bernie reached across the table and touched my hair.

For once, I was glad my curls were dark like my father's and not pale, like Shmuel's and Mama's. Otherwise the blood pulsing through the capillaries of my scalp would have turned my hair bright red. "I'm not a Dumb Dora like the girls in my class who act as if nobody's home."

"Science is discovering new things all the time," Bernie said. "No wonder you like it."

"Maybe I'll find the cure for some disease, like the Spanish flu." I told him about a dream I kept having, where I wore a long white lab coat and peered under a microscope.

Bernie squirmed. "I don't think women should work unless they have to, but it's good to learn what you can do to make the home a safer and healthier place." He sounded just like Leah.

"What about tikkun olam?" I reminded him, "the commandment to save the world?"

Bernie acknowledged that was important too. If he'd added "for men," I'd have stomped out. Instead, he pushed his soda to the middle of the table. I did the same. We bent our heads and sipped from each other's straws, a peace offering. Through lowered lids, I observed his dimples, no longer hidden by bad skin, and the arm muscles that swelled when his long fingers gripped my glass. I felt a flutter, but not from my heart's extra chamber. I refrained from taking a big gulp.

Advice column instructions quelled the flutter and percolated into my brain. *Ask about his work, his hobbies.* I asked Bernie what he wanted to do now that high school was over.

"Work at my dad's appliance store during the day, take business classes at night."

"That's what you *will* do. I asked what you *want* to do."

Bernie leaned forward. Our foreheads almost touched. "I dream about being a rabbi. My dad wants me to be a businessman. I'm more cut out to sell a big God than small appliances."

"What does your mother want for you?"

"Whatever my father wants." He sat back and shrugged.

"Aren't you disappointed that she doesn't take your side?" I wondered if boys sought their mother's approval as much as I craved my father's. I doubted it.

Bernie took time to consider his answer. "No, it's good for a wife to agree with her husband. I'm sure the tradition of sholem bayess, peace in the home, reigns at your house too."

"Mama is masterful at it. Personally, I wish she'd provoke a little conflict with Papa."

"In the long run, the mother being on the father's side is better for the marriage and the children." Bernie stuck out his chin.

"What if the father is wrong?" I asked.

Bernie's head snapped back, but then he tilted it, ready to listen.

"I think my father was wrong about Shmuel." Hearing myself say this for the first time I knew I was right. "Shmuel never wanted to be a rabbi. That was my father's dream."

"Your brother was a good student, like you. Scholarship is important for a rabbi."

"Yes," I conceded. "He liked books. But rabbis spend more time with people than books. They have to make the rich congregants happy." I thought of my uncle who always got his way. "And rich people never agree with one another, so the rabbi is always in the middle of a fight."

Bernie grinned. "I'm the opposite of Shmuel. I like people more than books. Even when they don't agree."

I grinned back. "So peace in the home is super, but peace in the shul is sacred?"

"A good rabbi makes everyone happy in the end."

"God willing."

Bernie laughed. "Yes. The all-powerful God—and powerful rich men—willing."

"My father isn't rich, but he tries to be all powerful. He didn't let Shmuel say no to being a rabbi. After Shmuel left, he got even stricter with my mother. She's barely allowed to lift a pot lid on Shabbas." I looked at Bernie to see if I was sounding too hot under the collar, but he nodded for me to go on. "Papa doesn't pay much attention to me," I admitted, "but when he does, it's always to tell me not to do something. He's a dictator!" I sat back and crossed my arms.

Bernie rocked like Gershon did before quoting the Talmud, and stroked what I imagined would one day be a soft, wispy beard. "Shmuel was two when your parents emigrated, dreaming of a better life. Think how much your father lost when Shmuel left. If he's grown more rigid, it's because his heart is broken. He's struggling to keep the family together so *he* doesn't fall apart."

It was my turn to admit I'd never thought of that. "You'll make a good rabbi," I said.

Bernie inched his hand across the table and put it over mine. "That means a lot, coming from you." I'd been wrong about him. He was virtuous, but not judgmental like Leah. In fact, he was the most understanding person I'd ever met. Warmth suffused my body. "Race you to see who can finish his root beer first," I said to recover. A few slurps later, we agreed it was a tie.

We stood outside the drug store under the rosy glow of a late afternoon sun. In the window where the Navy poster had once hung was an advertisement for Hall Brothers cards. "We help you say love to those you love." Bernie touched his lips to mine. I pressed back, not too hard. I didn't want to scare him off.

"Don't take any wooden nickels," I told him when we parted a block before my house.

"Don't worry. I know my onions." It was the first time I heard Bernie talk hip to the jive. With Shmuel gone, I hoped I could count on him to correct my slang and make sure I didn't say something hurtful. I felt his eyes watch me, protectively, as I walked to our stoop. I wished Papa would follow me with the same interest, not to hold me back but to see where I was going.

"Baloney!" Shmuel spurted inside his chamber. "This kind of attention is completely different." My brother was right, but thinking of him nearly arrested my heart with guilt. Was it wrong for his sister and best friend to have a good time together when he lay dead? I listened for his voice again, but Shmuel fell silent. I'd have to learn the language of romance on my own.

chapter 34

I hardly slept that night. Euphoria collided with my guilty conscience. Shiva had barely ended and here I was kissing Shmuel's best friend. Yet Bernie and I had been mourning my brother for over two years. Weren't we allowed to enjoy life again? I could hardly wait for school to let out on Monday so I could ask Leah. If someone as good as her reassured me I wasn't committing a sin, then I could stop worrying. Not that I was seeking her blessing, just a nod that it was okay.

My last class of the day was English, my favourite subject after biology. Language still bedazzled me. Learning a new word was like making a new friend. You discovered what the word did and the best way to be together with it. Searching for the perfect word was like picking who to spend the day with at Coney Island. Leah was my best friend, but sometimes other girls were better company. It was the difference between sweet and mellifluous, my newest word.

I still loved slang, of course, but using it got me into hot water. So the day I called the grungy guy who stiffed Bridget out of a cherry soda a piker, and Mrs. Whittaker held me back after class, I braced for a lecture. Instead she gave me *The American Language* by H. L. Mencken, with slang words from all over the country, like "bacon" for "money." I wondered if Jews were allowed to say that or if the expression "to eat your words" meant we had to speak kosher too.

Leah's last period was home economics. This year, high schools began tracking students and she was in domestic arts. I was one of the few girls in pre-college. If they'd had tracking in Shmuel's day, he'd be pre-college too. Same for Bernie. Yaakov would have been in vocational, learning how to dig manholes. Most girls in Leah's track didn't even graduate. They got married and had babies. I eavesdropped at the door while her teacher droned on about boiling diapers, washing hands, and isolating sick children. How did she expect families living in crowded, cold-water flats to do that? "Remember," she closed, "Ignorance breeds filth and filth breeds disease."

When Leah emerged, I harrumphed that, "poverty breeds filth and wealth makes health." I was quoting from a pamphlet my mother brought home after she marched on City Hall to protest tenement conditions. Leah said the government was trying to improve sanitation, but Jewish and Italian women wouldn't open their doors to city inspectors because most of them were Irish.

"They'd trust someone like you," I told her. "I still think you should become a nurse." I'd suggested the idea to her after Mama gave me a biography of Lillian Wald, a Jewish woman who founded the Visiting Nurses Association. Even though Leah wasn't in the academic track, she was smart enough to go to college. I said taking anatomy classes with her would be the bee's knees.

"That's not for me, Dev. It's enough to take care of my own family."

"Torah says to help others." Leah didn't need reminding, but I was annoyed she set her sights so low. Also, I wanted her with me in college so I wouldn't turn into a car without brakes.

"You're right," Leah said, chagrined. Then she brightened. "I can set an example with my own children and tell the women in Sisterhood to sanitize their houses and let the inspectors in."

"That's not going to heal the whole world. You should organize all the mothers at the Henry Street Settlement House to talk to the politicians about cleaning up the sewage."

"You sound like your mother." Leah knew I admired when Mama stood up for women, but got irritated when she didn't stand up to Papa. Like me, Mama craved his approval. I waited to see if he'd still loved her when she tested the waters, hoping I could dare to do the same.

"If all it took was knowledge and not action," I said, reluctant to abandon the argument and let Leah off the hook, "then Jews would be healthier than everyone else. Think how many laws the Torah has about cleanliness."

"Those laws are written for men to obey, and they apply to the temple, not the home."

"You're right, kiddo." I gave in. "There's nothing in the Torah about boiling diapers."

Leah smiled and slipped her arm into mine. Then we skipped home, taking the long way.

Our neighbourhood was an endless source of fascination. Skin colours varied from the freckled paleness of the Irish to the strong tea hue of the

Italians. Earthy smells of cabbage stewed with caraway seeds blended with the acidic sting of simmering tomatoes. Pushcart peddlers, selling wares from roasted chestnuts to sewing thread, shouted in a polyglot half-English, half something else. Horses either sashayed with pride pulling fully loaded carts or shuffled listlessly ahead of their equally dispirited owners. Animal tails and human hands flicked away swarms of flies as numerous and agitated as the bustling throngs competing for space and the cheapest prices.

Elevated trains clanked above us, spewing foul air, but also the promise of riding out to the unseen edges of the vast city. I looked up and around, dizzy with the sensations of the Tenth Ward and visions of the universe beyond it. Leah kept her eyes down, on the street.

"Dev, if you don't watch where you're going, you'll step in something."

"Such as?"

"Something ... nasty."

"Such as horseshit?" It was the first time I'd tried using that word.

"Dev!" Leah clutched her books to her chest as a protection against my naughtiness. She looked around to see if anyone else had heard. I smiled. I'd gotten her to lift her eyes.

"Poop, caca, crap, doodoo, dingleberries. Do you like those words better?"

Leah regarded me with suspicion. "Where did you learn them? Have you been spending time with Bridget?" I didn't admit that I wished I could pal around with Bridget as much as I used to, but she'd shunned me once we started high school. She said it was nothing personal, but that Jewish girls weren't fast enough for the likes of her. Maybe now I could prove I was different.

With as much superiority as I could muster, I told Leah, "For your information, Mrs. Grundy, those words are from a reputable source." Holding my other books and papers under one foot so they wouldn't blow away, I pulled out the Mencken book Mrs. Whittaker had given me. "See." I flipped to a page with a long list of slang words for excrement.

Leah glanced down, then averted her eyes. "It's just as bad to read them as to say them."

"Listen to this." I read the preface where Mencken says that prodding into the national idiosyncrasies and ways of the mind is always entertaining. I held the book out to Leah again. "Aren't you itching to know what absolutely everyone, everywhere, says and eats and wears and thinks and ... oh, everything else? In America we can scratch that itch."

Leah shook her head, like I might have expected, insisting she'd raise her children the same way she was brought up. The new opportunities were for *them*, not her. She repeated her bubbe's old saying, "It's up to the mama to turn plain potatoes into tasty kugel for the kinder."

"Our parents came here so *our* generation could have kugel, hash browns, spuds ..." I consulted my book, "taters, murphies, Idahos. We should also be eating strawberries and cream in January and roast beef instead of brisket on Shabbas."

Leah sighed. "So I'll cook those fancy things for my grandchildren."

"And pork roast and broiled lobster with drawn butter?" I teased.

"Shah, Dev." Leah laughed and bent to pick up my pile of books, which she straightened before handing them back to me. "You are too, too much."

"Beats being a flat tire, pill, or pickle."

We walked on, past Walhalla Hall where suffrage and union meetings were held during the week, and wedding music blared on weekends. "Did I tell you my Onkel Gershon is hiring three bands when my cousin Zipporah gets married next fall? The caterer is from uptown."

She grabbed my elbow, forcing me to stop. "Who did the shadchen match her up with? Where does the groom work? Where will they live? Will your aunt make the wedding dress or hire a seamstress? Has she picked out a china pattern? Silverware?"

"Hold your horses." I hadn't seen Leah this animated since we'd learned to roller skate. "His name is Jonah and my uncle does the accounts for his father's stationery firm. I suppose Jonah will take over the business. That's all I know." My cousin's nuptials didn't interest me, although I was a smidgen jealous over how much money would be spent on them.

Leah's face grew dreamy. "If I were rich like your relatives, I'd have a wedding dress with a ten-foot satin train and a hope chest filled with linen tablecloths and crystal candy dishes."

"Didn't your home economics teacher tell you that sweets are bad for children's teeth?"

"To tell the truth, Dev, I'm not learning much in school that I haven't already learned at home. Sometimes I don't care if I graduate. I just want to start a family."

Whenever Leah spouted such piffle, I had to restrain myself from shaking her. I touched the ringlets escaping from her scarf. "Women deserve more. You deserve more."

"God willing, the shadchen will find me a tailor or a baker so my children can wear nicer clothes and eat finer bread than me and you." Leah tugged playfully on my thick curls. "I don't want much, just to live my life being pious and kind."

"I know," I cried, "but you can be those things and still use your brains."

"I'm not like you." Leah stared down at her scuffed shoes. "My dreams aren't as big."

I stroked the spine of my science book, recalling the illustration we studied that morning. Vena cava sounded like a mysterious tunnel inhabited by a goddess. I admired the stubby aorta, carrying oxygen-rich blood to our muscles and relished the sturdy sound of "pulmonary." Maybe some day I'd discover why everyone's heart worked the same but their minds worked differently.

Leah and I resumed walking, past a stand selling daisy-shaped cookies with shiny white icing and yellow sugar crystals. "If we can't afford elegant weddings," I said, "let's treat ourselves to an elegant cookie. Split one with me?" Since Shmuel left, Papa had rescinded permission for Mama to pack store-bought cookies in my lunch box. Now everything had to be homemade. My mother was a good baker but her style was plain and simple. She refused to put on airs while others went hungry. If she'd ever aspired to adding a fillip to her cooking, Papa would have accused her of emulating my uncle's family and put the kibosh on her fanciness.

"They're probably made with lard. We shouldn't buy anything that isn't from the kosher bakery." Leah pinched her lips together, although her eyes devoured the pastries too.

"We don't always have to follow the rules. The man who wrote the slang dictionary says so, and anyone who isn't an old schoolmarm agrees with him."

"I'm sorry, Dev. I wish for your sake I could, but for God's sake, I can't." I almost bought a whole cookie for myself, but if I incurred Leah's disapproval for something so trivial, she'd never grant me absolution for the big sin of kissing Bernie.

We got to the Hester Street market. Mondays were quiet compared to Thursday afternoon and Friday morning, when housewives jostled one another shopping for Shabbas. Instead of carts filled with shimmering fish, fruits, and vegetables, today there were a few bedraggled peddlers hawking starched collars and dented tinware. Things were livelier at a corner café where Jewish labourers and students gathered to drink coffee and debate editorials in the *Jewish Daily Forward*. Arguments were loud but not violent. Unlike Catholics, Jews avoided saloons or speakeasies. It was said that even Irish policemen preferred patrolling our dry establishments.

"We could go to the Pilpl Café." Pilpl was the Yiddish word for a hair-splitting argument or debate, which was the café patrons' main pastime. "The coffee and pastries are kosher there."

Leah hesitated. It might be considered unseemly for young women to sit, unchaperoned, next to young men in a drinking establishment, even if the beverage was coffee, not giggle water.

"I have no intention of flirting," I reassured her, then winked. "There's a special reason why I'm on my best behaviour. If you come with me, I'll tell you."

Leah raised her eyebrows and followed me into the Pilpl.

I hadn't figured out what to say, so I stalled by suggesting we get tea and babka first. I gobbled mine in two bites. Leah nibbled hers and waited. I decided that if I acted like what I'd done was adventurous but nothing to be alarmed about, I could entice both her interest and her approval.

"Guess who I went to the movies with yesterday?"

Leah's face fell. "Bridget?"

"No silly. Not a girl. I wouldn't exclude you."

Her hurt look disappeared. The cookie stopped halfway to her lips and her eyes opened as wide as her mouth. I prolonged her amazement by pretending to brush cinnamon sugar off my coat, until I couldn't hold it in any longer. "Bernie!"

Leah returned the uneaten babka to her plate. "I'm surprised your father let you go."

I let her assume he had. "After the movie, we went out for root beer. It's kosher."

Leah grinned. "I know. What did you and Bernie talk about? He's so quiet."

"Bernie talks more when he's not around that big fat blabbermouth Yaakov. He told me he's working for his father but deep down he wants to be a rabbi. I talked about studying biology and my favourite words in the circulatory system."

"Marrying a rabbi would be even better than a tailor or a baker." Leah's eyes shone.

I'd scored a point, but I didn't want to win Leah's approval under false pretences. "I'm not marrying him," I said. "I plan to be scientist, not a rabbi's wife."

"Couldn't you do both?" Leah herself sounded sceptical.

"Bernie didn't sound enthusiastic about women working outside the home." Recalling his remark momentarily dampened my ardour, but I didn't let on to Leah.

"I'd give up a career to marry a rabbi," Leah said with certainty, "but I'm not sure you're well enough behaved to be a rebbetzin." She smiled. "Unless Bernie made you be good."

I should have smiled back, but the idea of a man telling me what to do was infuriating. "Bernie's not such a goody two shoes himself," I retorted. "We drank from each other's straws."

Leah clapped both hands over her mouth.

"Worried about germs?" Maybe a little teasing would sway her. I prayed she'd accept that people she considered good could occasionally transgress without becoming bad.

"I'm surprised a future rabbi would do that," she said.

"Bernie's an appliance salesman, not a seminary student."

"It's still not right. My bubbe says, 'Don't crack eggs unless you plan to make a cake.' You shouldn't even hold hands until you're engaged." Leah studied her hands, glanced at a table of students hotly debating the Red Scare, and then, taking a deep breath, leaned in to hear more.

Sometimes I wondered what made us friends. Maybe she was my Bernie and I was her Yaakov. The withdrawn person needed the livelier one to add excitement to his or her life. Not that I was loud and coarse like Yaakov, but we were both willing to take chances, relying on our counterparts to keep us from going too far, and to love us when we skirted the edge.

"Bernie and I kissed outside the drugstore." I grabbed what was left of Leah's cookie and crunched it between my teeth. Now I *had* gone too far. Leah would never condone my behaviour, but that familiar urge to shake her from her complacency was too strong to resist.

She drew back as if I'd slapped her. "If you're not careful, you'll be a mother before me and you can forget about being a scientist."

"I might not want to be a scientist after all. I told Bernie I dreamed of being a movie star."

"You're talking like a loose woman, Dev. Is that why he took the liberty of kissing you?"

"He didn't take anything. I wanted him to kiss me. We both wanted it."

Leah's nose was six inches from mine. "Your family is barely done sitting shiva. What would Shmuel say about his best friend and his sister ...?" She searched for the right word.

"Canoodling? Making whoopee?" I sputtered crumbs on the table.

We both stood up. I waved goodbye to a scraggly bearded student whose lips opened in surprise at the same time Leah pressed hers together in distaste. At the front counter, I bought a pack of Milo Violets. The colour drained from Leah's face. If her aorta didn't get busy pronto, she was going to pass out right on the floor of the Pilpl Café. My heart had stopped pumping too. I'd often shocked Leah, but I'd never made my best friend so angry at me before.

Outside, Leah headed home without looking back. When she reached the corner, I threw the cigarettes into a pile of horse manure. I'd never intended to smoke them. I bought them just to goad Leah, and to punish her for trying to make me feel guilty, or guiltier than I already felt. An erratic *lub, dup, lub, dup* percolated in my chest. I didn't know if it came from the four chambers of my own heart, or the fifth one where Shmuel knocked to chime in on the conversation.

It was already past time for me to help my mother with dinner, but the thought of going home crushed me. I was fed up with Mama's sadness, Papa's and Leah's disapproval, and my own guilt. "Talk to Ruchel," Shmuel whispered. He was right. My cousin would egg me on, not judge me. Tante Yetta would invite me to stay for dinner. The food would be kosher, but it would be more savoury than what everyone else was dishing out these days.

chapter 35

Ruchel had her own bedroom. I was envious. After Shmuel left, I had the front room to myself at night, but we all used it by day and my clothes were crammed in the hall closet with our coats and blankets. My only private space was a scarred wooden chest where I kept books, word lists, and keepsakes—a rag doll with faded yellow hair to whom I'd given the American name, Susan, and a tin of seashells I started collecting at age five, back when Papa took our whole family to Coney Island. He'd help me rinse them off in the ocean and when we got home, he'd put the shells in a bowl of water so their violet and mauve streaks would shimmer again.

My cousin graduated from high school in June, when Shmuel would have too. Now she was enrolled in a secretarial course, but her parents didn't take it seriously. Onkel Gershon said no daughter of his would need to support herself, but he paid the tuition in case Ruchel chose to help her future husband with his business before having children. Tante Yetta assumed Ruchel was just biding her time until Zipporah was married off, and then it would be her turn.

"Help me practice taking dictation?" My cousin sat at what she called an escritoire, or French writing desk, while I sprawled on her bed's lace coverlet, looking at the Gregg Shorthand Manual. It struck me as an odd approach to language, abbreviating words by sound instead of spelling. I could see the practicality, but for my mazuma, the longer a word, the better I liked it.

Using my deepest voice, I read the business letter Ruchel handed me while she scrawled away with a pearl-tipped fountain pen. "In regard to the aforementioned transaction, our sales department indicates blotters will be in short supply until October." She showed me her finished sheet of paper. I admired the unintelligible markings, and asked if I could make up a letter.

Ruchel agreed provided I used lots of vowels, which were tough to tell apart and required more practice. I thought a minute. "About our odious conversation on aortae, the obtuse and excessively obscure outlook is officious and archly elongated." Our giggling made it hard for me to speak and even harder for her to write. The litmus test was whether she read it back correctly.

She cleared her throat, peered intently at the page, and pretended to read. "In the modern era, the clothes of our fair sex are less form-fitting. Ergo, ladies' skirts reveal more ankle, shoes are supplanting boots, and buoyant bosoms blossom from unbounded bodices."

"Faithful secretary, thou hast earned a perfect score on the Sorenson pH scale."

"I aim to please, boss." Ruchel batted her eyelashes. "Seriously, what on earth is P-H?"

"Pure horseshit!" I said, deepening my voice further. Ruchel's eyelids stopped fluttering.

She turned on her radio. My uncle had bought three, one for the living room where he and my aunt listened to concerts, and one each for Ruchel and Zipporah who played popular music in their rooms. When I broached the idea of our getting a radio, Mama agreed it would be good for me. Not Papa. He said it was too expensive and would expose me to inappropriate ideas. He eyed Mama's pamphlets and I expected to hear a derogatory remark about women voting. Instead he said, "If Shmuel had kept his mind on ancient wisdom instead of modern warfare, he'd be alive today." My mother caught her breath, but said nothing, and the idea of buying a radio died too.

"A Pretty Girl is Like a Melody" came on the air. I glided across the floor and held out my arms for Ruchel to join me. Twice around the room we went, high stepping over strewn clothes and narrowly missing open drawers from which rumpled underclothes, blouses, and scarves spilled. I eyed them longingly. After my cousins grew up, I no longer inherited their hand-me-downs, although sometimes I got an outfit they'd gotten tired of.

Ruchel stopped dancing and turned up the volume. We listened to John Steel croon, "I have an eye for a maid, I like a pretty girlie." "What awful words!" Ruchel spat. I was surprised. Irving Berlin's lyrics were famous and he was Jewish. We weren't supposed to criticize our own. "He treats women like we're babies or baubles. It's ..." Ruchel looked around her cluttered room as if the word were hiding under a pile of wrinkled skirts.

"Demeaning?" I asked.

"Exactly."

I thought of "Alice Blue Gown," primping in shop windows. It seemed hypocritical for Ruchel, aswarm in clothes and jewellery, to sneer at other women's dreams. Didn't the poor deserve decent bread and an occasional rose too? "It's not bad to want nice things," I ventured, "if we can buy them ourselves instead of depending on husbands." My cousin conceded and we resumed dancing, striding like women marching for voting rights and better wages.

"Who needs fathers and husbands?" Ruchel tossed her head. "Not smart women like us."

"What about boyfriends?" I asked hesitantly. My cousin might scold me, not because of old-fashioned mores, but newfangled ideas about women's independence.

"Are you sweet on someone?" Ruchel, crimson-faced from dancing, returned to her desk.

"It's a theoretical question." I collapsed on the bed, hoping she'd take my blushing as a sign of exhaustion too. Still stung by Leah's outburst, I wasn't ready to trust Ruchel with my secret.

She reached way back into her top desk drawer. "Read this." She handed me *Family Limitation* by Margaret Sanger.

I turned too red then to hide my embarrassment. "Not that I plan on Barney mugging," I told her as I slipped the book between my English and math texts.

Ruchel winked. "Consider it part of your biology studies."

"I'm forever blowing bubbles, pretty bubbles in the air" blared from the radio. I loved the way a waltz rhythm slowed your heartbeat while tingling your fingertips. When the singer lamented that his bubbles faded and died like dreams, I hoped my dreams of Bernie wouldn't suffer the same fate. "They fly so high, they nearly reach the sky." It was sad to think that Shmuel had never had a girlfriend, that his bubbles had burst before they even floated to heaven. Perhaps he was up there now, gently catching my bubbles and blowing them back to me before they burst.

As I predicted, Tante Yetta asked me to stay for dinner. I offered to set the table. Ruchel rolled her eyes, like I was being a goody two-shoes, but I wanted to feel their ethereal china and hefty silverware. There were three forks per place setting—appetizer, main course, and dessert—and a small plate with a curved knife just for bread. My aunt had to show me where to put everything.

All through dinner, Tante Yetta beat her gums with a zillion questions about Zipporah and Jonah's wedding. Should the caterer put carrot crowns or radish rosettes on the chopped liver appetizer? Would guests expect kreplach or kneidlach with the soup course; stuffed potatoes or derma for the main course? Her biggest worry was whether anyone would be offended by men and women dancing together after the nuptials. Clearly, this was not to be an Orthodox affair.

Ruchel smirked at me across the table. "What do you think, Dev? You and your parents will be among the esteemed guests. That is, if your father graces us with his presence." Zipporah looked down at her lap and I felt bad that Ruchel was being such a killjoy. Not that I wasn't also worried about my father, but I didn't want to say anything that would upset my big, sweet cousin.

Yetta, reared like Mama on peace in the home, said, "Of course Avram will come to our simcha." Turning to me, she asked, "Petit fours or mandelbrot for dessert?"

"Both," I said. "Keep the bluenoses happy eating and they won't care who's hoofing it with whom." Everyone laughed, including Ruchel.

I couldn't imagine such high spirits in our house. My father had no patience for chatter. Conversation was meant for men, talking about Torah. With Shmuel gone, he had no one to talk to and nothing worth talking about. Meals were mute. Sometimes, to liven things up, I'd describe what we were studying in class. I figured the alimentary canal would get a rise out of him, even a disgusted "Feh!" Instead, he looked at me blankly and continued to shovel food into his mouth.

Meanwhile, my mother shuffled between the stove and table, refilling his plate. Lately, though, there was a tad more hotcha in her step. I think the energy she felt returning to protest marches carried over to her movements at home. If anything, Papa was more morose, like a needle stuck in the groove of a record on a Victrola, another musical appliance he refused to buy.

"Whatever makes you ladies happy." Onkel Gershon's grin went around the whole table. "Nothing is too good for my beautiful daughter's wedding." Zipporah's face was suffused with the glow of his praise. Ruchel cocked her head at me, but I directed my smile at Zipporah.

Tante Yetta, perhaps misinterpreting Ruchel's expression as jealousy, told her, "Don't worry, shayner maidel. You're next. And your wedding will be just as getsatske as your sister's."

"Call off the shadchen, Mother." Ruchel's dessert fork pinged the china plate. She flung her napkin on the table. "I've told you time and again that I have zero interest in getting married."

"I understand you want to finish secretarial school first, dear." My aunt refolded Ruchel's napkin. "It's always good for a woman to have a simple skill, God forbid she's widowed young."

"I don't want a simple skill. I'm thinking of going to college instead and being a teacher." She tossed her head as if she'd just tossed off this idea.

Onkel Gershon sat up in his chair and scrunched his napkin. "Since when?"

"Since I decided I don't want to work for a man. I'd rather teach letters to children who look up to me than take letters from a boss who looks down on women."

"Make up your mind."

"I will when I'm good and ready."

"As long as I'm paying, you decide now."

"Maybe I'll just pay for it myself."

"And how do you propose to do that, young lady?"

"I'll be a shop girl," Ruchel spluttered. "I'll find some poor widow to work for. It doesn't even matter if she's Jewish, as long as I don't have to answer to a man."

My uncle was apoplectic, Zipporah was near tears again, and my aunt stared in disbelief. I wished I'd eaten at home. A morose dinner was easier on the alimentary canal than a contentious one. Tante Yetta recovered first. She smoothed the tablecloth and asked if anyone wanted more dessert. Zipporah cleared the dishes and I volunteered to help wash them.

"Time for you to go home, Dev," my uncle said. "I don't want your mother to worry."

Ruchel stood. "I'll walk her."

"It's getting dark. I'll take her." Onkel Gershon pushed back his chair too.

"Why don't you both walk her?" suggested Tante Yetta. "Zipporah and I will clean up."

The Tenth Ward, hushed and empty at this hour, was like a stage set after the curtain goes down. Ruchel moved too fast for my uncle to keep up. I walked with her but felt bad for him. I admired Onkel Gershon for being a man of the world, unlike Papa. Ruchel didn't appreciate how lucky she was to have a father who paid attention to his daughters. And that had nothing to do with money.

After a block, when my uncle fell too far behind to hear us, I told Ruchel that if I talked to my parents the way she did, my mother would wash out my mouth with soap.

"Your mother is too modern to do something that old fashioned. Mine is so old world, I don't know why I bother explaining things to her." What a switch, I thought, Ruchel envies me.

"My mother thinks it's *her* job to explain life to *me*," I said. Ruchel wouldn't understand that having a mother who agreed that I deserved better made it impossible for me to stand against her. "Besides, she's not as enlightened as you think. She almost always caves to my father."

"We both have tyrants for fathers."

"Onkel Gershon is traditional, but otherwise he's nothing like Papa. Your father works at a desk and buys tickets to the Thalia. He personally helps people who are old and sick and poor."

"My father does that to prove how rich and powerful he is, not because he cares about the needy. If he was genuinely charitable, he'd give without any thought of recognition or reward."

Talmud says the highest degree of charity is when the donor and recipient don't know who the other is, but I saw nothing wrong in wanting thanks. Even God demanded it. And while lots of rich people only looked out for themselves, my uncle wasn't like that. He'd done so much to find Shmuel that he lost weight and business. I was convinced he did it because he cared about us, not just to show off he was a big shot. Papa sneered that Gershon persevered to prove him wrong, but I believed people worked harder going after their hopes than battling against their enemies.

Ruchel floundered without that focus. She didn't want to get married, but couldn't decide what she did want. It made her contemptuous of everything. Defying my parents' expectations wouldn't have been enough to satisfy me either. I was grateful to have a goal.

"My father is a fake." Ruchel raised her voice and glanced over her shoulder. "And so is yours. I don't owe my father any respect, and you don't owe it to Uncle Avram."

"I want to go my own way too," I said, "but I'd rather do it with my father's blessing."

"Then you're nothing but a good little girl disguised as a hipster talking jive." Ruchel spun around. Brushing past Onkel Gershon, she said he could walk me the rest of the way home.

Confusion burst all my bubbles. First Leah had judged me for being too bad, now Ruchel had criticized me for not being bad enough. Even Shmuel curled up wordless inside me. Feeling utterly alone, I waited for my uncle to catch up so we could finish our solitary journeys together.

part fourteen

Sam, 1919

chapter 36

The war on the Western Front was over. Sam was free to go home, but he stayed on, trapped by indecision. He lived on Mainland, the largest of the Orkney Islands, a block from Scapa Flow's harbour. The summer sun rose at 0300 hours and set at 2130, no-night days, called the simmer dim by the Scots, that suited his no-sleep nights. If he kept his eyes open, scenes of the fire couldn't play inside his eyelids. He found a job making coffins. Using his hands gave his head a rest. The carpenters worked around the clock, often outside at night, which felt safer than being confined indoors. The only drawback was being located next to a playground, where children skipped rope and chanted, "I had a little bird; its name was Enza. I opened the window and in flew Enza." The Allies had scored a military victory, but the Spanish flu was a worldwide medical defeat.

When he wasn't sawing, planing, and sanding, Sam walked the rugged coast, where sheep and cattle grazed on seaweed. Seals, dolphins, and the occasional whale were visible from shore. It was strange to wander a beach that bore so little resemblance to Coney Island's amusements. The wind blew constantly, often with gale force, creating tidal roosts and churning up whirlpools that matched the turbulence roiling inside him. There were virtually no trees on the island, but sea lavender dotted every surface. The flowers' pale purple was a stark contrast to the dark purple splotches that many flu survivors bore on their faces. Their scars could have made Sam less self-conscious about his birthmark, but its bright red colour still marked him as different. He let his hair grow even longer than it was in the Navy. Many Scotsmen wore theirs long too, pulled back with twine to keep it from getting tangled in a fishing net or saw blade, so in that way he fit right in.

Back in New York, Sam had doubted whether he was sociable enough to be a rabbi, and had been surprised to discover aboard ship that he liked his crew mates' company. Now, absent the hubbub of Navy life, loneliness seeped in. He missed talking with Tomasio as they swung in their racks at night, his friend grousing about officers and their rules. It reminded him of talking to Dev after their parents went to sleep, her chaffing at the restrictions they imposed on her. He felt an urge as strong as the Orkney winds to write her, but didn't know how without tipping off the rest of the family. Perhaps he could send the letter in care of her best friend Leah.

Dear Dev,

I am writing from across the ocean, living on one of seventy islands, in a peedie (from petite, French for small) flat. People here speak a sing-song dialect that makes them sound like the old men who daven in shul. The seabirds caw back in decidedly non-melodious voices. I'm what's called a ferry louper, or non-native. Can you figure out from these clues where I am?

Please forgive me for leaving without telling you. I am sorry to miss your growing up. If you need a big brother's advice, talk to one of my friends. Bernie is more steady and trustworthy, but given your rebellious streak, I expect you will naturally gravitate (a good word) to Yaakov.

I feel bad about hurting Mama. Please love her double and try not to argue with her so much. With me gone, I hope you'll now get the attention you always wanted from Papa.

Follow your dream to be a scientist. I'm not cut out to be a rabbi, but I don't know what to do instead. People here take me for a Christian. I neither say I am nor do I correct them. In New York, everyone knew I was Jewish. City people get sorted into categories, but in a small place, everyone assumes you share their beliefs. Unless you're a real oddball, it's easy to blend in.

On a separate sheet of paper, I jotted down some British slang expressions for you. It's okay to show them to Leah, but otherwise keep the words, like this letter, a secret between us.

Love,

It felt strange to write Shmuel, so Sam left the signature blank. After a week, he slipped the letter into the duffel bag beside those he'd never mailed Gershon. He imagined the ink fading, becoming as hard to read as the memory of their faces. Perhaps he was becoming equally invisible to them.

chapter 37

With the arrival of fall, the rhythm of time reversed. Long days unbroken by darkness turned into longer days without light. In November, after the Armistice, the gloom was lifted by the arrival of the German High Seas Fleet. Seventy-four battleships were interned at Scapa Flow to await the terms of the surrender and became a tourist attraction. Sam was offered a job captaining one of the sightseeing ferries departing Mainland six times a day, but his shipboard days belonged to the past. He watched the boats from afar, just as he stayed clear of the U.S. and British sailors who stayed behind to monitor the fleet in case Rear Admiral von Reuter, the German officer in command, attempted to restore honour to the Fatherland with a senseless act of revenge.

On the first day of summer, when days and nights again switched places, the German boats remained anchored in the harbour while Allied Forces debated their fate. It was a balmy Saturday, rays of sunshine piercing a bank of scudding clouds. The flu pandemic was waning and Sam had the afternoon off, the first time in months he hadn't worked on the Sabbath. Only it didn't feel like a day of rest. With nothing to divert his thoughts, uncertainty about the future left him restless.

He stood on the shore, one of two dozen locals and tourists basking in the fair weather. They watched a school group from nearby Stromness board the *Flying Kestrel* and cruise out on unusually calm waters to visit the massive fleet. Even at this distance, they could see the German sailors lining the glinting decks as the tour boat approached. Sam imagined their grim faces as a shipload of excited children came to gawk at the mighty vessels and jeer at the defeated enemy.

"Well, if it isn't his lordship, keeping a safe distance from the action."

Sam turned toward the familiar mocking voice behind him. Mikovski, his face once again ruddy with good health. The gold oak leaf on his collar meant he'd been promoted to Lieutenant Commander. Only recently had Sam let himself wonder what had become of him after the fire. Now he knew. Mikovski had remained in Scapa Flow with the U.S. Navy's monitoring force.

Sam had a split second to decide how to respond. As a civilian, he was free to ignore him or say something rude. If Tomasio were still alive and wearing civilian clothes, he would have fired off a sharp comeback. But Sam was too shaken by the sight of Mikovski and insulting him wouldn't bring back his friend. "Not much action to see these days, sir," he replied evenly.

Mikovski didn't goad him further. It was pointless, now that Sam had ceased being a threat. They stood in near-companionable silence, watching the tour boat chug toward the fleet. Mikovski's self-consciously erect posture betrayed his awareness that those on the beach admired him. He embodied the victory that gave them the right to babysit the once-proud German Navy.

Then, without warning, the ships began to list to port or starboard. Some plunged headlong into the water, their sterns raised like the tails of monstrous whales. Equipment spilled onto the decks and cascaded into the water. Sailors, tangled in loosened hammocks and empty life belts, flailed and cursed, their foreign words needing no translation for the horrified onlookers. A few managed to swim to the *Flying Kestrel* where tiny arms strained to pull them aboard, but most sank beneath the dark oil that oozed across the ocean's surface.

People onshore looked at one another in confusion. It made no sense that the ships were going down when not a single shot had been fired at them. In fact, the British Royal Fleet had headed out earlier that day for routine exercises. Mikovski was the first to realize what was happening. "They're sinking themselves!" he cried out. That can't be thought Sam, and the other stunned onlookers said as much out loud. Yet one by one it dawned on them that Mikovski was right. The order to scuttle the fleet must have come from the German Admiral himself. "Damn," marvelled Mikovski. "He'd rather sink his own ships than turn them over to Great Britain."

The sailors' pitiful pleas were soon drowned out by a dreadful roaring hiss as steam billowed from the ships' vents. Sam saw Mikovski brace for a fiery explosion, but there was only the slow, methodical submerging of the vessels. The first to go under, at 1200 hours, was the *Friedrich der Grosse*, the flagship of the Jutland Fleet that had attacked Hamble's crew three years ago. Sam tried to run up the beach in search of boats to help with the rescue, but Mikovski held him back. His arms, laced through Sam's elbows, were as unyielding as they'd once been wrapped around his ankles. This time, Sam didn't bother to struggle against them. He turned back, but unable to watch the nightmare at sea, stared at Mikovski's face. Now that he needn't fear fire, the lieutenant watched with satisfaction as the enemy drowned itself. Sam, as if hypnotized by Mikovski, stood there too, until the last ship to sink, the *Hindenberg*, went down at 1700 hours.

Summer daylight lingered well into night-time, but the shoreline was shrouded in the dark clouds of self-destruction. After the glow of watching Germany's demise, darkness descended on Mikovski too. His hands hung at his sides, and his chin sank as low as the vanished ships. "I guess the Brits won't want the U.S. Navy here anymore," he said feebly. "We're no longer necessary."

Sam couldn't bear to see another man go down. He tried to think of jobs Mikovski might be qualified to do. "They'll need someone to guard survivors, oversee salvage operations, or study the vessels to gather intelligence."

Mikovski shook his head. "Nothing I'd be good at, Lord. Time for me to go home."

"But you'll stay in the Navy?"

"I'm only good at fighting and training others to fight. War's over now. I'm back on the street." Mikovski eyed the debris drifting toward shore. "I never thanked you for saving my life." He extended his hand. Sam stared at the outstretched palm, loath to touch it. He'd never intended to save Mikovski. If not for the man's relentless grip, Sam might have rescued Tomasio.

Mikovski nodded and lowered his arm. "Guess I was a bit rough on you and your friend." He turned and trudged up the beach, his silhouette lit by the headlights of cars filled with late-arriving curiosity seekers. "Sorry," he threw back over his shoulder as darkness engulfed him.

Sam was sorry to see him go. It made no sense. Not until the eerie daylight returned did he begin to understand. A defeated Mikovski left him feeling unanchored, not victorious. There was no one left now, except his father, for Sam to define himself against. Would he self-destruct, like the Germans, rather than surrender to Avram's plan that he become a rabbi? Sam was safe on the shore, but he felt as lost at sea as the sailors who had drowned that day in a futile act of defiance.

part fifteen

Dev, 1919

chapter 38

Four days after my blow-up with Leah and the scene between Gershon and Ruchel, the peaceful routine of helping Mama get ready for Shabbas came as a relief. I watched her polish the brass candlesticks passed down by the grandmother I'd never met, too plain to be orchids but worth more than gold to my mother. I still puzzled over the silver candlesticks I'd found many years ago, beneath her braids, and peeked at again the day I discovered she'd saved Shmuel's payess too. I wondered what other secrets Mama was keeping from me. I wanted to ask, just as I now wanted to ask her about my feelings for Bernie, but not asking was my way of keeping secrets from her.

"I haven't seen Leah all week. I hope her bubbe isn't sick," my mother chattered.

"She's fine. Everyone's fine and dandy." I turned my back, but my voice was tremulous.

"Is something the matter? Did you girls have a fight?"

"I tried to talk her into being a visiting nurse," I said, sidestepping the real reason for our argument. It was only a half-lie. "It would be swell to take anatomy classes together in college."

"And how!" My mother laughed for the second time that week. Hearing her try one of my less jangly slang expressions made me smile. "What did Leah say?"

"She doesn't want to be a nurse. All she cares about is raising her own family."

"What woman doesn't want children? Let marriage and motherhood come first. Leah can become a nurse later if she wants." My mother set the two gleaming candlesticks on the table, and inserted the thick blue candles she usually saved for holidays instead of the plain white ones. I asked why. "To mark the first Shabbas after shiva," she explained.

I stroked the cold creamy wax, a sign our lives were moving forward in small steps. If only Papa would walk with us.

"I'll give these candlesticks to you when you get married. God willing, you'll have your own daughter to pass them down to as well." My fingers closed around the candle. "Why must being a wife and mother come first? Suppose I become a medical researcher before having a family? What if I never get married?"

"You know I've always been in favour of your studies." My mother patted my cheek, set the perfectly braided challah on the table, and covered it with the familiar embroidered cloth.

"But men rule?!" The candle snapped in my hand. "You don't stand up for me and you kowtow when Papa orders you around. You even let Onkel Gershon dictate what you do." Leah and Ruchel's opinions ceased to matter. I wanted my mother's reassurance that my feelings for Bernie were allowed, that I was entitled to have a career *and* get my father's approval. I wanted to be a woman like her, while at the same time, I didn't want to be like her at all.

"You even loved Shmuel more than me because he was a boy."

My mother's legs shook. She collapsed in Papa's chair and I ran to kneel by her side, my tears watering the tiny silk flowers sewn on the hem of her Shabbas apron. It was the first time in three years that she'd worn it. "I'm sorry, Mama. That's not true. I don't know why I said it."

Just then my father came in the door. In a lachrymose blur, I saw how his hair had turned gray and his shoulders stooped beneath his thin coat. He no longer gave my mother the traditional Friday night kiss to welcome the Sabbath bride into our home. With a blind nod in our direction, he went into the bedroom to change out of his work clothes.

My mother stood and pulled me up after her. "One handful of dirt doesn't fill a grave. It will take years to fill in the hole Shmuel left." She melted the broken halves of the candle back together and rested her hand on my head, a gesture of blessing. "In the meantime, sholem bayess. Peace brings healing. Healing brings peace."

Minutes later, when my mother handed me the matches to light the candles, my father didn't object. Nor did he mention that they were blue. He stood at the head of table with Mama sitting opposite him, and me on his left. Shmuel's empty chair, on his right, was a grave marker in the kitchen. One evening I moved the chair next to the couch and laid out my next day's clothes and books on it. When I got home from school, the chair was back at the table. I let it be after that.

Wrapping his Shabbas tallit around his shoulders, my father recited the prayers over the wine and bread. I wondered again what had happened to the prayer shawl he'd worn the first time he sat shiva, the one he'd been saving to give Shmuel on his ordination as a rabbi. It was as big as a blanket, and shot through with gold threads, so it should have been hard to hide. But it wasn't stashed in the bedroom closet with my mother's treasures, or behind my father's cracked old boots in the hall closet. That tallit had disappeared as finally and completely as my brother.

"Amen," my mother and I said when my father finished the bruchas. I sipped the thick, sweet wine, no longer restricted to grape juice or watered-down alcohol like a child. Papa broke off the last twist of challah and passed portions to us. Following tradition, only after the prayers were done and everyone had swallowed, could we talk to one another. Otherwise we would have interrupted the sacred thread that linked us to God's generosity. Around our table, however, the silence often continued well into the meal. Rather than prolonging our connection to God's bounty, the absence of conversation only reminded us of what He had taken away.

We'd finished the soup and gefilte fish, and were onto the main course, when my mother finally spoke, a peacemaker's attempt at conversation. "There's a march on Sunday to demand the release of Lillian Wald." I already knew from Mama that Wald had been arrested as a Communist agitator for bringing health care to the poor. "I thought we'd go as a family." She spoke to Papa, then looked at me for confirmation. I nodded, thankful for a chance to make amends.

Papa pulled a leg off the chicken and chewed it slowly. He wiped his hands on his napkin before picking up his fork and cutting off a bite of kugel. We watched him eat. At last he said, "I have to work." Addressing my mother, he added, "You'd be better off working too. We ran out of bread last week and you had to get store bought. If women spent less time marching and more time looking after their families, we wouldn't need meddlesome nurses sticking their noses into our business." I waited, and hoped, that he'd scold me to stay home too and work on my studies.

"The march doesn't start until five o'clock. I'll bake in the morning, an extra loaf. You'll be done with work by then, so you can meet us at City Hall."

"I'm coming straight home and I expect you to be here." Papa measured out his words.

"The entire Sisterhood from synagogue is going," my mother said. "Even Yetta and the girls are marching. Lillian Wald is a Jewish woman and we have to stand together to defend her. You know Jews are being singled out for persecution in this meshugga Red Scare."

"I know Jews have to stay silent and invisible or else we'll be singled out more. They don't want us here, except to sweat in their factories and sacrifice our sons in their wars."

"This has nothing to do with Shmuel. I'm trying to make a better life for us. And for our daughter who, God willing, will live in America with her family long after we're dead."

"Rivka, I forbid it!" My father slammed his hand down so hard that wine sloshed out of his glass onto the tablecloth. My mother jumped up to put salt on it, but my father yanked her arm and stopped her. I watched as the resistance left her body and my father loosened his grip. She sprinkled salt on the blood-red stain that meandered between the cross-stitched threads. Their eyes locked, his beseeching hers for forgiveness, hers hard and unblinking.

My father turned to me and barked, "You will stay home too."

I was thrilled to be included in his admonition, yet furious at his handing down the law. My fingers itched to overturn my wine glass until I remembered what Bernie said about my father losing his dream. I reminded myself to be more compassionate, an action that might earn me Bernie's respect and Papa's love at the same time. I could never be the rabbi he wanted Shmuel to become, but if I could persuade my father to accept my dream, I'd settle for being his second best.

"I have a biology test on Monday. If I stayed home to study, I'd get another A." I glanced at my mother and her eyes forgave me. She thought I was capitulating for sholem bayess.

"*Another* A?" Papa's raised eyebrows relaxed until the wrinkles etching his forehead smoothed out. Mama sat down and we all began to eat again.

"Yes," I said. "I got the top score on every test. Higher than the smartest boy in my class."

"This is good, you're doing well in school, though maybe not so good you're doing better than the boys." He actually smiled, an itsy bitsy bit.

"If I want to be admitted to the medical research program at Hunter College, I'll have to graduate at the top of my class."

Once more, my father stopped eating. "Who says you're going to college?"

My mother clutched the stem of her wineglass and mine. She couldn't reach his across the table. "Hunter is all-girls," she reminded him. "Dev wouldn't be competing with boys."

"No college." My father's voice rumbled softly, like far-distant thunder. "Marriage and children were good enough for your mother," he said to me. "They're good enough for you."

"Not good enough!" Now it was my mother's turn to pound the table. "My child is gone and my husband might as well have abandoned me. We didn't come here for Shmuel alone. We came to make all our lives better, from generation to generation." She spoke the Aramaic words, "l'dor vador," from the Amidah, an old prayer of praise. "Dev is our only remaining hope. She deserves the opportunity and it's a mitzvah, a commandment from God, that we support her."

"Don't tell me what God demands of us. You still have your daughter, good for you. I lost my son. Or my son lost himself. God hasn't told me why, but as long as I remain the head of this household, I will issue the commandments and you will obey my laws." He swept into the bedroom, the wind created by his tallit fanning the flames of the candles. The door slammed.

My mother and I sat in silence until the blue candles sputtered, leaving a sinuous trail of wispy, white smoke. Still we didn't leave the table. I used to associate fire with nourishing the hungry and cauterizing the wounds of the hurt. But now I realized that fires eventually burn out, unless, as in the ancient temple, they are continually fed by animal sacrifices. With Shmuel gone, my parents at war, and me split in two, our family had nothing left to slaughter.

The silence continued the next day, even after Papa returned from services and we lit the havdalah candles marking the end of Shabbas. I lay awake Saturday night too, until I heard the first peddlers wheeling their pushcarts after their day of rest. Newsboys sang the headlines of the *Jewish Daily Forward* to the earliest workers, although there was barely enough light to read the paper. Hearing their cries gave me the idea of writing a letter to Bintel Briefs, the newspaper's advice column.

Worthy Editor:

I write as a fourteen-year-old daughter of immigrants, the first person in our family born here. My older brother left home without telling anyone and is a casualty of the war. It broke my parents' hearts. My mother, a modern woman, is rediscovering her zest for life. My father, who wanted his son to be a rabbi, is mired in anger. He criticizes my mother and ignores me.

I am a good student. I love biology and dream of going to college to become a medical researcher. Someday I may discover the cure for a deadly disease. My mother is in favour of my having a career. I am happy she feels this way, but sometimes I think she is a hypocrite about women's rights because she doesn't stand up to my father, who is opposed to the idea. He wants to me get married and have children. I am torn about which way to go. If I stay home and do what he expects, will that help him heal and repair the rift with my mother? Or should I pursue my own ideals and try to heal the world? What is my responsibility as a good Jewish girl?

Respectfully,
Trying-To-Be Dutiful Daughter

When I finished the letter, the smells and noises from below filled the apartment. I listened at the bedroom door, but couldn't hear Papa's loud snores or Mama's gentle breathing. Shmuel slept silently inside me as well, while the lub-dup of my own heartbeat was as irregular as the clip-clop of a peddler's lame horse. I crawled back under the blanket, faking sleep. If my parents saw me looking peaceful when they woke up, that tranquillity might flow back toward them. I refused to believe that the poisoned blood coursing through my family was what science, or God, intended.

chapter 39

That afternoon, I met Bernie at the station and we took the subway uptown to the Metropolitan Museum of Art. We were going to see the Egypt exhibit, which the entire city was abuzz about. Before Shmuel left, my father sometimes took us to the museum on summer Sundays after he got off work. It was late afternoon by the time Papa got home, but there was still enough daylight for us to stroll back downtown afterwards or even catch a free outdoor concert in the park.

"Yaakov saw the exhibit last month," Bernie reported. "I asked him about the carvings and paintings, but all he wanted to talk about was the gory details of the shrivelled mummies."

"Ooh! What did he say?"

Bernie blushed. "It's not for sharing in polite society."

"Do you think it's wrong for Jews to be interested in the glories of ancient Egypt?"

Bernie took time to answer. "The exhibit can help us understand why Pharaoh wanted to keep us as slaves. We'll get a sense of how our ancestors lived too."

"You mean we'll appreciate why, after the Exodus, the Hebrews pined to go back to the leeks and garlic and fish of the Nile instead of subsisting on manna in the desert?"

Bernie laughed. "You know your Torah." Never before had I heard a man say this with praise instead of scorning a woman for being uppity. My heart flip-flopped with pride.

He continued. "Manna was God's food, sustaining us for forty years of wandering in the desert while we learned the value of freedom. In all that time, even our sandals didn't wear out."

We looked down at our shoes, obviously polished for our date, but which nevertheless bore the chaffing and cracks of poverty. I held out my foot, revealing a bit of ankle for Bernie's closer inspection, but he glanced out the window "We don't want to miss our stop," he said.

The Egyptian wing of the museum was filled with thousands of orchids, making Onkel Gershon and Tante Yetta's swanky apartment look like beggar's quarters by comparison. I ogled the most beautiful necklace I'd ever seen, strung with carnelian, amethyst, turquoise, and quartz. "Those are four of the twelve stones embedded in the breast-plate worn by the high priest in Leviticus," I commented, showing off more of my Torah knowledge. Together Bernie and I named the other eight. I wished my father were a fly on the wall to overhear how much I knew.

The next display case held a carved bronze ankle bracelet. "Do you suppose ankle bracelets will become fashionable now that skirts are getting shorter?" I asked Bernie.

"Goodness, Dev. I deal in small electric appliances. I leave it to you to ponder fashions."

My blood raced to hear him say my name. Mama must have once felt that way about Papa.

"I'm ready to see the tombs and mummies if you are," I said, louder than I intended. Moving from the sparkling glass cases to the hushed cave-like enclosure where the burial rituals were displayed, we stared in uneasy silence at images of the deceased, painted on dark wooden coffins. Gesso, sarcophagus, amulet. I added these magical words to my vocabulary list to keep the creepy feeling at bay, but after a while, the sense of eeriness gave way to one of calm.

"Too bad Jews don't put pictures on grave markers," I sighed, wishing I had an actual portrait of Shmuel to talk to, not just an anonymous sailor on a poster. It would be terrible if I forgot what he looked like. I was also touched by the food mourners buried to sustain the dead on their journey to the afterworld, and the clothes and ointments to assure they arrived in splendour.

"I sometimes wish we believed in an afterlife," I said.

"It would be easier to accept death," Bernie agreed and shivered.

"Maybe we'd kvetch less about our troubles in this life too," I said to lighten the mood.

Bernie's laughter rewarded me. "I guess Jews have to be satisfied with being remembered through the children we leave behind..."

"What about people who don't have children, or whose children die before their parents?"

"They still live on through their good deeds."

"So it's not incumbent on us to have children provided we do good deeds?" If my medical research saved humanity, would I be spared God's judgment for not having children?

Bernie's face darkened. "Maybe it's not such a good idea to spend an afternoon with the dead so soon after sitting shiva for Shmuel." He turned back toward the light-filled hallway.

"Wait," I said. "My father turned away too quickly, but instead of getting past the pain, he's stuck there forever. My mother let the grief seep in and absorbed it so she could move on."

Bernie slowly pivoted, taking in the hundreds of paintings, containers, and gifts that had outlasted four millennia of decay. "Spoken with the wisdom of a rebbetzin," he said.

On our way out of the museum, we passed through galleries filled with the sculptures of ancient Rome. I stopped to look at figures of naked men and women, but Bernie tried to hurry me to the exit. "Just like my father," I joked. "You think that by scurrying along, we'll get past our discomfort. I'd rather stay and let reality sink in. There's always something to learn."

Bernie's flushed cheeks looked twice as red against the cool white marble of the statues. "I don't think these have the same educational value as the Egyptian exhibit," he mumbled.

"Not for an appliance salesman, but remember, I'm going to be a biologist."

Our short walk to the subway station turned into a foot race. I let Bernie win, but only by a little. Standing on the platform as the train shot out of the tunnel, I felt the wind whipping my hair. My thick curls trapped the warm gust and a sense of heated exhilaration swirled around my head.

The train hurtled us from ancient Egypt to the Lower East Side, a journey traversing six thousand miles and four thousand years. Bernie and I sat next to each other, bouncing in unison, on the shiny woven seats. Three stops before ours, the car lurched to a stop. I was thrown against him, one hand on his chest and the other on his thigh.

"Ups-a-daisy." Bernie gently pushed me back into an upright position.

This pas-de-deux was repeated at the next stop. We lingered a second until Bernie edged away and I sat up straight again. At our station, we climbed to the street level and Bernie walked stiffly ahead. I reached for his hand to stop him, and lifted my face. I was hoping for a replay of our first kiss, curious whether our second might be a touch firmer and last a bit longer. It would have to happen while we were still a few blocks from home and the prying eyes of our neighbours.

"We can't, Dev." Bernie's voice trembled.

This time, hearing him say my name made me angry. I remembered my mother slapping me when I got my first period, the same day Shmuel disappeared. She told me it was a tradition intended to "make the blood flow," but I worried that it was a warning not to bring shame on the family. Even then, I believed I was capable of it. The proof was that I wanted to go further with Bernie now. I was curious about sex, feeling a force stronger than blood pumping through me, but I was motivated by more than desire. I wanted, above anything else, to simply be fully alive.

"Why not? Where in the Torah does it say, 'Thou shalt not feel good?'"

Bernie gently pried my fingers loose. "I'm thinking more seriously about being a rabbi. You're the one who inspired me, last week, with what you said about following our dreams."

I was thrilled to think that what I'd said had been so important to him, but furious that yet another person was trying to make me feel guilty about wanting something. "Fine and dandy," I retorted. "You go your way, I'll go mine, and we won't see each other again." I walked past him.

This time Bernie held *me* back, with a light touch on my shoulder. "Let's be friends, Dev. At first, I thought seeing you would fill the hole left by Shmuel, but I care about you for yourself. I never met a girl I like talking to as much. You're smart and funny. You teach me what it means to enjoy life. You have a force inside you that's important for a rabbi to know and understand."

I shrugged my shoulder, but not hard enough to dislodge Bernie's hand.

"There is no mitzvah against feeling good," he continued, "only one to do good. We're different people, but we're both committed to pursuing our dreams. We can honour them, and stand with virtue before God, if ours is a relationship of minds, not bodies. At least, for now."

Bernie lowered his arm. We stood face to face, hands at our sides, then simultaneously turned in the direction of home. Minds, not bodies. Brains, not blood. It sounded dry to me, like the static words of Talmud. I wanted animated diagrams. I walked the last block alone, Bernie's eyes on my back the same as last time, but this evening he was protecting himself as much as me.

Two weeks later I read my answer from Bintel Briefs in the newspaper:

Dear Trying-To-Be Dutiful Daughter:
   Immigrant parents come to America with dreams for their children. Follow your dream, and your father will eventually join your mother in kvelling with pride. As for romance, proceed with caution. We are born with many talents and opportunities, but only one heart. Career paths are easily rerouted, not so the road taken in love.
   The Editor

part sixteen

Gershon, 1921

chapter 40

"Hurry," Yetta told Gershon. "The march starts at five." She adjusted the purple cloche with its spray of seed pearls over her springy gray curls. It was the fourth hat she'd tried on to wear to the Women's Trade Union League protest rally. "Does this hat make me look too rich?"

Gershon slumped on an overstuffed chair in their bedroom. He wore an undershirt and trousers grown so loose in the two years since he'd failed to find Shmuel, that the waist flapped between his suspenders. He longed to lie down. Only Yetta's insistence that their maid Margaret make the bed each morning got him out from under the covers before midday. "I already told you, I'm not going on this cockamamie march."

"Rivka and Dev are meeting us at the corner of Orchard and Rivington. Ruchel already left to pick up Zipporah." Yetta counted on her plump fingers. "That makes six of us."

"Five." Gershon sank farther into the chair.

"Mr. Stubborn." Yetta stood over him and crossed her arms over her corseted bosom. "Shame on you. You don't help no one no more since you resigned as president of the shul."

"It's a march for women." Gershon crossed his own arms over his sagging chest.

"Nu? Women aren't people? You got a wife and two daughters. Someday, God willing, a granddaughter. We don't count?"

"I'm not saying women don't count. You run the home."

"Hmph! Some women got to go out and work too."

"Thank goodness, not in our family. Even with the next-to-nothing Avram makes, Rivka stays home to raise the children." Mortified, Gershon let the plural hang in the air.

If Yetta also thought "child," not "children," she didn't correct him. She pulled him from the chair and laid out his clothes on the bed.

"Meanwhile, you stay home when you don't got to. So today, I'm making you go out. It's past time you did poor people a bissel good again."

His wife was right. Torah commanded him to care for the poor, widowed, and orphaned, just what the women's march to raise wages and end child labour demanded. But if he ignored that commandment, could God punish him worse than He was already doing? Being reminded of his failure made Gershon obstinate. He kept his elbows stiff as Yetta tried to force his arms into a freshly-ironed shirt. "It's bad enough Rivka calls herself poor. Must she drag you along?"

"You should thank God Rivka is getting out of the house, after being so dershlogen since Shmuel's funeral. Marching gives her what else to worry about." Yetta stuck a finger in the gap between the top button and Gershon's scrawny neck. She tsked. "It would do you good too."

"You're giving *me* what else to worry about." Gershon squirmed as she tucked in the folds of his shirt and slipped on his suspenders. "The neighbours will see our entire family link arms with Margaret Drier Robbins and her Communist rabble. It's one thing for me to help the needy behind the scenes, another for a matron like you to make a public spectacle of herself."

"Does that mean you approve of young maidens like Dev and our girls marching?" Yetta stroked his cheek and smiled so coyly that he struggled to look stern.

"If Avram can't control Dev, that's his affair." Gershon sat back down. "Zipporah is a married woman now and belongs at home with Jonah. As for Ruchel, she should figure out what to do with her own life instead of telling others how to live theirs." Gershon was ready to tear out what was left of his hair over her. She'd quit secretarial school, decided college wasn't for her after all, and was a salesgirl in a hosiery shop. She bragged that working for a woman, even in a menial job, was less degrading than being supported by her father. It irked him that she ignored the fact that all she paid for was her clothes. He put a roof over her head and food in her mouth.

In some ways, life had been easier in Lemberg, where even a poor man like himself could dictate seemly behaviour for his wife and daughters. True, Yetta had fallen in love with Gershon, but their marriage wouldn't have happened without her father's permission. Here in America, even a rich man trying to control the women in his family could no longer count on the approval of the community. A new wave of impatient immigrants was breaking the old rules.

"It's a shanda!" Gershon catapulted from his seat with outrage. "Have they no shame?"

"So nu," Yetta said, slipping her arm into his and marching them to the door, "if you're so worried we women will bring disgrace on ourselves and you, come along as our chaperone."

Lower Manhattan smelled of summer sweat and fruit rotting on push-carts. Gershon wanted to cover his nose, but in this crowd he was self-conscious about his silk handkerchief. He settled for taking short, shallow breaths, which left him light-headed. Yetta pulled a small ivory fan from her purse but quickly put it away too. Children, naked or in rags, ran squealing through the clear gushing water of an open fire hydrant. Mothers in faded dresses, and a few fathers stripped to their undershirts, tried to herd their little ones toward City Hall, where the rally would soon start.

A phalanx of police officers and spectators lining the curb forced the protesters to walk in pairs. Yetta sought out Zipporah, eager to hear how she was adjusting to married life, while Dev and Ruchel gravitated toward one another as the two youngest members of the family. Gershon found himself beside Rivka, their first time alone since the final admission of his failure to find Shmuel. He had trouble keeping up with her brisk stride and lively patter. Yetta was right that these marches had restored his sister's vigour. He was reminded of her as a girl back in Lemberg, racing him through the priest's orchard with stolen pears tied up inside her skirt.

Soon men, finishing their shifts at the factories and sweat shops, began to swell the ranks of the women protesters. Rivka's head swivelled from one side of the street to the other. "Do you see Avram?" she asked. "I was hoping he'd join us when he got off work."

Avram, here? Gershon panicked. Was Yetta unaware he might show up or had she kept it from Gershon? "I didn't think my brother-in-law made political appearances," he said.

Rivka laughed, a sound Gershon hadn't heard in years. "I'm not really expecting him to come, unless it's to keep an eye on me and Dev." She hugged him, something else that had not happened in a long time. "I'm surprised you came, but it matters a lot to me. A sheynem dank."

He stopped himself from saying Yetta had made him come for his own sake. Let Rivka think he'd come for hers. "It's good to see you less ..." He hesitated, afraid to sound accusing.

"Depressed? Downhearted?" Rivka pulled down the corners of her lips in a mock frown. "Grummy?" She pointed ahead of them to where Dev was walking with Ruchel. "Dev's slang can be a trial, but the wild expressions she uses make you take a more honest look at yourself."

"Then I should apologize for being such a washout. Is that the right word?"

Rivka looked up at him, not understanding.

Gershon hated to dampen her mood, but he had to unburden himself. "A disappointment. A loser. I should have made the Navy find Shmuel and send him home. I'm the big brother, the big macher in the community. It's my job to make things right." He choked back tears. "Avram's justified in spitting on me now. I wouldn't blame you if you thought I was nothing too."

They stood still, facing each other. Marchers flowed around them, shouting slogans, but Gershon was deaf to everyone except Rivka.

"Nothing?" She expelled the word. "I look up to you more than anyone in the world."

"How can you? I failed you when you needed me the most."

"You did everything you humanly could. More." Rivka gently pressed her fingertips into his hollow cheeks, then rested her hands on his sagging shoulders.

"It wasn't enough to save your son." Gershon's memory was flooded with an image of Shmuel at his bar mitzvah, singing his Torah portion in a sweet but quavering voice.

"Fate is for God to decide. All we can do is act as though every deed matters."

Gershon thought of the quote from the Talmud. "Pray as if everything depends on God. Act as though everything depends on you." He'd lost his belief in action along with his faith.

Rivka lifted his chin and stared fiercely into his eyes. "I'll always look up to you. If you hadn't had the courage to move to America, Avram and I would still be nothings in Lemberg. There's a good chance I'd have died in childbirth or that Shmuel would never have lived past infancy. It's true I lost him, but not before I had the joy of knowing him for sixteen years."

"You're not much better off in America than you were in the shtetl. It's still a struggle to put food on the table."

"Here we can hope for change." Rivka pointed ahead again, where Dev and Ruchel were saving the family a spot at the front of the rally. "Your success gives me hope for our daughters. Think how many people you've helped. Now that I'm finally getting better, I want to make a better life for others too. Looking up to you has been and will always be my inspiration."

Rivka's embrace opened a floodgate of relief in Gershon's chest. He took a deep breath, not caring that he was drawing the tenement's polluted air into his lungs. "So you forgive me?"

"What's to forgive? All I ask is that you stay strong for me while I finish healing. It's been four years since Shmuel left, two since I sat shiva. Recovery is slow. Be patient with me."

Gershon again thought guiltily of their childhood, wondering if hereafter he might finally forgive himself for nearly causing his sister's death. Was it possible that Rivka's insistence on seeing him as a hero had given her the determination to get better then too?

"I ought to help more." Gershon cupped Rivka's elbow and steered her to the grandstand, where Yetta and Zipporah now stood with Dev and Ruchel. "For one thing, I should stop putting you in the middle between Avram and me. A wife's loyalty belongs with her husband."

"Avram is a good man," Rivka said. "He can't help being jealous of you."

"It's been that way since we were boys. Time we got over it."

"You're both stubborn." Rivka smiled.

Gershon shook his head. "Two alter kockers stuck in our ways."

"Except that Avram's stubbornness keeps him rooted in place, while yours pushes you ahead." Rivka held Gershon back while she finished speaking. "The point isn't to get the most nuts in the hole or quote a wiser passage from Talmud. You win simply by daring to take up a worthy cause." Waving to Yetta and the girls, Rivka now led Gershon to the front of the rally.

The speeches lasted nearly two hours. Robbins and other League officials harangued the crowd to petition Congress for better treatment of women and children. A few councilmen spoke to show they sided with the poor. Stepanic and his fellow board members were nowhere to be seen.

Gershon wilted. Not since Shmuel's funeral had he walked as far or stood outside as long. Others grew restless too, hoping for a rousing speech that would end the rally, but everyone on the makeshift podium had said his piece. Gershon closed his eyes, waiting to be dismissed. When he opened them, Ruchel was approaching a nearby family gathered around a woman twisting a handkerchief. She looked old, but judging from the ages of the adult children comforting her, she must have been Gershon's age. Poverty had worn her down to wrinkles and bones.

Ruchel patted the woman's wrist and marched up to the stage. Her heels, unlike the rundown soles of the workers' boots, clicked smartly on the rickety steps. She grabbed the bullhorn and faced the crowd, nostrils quivering with determination. The setting sun, released from behind a cloud, backlit her shiny black hair, making her look like an avenging angel.

"Wives, mothers, widows," Ruchel called out. "Young and old." A pause. "Even men!"

A burst of laughter was followed by silence. Children stopped whining, women's heads snapped forward, men strained to see the girl whose clear voice cut through the murky air.

"It's been a decade since the Triangle Shirtwaist factory fire." Ruchel waited for them to remember the young Italian and Jewish immigrant women who perished. "The sister and aunt of one of my fifth-grade classmates were burned to death." Gershon recalled paying for their funerals. Ruchel nodded toward the family of the weeping woman. "The fire was put out but their grief will never subside." People craned their necks to see the circle of mourners. Several shouted out that they'd lost relatives too. In a way he couldn't have done then, Gershon understood their pain.

Ruchel let everyone vent their rage before she continued. "Conditions now are marginally better. Women aren't trapped behind locked doors, but they're still trapped working fifty-four hours a week and earning half the pay of men." People booed until Gershon grew alarmed for Ruchel's safety before recognizing they were expressing solidarity with her. The wind died down, letting her voice reach the crowd without the bullhorn. "Men who rule the unions won't speak out *for* us or *against* child labour. Now that women have the vote, we must use it to elect candidates who *will* fight on our behalf." She raised her arms for quiet and spoke to a knot of labourers milling up front. "Men, when conditions improve for your wives, sisters, and daughters, yours jobs will get better too. Everyone will benefit when women are truly emancipated from slave labour."

The assembly chanted, "Vote women's rights!" and, "End child labour!" Gershon panicked they'd lift Ruchel and carry her out on their shoulders. Instead, they parted like the Red Sea to let her walk with dignity down the steps. In unison, the stirred-up crowd turned and marched with resolve back to their dilapidated tenement buildings. Gershon's shaking fingers closed his gaping mouth. His daughter had saved the rally from petering out and spurred a call for action. She'd given a speech more effective in its passion than any sermon he'd heard in synagogue.

Flushed and happier than Gershon had seen her in months, Ruchel accepted the embraces of Rivka and Dev. Yetta, awkward before her own daughter, patted her perspiring cheeks and beamed. Zipporah grinned with pride for her little sister. Gershon wanted to congratulate her too, but was afraid he'd be met with scorn. He didn't know if Ruchel saw him as the enemy or as one of the men whose support would help the women's cause. Years ago, he'd have taken her regard for granted. Now, he had no reason to believe she'd see him in a better light than he saw himself.

The women turned toward home, five abreast with Ruchel in the middle. Dev skipped beside her like a proud puppy. Women, who an hour ago looked ready for the grave, marched with a bounce in their step. Young men tentatively smiled or waved. Ruchel responded to no one, but the lift of her head told Gershon she was aware of the attention. He was content to walk behind the women in his family. It was a relief to hide in their shadow, concealing his own shame, but also gratifying to see them in the spotlight. Where but in America could such a thing happen?

After a block, Yetta fell back to join him and linked her arm in his. They walked together in comfortable silence until she asked, "Are you happy I made you shlep to the rally?"

Gershon pulled his wife closer. Her body felt warm and soft beside the stick figure he'd become. "Ruchel spoke well," he said. "Who knew?"

"She can make your hair go gray, but we raised a good daughter."

Yetta leaned against him and for the first time in months, Gershon let himself think he might regain his strength. He sensed his appetite returning for Yetta's cooking, for her.

"You deserve the credit," he said. "Like you, Ruchel's generous the way only a rich person who's been raised unspoiled can be. I shouldn't have been so quick to doubt her."

"Did you ever think maybe she gets her goodness of heart from you?" Yetta asked. "After you got rich, you didn't stop taking care of the poor."

Gershon squirmed. He had stopped, ever since he'd failed to find his nephew.

"And making such speeches?" Yetta continued. "She doesn't get that from me."

"I still think you deserve the credit," he told Yetta.

"Since when it is a contest?" she asked. "Why can't we both kvell and shepp nachas?"

The dream of all parents, thought Gershon, to revel in their children's accomplishments. Perhaps his daughter's outspoken defiance was proof he'd succeeded with her after all. He watched Dev giggle and frisk in the aura of Ruchel's success. Unlike his relationship with his niece's father, Gershon was not in competition with his wife. They'd built a solid marriage and their memory would live on through the good deeds of their children. "You're right, we'll share the credit," he told Yetta. "As our niece likes to say, you know your onions."

chapter 41

With Ruchel's impassioned speech playing in his ears, Gershon vowed to call the synagogue and resume his charitable work. Only it had been so long since he'd helped anyone that he wasn't sure the members would trust him. To restore his self-confidence, he went back to work first and, upon hearing how happy his clients were to see him again, began to wake up early each morning and relish a hearty breakfast. Yetta, delighted at the return of his appetite, packed big lunches too — herring with onions, half a roasted chicken, and enough babka to feed the pigeons on every train platform from the Lower East Side to Coney Island. Gershon soon filled out his clothes once more and didn't need the enticement of Yetta's hand mirror to make love to her on Shabbas. Still, something held him back from making that first helping call. Perhaps it was the memory of Ruchel speaking over his head to address the crowd. He felt invisible in her presence.

On Wednesday night, ten days after the rally, Gershon came home wondering whether the resumption of midweek lovemaking with Yetta would be the last step in building back his courage. Before he'd opened the door, the heavenly aroma of his wife's baking took him far from the garbage-filled streets around the train station. Even though she tucked cakes and cookies into the meals she delivered to hungry immigrants, Gershon had always fancied that she prepared her tastiest treats for him alone. So he was surprised when he saw the dining room table laden with trays of her best pastries. Had she overestimated his appetite that much? Gershon reached for a slice of marble cake and was even more surprised when she playfully swatted his hand away.

"Not for you. For the women's meeting. You can have some later, if there's any left."

There wouldn't be. Yetta's marble cake was swirled with twice as much chocolate as the recipe called for. Gershon was stung. A mouthful of useless saliva made it difficult for him to talk. "What meeting?"

"I told you." Yetta shooed him into the kitchen, where she pulled another sheet of cookies from the oven. "Ruchel organized the women on our old block and Rivka handed out pamphlets in her building. Margaret talked to the Catholic ladies at her church, they should come too."

"Come where? You're carrying all this to Walhalla Hall?" Gershon glanced longingly toward the trays in the dining room. She couldn't leave a little plateful behind for him?

"No, Mr. Forgetful. We're meeting here."

"I thought Ruchel was busy organizing factory workers. Don't the women coming here tonight stay home?"

"Yes, but they don't got it any better. There's four apartments on each floor what share two toilets. Most buildings still don't got electricity. The meeting is to organize them too, they should rise up against the landlords."

"I'm a landlord."

"A nicer one than those other gonifs, thank goodness." He watched Yetta carry a plate of almond cookies into the dining room. When she returned, she touched his cheek. "Even so, we got our own private bathroom while upstairs two apartments share. Also, we got a refrigerator and fancy-shmancy chandeliers, while our tenants got maybe a lamp or a bulb on the ceiling."

Gershon's pride turned to resentment. It was one thing for his daughter to defend the less fortunate. But now she'd gotten his wife and even their maid to go after men like him, who were just trying to make a decent living for their own families. His stomach grumbled. "But I'm hungry."

Yetta took a bowl of cold borsht and a plate of sliced pot roast out of the refrigerator he'd recently bought her. Didn't she realize it was the rent he charged, a fair one he thought, that had paid for this newfangled appliance? "Essen." She handed him a set of silverware.

"Here? Alone in the kitchen? Where Margaret eats?"

"Hurry. I have to finish getting ready. And when you're done, you'll stay out of there?" Yetta nodded toward the dining room.

"I promise I won't eat the cake and cookies until you give me permission." She was treating him like a child and he was beginning to feel like one, a neglected and very angry one.

"Ruchel's afraid the women won't talk up in front of a man."

"So you're banishing me to the bedroom?" It made no sense. His wife had spent weeks urging Gershon to get out of bed. Now she was sending him back there, and not with the purpose he'd been fantasizing about earlier in the afternoon. His hunger for food, for her, was gone.

"Who's saying the bedroom? Go to your study, read Talmud, pick up the telephone."

Was she pressuring him to resume his charitable work too? "I will not be restricted to certain rooms in my own house." Gershon banged the heavy silverware on the table. He wanted Yetta to take it from him, to help him calm down. He didn't care if he was acting like a child.

Instead she flapped her apron in a gesture of impatience. "You got a choice where to go in this apartment—our bedroom, your study, Zipporah's old room, the bathroom. The ladies what's coming here tonight got ten or twelve people, maybe more, living like animals in two rooms."

Gershon knew this was the perfect opportunity to spend an evening in his study, calling around to find out who needed help. Here was his wife, no longer just bringing food to their poor old Jewish neighbours, but taking up social causes for Irish and Italian Catholic families too. Yetta was venturing out while Gershon stood immobilized. What was holding him back?

The cold meal sat before him on the kitchen table. He couldn't smell the earthy aroma of the beets or the spicy paprika dusting the edges of the meat. All he could inhale was the butter and honey of the desserts in the next room, a sweetness denied to him. For nearly three decades, Yetta's main job was taking care of him. Now Gershon was being asked to share her. He'd never worried about competition from another man. Was he going to lose out to a battalion of women?

"As long as I'm the breadwinner in this house," he declared, "I'll decide what room to park my tuchus in and what food to put down my gullet." He grabbed two cookies off the sheet Yetta had just taken from the oven and crammed them into his mouth, burning his tongue.

She didn't rush to get him a glass of cold water, or try to soothe his temper, but in a rare flash, displayed her own. "Just like Ruchel said." Yetta shook a rigid, flour-coated finger at him. "As long as women take orders from men, they're no better off than the slaves in Egypt."

"Don't quote my daughter or the Torah to me." Gershon tried to sound defiant, but when his wife's finger wagged just beneath his nose, he stepped back in alarm.

She retreated too, and busied herself unloading the rest of the cookies onto a china plate. In a softer voice, she said, "A true man is not afraid to stand up for the rights of women. I always thought you were that kind of man, a real mensh what doesn't need to make himself look big."

"And now?"

She wiped her hands and looked at him. "Nu, sometimes I don't know you anymore."

"I'm still the same man you married."

Yetta shook her head. "The man my father gave me his blessing to marry quoted Talmud, not from his head, but with his whole heart. I married you for your goodness, not your money." Here she gave a quiet laugh, as though recalling the poor boy who didn't know what utensil to use the first time he ate dinner at her house. "You used to be a man of such wisdom, Gershon."

"And now?"

The door opened and Ruchel and Margaret entered, leading a dozen women into the dining room. Yetta took off her apron and joined them. Gershon retreated to the darkened bedroom after all, where he crawled under the covers and quaked in fear at the thought of losing Yetta. His love for her had been the sole impetus to excel in his studies, cross an ocean, strive for success. Without her, he was nothing but a poor shopkeeper's son from a stinking shtetl.

Where would his wife go if she left? To live with Zipporah and Jonah, or even stay in a hovel with Ruchel? Being poor wouldn't bother Yetta. He remembered how, when they got to America, she'd adapted to tenement life better than he had. What he saw as a setback, she saw as a challenge. No chairs? No problem! Drape a shmata over a milk crate. Yetta's confidence kept her warm; she fed off the righteous passion of her mission. He was no longer stoked by that fuel.

Gershon had to do something to win her back, to prove he could still use his influence to help those in need. Especially women. He flung back the covers and hastened to his study. He opened the Talmud for inspiration, but the words swam on the page. His hand reached toward his heart, then grabbed a pen. When, an hour later, he made a phone call, it was not to a needy Jew.

Two nights later, Gershon stood before the Community Board. His speech was in his pocket, but he knew what he wanted to say without reading it. Stepanic had put him last on the agenda so the men were eager to go home by the time he was finally called to address them.

"Gentlemen, my petition tonight is not personal. I speak for immigrant women, many of whom cannot yet converse in English, to beg you to consider the plight of their poor children."

Stepanic's raised eyebrows circled the table, inviting his fellow board members to join him in ridicule. Instead, they listened intently. Gershon had calculated, correctly, that they'd be intrigued by someone speaking on behalf of others, not for himself. Flattery would help too.

"In your esteemed positions, you have the power to urge landlords to drastically improve conditions in the tenement buildings where mothers are trying to bring up their young."

Stepanic interrupted, prepared to dismiss him. "City laws already force owners to upgrade the plumbing and electricity. Conditions are getting better without the board's interference."

"Not better enough, and not fast enough," Gershon leaned forward before Stepanic could lower his gavel. "True, there's indoor plumbing now, but it's only cold water, and there are just two toilets per floor. Electricity hasn't been installed in half the buildings and what power exists is barely enough for one small family, let alone a dozen large ones."

"Compared to the mud huts and outhouses they came from, people here have it pretty good." This remark, spoken by a board member, not in anger but as fact, was Gershon's opening.

"What the women ask for is not unreasonable. In fact, they are quite humble." Without quoting scripture, Gershon nevertheless drew a parallel between the biblical Exodus and the vast migration to America's shores. "After four hundred and thirty years of oppression, it took time for people to learn how to live in freedom. At first they were grateful merely to have food and water, the same bare necessities their taskmasters gave them Egypt. Only later did they feel entitled to a more decent life, provided they accepted a new set of laws and became good citizens. That's what the women want now, not so much for themselves as for their children." Gershon looked each man in the eye. "Isn't that why we all came to America? To make a better life for the next generation?"

Stepanic changed tactics. His slimy lips curled in a conciliatory smile. "I haven't heard any complaints from the women, or their husbands for that matter." When several men laughed, he continued. "They seem happy enough going to church suppers and free concerts paid for by these so-called greedy landlords. Heck, the board even organizes parades and parties at Walhalla Hall. Lazlo here danced a polka with his wife last Christmas." There were hoots and guffaws. Stepanic, looking satisfied, asked, "What more do the ladies want?"

"You give them Sunday entertainment as an escape when what they need is an escape from day-to-day poverty." Gershon's stern expression wiped the smiles from the men's faces.

Stepanic pressed his lips together. His eyes narrowed. "You're speaking up for Commie Jews, just like you. A bunch of cowardly men who hide behind their women because they're too ashamed and sissified to admit their own weakness. If they'd served in the Army before slinking onto a boat bound for America, it would have toughened them up enough to face hardship here."

Gershon harked back to Ruchel's words when he answered. "Men grow bigger, not smaller, when they have the guts to stand up for the rights of women. Dignity is the due of all those who come to these shores, and that includes God-fearing Catholics as well as Jews."

Heads nodded, except for Stepanic's. The veins in his neck bulged. "I'm a landlord, Mr. Mendel. So are you, if I'm correct?" Here he inclined his head with a sly smile. "Don't you agree that the buildings on the Lower East Side look better now than the day we got off the boat?"

"The outsides are done in Queen Anne, Greek Revival, and French Renaissance." Seeing Stepanic's face go flat with ignorance, Gershon pressed his advantage. "Builders make names for themselves with fancy facades, but the insides stay rotten. Unlike in the bible, families shouldn't have to wait forty years for living conditions to improve. They're already in the promised land."

Lazlo called the vote. All, save Stepanic, voted to require landlords to double the number of toilets and electrify every tenement within two years. The men thanked Gershon for reminding them that they had also started out with nothing. He didn't know if he felt pride or humility over his success with them, but it didn't matter. All he cared about was what Yetta thought.

chapter 42

Yetta was in bed when Gershon got home. It was unusual for her not to wait up, a cup of tea and a slice of cake set out for his return. She didn't stir when he slipped under the covers beside her. He touched her shoulder hesitantly. Yetta did not shrug him off, but neither did she roll closer.

"I'm tired," she said. "Ruchel schlepped me to another of her meetings. All those ladies talking and making plans. So many words, my head got dizzy from listening."

"Next time, you can be the one to speak," Gershon told her.

"Me? What would I say?"

"Tell them that by the year after next, every family will have a toilet and electricity."

"And by what miracle is this supposed to happen?"

"No miracle. I talked the Community Board into passing a resolution. If landlords don't comply, they'll be reported to the City authorities and fined. Maybe even jailed."

His wife sat up and planted a big kiss on Gershon's dry lips. Tears ran down his cheeks. "So you're not going to leave me?" he asked.

"What in God's name are you talking about?"

Gershon hesitated. Was he crazy to have imagined Yetta was fed up with him? Had two years of searching for Shmuel, followed by two years of remorse for failing, made Gershon lose his mind? Half embarrassed, half desperate for reassurance, the words tumbled out. "Now that you see I still have influence, you won't move out with Ruchel or move in with Zipporah?"

Yetta got on her knees and turned to face him. Light from the street lamp illuminated the window shade behind her, making her look like an actress on a movie screen, but her words were better than a script. "What did I ever care if you were rich or poor, a big macher or a little pisher? Money I had growing up. You I married because I wanted an adventure. You gave me a life in America I never would have had in Lemberg. Here I learned everyone is a worthwhile person."

"Including me?"

"Especially you." Yetta held Gershon tight. "I love you, not for winning, but for being a mensh. You stand up for others, even if it's a losing cause."

"I'd rather win." Gershon unpinned Yetta's hair, whose silvery strands tumbled down in the moonlight. Tomorrow he would buy her an expensive gift to celebrate.

"Nu, there's nothing wrong with winning." Yetta touched his chest like the flirtatious girl who'd slipped her handkerchief into his pocket at the bakery thirty years ago. "You won me."

Not a fancy present, Gershon reconsidered. Tomorrow he'd bring home a watermelon.

A week later, Gershon had just gotten off the phone after arranging housing for a family newly arrived from Russia when Yetta and Ruchel came home from a women's tenement association meeting at Walhalla Hall. Ruchel had persuaded the men's American Federation of Labour union local to let the women use their reserved space that night. They'd even donated a coffee urn and paid for the rented chairs.

Yetta had been excited but nervous about announcing the board resolution to the group. "What do I know from making speeches? Why can't you explain it to Ruchel, she should tell them?" she'd asked. Gershon couldn't admit that he was scared to tell his daughter. Suppose Ruchel resented his interference or taunted him for bragging? She might dismiss its significance, along with him. Instinct told him it was better for Ruchel to hear about the resolution from Yetta.

Usually Ruchel went to her room when they got home, while Yetta stayed up with him. Tonight, however, Yetta nudged Ruchel toward the kitchen while she went into their bedroom without saying anything. Gershon was afraid things had gone badly. Ruchel asked if he'd like a cup of tea. Stunned by her offer, Gershon could only nod. He watched his daughter fill the kettle, not bothering to wipe the water she dripped on the floor, and take down a china plate reserved for company, on which she arranged an assortment of cookies. They were both silent waiting for the water to boil. Before the tea had fully steeped, Ruchel brought their cups to the table. Gershon asked her for the sugar cubes. She stared around the kitchen, until Gershon got them from the cupboard where Yetta kept them in a cut glass dish and brought them to the table himself.

Gershon took a rugelach but his throat was too constricted to swallow. He wanted to wash down the cookie with the weak tea, but it was too hot. He blew on it, hoping it would cool off quickly. He prayed for Yetta to emerge from the bedroom and fill the kitchen with her chatter.

At last, Ruchel broke the silence. "It should have been a woman who addressed the board and got them to pass the resolution." She demolished a cookie in two bites, dropped three lumps of sugar in her tea, and took a gulp, apparently immune to the scalding water.

Gershon shivered, his body tensed for a scolding.

"But until more women find their voices, we still need men willing to speak up for us." She slid the sugar dish back toward him. "So, I suppose I should thank you."

Gershon took a tentative sip of tea, slowly emptying his cup before trusting himself to answer. "The words I said to the board were the same ones you spoke at City Hall. I couldn't have said it better. They were ready to take action, just like the crowd who cheered at your rally."

Ruchel's face flushed. Gershon hadn't expected his praise would matter to her. "Maybe you should reconsider being a teacher," he told her. "Think how many girls you could talk into making something more of their lives."

"I thought you and Mother wouldn't rest until I got married." Ruchel snorted and refilled their cups. "I don't want to be responsible for our family being the subject of gossip."

"I'll persuade your mother that marriage can wait, especially if Zipporah and Jonah give her a grandchild. Besides, Mama's stronger than she looks." Stronger than me, Gershon thought.

"And you?" Ruchel asked. "Will you be ashamed before the whole community?"

"I'll be happy to see you find a purpose in life." Gershon stopped, afraid she'd see him as pushing her and deliberately reject his suggestion.

Instead Ruchel laughed and looked at the puddle on the floor and crumbs scattered on the counter. "I'm not marriage material anyway."

Gershon let out his breath and savoured a cookie. He'd settle for Zipporah alone carrying on his wife's talent in the kitchen. "I'll pay your tuition. You can quit your job at the hosiery store."

"What's wrong with my working?"

"Nothing," Gershon sputtered. Somehow she'd scrambled the gist of his words. "I meant, I don't mind paying. I want to encourage you."

"I'm going to keep working, Father. I refuse to lose touch with women who don't have a choice." Ruchel paused and scooped up the crumbs. "I might be willing to accept a loan."

Gershon risked a smile and quoted Leviticus. "When you lend money to a kinsman, do not charge interest or otherwise take advantage of him."

"What about a kinswoman?" Ruchel's voice was edged with impatience.

"We're family!" Gershon said, getting mildly annoyed himself.

Ruchel leaned forward, all childish petulance suddenly gone. "Suppose I wanted to start a school for girls only? Not to teach them homemaking skills, although I'd make sure they learned the latest information about health and hygiene, but to enrol each one in a precollege track."

"I'll underwrite your school." Gershon reflected that in Lemberg, poor boys were forced to end their education at thirteen. Here in America, poor girls had a chance to go to college. What immigrant, even in his wildest dreams, had imagined such a thing?

"You'd acknowledge that I was the headmistress and let me make the rules?"

"Agreed. I'd stay in the background, even moonlight as the invisible night-time janitor."

"If you behaved, I might let you teach a course in accounting."

"So you're going to encourage young women to become capitalists?"

"I'm going to encourage them to become whatever they want. That's how it works here."

"Yes. That's how it works in America."

Gershon sat alone in the kitchen late into the night. Ruchel thought the way he had upon arriving in this land of opportunity. Power meant money and running the lives of others. In the last year, he'd come to a different understanding. Success did not depend on accumulating wealth or status. Gershon's ultimate achievement was to stand alongside the poor and disenfranchised and, above all, earn the love of his family. Genuine success called for humility.

He hoped that someday Ruchel would learn the true meaning of being an American too. That would be the ultimate proof that not only had Gershon himself arrived, he'd passed along his wisdom, l'dor vador, from one generation to the next. Like the contentious Jews in the Torah, railing against authority was a necessary step on the road to the Promised Land. Henceforth, Gershon would take pride in his daughter's rebellion. Even when it hurt, he'd remind himself she was continuing the journey he started.

part seventeen

Dev, 1922

chapter 43

I'd just finished my homework on the Islets of Langerhans, the pancre-
atic cells that sounded to me like an exotic Scandinavian retreat, when
Bernie let himself into our apartment. He called to the kitchen to
thank my mother for the tea and cookies she'd left him as a snack,
and sat on the couch beside the steamer trunk I used as a desk. He'd
be staying for dinner too, after which he and my father would study
Talmud together.

Following Shmuel's funeral two years ago, Bernie had continued to
visit my parents. For the first month after our trip to the museum,
things between us were strained, but since we were never alone after
that, it was soon copacetic for us to be around each other. Yaakov
dusted out, which was jake with me. His ogling gave me the heebie-
jeebies, and I'd heard he was hanging out with Meyer Lansky and
Benny Siegel, who were bound for trouble. My mother was grateful to
Bernie for staying in touch, but my father ignored him until last year
when he began rabbinical studies. Overnight, Bernie was transformed
from a shmendrick into a Solomon in his eyes. Once Papa invited
Bernie to study with him, it was like the old days when he and Shmuel
sat, heads bent over the text, dissecting ancient miracles. What I did in
biology lab, they did at the kitchen table. Only now they did it under
the electric lights that had finally been installed in our building.

Not long after their nightly study sessions began, my mother
suggested Bernie come early and eat dinner with us. He quickly
became a regular, more family member than guest, and having a young
man with a hearty appetite at our table again was like medicine to her.
I was glad there was no longer an empty chair staring back at me across
the table. Soon Bernie was even attending Shabbas services with Papa.
I was surprised he didn't spend Friday night with his own family, but
his father snapped a cap when Bernie announced he wanted be a rabbi

instead of working in the appliance store. Woman's intuition told me that Bernie was hurt when his father practically disowned him, but he was clearly thrilled that my father had as good as adopted him.

"So, what did you learn in school today?" Bernie asked me now, careful to eat over his plate. My mother trusted him alone to eat food outside the kitchen and not leave crumbs.

I handed him my biology book, open to the page I'd been reading. "Dr. Frederick Banting of the University of Toronto recently discovered that insulin, extracted from the pancreas, can treat diabetes." I loved learning about the body's intricate and interconnected parts. It was like watching a play in which each scene was more dramatic than the one before.

Bernie leaned forward to study the illustrations and marvel at God's creation too. Almost as much as my brother had, he enjoyed seeing me excited about my classes.

"Do you think I'll make a life-saving discovery some day?" I asked. With Shmuel gone, Mama too ready to praise, and Papa indifferent, Bernie's encouragement mattered.

He spread out his arms. "I can see the headline in the *Jewish Daily Forward*. Doc Dev Lev Discovers Cure for Gout! Jews Urged to Renounce Schmaltz!"

"I'm serious."

Bernie lowered his arms. "I didn't mean to make fun. Seeing you inspired is contagious." I smiled to show things between us were ducky again and asked what inspired him. He told me about Rabbi Bernard Revel, still in his thirties, who'd radicalized the curriculum when he became president of Yeshiva University. Now, in addition to studying Torah and Jewish laws, Bernie and his classmates took practical subjects too, like how to write sermons and do pastoral counselling. "We're even learning the business of running a synagogue," Bernie said. "Rabbi Revel used to manage his wife's family oil business in Oklahoma."

"There are Jews in Oklahoma?" I clapped my hands to my cheeks.

Bernie playfully slapped my hands down. "I'm serious too. I want to be a modern rabbi, not stuck in the old-country ways." I nodded, ready to hear more. If being modern meant having enlightened ideas about women, then my father, who seemed to respect Bernie, might begin to think that way too. Bernie inhaled the aroma of Mama's brisket wafting from the kitchen before continuing. "I don't think rabbis should hold themselves above others even though the Mishnah says that those who teach another even a single letter of Torah must be treated with honour."

"What *does* it mean to treat a rabbi with honour?" I wondered if my relationship with him would have to become more formal after Bernie's semicha in a few weeks. The ordination would mark a turning point in his life, and perhaps in mine.

"For one thing, you're supposed to stand in his presence."

I stood. Bernie rose and gently pushed me back down, letting his hands rest on my shoulders. "I'm not interested in that kind of honour. Besides, a rabbi's wife is considered his extension. She doesn't have to stand. In fact, people are supposed to get up in her presence too."

I stood again, making a game of it, but having said, "wife," Bernie pulled his hands away from my shoulders, as if they'd caught fire. It was discombobulating. I had long since stopped being stuck on him. Not that I'd lost interest in nookie. I liked to neck under the gym risers. But I refused to go goofy over boys. I planned to wear a white lab coat some day, not an apron.

"Are you modern enough to approve of the bat mitzvah of Rabbi Mordecai's daughter?" I asked, to change the subject. Rabbi Mordecai was the leader of the Reform movement, which was so liberal that people like my father didn't even think of them as Jews. Our shul considered his daughter's coming-of-age ceremony nearly as scandalous as marrying outside the religion.

Bernie pursed his lips. "It's one thing for girls to read biology texts, quite another for them to be called up to the bima to read Torah. Some learning is best left to boys and men."

Says you, I almost blurted out, but for once I kept my big yap shut. An argument might only harden Bernie's position about women, and I still hoped to persuade him to influence Papa in my favour. Instead, I asked him brightly, "So what did *you* learn in school today?"

"I learned that Babe Ruth signed a three-year, $52,000 per year contract with the Yankees."

"Are rabbis, even modern ones, allowed to be interested in baseball?"

"If we want to reach our congregants. Baseball is the universal religion of America."

"I heard it was being challenged by a new sport called water skiing."

"Are you pulling my leg?" Bernie frowned. I think he regretted his choice of expression.

"I heard it on the radio at my cousin's. My uncle bought three sets ... from your dad." Bernie laughed. "A man named Ralph Samuelson was the first to ski on a lake in Minnesota."

"It'll never catch on among our people," Bernie said. "Jews aren't good in the water." We grew silent, thinking of Shmuel. Then he asked how water skiing was different from snow skiing.

I was glad to get back to sports. "The way the announcer described it, you keep your body stiffer and lean back. If you bend at the knees and lean forward, like snow skiing, you end up face down in the water." I stood in front of the window holding a pencil between both hands like a tow bar. Seeing a horse-drawn pushcart down on the street, I imagined a boat pulling me across the waves. With knees locked, I rotated my upper body back and forth and skimmed toward the horizon. Bernie came up behind me and held the ends of my makeshift tow bar too. His chest pressed against my back and he exhaled into my hair. I let go and turned around so that his arms encircled me. This time, there was no mistaking his thoughts and feelings. Or mine.

"I'm sorry Bernie," I stammered. "I don't ... I mean," I took a deep breath. "You're like a brother to me now." His face fell along with his arms. Half a minute later, when my father came home, we were still facing each other, wordless.

"Dinner's ready," my mother called from the kitchen. Bernie went with Papa to perform the ritual washing up before the meal. I helped Mama carry the food to the table.

After we ate, the kitchen became Papa and Bernie's private yeshiva. My mother sat on the couch mending my father's collars. I perched at the steamer-trunk to finish my homework. Tonight's English assignment was using prefixes to turn a word into its opposite. Regard and disregard, sense and nonsense. It didn't always work the other way; you couldn't be combobulated or descript. To immigrants like Tante Yetta, the language was a minefield, but I continued to love its complexity, second only to my obsession with science. Mathematics, alas, held no such fascination. Faced with a geometry proof, I eavesdropped on the conversation in the kitchen.

The reading was Deuteronomy, Chapter 12. After wandering in the desert forty years, the Jews are finally about to enter the Promised Land. Moses tells the people that God wants them to "smash the idols and obliterate the name" of the nations they are about to kick out. Tonight was Bernie's turn to open the debate. In an earnest voice, he asked what God meant. My father quoted the medieval commentator Rashi, who said Jews must destroy all the places where other peoples worshiped their gods, even "upon the lofty mountains and hills, and under every lush tree." He cited another verse that said Jews could only worship in the sacred places the Lord designated.

Papa's sure voice implied there was little room for interpretation, but Bernie said, "That works in an ancient agricultural society, but here in America, Jews often take over old buildings, even churches, and convert them into synagogues. We can't afford to destroy those structures."

Now papa sounded aggrieved. "God forbid we should make a shul from a storefront or church. Or that you end up serving in one as a rabbi. Scripture is clear on this." He again recited Rashi. "Only to the place which your Lord God shall choose to set his Name shall you bring burnt offerings."

"We no longer bring burnt offerings. We give money," Bernie said.

"Exactly the kind of worship God warns us against." I heard my father pound the table. "Jews today lust after Mammon. In the shtetl, we were poor, but we adhered strictly to Torah. In America, we've turned away from the most basic commandments. It will be our downfall."

"At least we're not following Moloch and sacrificing our children." I think Bernie meant the remark as a joke, to lighten the conversation, but it was followed by a heavy silence.

"We *are* sacrificing our children." Papa's voice rose. "They go to school with Gentiles, they want to eat the same trayf as them. Boys come home with ideas for going off to war."

"I don't see what Shmuel ..."

"Girls announce they want to go off to college." My father's voice got more exasperated. Bernie tried to intercede again, but Papa, reading aloud the rest of the chapter, overpowered him. "Beware of being lured into their ways after they have been wiped out before you! ... You shall not act thus ... for they perform for their gods every abhorrent act that the Lord detests."

"Surely you don't claim all Americans are idolatrous?" Bernie's question hung in the air. With my father now silent, Bernie continued. "Some American practices must be allowed under Jewish law. A leader's job is to figure out which ones, otherwise we'll never be accepted here."

"Show me the Talmudic passage where it says that."

"There is no commentary. That text was written two thousand years ago. Today is today."

"The ancient words served our forefathers for five millennia, through more change than you or I will see in our lifetimes." Pages rustled. My father trusted the text. He had no patience for speculation. Although, when he and Shmuel had similar arguments, my brother had a knack for quoting passages that made ancient writings sound as if they'd been written for Jews today.

The one I remember best was in Numbers, when the five daughters of Zelophehad protest that because their father has not left behind a son, they should be allowed to inherit the family's share of land. Moses agrees, provided they marry within their own tribe and turn the property over to their husbands. Shmuel argued further, citing oral law from the Zohar and Baraita, that the daughters were God-fearing women who could themselves be trusted as stewards of the land.

"Only until they married their cousins," my father repeated, his finger still on the Torah. "Even if they never married," Shmuel said, holding forth his sources. "Their right derived from their righteousness, not from their family lineage." Papa still didn't buy his argument, but because my brother had quoted the ancient sages, he was at least willing to consider the idea.

Bernie's scholarship couldn't hold a candle to my brother's. He'd admitted to me that he grew bored with nitpicking arguments. A rabbi today had to help his congregants retain their faith while adjusting to the new world, not harking back to the old one. I approved of his intentions, but couldn't help seeing my brother as superior to Bernie. Shmuel could nitpick *and* make a case for modernism. I took my father's impatience as a sign that he saw the difference between them too.

I waited for Papa to quote more Talmud, but a series of thuds signalled that he'd closed the books. "Interesting questions, but enough studying for tonight." He called to my mother for tea and cake. She bit off the last piece of thread and hurried into the kitchen. I was angry at her for accepting my father's right to treat her like a slave, and angry at my father for not holding Bernie to the same high standards he demanded from Shmuel. But in his own way, Papa had become a practitioner of sholem bayess, seeking peace in the house, or at least around the kitchen table, by capitulating to Bernie's limitations. I understood that he didn't want to push him, or push him away, and risk losing another son. It was a sane response, but I saw it as a betrayal. It seemed that as my mother healed and my father softened, I was becoming more easily hurt and harder.

chapter 44

Three months later Bernie was ordained as a rabbi. The semicha was held on a Thursday night at Yeshiva University, a few blocks from our house. Bernie's parents attended the service, even though, according to him, his mother practically had to shlep his father there in a wheelbarrow.

"I wish I could invite you in my old man's stead," Bernie told my father, and Papa would have gone too, if my mother hadn't told him to get off that trolley. What she actually said was that people would gossip because it wasn't appropriate for him to substitute for Bernie's real father. Yet she didn't think it was wrong for Bernie to take Shmuel's place as my father's son.

My mother also thought it was legit for her to make a special Shabbas dinner at our house the night after the ordination, where my parents could kvell in private, as if he really did belong to them. Earlier, at shul, Bernie had been called up to the bima to chant the Torah and deliver the sermon. Then the sisterhood threw an oneg in his honour in the social hall. According to Ruchel, it wasn't a hotsy-totsy affair—they served schnapps in addition to wine—but it was clear that our synagogue was proud of him. I was sorry to miss it, but I was helping Mama get ready at home. She'd spent a week cleaning and baking, despite the heat, and the house was redolent with gefilte fish, freshly grated horseradish, and chicken soup liberally laced with dill.

For a few weeks after I'd declined to water ski with Bernie, we were awkward with each other again. He came later each day and sat stiffly on the couch, covering his lap with tomes of Torah commentary. I glued my eyes to the textbooks spread before me on the steamer trunk, and if Mama came in to refresh his tea or ply him with homemade cookies, we'd both look up and smile brightly. I don't think she suspected anything. Pretty soon, the charade convinced us too. Bernie resumed asking what I was learning in school, and I opened my book so he could trace the blood vessels that branched from the heart to the teeniest capillaries of the fingertips.

The night of the dinner, as we waited for Bernie and my father to get back from shul, my mother was anxious that everything go just right. It was as if she felt that if something were to go wrong—two noodles stuck together, a wrinkle in the tablecloth—she'd be dishonouring God, or my brother's memory. She opened the door before they reached the top of the stairs, held the enamelled basin and pitcher while they washed their hands, and urged them to sit down. Bernie took Shmuel's old seat, to my father's right. Papa deferred to him to make kiddush over the wine and say motzie over the challah. I still clung to the hope that my father would bestow on me the Sabbath blessing given to children, the one he used to reserve for Shmuel. But since that night five years ago when I'd gotten my first period, the same night my brother disappeared, the special prayer had ceased being part of our family's weekly ritual. When Bernie began to eat Friday dinner with us, I half expected Papa to bless him, but Bernie was already an adult by then so Papa was silent. I was relieved. Not that I was ever jealous of Shmuel, but I would have resented Papa blessing Bernie when he continued to ignore his real child, me.

While the rest of us ate Mama's cooking, my father talked with Bernie about his sermon. In that week's Torah reading, God tells Moses he won't be permitted to enter the Promised Land. Only those born in the wilderness, not the generation who'd been slaves in Egypt, would cross the Jordan. Bernie had drawn an analogy to immigrants coming to America, leaving their elderly parents behind. My father sought a more scholarly interpretation. "Moses takes this news calmly," he said, "and merely asks God to appoint a successor. Why is it that Moses does not protest?"

Bernie smiled at my mother as she ladled the last meaty kreplach into his soup. "It's natural. The old step aside, the young step in. Moses accepts that Joshua will take his place."

"But why doesn't Moses voice his sense of injustice?" my father asked. "He's spent forty years leading the rebellious Israelites toward this goal, only to be denied entry at the end."

My mother and I cleared the table and served the fish. Bernie watched until we sat down again. I wondered if he was being polite or stalling for time. My father couldn't wait. "Because Moses is confident he's passed down his wisdom to Joshua." Having answered his own question, Papa smiled triumphantly. Bernie looked grateful to be off the hook. "But ..." My father held up a finger. "God also says that Moses should invest Joshua with only *some* of his authority." Papa picked up his fork and everyone took it as a signal to begin the second course.

Except me. "So," I asked my father, "Is the Torah saying knowledge and power diminish with each succeeding generation?"

Papa didn't answer, but Bernie did. "Torah says here what it says at the very end. 'Never again did there arise in Israel a prophet like Moses.' No one could match him." My father smiled his approval that Bernie was quoting scripture to make his point.

"What about all the discoveries made by a young generation of scientists?" It was my turn to argue. "Doesn't new knowledge give us more wisdom and power than our ancestors?"

My father ignored me and spoke to Bernie. "I read in the *Forward* that a memorial to President Lincoln was dedicated in Washington. He too was a great leader who freed the slaves."

Bernie looked at me in silent apology for Papa's rudeness, but he still addressed his next question to my father. "Will there ever be a monument to Moses for helping to free the Jews?"

Papa answered without hesitation. "It would be wrong, since it was truly God, not a human being, who performed the miracles that ended our slavery."

I refused to keep my yap shut like a lump of gefilte fish. "What about a monument to Susan B. Anthony now that women finally won the vote?"

This time my father did speak to me. "Ending slavery is a good thing. I'm not sure that women's suffrage is."

I waited for my mother to contradict him. Instead she said, "I made a special dessert," and fetched a poppy seed kindli from the oven. Why did my father have to be so controlling and my mother so meek?

Now Bernie played peace-maker. How many defenders of sholem bayess did my family need? "Perhaps it's unfair for a monument to single out one individual," he mused. "Every major accomplishment comes about from many people working together."

"Yet tonight we're singling out you." It was my father's turn to retrieve something special. He came out of the bedroom with a wrapped parcel. Mama's eyes widened. Whatever was inside, Papa must have hidden it well for her not to have found it during the past week of frantic cleaning.

Bernie's hands trembled as he undid the brown butcher's wrap, then folded back a layer of yellowed tissue paper. He pulled out the silk tallit, glinting with gold thread, that had belonged to my great grandfather and that Papa intended to give Shmuel when he was ordained. For five years, the prayer shawl hadn't seen the light of day, buried as deep in the closet as Shmuel was at sea.

"Thank you, but I can't accept this." Bernie stroked the delicate embroidery and fragile tzitzit, the longest fringes I'd ever seen on a tallit. He held it out to my father.

"You have to," my father said. "It's the least I can offer you for giving me back my life, and for making my journey to America worthwhile."

I was startled when my father put his left hand on my head. Was I at long last to receive his blessing? And if so, for what? Instead, he continued speaking to Bernie. "Now that you're a rabbi, you'll need a rebbetzin. I wish I could give you my daughter too."

I stared down at the honey, flecked with black seeds, crystallizing on our plates, assuming Bernie would do the same. Instead, I felt his eyes on me. When I looked up, I saw the hope on his face.

I should have put the kibbosh on it right away. Bernie was like a brother to me. Yet I said nothing. I thought of our first date, when I'd admitted how Papa's obsession with Shmuel made me feel like the sibling of an only child. Knowing how I craved my father's love, did Bernie think I'd accept his offer as a way to finally win it? Would I, in fact, consider such an idea myself?

My brain was in such a turmoil all week, I severed two frogs' legs in biology lab. Suppose I did marry Bernie. Would he let me have a career or insist that being a rabbi's wife filled the bill? What about Papa? If Bernie agreed I could work, would my father think less of Bernie instead of approving of me? In that case, the point of marrying him would be lost. I needed help to clear up the muddle, but I wasn't sure who to ask. Not Ruchel. She was anti-marriage, whereas I was pro-career. I thought I could manage both. After all, I was better organized than my distracted cousin.

In the end, I talked to Leah. We'd long ago patched things up again and learned how to be more careful with each other. I only confessed to minor transgressions and she tried to judge me less harshly. Leah alone knew me well enough to understand why I was torn about marrying

Bernie. She was also very practical and I counted on her to help me figure out what to do.

"I'm going to shvitz a bucket," I announced as soon as I walked into her apartment, which was as hot as mine. I lifted my skirt to fan some air between my thighs. Leah gently slapped down my skirt and held my hand firmly as she dragged me two blocks to the playground of our old elementary school. Sitting on the swings, we could imagine we were creating a slight breeze.

"It's a shame you missed Bernie's sermon Friday night," she said. 'His D'var Torah about leaving parents behind to come to the new world made half the congregation cry."

"The older half, no doubt. The younger ones were probably praying their parents would go back across the ocean and leave America to them."

"Shush!" Leah's laughter jiggled her swing. "Disrespecting parents is against the fifth commandment."

"I'll borrow Bridget's rosary beads and say a zillion Hail Mary's."

"I'm happy my bubbe and my parents are here. I'll have three generations at my wedding."

"Did your parents speak to the shadchen yet about finding you a suitable match?"

"They promised to do it when the High Holy Days are over, so there'll be enough time to find someone this winter and then have the wedding right after graduation next spring."

"Maybe your parents can throw one party for both simchas and save money."

Leah shook her head. "Who's got money to spend on one, let alone two? I just hope whoever he is earns enough for us to have our own apartment." She got that dreamy look that clued me in she was imagining setting the Shabbas table and lighting her own set of candles.

"I hope for your sake, he's a good kisser."

Leah blushed, but she smiled. A little sex talk was permissible, as long as it was in the context of marriage. I decided not to push my luck.

"Tell me about the dinner your mother made for Bernie," Leah said, changing the subject back to Friday night. "Did he talk about his sermon or was he too modest?"

"My father pressed him to cite ancient commentaries that supported his modern position."

"Did Bernie come up with an answer that satisfied him?"

"I'm really not interested in talking about this week's Torah portion." Leah looked hurt. I'd spoken more abruptly than I meant to. "I need your advice," I said, dragging my feet on the ground to slow down the swing. She stopped pumping too and turned to face me. Things between us were copacetic again. "You know how Papa has basically adopted Bernie as his son?"

Leah nodded and touched my hand. "You said your father's been less angry since they began studying Torah together. And your mother finally snapped out of her depression."

"I think women's rights more than men's Torah study was responsible for Mama getting better. But," I winked, "let's not get in a pilpl over it." Joking about the name of the café where we had our fight always made us back off another argument. "After dinner, Papa gave Bernie his grandfather's tallit, the one he'd been saving to give Shmuel after his ordination."

Leah's eyes narrowed. "No one can ever replace Shmuel. Is that why you're upset?"

"I do feel bad my parents treat Bernie like a son, yet I also kind of see him as a brother."

"So what's the problem?" Leah fanned her face, then mine.

I took a deep breath and forced out the words, quickly. "My father also wants to 'give' me to Bernie as a wife. And Bernie seems to like the idea."

Leah rested her chin on her hand. "I don't understand. Not long ago you were carrying a torch for Bernie." That was an expression I'd taught her. "Why wouldn't you say yes? Or are you hesitating just to rebel against your father?" She gave my swing a playful push.

"Just the opposite. I'm *not* stuck on Bernie any more, precisely because he's like a brother to me. Marrying him would feel incestuous. On the other hand, my father would ..."

"Give you the love you always wanted from him." Leah finished my sentence.

I swallowed the lump in my throat. It was too hot to cry.

"You could try to think of Bernie more like a first cousin than a sibling. People in the old country married their first cousins all the time."

"Ugh!" Maybe for Leah, to whom lovemaking was a marital

commandment, sex with a relative would be palatable. Not me. "Besides, you'd be the first to admit I'm not cut out to be a rabbi's wife. Can you picture me as a well-behaved rebbetzin?" I cocked my head demurely and was rewarded by Leah's wry smile. "I want to *look* under a microscope, not *live* under one."

"As a rebbetzin, you could bring science to the women in the congregation, making their homes healthier and safer. That's a mitvah as worthy as discovering the cure for some disease." The argument was similar to one I'd used with Leah, unsuccessfully, whenever I'd tried to talk her into becoming a visiting nurse instead of just getting married and having her own family.

"I don't want to work quietly behind the scenes. I want to be out front, getting money and recognition." I was shocked to hear myself say this, after always believing in my own altruism.

Leah's face twisted, along with the chains on her swing, when she turned toward me. "For shame, Dev. I knew you were ambitious but I never thought you were selfish."

"What if I am? Where does Torah say that doing good and doing well cancel each other out? In fact, doesn't God say that if you do good, you'll be rewarded?"

"Doing good means following God, not money. Success and rewards come *after* piety."

"I don't want to be pious. I want to lose myself in work, not worship."

This time Leah didn't smile at my turn of phrase. She scowled. "You've changed, Dev. If Shmuel were alive today, he wouldn't recognize you. Your brother was as smart as you, but he was modest about the gift God gave him. You act like you created intelligence all on your own."

"Just because you're wasting the intelligence God gave you doesn't give you the right to say anything about Shmuel and me. You haven't even lost so much as an old grandmother."

Leah untwisted her swing and spoke in a calmer voice, which I saw as a lame attempt at sholem playground, peace in the schoolyard. "What if you got married and started a family first. Your father would be thrilled and your mother would get over more of her grief. Start a career after the children start school. You'd have to forego a fancy degree, but you could work in a lab."

"If you remember, Bernie wasn't in favour of women working outside the home."

Leah pondered and dismissed this problem too. "That was two years ago. He's not so old-fashioned now. You should have heard him on Friday night. Bernie is a modern man."

"Not that modern. He's still an Orthodox rabbi with traditional ideas."

Leah started swinging again. "Whatever I say, you say the opposite. You never used to be so contrary and narrow-minded."

"You're the one whose mind is closed." Every overheated fibre in my body wanted to dispute and insult her. After two years, I was tired of putes and sults. "Just because all you want is to marry and have babies, you can't understand that I'm driven to change the whole world."

Her swinging got faster. "I can't understand why you'd throw away a chance to marry up, make your poor parents happy, raise healthy children, and help immigrant women do the same."

Leah jumped down and ran to the schoolyard gate, her empty swing bouncing erratically behind her. I grabbed it just before it crashed into me and waited for the swing, and my heart, to settle down. The pavement baked the soles of my shoes as crisp as the cookies my mother made for Bernie. Leah and I were having more than a pilpl. This was a full-blown krig, and if my father had pressed me, I couldn't have cited an old commentary with something helpful to say about life in the new world. The laws for wandering in a barren desert, heading to one special place, were useless in helping me decide which path to take in a teeming city with a multitude of choices.

Still burning inside and out, I walked home through streets as deserted as the schoolyard, not teeming at all. The stillness came as a relief and I looked forward to the quiet of our apartment to sort out my thoughts. I couldn't believe my mother was baking when I walked in the door. The aroma was pure heat; it didn't even smell like food. "Are you daft in the noggin?" I asked.

"Sunday is baking day, whatever the weather." She set two loaves of bread on wire racks to cool, put two more in the oven, and wiped her brow with her apron.

"I'll shop at the kosher grocery on the corner," I offered. I used to think Papa wouldn't allow store-bought in the house for religious reasons, but lately I felt his real motivation was to enslave Mama. "I don't understand why you let Papa make all the rules. Don't you get a vote?"

My mother filled the cookie pan with crescent-shaped rugelach before straightening up and studying me. "You look upset. Did you and Leah have another fight?"

I pinched off a piece of the raw, cinnamon-dusted dough and sucked it from my fingers.

Mama sighed. "I thought you two were past the age of having fights."

"You don't outgrow fighting," I said. "At least not when you're stuck in childish patterns of thinking, like Leah."

My mother sat at the table and patted the chair beside her. I remained standing. "Do you want to tell me about it? I'm a good listener."

"Just because you listen to Papa doesn't mean you're hip to the jive with me. You and I don't speak the same language, and I'm not talking about Yiddish and English."

"Suit yourself," she said, using an expression I regretted having taught her. "Do you want a slice of cake?" She removed the dish towel meant to keep off flies.

I knew she was pretending my refusal to confide in her wasn't upsetting, but I'd long ago learned to recognize when I'd hurt her. A tiny wrinkle formed next to her left eye, as though she were trying to wink away the pain. "Since when are you interested in my life anyway?" I asked.

The skin around my mother's wrinkle began to pulse. Truth be told, she'd always been interested, but I was itching for a screamy-meemy fight. Leah had won ours by walking off first and I wanted to be a winner too. I didn't know what victory meant at that moment, other than making up my mind about Bernie, and I was no closer to a decision than when I sought out Leah.

My mother took the bread out of the oven and picked up the loaded cookie pan.

I took a step toward her. "Just because I'm the only child you have left doesn't give you the right to cling to me just so you can feel you're still useful as a mother."

The pan clattered to the floor at the same time we heard my father coming up the stairs.

"An accident," my mother said, as my father entered with a look of alarm.

"I'll make another batch of dough," I told my mother, kneeling to clean up the mess.

"No, you were right, Dev." She took the dish rag from me. "It really is too hot to bake."

I turned to my father. "I'll run to the store. Can't you make an exception in this heat?"

"One exception leads to another," he said, watching my mother wipe up the cinnamon sugar that had sprayed across the cracked linoleum.

"We're not talking about a golden calf," I said, "just a bag of cookies."

"Let Dev finish the baking," he told Mama. "It wouldn't hurt her to practice cooking." Then he faced me. "You can't serve your family frogs' legs left over from the dissecting lab."

I stared back at him. "I didn't think you listened when I talk about what I do at school."

"I listen to you." My father walked around my mother, still on the floor, to sit at the table.

But did he hear what I said? Please God, I prayed silently, make it so.

"I'm listening now." Papa tapped the same chair my mother had. This time I sat.

"Tell me," he said, "have you thought more about my offer regarding Bernie?"

I sat on the edge of my seat. "*Your* offer of *my* hand in marriage?"

Papa pulled his collar away from his sweaty neck. Mama brought him a wash cloth and said, "Your father just finished a ten-hour shift slaving over a pressing machine. Let him be."

He motioned her to back off. "Let Dev talk, Rivka. Maybe she has a point. I don't listen to her enough." He regarded me expectantly. I recognized the look as one he gave Shmuel when he anticipated an answer whose wisdom would satisfy him. It was not a look he gave Bernie.

My kishkas coiled inside me like the chains on the swing. I wanted to keep stoking my anger, but I was lured by what I took for Papa's genuine interest in what I had to say. "You can't make me marry Bernie." I was prepared to dredge up a Torah passage if need be.

"I would never make you marry anyone. Forcing a woman to marry goes against God." Papa smiled kindly. I smiled back, happy that he had found the Talmudic rationale himself.

"But I see how the two of you get along," my father said. I must have raised my eyebrows because he chuckled and continued. "Your father sees as well as listens. Even when Shmuel was still alive, you and Bernie had special looks for one another. I'm right, yes?" The look on Papa's face was one I had not seen before. What I'd taken for interest was in fact smugness.

"You don't listen or see." I pushed away from the table. "You want your real daughter, who you don't care about, to marry your adopted son, who's a poor substitute for your real one."

My mother gasped.

"Well, my learned father, Leviticus 18:9 forbids carnal relations between brothers and sisters, and the answer to your offer is no. Are you listening? Negative! Never! Neyn!"

I stopped talking but even if I had gone on, my father wouldn't, or couldn't, have listened. He held his head as though waves of blood were crashing between his ears. Every visible inch of skin on his head and hands was bright red, heated by an equal mix of hot, humid air and boiling rage. "Out!" he screamed, his thick finger stabbing toward the door. "Leave! Go! Avekgeyn!"

I stormed from the apartment and embraced the fiery blast of air that greeted me. Shmuel had left home of his own accord. I'd been ordered out, but in truth it was my own choice to go.

chapter 45

The day had cooled off by the time I reached Ruchel's, for which I was grateful. So had my self-righteousness, for which I wasn't. I wanted to stay angry and counted on my cousin to help me do that. "I've left home," I said when she opened her apartment door. She was living on her own now, going to college to become a teacher. Onkel Gershon paid for everything.

I plopped myself down at a table littered with dirty dishes and newspapers. "I can't marry Bernie just to make Papa happy, but it might be okay if I could go to school too. Mama would be relieved because she wouldn't have to choose between me and Papa anymore. I wish I knew how Shmuel would feel about my marrying his best friend. Oh, I'm all balled up." I put my head down on my outstretched arms and wailed.

"You need a drink." Ruchel winked and got two bottles of Coca-Cola from the electric icebox. I didn't think they were kosher, but I gulped one down like a dried-out alkie reunited with his hooch. "Your father's an old-fashioned tyrant." She wiped her mouth with the back of her hand. "But this dustup will blow over. Aunt Rivka's good at calming Uncle Avram down."

After what I said about me and Shmuel, and Shmuel and Bernie, I wasn't so sure. "It could be a couple of days before it's safe to go back home. Is it okay if I spend the night here?"

"Why go back at all? Move in with me. I'll show you the latest dances and fill your head with propaganda, while you help me with my science classes."

"It sounds divine, but ..."

"Don't worry about the money. My father already pays the rent and my mother brings enough food each week to feed a union hall. You can even invite your friend Leah for dinner."

Still, I hesitated. Money was a problem, and maybe the solution was as easy as Ruchel said, but something else was eating at me that I couldn't explain, a vague fear that if I left home without my parents' blessing, like Shmuel, I'd cease to exist too. My mother might send my uncle after me, but my father would immediately write me off for dead. And then, like my brother, it would turn out I really was dead. Papa wouldn't even feel a sense of loss like he did with Shmuel. He'd think, "Good bye and good riddance, daughter." Maybe that's what he was thinking now.

Well if he didn't care that I was gone, then I wouldn't care about returning home. "Deal," I said. "I'll get my things tomorrow when Papa's at work and Mama is out shopping."

"Why bother? I've got plenty of clothes. You won't need your school books until the fall. Face it, your father is hopeless. It's time to give up and move on with your plans for a career."

Part of me—a blood vessel, a muscle— wasn't yet ready to abandon hope. "Onkel Gershon used to feel the same way as Papa about women getting married, but he changed."

"Yes," my cousin said, "but my father never had a son to pin his hopes on."

Ruchel found bed sheets that weren't too dirty so I could sleep on the couch, but we expected to spend nights on the fire escape until the heat broke. Pretty soon Onkel Gershon and Tante Yetta came over for their Sunday evening visit. My uncle handed over a week's spending money, while my aunt unpacked enough chicken and brisket to feed an emperor's army on a fortnight's march. She grimaced when she saw the Coca-Cola and silently poured it down the drain. Ruchel winked again and wiggled her pinky toward the cabinet under the sink, where she kept a stash.

Despite the heat, my uncle wore a short suit jacket with narrow lapels. I surmised Ruchel had been giving him sartorial advice. He pivoted for her approval, but it was my aunt who wolf whistled. "Show Ruchel the full effect," Tante Yetta said, handing him his straw boater. "Nu, isn't he a dapper ducky in his glad rags?" He in turn pecked her on the cheek and she blushed like the young bride I was reluctant to become. I couldn't imagine my parents flirting in private, let alone in front of me. I felt cosier with this family than with my own.

On their way out, Tante Yetta picked up the sheets, assuming Ruchel had left them there for her to take home and wash. I stopped her, saying that I would be staying the night, maybe more.

"How many more?" she asked.

"A few," I stammered.

"How many a few?" My aunt's arms crossed her bosom, awaiting my answer.

"She's moving in with me," Ruchel said.

Tante Yetta continued to look at me, not at Ruchel. "This is true?" I nodded.

"You had a fight with your parents?"

"With Uncle Avram," Ruchel said.

"Shah, let your cousin speak for herself." My aunt tapped her foot, which was muted by the thick Oriental carpet she and my uncle had given Ruchel, along with their other cast-offs. I confirmed that I'd taken Papa at his word when he ordered me out of the house. I wouldn't go back, even if he asked three times for forgiveness, as was customary among observant Jews.

"I'll let Rivka and Avram know you're staying here. They'll be worried."

"Hah! My father doesn't care a fig about me."

"He likes dates better? Or he cares raisins about you?"

"It's an expression, Tante Yetta. It means my father ..."

"I know what it means. I'm in this country over twenty years, I know American sayings."

"Like 'Don't take any wooden nickels' and 'You slay me,'" my cousin teased.

"Like whatever is eating you," my aunt held my cheeks in her plump hands, "you should know that your father cares a whole bushel of fruit about you."

"He has a strange way of showing it, or not showing anything at all." I turned away.

"Men take a long time to heal. Women recover faster. We're stronger." My aunt looked at my uncle for confirmation. He looked at the carpet.

"Papa never cared about me even before Shmuel left. He just doesn't love me." I plunked down on the couch and balled up the sheets in my lap.

"Nonsense, mamele, of course he does." Again, Yetta looked toward her husband, who remained silent. She grew impatient. "Gershon, tell your niece that her father loves her."

"You tell me if you need anything," he said to me. "Clothes, school books. You want to apply to college next year, I'll pay your tuition.

Come, Yetta. I'm sure the girls, excuse me, the young ladies, have a lot to talk about."

He offered my aunt his elbow and led her out the door.

chapter 46

A week passed and Mama didn't come to Ruchel's to persuade me to go home. I hated to admit it to myself, but I was disconsolate, wondering whether she sided with Papa or was just glad for the peace and quiet with me gone. By the second week, I told myself to feel consolate about my freedom and the whirlwind excitement of living with my cousin. It was a relief not to exist in a state of inhibition, anxious I'd say or do something to plunge my mother into a sad memory or elicit my father's disapproval. Ruchel, for all her strong opinions, didn't judge me. Either that, or I was immune.

For the first time in my life, I was surrounded by orchids—hand-painted china, fringed lampshades, and upholstered chairs— although the plain furnishings at my house were cleaner and better cared for. Tante Yetta attempted to straighten up when she visited Ruchel's, but the place was dirty again by the next day and my cousin thought nothing of ruining things I would have treasured. I hated to think I missed Mama's housecleaning, so I reasoned it was the methodical scientist in me who was offended by my cousin's carelessness. I was orderly in the lab, but it would be liberating if I could let myself act the slob, at least a smidgen, at home.

Even better than pretty objects were the closets and drawers over-flowing with Ruchel's flapper clothes, which she shared with the same generosity as her opinions on women's rights. I copied everything about the way my cousin dressed and did her makeup, except for how I styled my hair. She'd bobbed and marcelled hers to fit underneath her collection of cloche hats in every conceivable colour. Chopping off my hair would have solved the problem of its unruliness, but it had become a symbol to me. Permitting my mother to wear her hair long was my father's sole flaunting of Orthodox tradition. If he could relax this rule, I hoped he might ease up on others.

"Listen to this." My cousin's outraged voice carried from the living room where she was reading the newspaper, to the kitchen, where I was forcing myself not to do the dishes. "A bank in New Jersey has banned women from entering the premises unless properly attired. Patrons and employees are forbidden from wearing feathery scarves, rakish hats, champagne-coloured hose, sleeves above the elbow, or hemlines more than a foot above the ground. The Federal Reserve also banned females from wearing makeup and, while short hair is permitted, workers may not fluff it on the job. Anyone who defies the dress code will be fired with no recourse or appeal."

"Flapper flap," as the incident was dubbed, soon spurred a protest rally. My cousin and her friends chartered a street car to take us and other marchers from our district to Fidelity Trust Bank, across the Hudson River, where the whole to-do started. Waiting on the corner early Monday morning with a throng of women dressed in outrageous outfits, I was surprised when my aunt took her place beside us. Ruchel hadn't told me she was coming. Tante Yetta wore a sedate dress, but she'd adorned it with a fluffy scarf and tucked her Orthodox wig under a pert little hat.

"What? You think marches are only for the young?" she asked. "These ladies work hard to feed their families. If they had smarts in the keppe," my aunt tapped her forehead, "these big-shot banker bosses would know that showing a bissel flesh was good for business."

Ruchel hugged her. "I never thought I'd see the day you spouted economics in support of women's rights." I couldn't help feeling envious. I hadn't seen or hugged my mother in weeks.

"What does Onkel Gershon think about your going on the march?" I asked my aunt.

"I was going to keep it a secret." She glanced up the street like she expected him to swoop down and order her home. Instead she smiled and said, "When your uncle found the scarf I bought to wear, he teased that he was going to come too and act as our chaperone."

"What stopped him?"

"I forbid it. I said I didn't trust him around sexy young women in flapper clothes." Yetta giggled. "He said he was happy to settle for unwrapping a new scarf from off his old wife." Even Ruchel raised her eyebrows at that. I wondered if my aunt and uncle, already affectionate, felt free to touch more since their daughters had moved out. Would my parents act differently toward each other without me around? I remembered the old days when Mama bathed on Friday afternoons and Papa stroked her hair.

The street car came into view and my aunt stood on tiptoe, looking not toward her house, the richer end of the Lower East Side from where my uncle would approach, but the poorer neighbourhood where my parents lived. Her pursed mouth broke into a relieved smile. Hurrying toward us, wearing her zippered skirt, was my mother. I felt betrayed and glared at my cousin for not telling me she'd invited her, but Ruchel looked surprised too. Only after Tante Yetta began to wave and chant, "Yoo hoo, over here!" did I realize it was she who'd asked Mama to come. Yetta grinned broadly as my panting mother raced toward us and enveloped Mama when she got there.

My mother pulled back, but addressed my aunt politely. "I had to wait until Avram went to work before I could leave." She peered at me sideways but I refused to return her gaze.

"Not to worry," my aunt said. "You made it in the kick of time."

"Nick of time," Ruchel corrected.

Yetta pulled Ruchel up the steps of the street car, pushed her into a window seat, and took the aisle seat next to her. I was forced to sit with my mother instead of with my cousin. We took the row behind them and sat in silence, looking out the window as the driver headed uptown and crossed over the river into New Jersey. After ten minutes, my mother took my face in her hands and turned it toward her. "I was worried you'd get too thin."

"Tante Yetta brings us plenty of food."

"I'm sure it's better than what I can afford to cook." Next my mother gently fingered the beads on the shoulders of the lavender chemise I wore. "It's a pretty dress."

"Ruchel is generous with her wardrobe."

"But not so generous with the soap and water," she whispered, passing her finger over a small stain above the elbow. We looked at the back of my aunt and cousin's heads, then leaned into each other, muting our laughter.

"What will you do when school starts?"

"Stay with Ruchel. It's not as quiet as at our house, but a lot of her classes are in the evening so I can study then." I took Mama's hands and squeezed them. "I'm reading her science textbooks. When I start college in a year, I'll already be ahead of the other students."

My mother touched my hair, which was as wild and curly as ever. "No short flapper do for you?" she asked.

I stroked her thick golden waves. "I can't," I said, "and you shouldn't."

"Do you want to come home?"

Two weeks ago I would have said no; standing in line for the bus when my aunt and cousin joked and hugged, I would have murmured yes. Now, sitting beside Mama, part of me wanted to bury my head in her breast, tell the driver to turn around, and go home right away. Yet another part told me that having broken loose, I should let the scar heal and move forward. "I can't go back, Mama, but I'm ready to have you come visit me in my new home."

"You're there during the day, at least until school starts in the fall?"

I realized she was figuring out how to sneak away when my father wasn't home.

"All day Sunday, too. Ruchel isn't in class and you can visit with both of us."

"Come Sunday before Avram gets home from the factory." My aunt turned and peered over the seat rest in front of us. "For dinner. Gershon and I will come earlier than usual too."

"You bring the main course," my mother said. "I'll bring the soup and dessert."

When we arrived in New Jersey, there were so many women on the street that the driver had to park several blocks away from the bank. We marched to the rally twelve across, me and Ruchel in the middle, our mothers on either side of us, and a colourful throng linking arms curb to curb. "Don't fire flappers" and "Freedom for dresses and tresses," we chanted. "Bankers are bullies" and "Who cares about hair?" cried the women approaching from the other direction.

My father's a bully too, I thought, but thank God my mother cares. It wasn't a perfect deal, but unlike the bank women fired for changing with the times, I needn't fear going hungry.

chapter 47

My mother couldn't prepare extra food at home without my father knowing, so she came to our apartment early Sunday afternoon to cook for us. Tante Yetta started coming earlier too, with Onkel Gershon arriving at five. He and my aunt would then walk Mama home before Papa returned from work. The subterfuge was thrilling, like a spy movie, but going behind Papa's back also made me sad. On days when the heat was oppressive and the sweat I pictured pouring off him was a poor substitute for the tears he needed to shed, the ache in my heart nearly zotzed me.

Not enough to dampen my enthusiasm for the weekly mother-daughter cooking sessions, though. Tante Yetta hoped Ruchel would pick up some domestic skills, but my cousin nibbled absent-mindedly on scraps of bread dough or the celery stalks used to flavour the soup. I, however, watched the proceedings with interest. Our mothers' skills in the kitchen were like those of a chemist mixing potions in the lab. The only thing stopping my own experiments with cooking was the fear that my cousin would deem me insufficiently feminist.

While the mothers chopped and stirred, the four of us talked. Yetta spoke about growing up a rich girl in Lemberg; my mother described what she'd endured being both poor and female. Ruchel, lamenting the political struggles of women in America, was happy to find an ally in my mother. Because of the tension between my father and uncle, Ruchel and Mama had never spent much time together. So, an unexpected consequence of my rift with Papa was that his wife and his rival's daughter crossed a generational divide. Usually the loquacious one in a group, I was mostly silent at these gabfests. I absorbed the other women's experiences along with the smells of baking and boiling, while imagining what my life as an American woman would be like.

"I was given clothes, trinkets, and a private tutor," Yetta told us. "Of course, I was an only child. I wonder, if I'd had a brother, whether most of the attention would have gone to him."

"Even with an older brother," Mama told Yetta, "I never felt Gershon received special treatment from our parents. We couldn't afford for anyone to get more than the bare essentials."

"Yet only Onkel Gershon was allowed to go to school, right?" I asked.

"Yes," my mother said, "but that was true for all the boys. And since Gershon was the smartest, he brought honour to our whole family." What was honourable about having brains if they made others bitter, I wondered, thinking of the trouble between him and my father. "I never resented Gershon's education," Mama continued, "nor did I mind doing extra chores so he could study. When you grow up poor, being a scholar is the only road to recognition in the community."

My cousin fixed her eyes on my mother. "Education is the way to move up in America too. Jewish girls today still get less education than Jewish boys. They'll be as downtrodden here as they were in the old country if we don't work to open up opportunities for them."

Yetta looked at her daughter with pride. "So you'll become a teacher and tell them they should study hard. Girls will see you and know they can succeed too."

Ruchel blushed under her mother's praise. "It's easier for me because I grew up rich, like you. Also, Zipporah and I didn't have to compete with a brother."

My aunt's lips quivered. "You think if we'd had a boy, we'd have given you girls less?"

"Not Father," Ruchel answered. "He adores being surrounded by women. You, Mother, I'm not so sure about ..."

"Ptooey! Get away with you!" My aunt shook a celery stalk at my cousin, who snatched it and chomped down with a loud crunch.

"Dev grew up poor, like Avram and me," Mama said when we all stopped laughing, "but she's going to college too." Her eyes glistened like the fat globules on the surface of the soup.

"That's why her education means more than mine." Ruchel sought, and got, an approving look from my mother. "She's the kind of role model the students I'll be teaching need." Inspired, she waved the celery stalk at me. "Can I bring you to school for show-and-tell?"

"You're going to teach high school. Isn't that too old for show-and-tell?"

"The four of us show and tell every Sunday," Yetta said. "You're never too old to learn."

"You can show and tell me all you want," Ruchel teased. "I'll never learn how to cook."

My aunt shrugged. "These days, who needs to, when you buy ready-to-eat from the store?"

"I wish I could," my mother said, "but Avram worries the food isn't kosher."

"He wants you busy at the stove so you don't have time to go on more protest marches." Ruchel sounded certain, but Mama wasn't ready to admit she was right.

"When I'm a scientist," I told them, "I'll invent a way to make store-bought kosher foods. Saving women from death by cooking would spare more lives than finding a cure for cancer."

"I don't want to speak bad on your idea, mamele, but nothing you invent could ever be as good as your mother's honey-nut cake." Tante Yetta raised her eyes to the ceiling in praise.

"Or your aunt's noodle kugel." Mama grinned.

For the first time in my memory, my aunt and mother exchanged a look of pure affection.

Mama sliced the two end pieces from a loaf of bread and handed one to Yetta. "I didn't resent my brother growing up, but I hated you for being rich. I assumed you were spoiled."

"I probably was, but not as much as the children of the other merchants. My mother was strict. She made sure I learned how to cook and run a household. My father pampered me, but he taught me it was important to care about those who didn't have as much as we did."

"You were poor when you first came here, Yetta. My brother struggled to earn money."

I felt like I was eavesdropping on a private conversation between my mother and my aunt, but I wondered if part of them wanted me and Ruchel to overhear them. Each word was a gift.

"For me, it was an adventure," Yetta said, "figuring out how to make a small potato fill a big belly. But when you're busy taking care of others, you don't worry so much about yourself."

"That's why women handle adversity better than men," my mother said. "We don't have time to feel sorry for ourselves."

"Emes, that's true." Yetta bit into a noodle to see if it was done. "Now I got plenty. It feels good I should do for those who have less." She drained the pot and stared into the sink before continuing. "I always wanted to do more for you Rivka, but you wouldn't take nothing from me. I didn't know if it was because I was rich, or because you were being loyal to Avram."

My mother thought this over for a while. "Probably both."

"It must be hard." My aunt beat the eggs for the kugel. "You love your brother and you love your husband, but for sholem bayess, it's right you should put Avram first."

Mama slowly stirred the soup. "All these years, I was wrong about you. I'm sorry."

Tante Yetta walked to the stove, tasted the soup, and dipped a spoonful for my mother to try. After Mama sipped and nodded, my aunt said, "Why apologize for yesterday's tsuris when God gives us such glik today? We got two smart daughters what will change the world."

A sigh of contentment passed between the two women. I was momentarily satisfied too. Their late-life closeness was another unintended but good consequence of my leaving home.

When school resumed that fall, I applied to Hunter College. Ruchel was attending Barnard and Onkel Gershon offered to pay my tuition there, but I didn't feel comfortable accepting that much money from him. Hunter was part of the city's university system and it was free. He could pay my lab fees and continue to cover my living expenses and that was the berries enough for me.

Hunter had high standards and I worried about being admitted, but the guidance counsellor reassured me I was a shoo-in. Ruchel said so too, and I trusted her judgment. My scatterbrained cousin was smarter than she appeared, and aced most of her classes. Science was a struggle only because it didn't interest her. On the other hand, economics came easily to her because it was important to women's rights. Ruchel had inherited Gershon's financial acumen (one of my favourite new vocabulary words) and planned to teach girls how to start their own businesses.

The only stumbling block was that the application form required a parental signature. My father had, if anything, grown stronger in his opposition. My refusal to marry Bernie was part of the reason, but he'd thrown an ing-bing about my going to college long before then. Late night discussions with my cousin hadn't helped me figure out why he was against the idea, but after Mama and Tante Yetta reconciled, I had an inkling. Papa was ashamed of being poor. It was bad enough that he'd been bested by Gershon, then lost his chance at respectability through his son becoming a rabbi. For his daughter to show him up would be the ultimate shanda.

"I'll sign the application as your guardian," my uncle said.

"You're already doing enough," I told him. "Suppose you got arrested for forgery?"

"She's right, Father," Ruchel said. "How would you pay her bills from behind bars?"

"My practical daughter. Maybe it's my ability to pay your bills that has you worried?"

"I could forge his name myself," I suggested. "So many immigrant parents have illegible signatures, if they can write at all. Who's to know the difference?"

My mother put the kibosh on that idea. "I'll forge Avram's signature. Better that I get into trouble than you if the school finds out. You can say you didn't know I did it."

Tante Yetta turned to Mama. "Rivka, why can't you sign it with your own name? You're Dev's parent too. Where does it say on the form that it has to be her father?".

Ruchel whooped with glee. "We spend every Sunday talking about women's rights and all of us, except my mother, fell into the trap of assuming it had to be a man."

Tante Yetta found a pen among the jumble of books and papers on the kitchen table. "Go mamele." She shooed me toward the desk in Ruchel's bedroom. "Make us all kvell with pride."

I worked on the application the following Sunday, pausing to listen to the talk in the next room. I grew wistful, thinking it might not be so bad to spend my life in the kitchen with women. I even got grummy missing Leah. Then I re-read the college catalogue, including the part about the new science lab, and got more excited than ever about having a life that was different from theirs.

"Ta da!" I twirled around the kitchen, waving the completed form above my head. Tante Yetta cleared a spot and wiped the table with her apron. We all sat down as my mother made a ceremony of signing her name.

"I should have brought something special for us to celebrate," my aunt said.

"I did." My mother reached deep into her shopping bag and brought out the ornate silver candlesticks I'd long ago seen buried in the closet beneath her braids and Shmuel's payess. Tante Yetta gasped when my mother set them on the table. Tears streamed down Mama's face. Baffled, Ruchel and I looked at each other, and then at our mothers as they embraced.

"They were a wedding gift from Yetta," my mother explained. "I never used them. Only now, since I've come to love your aunt, can I not only accept them, but pass them down to you."

"What about your mother's brass candlesticks?" I asked. They were the ones Mama used every Shabbas and were my only connection to the grandmother left behind in Lemberg.

"You'll get those too someday. They'll be your old heritage; these will be your new ones. It's up to you to decide which pair to use."

It wasn't Shabbas but we put a fresh pair of candles in the gleaming holders and said the Shehecheyanu. "Thank you God for giving us life, sustaining us, and enabling us to reach this season of celebration." The prayer is traditionally chanted on the first night of a holiday.

"Tonight is its own kind of first," my mother said as the four of us held hands and stared into the flames. "Dev will be the first woman in the Levinson family to go to college."

"I have to be accepted before you can say that." I was still a little worried.

"And this is the first time the candlesticks are being used." Tante Yetta beamed.

"There's no longer any question that I accept your gift," my mother said to her.

"Or that I accept yours," I said to my mother.

That night, after the women had left and Ruchel was asleep, I gazed at my candlesticks. I considered giving them to Leah to heal our friendship. Once she married, she'd make Shabbas dinners fancy enough to justify their use. Then I decided to keep them. They told the history of a generation of women and I would be adding to that story. I'd always wanted an orchid and I didn't need marriage to make my own Shabbas dinner every week. I could light the candles, even cook, for the friends and family members who accepted me. Maybe someday my father would accept my decisions, but whether or not he did, I would learn to accept myself and light up the world.

part eighteen
Sam, 1922-1925
chapter 48

Gavin, the newest employee in the carpentry workshop where Sam taught shell-shocked veterans, threw his jig and hammer across the room. "I'm pure scunnurt mitering this fucking butt joint!"

Sam calmly handed the hammer back to Gavin. "Outside with you, then, and go pound nails in the blooter board."

"Are you gowk, man, sending him to skelp nails in this weather? It's peltin doon not even fit for a fannybawbag." Tavis threw down his tools too, followed by Brody and Eilig.

Sam looked through the open door at the sheeting rain, sympathetic to their frustration. For six years, he'd been teaching these damaged men to make furniture for young families eager to start households now that the war was over. They built beds and tables for people who took for granted the kinds of normal lives his fragile crew could never hope to have themselves.

"The fucking pine boards leave splinters in my blighty fingers," Gavin whined. "When can I get my hands on some braw oak?" The men were impatient to work with oak, but Sam started them on pine. Mistakes mattered less on cheaper wood, and even these were costly. All the lumber was imported from England because the Orkney Islands, where Sam had stayed after the war, had few trees of their own. The braying winds that swept across fertile fields, dense with ripening grains and grazing sheep, made it impossible for anything to grow taller than a child.

Ian piped up next. "Haud yer wheesht, silly twally. Your balls will freeze in hell before Mr. Lord lets you make an oak bookcase for some minted dobber. We're lucky to make chairs for poor numpties to park their arses on." Sam smiled at the colourful language his men used to show their envy for the rich. Dev would have loved it. Class resentment here was the same as in America.

Gavin pouted and sucked his thumb. Like toddlers after a tumble, his battle-scarred men needed a cuddle from their mums, but made do getting tight at the pub every night and pitching tantrums by day. The rhythmic sound of sawing often smoothed their rough edges, and while hammering sometimes jarred them, like bullets flying over the trenches, it could also calm them. Sam would send them outside to pound nails into what they soon called the "blooter" or "drunk" board. For this he sacrificed a piece of hard oak each week, which absorbed their rages better than the squishy pine. They'd whack at it and come inside ready to pick up their tools and go back to work, until a day or two later, when they would detonate again and repeat the cycle.

That's not how the furniture workshop was supposed to function. Lord Cameron, the philanthropist who created it, wanted to give traumatized soldiers a place to heal before sending them back into society, becalmed and employable. Since the treeless Orkneys had no tradition of woodworking, it would be a new industry for the war weary islands as well as a fresh start for its shattered vets. Sam heard about the workshop from Hamble Weir, who he'd run into at the docks a year after he met up with Mikovski at Scapa Flow. Hamble had escaped the Spanish flu and spent the rest of the war helping U.S. ships navigate the mine-infested waters en route to Europe.

"Wish I'd been there with you to see the sinking of the German fleet," Hamble told Sam. "It would have warmed me chilblains better than a hot toddy to see the *Friedrich der Grosse* go down. She was the flagship of the Jutland Fleet that attacked us early in the war." Hamble's story of the men in the Lutzow's boiler room being burned alive continued to haunt Sam, especially on days when he wandered the beach questioning why he'd been spared in the schoolhouse fire.

Sam shook his head, remembering the unsuspecting German sailors scrambling for their lives as one by one the German fleet sank under the assault upon itself. "I still can't fathom why commanders would sacrifice their own crew rather than turning their ships over to the British."

Hamble didn't think it was strange. "Power goes to men's heads. Mikovski wasn't above sacrificing American boys to prove his superiority. I always wondered if you'd grow the guts to stand up to him." He chuckled. "Tomasio wasn't afraid to scuttle the bastard by mocking him."

Sam laughed ruefully. Hearing Tomasio's name, he felt obligated to confess how he'd saved Mikovski while being powerless to rescue his friend. It was the first time he'd spoken of the death and was afraid he'd choke on the words, but his lungs felt clearer than they had since getting the Spanish flu. Jews confessed only once a year, on Yom Kippur, whereas Catholics admitted their sins weekly. Their way was better, Sam decided. Holding onto guilt was suffocating.

"The wrong man died," Hamble said, launching a torpedo of spit. "Tomasio was the hero. He joked rings around his enemies. Mikovski confused bullying with bravery. He was useless."

Sam disagreed, but kept quiet. Mikovski, for all his flaws as a human being, was a good teacher. He made men angry enough to spite him by surviving. Only after the war did he find himself useless. Sam felt useless too. As if reading his thoughts, that's when Hamble told Sam about the carpentry workshop. In the same way that Hamble had escorted ships through mined oceans, the Veterans' Service had enlisted him to accompany men to woodworking training before they too blew up. Hearing that Sam spent the final months of the war building coffins, Hamble suggested he apply for a job with the program. There was an opening for a specialist in joinery.

Sam's carpentry skills were rudimentary, but with mail-order manuals, he taught himself the different kinds of joins: mitered butt, tongue and groove. It was like learning sailors' knots in boot camp. His hands, practiced at twisting yarn and tying fringes on the tallit he'd discarded eight years ago, were equally agile cutting wood. He built himself a dresser, working Saturdays as well as weekdays, letting the pleasure of executing half-blind and sliding dovetail joints over-ride the guilt that still tugged him about working on Shabbas. When the dresser was finished, he got the job and felt it was a small step forward. He quickly learned, however, that rather than getting on with their lives, the men he taught were as locked in place as the joins they fastened.

There was one exception, Laird, who claimed that finding religion had helped him get better. Others called the Church havering hogwash, their faith destroyed by the smell of feet rotting in flooded trenches while cannons boomed overhead. Laird, whose upbringing was least dogmatic, discovered solace in simple rituals. "My parents were take-it-or-leave it Christians," he told Sam. "As a wee bugger and after the war, I left it. But coming here, I thought I'd give it another try."

Sam asked Laird what made him change his mind.

"I dunno. Sniffing glue?" He inhaled the drawer he'd just cut. "Or maybe it was the smell of clean wood when the router sliced through it." Laird smiled. "Are you a church man?"

Like everyone else Sam had met since the war, Laird had assumed he was Christian. It was easy to pass as one. Away from the ship, his skin had turned pale again and his red hair was sun bleached. Sam wore it long to hide the strawberry mark. With no mirror in his cottage, he barely thought of it. Only when he prowled the beach, and the relentless Orkney wind blew his hair back straight as a board, did Sam instinctively hold his hand below his right ear to cover up the stain.

"My parents were non-denominational," Sam told Laird, the succinct answer he usually gave, but Laird's interest prompted him to say more. What he said was technically true, if not forthright. "My father was strict, though, quick to label unorthodox thoughts and behaviours as sinful. He judged me and others as unworthy if we weren't devoted to extolling the Almighty."

"Not my old man," said Laird. "He liked to say, 'We're all Jock Tamson's bairns,' by which he meant no one is better than anyone else. Genesis says that God created man in His own image. If you believe in our Lord's beauty and goodness, you believe it to be true of all men."

"There is neither Jew nor Greek, there is neither slave nor free, there is neither male nor female; for you are all one in Christ Jesus," Sam responded.

Laird smiled. "Galatians. Your father taught you at least one important truth."

It was actually Tomasio who'd taught Sam the New Testament quote to convince him that not all Christians were Jew haters. "Unlike Mikovski," his friend had added, "who hates everyone, even other Catholics. Although he'd torture you worse if he knew he was being bested by a Jew." Sam agreed.

"Maybe someday you'll give religion another try, like me," Laird said, admiring the joins on the finished drawer. "You might find a way back to your faith that works for you."

"Not likely," Sam said. "My father spoiled it for me for good." He watched Laird select a fresh board. "Your father gave you a choice. That's why you were able to change your mind."

Laird looked at two veterans skelping nails in the nearly full blooter board. "Be thankful you're not radge-brained like them. Whatever you lost during the war, it wasn't your marbles." He measured twice before cutting the wood. "Religion isn't as precise as carpentry, but just like a drawer gives you a place to keep your things, religion gives you a box to store your thoughts."

"You pull out what you need, when you need it?" Sam asked.

Laird sanded the edges. "That's the ticket."

"What do you do when whatever you pulled out gets dirty?"

Laird shrugged. "You wash it and put it back until you need it again."

In the three years since Laird had left the workshop, he occasionally wrote to Sam. He soon got a job with a high-end woodworking firm in London, and then met a nurse who shared his beliefs. After they got married, Laird filled their house with the furniture he built. His faith made him happy and secure, but he never proselytized. Sam sometimes regretted that he hadn't been more honest with Laird about his own religious upbringing. At the time, he thought it was his instinct for self-protection. Later he wondered if he was trying to protect Judaism itself. Although Jews had lived in Scotland since the Middle Ages, no one on the islands appeared to have known one. Sam didn't want them to think all Jews were as rigid as his father. Just because he no longer called himself Jewish didn't mean he was willing to cast a bad light on his people.

In a way, it was too bad there were no Jews among the worst-off survivors of the war. Hebrews saw suffering as a privilege God had chosen for them. Pain was their goad to improve the world, even if they never expected to succeed. Maybe Sam had inadvertently transferred his own low expectations to his men. Teaching them to work with their hands muted their demons, but he wasn't taking care of their souls. Aboard ship, when his mates were facing death, the facts and knots Sam taught them bolstered their confidence in their chances of survival. Here, trying to help men who'd survived the horrors of war, he'd failed to make them believe they weren't as good as dead already. How could he help others heal when his own spiritual drawer was empty?

chapter 49

Ian, his stubbled face ashen, knocked on Sam's door an hour before the workshop opened one Wednesday morning. Outside it was even more blustery than usual and bullets of rain pelted the windows of Sam's drafty cottage.

"Mr. Lord, it's Gavin."

Ian tried and failed to light a cigarette. Sam's steady hands lit it for him.

"Gowk numpty got blootered last night and fell and skelped his head on a rock down by the beach," Ian said after taking a deep drag. Sam was surprised to see his shoulders shake with silent sobs. The men were bound together, but never dared show feelings toward one another besides anger and scorn.

Sam threw on his old Navy peacoat and raced outside, heading toward the water. Ian stopped him. "Too late, sir. He'd already bled to death by the time the beachcombers found him, about an hour ago. One of 'em knew me and Gavin shared a room so he came and got me."

"Do the others know?" Sam asked, wishing he too smoked so he could suck the heavy fog of loss into his lungs and let it permeate his body. Better thick air than emptiness.

"I thought it best if you told them," Ian answered. "Gavin ain't got no family so it'll just be us dobbers at the funeral. Maybe you could say a few words? It'd be more fitting than some man of the cloth who didn't know him talking mince over his corpse."

Sam had already started on Gavin's coffin when the others wandered in. He used his best oak and continued working when the men, curious but wary about what he was doing, gathered around awaiting an explanation. He kept his voice steady when he told them, relieved that his forced sense of calm nevertheless averted an eruption from the men, at least for the moment.

They watched Sam measure three times before he cut each board. "Looks like Gavin will own a piece of our furniture after all," snarled Brody, "and the twally's getting it for free too."

"He paid a high price," Sam said. "I thought I was done making coffins when the war ended. I don't intend to sell or give away any more after this one. If I can't stop you from getting drunk, then have the good sense not to walk home alone. Find yourselves a buddy." The men surveyed one another warily until their eyes lit on the person they felt least uncomfortable with. Sam wondered if a few might actually make an attempt at friendship.

Three days later he wrote to Laird, telling him about Gavin's death and the eulogy he'd delivered as the men stood, half of them drunk, the rest cold sober, listening in silence:

I wish you'd been here to speak instead of me. It was hard to say something meaningful about a life so wasted. I told the men, "Don't let others define who you are. You're not the war's trash to be thrown away. The workshop is a way station, a temporary port. Take what you've learned and leave. If Gavin's tragic end saves your lives, he won't have died in vain." I felt like a hypocrite, trying to inspire them to be better than what I knew I was. Then it hit me that I could leave too. I'm still not sure what I learned here, but I have to trust that the lesson will become clear on the long voyage home or soon after I arrive.

A week after mailing the letter, Sam visited the Stone of Destiny, a Scottish treasure taken by the British six hundred years ago and now in Westminster Abbey. It was a religious relic, said to be the pillar where Jacob, fleeing the wrath of his brother Esau, had prayed for God's help to return safely. Many years later, God had fulfilled His promise. Sam, like Jacob, had sojourned for a long time, far from home. He'd accumulated a pile of dirty laundry. It was time to wash it, put it back in the drawer he'd painstakingly built, and find his way home to America.

part nineteen

Dev, 1922

chapter 50

"Let's have a Chanukah party," Ruchel announced in early December. "We'll invite my parents and your mother to thank them for their help. Also Zipporah, Jonah, and the baby. My poor sister never gets out these days." She hesitated before asking, "Do you think your father would come?"

"You're tooting the wrong ringer if you think I know." Usually I avoided slang around Ruchel, ever since she said it made me sound like a ninny. The last thing I wanted to do was aggravate her. Now, however, I was trying to sound casual, hoping to avoid the black hole I fell into whenever Papa crossed my mind. It didn't work, but I had an idea. Maybe doing something domestic, like frying potato latkes and jelly donuts, would convince him I was redeemable. He might come out of curiosity.

"We've never boiled an egg between us," I said, looking around the dirty kitchen. "How are we going to cook a holiday meal for all those people?"

"You're the scientist. Read the recipes in the paper and experiment." Ruchel winked. "Besides, I see your fingers twitching to chop vegetables and massage the dough when we watch our mothers cook." My secret was out and Ruchel didn't condemn me for it.

We posed the idea to Mama and my aunt that Sunday. "Who cooks from recipes?" Tante Yetta scoffed. "Rivka and I will make the food. You set the table. I'll bring clean napkins." My aunt was already straightening the kitchen in anticipation of the dinner that was two weeks away.

Ruchel stopped her. "You're missing the point. We want to do it ourselves to thank you." Then she said conspiratorially, "Think how surprised Father will be to eat a meal prepared by his younger daughter. Even my big sister's jaws will drop." She and my aunt giggled.

My mother and I looked up from our private thoughts. She shook her head and answered the unspoken question. "I don't think he'll come," she said, "but I'll ask him if you want me to." I lifted my chin in response, not knowing whether that signalled yes or was a gesture of defiance.

"Of course Avram will come." My aunt's optimistic voice carried the same assurance as her busy hands. "A family gathering during the holidays is the best time to make up." Or create a disaster, I thought. Mama's puckered mouth told me she harboured a similar worry.

Ruchel and I divided the chores, the same way women at her meetings each volunteered to do what she was best at. The problem was that neither of us was good at anything we needed for the party. So we decided who was least worst. Ruchel was in charge of cleaning. Her solution was to throw everything in drawers, which only made it harder than usual to find things.

Shopping and cooking fell to me, so I did a few trial runs. The first time I grated potatoes, I scraped my fingers until blood ran into the batter. I would have asked Leah if there was a better way to do it, but the timing wasn't right. We'd repaired our rift again, and as often happens after a fight, we were closer than ever for a while. For reasons I didn't understand though, she'd been distant lately. It might have been the feminist rhetoric I spouted, courtesy of Ruchel. Maybe Leah thought I was condemning her choices the same way I believed she was critical of mine.

In the end, I didn't need my friend's help. On the fourth try, I'd deduced the two variables critical to making perfect latkes: enough bread crumbs to hold the batter together and waiting to flip them until their edges were just past medium brown. Ruchel was so impressed by how good they looked and tasted that she agreed to peel apples so I could cook applesauce to go with them.

The fried jelly donuts were trickier. They disintegrated into a gooey mess. Our mothers paid us a surprise mid-week visit the evening I was trying to scrape the pot clean. "Nu, mamele," Tante Yetta asked, "maybe you'll change your mind and let me or Rivka make the donuts?"

"No." I threw the steel wool in the trash and shoved the sticky pot under the sink. "I'm going to get store bought." Since I'd never made them before, my father wouldn't know the difference between mine and the baker's. That is, if my father came. My mother hadn't said.

"Mama," I asked, inspired by my own subterfuge. "How come you never bought ready-to-eat food and pretended to Papa that you made it yourself?"

"After all these years, your father knows my cooking from store-bought." I told her that was too bad. "It would be worse if he didn't," Mama said. She and Yetta smiled at each other.

A light snow was falling the night of the Chanukah party. Ruchel's family lived a few blocks away and wouldn't have far to walk. I'd grown up in a poorer section of the Lower East Side, distant in more ways than one. The trip would be longer and colder for my parents.

My aunt and uncle arrived first, bringing a gold menorah and hand-dipped candles. My cousin forced her mother to sit in the dining room so she wouldn't meddle in the kitchen, although she still managed to "help" by substituting an ironed, lace-trimmed tablecloth for the wrinkled one Ruchel dug out of our closet. Zipporah and Jonah came next, apologizing that a last-minute diaper change had made them late. Baby Yitzak took after his father. He was bald and his skin was so pale you could see the tiny blood vessels underneath, but he had a happy disposition. My aunt, busy kvelling over her grandson, was finally distracted from what I was doing in the kitchen.

Ten minutes later, I heard footsteps on the stairs. I tried to count the number of people but the sizzling of latkes in the frying pan was too loud. Yetta opened the door and she and my mother said hello like long-lost sisters. I listened as the women made a fuss over the baby.

"Avram, it's good to see you," I heard Yetta say. "Give me your coat, I should hang it in the closet." The clamour of my thumping heart over-powered the sound of the bubbling oil. I was happy Papa had come, but scared the evening would fall apart, like my first batch of latkes.

There was silence as my parents took off their things, then my aunt exclaimed "Oy vey!" as the papers and boxes Ruchel had crammed on the closet shelf came tumbling down. The noise made the baby cry, but it broke the tension. Even Papa laughed as he helped Yetta pick up the fallen things. Audible greetings followed, except between my father and Onkel Gershon. I hoped they at least nodded at each other. I rearranged the latkes, now draining on the dishtowel, too nervous to go out and see for myself. At last, taking a deep breath, I walked into the living room, spatula in hand, as my father and mother settled on the couch. "Hello, Papa," I said, "Happy Chanukah."

He ran his finger inside his shirt collar, cleared his throat, and wished me the same. "It smells good. Your mother tells me you've taken up cooking."

"Just Chanukah specialities so far, but I'm an expert on them." I excused myself to fetch the food and Ruchel ushered everyone to the table.

There was an awkward moment when it wasn't clear who should light the candles in the menorah and say the Chanukah blessings. This was traditionally done by a woman, but which of the five of us would have the honour? My aunt handed a match to me and the matchbox to Ruchel.

"Together," she commanded, so that's what my cousin and I did.

While Yitzak slept, nestled in a pile of pillows next to the sideboard, the rest of us ate and talked. The latkes were the best batch ever and my father sang their praises. Ruchel joked that she'd not only peeled apples for the applesauce, but had added honey, sprinkled in cinnamon, and stirred the pot a couple of times.

"Who knew my sister could cook?" Zipporah glowed as I'd never seen her before. She and Jonah occasionally gazed at the baby, then smiled at each other. At one point, they grasped hands under the table, a most unorthodox public display of affection. Onkel Gershon looked like a satisfied patriarch presiding over his family, while Yetta beamed like a benevolent queen on her throne. Only my father appeared stiff, avoiding looking at my uncle across the table, while my mother looked warily between her husband and her brother. Everyone ate heartily, except Mama and me. Still, sholem bayess prevailed. My eyes sought Ruchel's to congratulate ourselves on the party's success. I brought out the donuts, arrayed on a thick, hand-painted china platter.

"Good!" my father pronounced, eyebrows raised that I'd mastered something so difficult. He handed me his plate for another.

"I'm glad you like them Papa." A current passed between me, Ruchel, and our mothers.

"Did you hear Annie Oakley set the woman's record in marksmanship?" my cousin asked, before he could inquire how I'd made the dessert. "She broke ten clay targets in a row."

"Sounds like the kind of woman we need on our side the next time this country goes to war," said Onkel Gershon, helping himself to another donut.

"Better a woman should fill holes with jelly than shoot holes in barn doors." My father took a third donut. My uncle did too. And so it went until Gershon grabbed the last one.

"What do you think of Hungary joining the League of Nations?" I asked, hoping that talk of their shared homeland would unite the two men. "We're reading about it in social studies."

"It's too soon after the Empire split up," said my father. "I don't trust them."

"The Hungarians were never as bad as the Austrians," Tante Yetta said. "Besides, people can change for the better, even in Lemberg."

"The whole world is changing," said Onkel Gershon. "Who would have thought President Harding would sign a resolution two months ago to establish a Jewish homeland in Palestine?"

"Signing something is not the same as making it happen," my father said, addressing my uncle directly for the first time that evening. I thought of Mama signing my college application.

"Women can vote now that the Nineteenth Amendment was signed into law." Ruchel rose slightly in her seat. I gently tapped the table to signal her to pipe down, but she ignored me. "And our Dev is going to change the world by discovering a cure for cancer."

"Not unless she goes to college, and I can't afford that."

"Hunter doesn't charge tuition, Uncle Avram." Ruchel was standing now.

"She still has to pay for books and whatever else those goniffs charge the students."

Ruchel agreed. "She'll have to pay lab fees. Transportation. Living costs. But it won't be a problem because my father is going to pay for it all." Ruchel sat down in triumph. Papa looked at me. I nodded to show it was true, but I wished Ruchel could take it back. The lone potato latke I'd eaten backed up my digestive tract. I wanted to fry Ruchel in hot oil.

Tante Yetta started clearing the table, but the clanking silverware heightened the uneasy silence creeping around the table, so she stopped. We listened to the baby's rhythmic snore. I hoped it would calm things down, but Papa's breathing quickened until he rose and lifted the empty donut platter above his head. Jonah draped a protective arm around his father-in-law's shoulder.

"Our forefathers wrote that stealing the love of children from their parents is as bad as sacrificing our offspring to Molech." Again, my father spoke straight to Onkel Gershon.

My uncle snorted. "Talmud says no such thing, Avram. You always were a lousy scholar."

Papa slammed the plate on the table, sending a small chip flying toward my uncle. Yetta hugged the platter to her breast, surreptitiously examining the underside for more chinks. Ruchel gently pulled it from her mother's grasp and laid a steady hand on Yetta's shaking one.

My father's chair toppled as he pushed back from the table. Boxes thudded to the floor again while he got his coat, and the wine in our glasses sloshed as the door slammed. Mama trembled, her face whiter than the linen tablecloth. Without a word, she rose and followed him out.

I walked to the front window and watched them trudge through the now heavy snow. Papa strode into the blowing wind, his head held high. Mama, eyes cast down, was a few paces behind. Reflected in the window, behind me, the three generations of the Mendel family sat silently around the table. Jonah leaned over Zipporah as she soothed the baby, startled awake by the noise. Gershon and Ruchel stood on either side of Yetta. Above her head, they exchanged the relieved look of a father and daughter who had managed to reconcile.

I was furious that Ruchel's big mouth had ruined that possibility for me. Of course, Papa would have found out eventually that my uncle was paying for me to go to college, but he would have heard it from my mother, in private. The news would have gone down more easily than hearing it from Gershon's daughter, in Gershon's presence, with the whole family around him. Ruchel's brashness helped women gain their rights, but it didn't help families set things right. I wanted to hurl every slang epithet in Mencken's book, and then some, at her.

"Come mamele, sit with us," my aunt urged. "I'll wash the dishes."

"It's okay, Tante Yetta, I'll do it. Cleaning the apparatus is part of being a scientist too." I stared out the window until my parents turned the corner. Then, turning back toward the happy Mendels seated around the table, I picked up the empty donut platter and carried it to the kitchen.

chapter 51

I had to tell someone how my family was going from bad to worse. I considered calling Bernie, who no longer seemed to begrudge my refusal to marry him and might help me understand my father better. In the end, I rejected that idea. We were more than civil to each other, but things were still a bit touchy between us. Ruchel was useless too. I still itched to zotz her for blurting out what she knew would send Papa into a tizzy. I also resented how peachy her life was. Envy made me feel guilty, but I couldn't shake it. Nor did I want to. The combination of anger and self-pity was satisfying. It was childish, but technically so was I, even if I no longer lived with my parents. That left Leah. She'd been standoffish lately, but I hoped she'd hear me out since I wasn't going to talk about Bernie or sex.

Horses and people hadn't yet turned the snow to slush when I left for her house the next morning, trudging through the same hushed streets my parents had taken the night before. Leah's mother answered the door. "Oh, Dev. I was expecting, I mean ... Come in dear, we haven't seen you in a while. Can I get you a cup of tea? A jelly donut?" A plain tin menorah sat on the table, the candles for the second night of Chanukah already wedged in place.

I declined the offer and made straight for the back room to unburden myself. As soon as Leah hugged me, it all poured out. "Shmuel's dead, my father hates me, and my mother's taken my father's side. I have no family anymore." I accepted her freshly-ironed handkerchief.

"Your brother's gone," Leah commiserated, "but your mother will be back on Sunday to cook for you and Ruchel, and your father will come around eventually."

I sniffled. "No, he won't. Papa's angry because my uncle is paying for me to go to college. Ruchel spilled the beans and now Papa thinks I'm in cahoots with his enemy." My misery was genuine, yet I couldn't help admiring my woebegone performance, good enough to rival Theda Bara. I waited for another hug and a sympathetic tsk, tsk from Leah.

Instead, she glanced at the clock on her dresser. "I wouldn't be surprised if your mother feels bad and is on her way to see you right now," she said. Her ticking clock matched the sound of pacing coming from the front room. Something hinky was going on. The doorbell rang.

"Good morning, dear," I heard Leah's mother say when she opened the door. The voice that answered was Bernie's. "Here's the radio. Not your usual engagement gift, but my father gave us his most expensive model." My jaw dropped and this time I wasn't performing.

"It's lovely," Leah's mother said. "You can put it on the credenza when you two find an apartment." There was muffled talking whose gist I had no trouble filling in. "Leah, dear, come see what Bernie brought."

I glowered at Leah. Tears leaked from her eyes. "I didn't know how to tell you, Dev. The last thing I ... we ... wanted was to hurt you. Even though it's not as if ..." Leah gave up.

"As if *I* wanted to marry him." I finished the thought, the same way Leah and I had once completed each other's sentences as children. She nodded. Now I understood why Leah had grown distant again the last few weeks.

Over the thudding of my heart, I heard Bernie tell her mother, "My father has to work on inventory, so my folks wondered if we could come to dinner an hour later tonight." He stopped as Leah and I entered the room. "Fine," said Leah's mother. "Or wait until tomorrow. Chanukah lasts eight days, plenty of time for our families to celebrate together."

Leah started to move toward Bernie, but stopped midway. My eyes drilled into him until he looked down at the worn carpet. I returned to the back room, waiting for Leah to say goodbye to her fiancé and then talk, really talk, to me.

"How soon after I turned him down did Bernie turn to you?" I put it to Leah bluntly.

"I don't remember, Dev. Does it matter?"

It shouldn't have, but in my anger at the world's unfairness, I wanted to grill her until she twisted and curled in on herself like a skewered shrimp roasting over an open flame. Leah, eager to tell me whatever I needed to hear to forgive her, alternated between apology and ecstasy.

"Bernie gave another D'var Torah at Friday night services, maybe two months ago, and at the one afterwards, my bubbe congratulated him. Bernie and my grandmother were still talking when I brought her some tea and cake, and he asked me what I thought of his sermon."

I imagined Bernie lecturing the congregation to get with the times. "What did you say?"

"That his talk was interesting, something like that."

"Come on Leah, Bernie's ideas are too modern for you."

Leah looked dreamy. "To tell the truth, I was staring more than listening when he spoke."

I snorted. "Leah, I am shocked at you. What on earth was going through your mind?"

She blushed. "It doesn't matter if Bernie's ideas are different than what I once believed. He's my rabbi, and soon he'll be my husband, and it's my place to follow him."

Nothing modern in that, I thought.

"We do agree our household will be traditional. We both want children, God willing." Leah giggled. "We argue over who we want the children to look like. I say him, and he says me."

I'd heard enough. Seeing Yitzak last night had made me marvel about the miracle of procreation, but it hadn't made me yearn for a baby of my own. So why did hearing Leah burble about the children she would have make me jealous? And why did her swooning over Bernie make me want to bust up their courtship? Maybe I was just lonely at the moment, afraid love would always elude me and sad that I'd never have or make a family as close as the Mendels. Worse, maybe I was scared that a career as a scientist would feed my brain but starve my heart.

While I put on my coat, Leah grabbed my hat and scarf to stop me from leaving. She searched for something to say to prove she was still my friend, and concerned with my happiness. "Your father will get over your not marrying Bernie now that he's engaged to someone else."

"You know Papa better than that. Bernie marrying my best friend makes it worse. To come close and miss at the very end is like Shmuel almost becoming a rabbi, and then dying."

"That's not fair, Dev. Your father substituted Bernie for his dream of Shmuel becoming ordained. Why can't he substitute you for his dream of a child succeeding in America?"

"Because that never was my father's dream. He wanted a rabbi, not a success story."

"Nonsense. It's the dream of every immigrant. Bernie's been assigned a shul in the Bronx filled with people moving up from the Lower East Side. He'll be an example for them."

"Bernie's a Yankees fan," I said, eager to divert Leah from what my father wanted and pinprick her bubble. "I'm sure living in the Bronx will make him happy." The Yankees were building a new stadium and I hoped Bernie and Leah would live right near it, under the elevated train that ran past. The vibration would keep them up at night and they'd be too tired and grummy to make babies. Or they'd make so many, Leah would come to hate them.

"Bernie likes baseball?" Leah looked like the odd child out in a schoolyard threesome, excluded from the secrets I shared with Bernie. I wondered what else she didn't know about him, like his not-quite-kosher imitation of immigrants butchering English. Or his love of root beer.

"We both hope you'll give us your blessing." Leah, sounding meek now, handed me my hat. I jammed it on my head and flung my scarf around my neck.

"Your bubbe will dance at the wedding. There are more appliances where the radio came from. You two have everything you need. Why do you care about my blessing?"

"Because I still need a best friend and Bernie needs a sister. We're both only children and want you to be like an aunt to ours. Besides, we're as excited about your future as we are about ours. Bernie and I expect to kvell with pride someday when you make a great discovery."

I was tempted to retort that I was an only child too, but I wouldn't take vicarious pleasure in their becoming parents. Nor did I believe they'd take pride in my achievements. Then I saw Leah's pleading eyes. I used to think I needed her absolution for my sins, but now I wondered if Leah counted on my approbation more than I depended hers.

Squeezing Leah's hands, I wished her and Bernie a lifetime of sholem bayess and said she'd make a perfect rabbi's wife. I didn't say she might someday have doubts about her dream-come-true marriage. Bernie was what she'd always wanted, but she was his second choice. Then again, I'd have settled for being second best in Papa's eyes. Instead, he chose not to see me at all.

chapter 52

Roiling over Bernie's and Leah's engagement, I turned for distraction to my classes, especially advanced physiology lab. We were studying platelets, small clear discs without a nucleus that helped to repair connective tissue. I felt as if I too lacked a centre, and wanted desperately to be reattached to my family. That's when I thought of my aunt's uncanny ability to sympathize with Mama's need to find a balance between her brother and her husband. Maybe Tante Yetta could teach me how to simmer instead of boil, the same way she knew when to do what in the kitchen.

"I'm no scholar," my aunt said when I confessed reluctance to give Leah and Bernie my blessing. "So I never understood God's refusal to forgive until the third or fourth generation. I say the sooner you let bygones be gone, the sooner you sleep better."

"But they have each other, Tante Yetta. I lost another brother and my best friend."

"I'm not saying it shouldn't hurt. Only that it will hurt less if you don't hold it against them."

"Do you think when I'm older I'll find a new best friend, like you and Mama did?"

My aunt kissed my forehead. "Don't give up on Leah yet, but you'll make new friends in college. God willing, they'll become as special to you as your mother and I are to each other."

"Sometimes I'm not sure about going to college. Look how much it's cost me already."

"Your uncle ..."

"I don't mean the money, Tante Yetta."

"I know mamele. You miss your friends. More than that, you miss your parents."

I nodded, unable to speak. When the unspent tears receded, I asked my aunt what to do.

"I'm old enough to know time helps, wise enough to know that's not a good answer for a young, impatient person. You need to talk to someone who understands your generation." She sent me home with a bag full of babka and a mind as full as an oven before sundown on Shabbas.

Forgiveness was a tall order for a kid. Most adults failed at it. My father hadn't been able to forgive Shmuel nor would he and Gershon ever forgive each other. I supposed I'd eventually absolve Ruchel for speaking the truth, but unless I cut Leah and Bernie out of my life, every encounter with them would reopen that wound. Could there be forgiveness without healing?

Maybe it was myself I needed to forgive. I still felt guilty for not keeping Shmuel home. I didn't stand behind Mama as much as she stood behind me. And now I doubted my own choices. I was putting Mama in the middle and depriving Papa of the one thing he wanted, a rabbi in the family. Was I acting selfish? Or was I meant for bigger things? If I forsook a chance to heal the whole world, and instead repaired my little family, would God forgive me?

When I got back to the apartment, I washed a plate for Yetta's cookies and cleared a space on the table. Buried under Ruchel's term paper about suffragists was *Reader's Digest*, a new magazine she liked because every issue featured a tribute to a woman. This one was about a farmer's wife. Looking for something more useful, I turned to an article on how to get ahead in life. "Common sense and a grasp of the facts are society's great equalizers," it said. I crammed two babkas in my mouth. *Reader's Digest* must be written for native-born Americans, I concluded. Immigrants and their children depended on good sense and it wasn't enough to make us equals. Then I wondered about "a grasp of the facts." That could mean education, but would college separate me from my family and friends? I closed the magazine and shoved it back under the mess.

In an effort to calm myself, I cleaned up the kitchen. I carried Ruchel's school things to her bedroom, washed and stacked the dishes, then tackled the clothes and papers strewn around the front room. That's when I came across a month-old copy of the *Jewish Daily Forward* that Tante Yetta had used to wrap a crystal candy dish she'd given us. Two years ago I'd written Bintel Briefs for advice. The editor had been wrong about my father relenting, but right to urge that I use caution in matters of the heart. Perhaps it was worth writing him again. His columns blended my aunt's old-world wisdom with an understanding of an immigrant's life in America today. If nothing else, I was more likely to get suitable advice from him than from *Reader's Digest*.

Wise Editor:
   My best friend is marrying the man I turned down, my father is angry that I want to go to college instead, and my mother is caught between my father and me. I'm in a tumult about what to do. This seems a uniquely American dilemma. In the shtetl, there were no choices. I'm not asking for help to solve the problem, but to figure out what the problem is. My biology teacher says a scientist's most important job is asking the right question. What should my question be?
   Sincerely,
   Muddled Maiden

I used part of the spending money I got from Onkel Gershon to buy the paper each day until I got my answer. Fortunately, I didn't have long to wait:

Dear Muddled Maiden:
   In the desert, Moses asked, "What will make God happy?" In the shtetl, our parents asked "What will make the community happy?" Here in America, people ask, "What will make me happy?" It is the hardest question to answer because there are no books or elders to offer advice. The land of opportunity is a country where you decide for yourself.
   The Editor

Another letter arrived soon after, this one in the mail, saying I'd not only been admitted to Hunter College but accepted into the honours program. Ruchel was there when the mail came, but I swore her to secrecy until I told our mothers and her father on Sunday. Leah and Bernie invited me over midweek, the first time we'd spoken since I heard of their engagement, so I told them next. Leah jumped up and down like we did when we got excited as children and Bernie recited a blessing. They were happier for me than I was for them, but I hoped that by the time of their wedding, my congratulations would be sincere. The only person I didn't tell, the one I most wished I could, was my father. Mama would kvell to him, but my heart ached that I couldn't tell Papa myself.

Ruchel wanted to celebrate with another party, but all I could think of was how badly the last one ended. My headstrong cousin refused to be dissuaded. "You earned this. If you won't have it here, I'll rent Walhalla Hall and invite the whole neighbourhood to show and tell." "Horsefeathers. You wouldn't." I threw a dirty dish rag at her. She threatened to dump flour and sugar on the floor until I cried uncle and agreed to the party, provided she cleaned up the house for real.

It was also Ruchel's idea to serve store-bought food, but I wanted to cook the meal myself. Only this time, rather than studying recipes in the Jewish newspaper, I went to the library to look up classic American dishes. I'd prepare them kosher, but we'd eat meatloaf instead of brisket, and spaghetti with tomato sauce, not noodle kugel. The cat's meow would be apple pie for dessert.

We scheduled the dinner for Sunday so I'd have the whole day to experiment. Despite my reassurances, Tante Yetta couldn't stop herself from coming over to help. She said Mama hoped to arrive early too. I shooed my aunt out of the kitchen and ordered her to help Ruchel straighten up. Yetta decided the windows should be washed. To everyone's surprise, especially Ruchel's, my cousin enjoyed this chore. The days were growing longer as winter came to end, and cleaning the panes let in the light, an apt metaphor for what today's women were trying to accomplish.

As I took a perfect meatloaf out of the oven and slipped in the pie, Onkel Gershon and the building's superintendent came huffing up the stairs, carrying a desk, which they plunked down under the window in the front room. The oak wood gleamed golden in the rays of the setting sun.

"You'll need a place to study besides the kitchen table," my uncle said, tipping the super. Yetta warned "Hanten avek!" and shook a finger at Ruchel, who swore to keep her hands off and her papers too. The desk was brand new, not a hand-me-down from the Mendels' apartment. I now owned a second orchid. I ran my hands over the cascading grain and smelled the beeswax polish. The drawers slid smoothly and the top one had a heart-shaped lock with a tiny gold key.

"To hide the notes about your secret discovery," my uncle teased.

I turned the key while glancing at the darkening sky, hoping to see my mother hurrying down our street. Instead I saw fathers coming home from sweat shops, met by wives and children tumbling out the doors of their crowded apartments. Whole families strolled past, buoyed by the promise of spring. I retreated to the kitchen to give the tomato sauce one last stir.

Zipporah and Jonah arrived next, with the baby, who'd begun crawling. In five minutes, he was chewing the toe of one of Ruchel's silk stockings, which he'd found under the couch. "I can't miss a thing when I clean either," Zipporah said. "Whatever Yitzak finds goes in his mouth."

"And it's getting impossible to take it away and distract him," Jonah added with pride.

Onkel Gershon bent down to pat the baby's head. "My grandson is a persistent investigator. You can hire him as a research assistant when you open your own lab, Dev. I'll put up the seed money."

The streetlights came on. It was Yetta's turn to peek out the window. She looked back at me with a small shrug and put her hand on my arm. I let her help me bring the food to the table. When we sat down, Onkel Gershon gave Jonah the honour of saying the blessings. I thought I'd have to explain what the dishes were but Tante Yetta pointed and called out their names: chopped beef, pasta with marinara sauce. I asked how she knew what everything was.

"When your uncle and I first came here," she said, "our building had immigrants from all over. As I figured out how to shop and cook in America, I showed them. Even after we moved to a better place, I went back there. In return, the women taught me the dishes they grew up with. I learned more from them than they learned from me."

My big uncle put a small piece of meatloaf in his mouth, chewed slowly, then followed it with a big forkful. "So how come you never cooked this delicious dish for me?" he asked Yetta.

"You want? I'll cook!" She smiled. "A wife's job is to make her husband happy."

That's when I heard footsteps on the stairs. I threw down my napkin and ran to open the door. My mother came in, alone. I looked behind her but she shook her head. "It's just me," she said, "and I'm going to stay for the whole meal."

I heaped her plate with spaghetti and a thick slice of meat. Half a loaf was better than none, I thought, and there was still a whole pie to go. It too had emerged perfect from the oven.

That night, too wound up to sleep, I sat at my new desk, opening and closing drawers. Issues of *Reader's Digest* were stacked in a neat pile on the table next to the couch. Despite misgivings, I picked up the latest issue. The tribute article was about Sara Josephine Baker, the public health doctor who'd invented a sanitary way to package the silver nitrate put on newborns' eyelids. As a result, infant blindness from gonorrhoea had been virtually wiped out. Could I do for grownups' hearts what she'd done for babies' eyes? Hearts were more complicated. Blood vessels clogged; muscles stopped pumping. Hearts went on the fritz when people fell in love and weren't loved back, when a parent lost a child, or a child ached for the love of a disapproving parent. Discover how to cure any one of those and I'd earn a nod from God and a Nobel prize for medicine. More important, I might discover how to make myself happy. The land of opportunity didn't mean you got everything you wanted, but most immigrants agreed it was better than what they had before.

I read the rest of the magazine, prepared to accept its advice and leave Bintel Briefs to greenhorns. I had my aunt's common sense, my uncle's grasp of facts, and my mother's resolve. It was a recipe for success. My doubts began to disappear, like vapour from a heated test tube.

Disappear, I realized, was that rare word that offered two positives: appear and reappear. Of course, the appearance of a verb didn't mean the action would happen. Shmuel was not going to reappear on the shore. I'd have to set sail myself. Not only was I the first Levinson born in this country, I was the first to run toward, rather than escape from, a way of life. America was the most valuable orchid ever and it was mine. All I had to do was reach for it.

part twenty

Sam, 1925

chapter 53

Six years later and one friend shy of the reunion they'd pledged to
have on their last night of boot camp, Sam met Ryan at Boston's
Green Dragon Tavern, the pub where a soused Paul Revere and John
Hancock were said to have plotted the American revolution. The red
and gold sign over the door promised "Hospitality for the weary trav-
eller." Sam had journeyed a long way out and back to get here, but he
was too keyed up to be tired. Through the multi-paned windows he
saw smoky amber lighting, meant to evoke to the lamps of colonial
days. Once inside, he walked past the long, dark bar and chose a quiet
table at the back.

Ryan arrived exactly a minute after Sam, at 1701 hours. Clasping
hands, they joked that Navy punctuality would dog them the rest of
their lives. Sam had proposed dinner at an Italian restaurant, in honour
of Tomasio, but Ryan thought that sounded morbid. "Besides," Ryan
said with a confidence he'd lacked before the war, "I need to get home
by six, civilian time. I got a two-year old son to feed, another baby on
the way. You know how it is with the wife." Ryan grinned. "Or you
will, someday."

Sam had rehearsed the words to explain where he'd been the last
eight years and why he'd waited until now to come home. The speech,
which he launched into quickly to get it out of the way, was truthful
about what he'd done, even if it muddied the reason why. The story
went that when the war ended, Sam was still weak from the Spanish
flu and the brisk Orkney air helped heal his lungs. He found he enjoyed
working with his hands and took up carpentry, an easy life that let him
put the horrors of death behind him. Sam hadn't contacted anyone for
fear they'd urge him to return home before he was strong enough. Now
he was ready to get on with his life. He wasn't sure what he would do,
but he wasn't worried about finding a job. The country was prospering.

Ryan, having been through the war himself, seemed to accept Sam's explanation. He'd come home soon after the Armistice and found work as a stock man on the Boston and Albany Railroad. "A job on the docks wasn't for me," he said. "I had my fill of water in the Navy."

"I thought you'd be a fireman or a policeman. Most Irishman in this town join the force." Sam sipped his beer from an old-fashioned glass tankard. He'd learned to drink to be sociable, but alcohol still felt more taboo than pork or shellfish. The one exception was the syrupy kosher wine Jews drank on holidays to celebrate the sweetness of life. Now that he'd be able to buy kosher wine again, he wondered if a sweeter life was in store for him. The men he'd known these last few years had used alcohol to escape life's bitterness.

"I wasn't interested in being a fireman or a cop, either." Ryan gulped half his mug. "I saw enough fire and blood in the service to last a lifetime too."

Sam nodded. "Remember before we shipped out when you bet Tomasio and me you'd end up in Paris and spend the war carousing? Tomasio was jealous, and said he was the only one of us three with the know-how to appreciate the French ladies you'd meet on shore."

Ryan laughed. "He was right about the women, at least back then, but I was wrong about where I'd serve." Sam had to prod before Ryan said his ship had patrolled in the Mediterranean, blocking German subs from entering the Atlantic. Sam pressed again, asking if Ryan had seen any action. Ryan emptied and refilled his glass from the pitcher before answering. "We did support for the USS Druid and a fleet of British ships near the Strait of Gibraltar. Blew up a mess of U-boats. Rescued a few Gerries, but saw a hundred more bodies floating on the water."

Sam thought of the dead who simply went down when the Leviathan sank their sub, never to resurface.

Ryan gazed at the wall above Sam's head, decorated with etchings or photographs of the first immigrants to land on these shores to the most recent arrivals. "Decent pay, though."

"In the Navy?" Sam was puzzled. Rank determined pay, and no amount compensated for a lifetime of nightmares filled with burned and bloated corpses.

"No, at the railroad yard." Ryan looked back down at Sam, his face green. Sam thought it was the beer until Ryan took another healthy swig. "Sorry, I don't talk much about the war. You?"

"Scapa Flow. Blew up one sub before it attacked us. Otherwise, uneventful."

"Why'd you stay over there instead of coming home right after it was over?" Apparently Sam's story hadn't satisfied Ryan.

Sam shrugged. "Nothing I can really talk about either. Tell me about your family."

Ryan shoved aside the pitcher, wiped the table dry, and pulled out pictures of his wife and child. Red hair and freckled cheeks on both. He put his son's photo in Sam's hand. "Smart as a whip, like you." Ryan took back the picture. "Gonna do better than his dad, that's for sure."

"You said you were doing well."

"Decent ain't the same as well." Ryan put away the photos. "I'm not complaining. I've got a great family and my kids have a future. I'm happy enough. More than enough."

Sam studied Ryan's hands as he poured the remaining beer into his glass. His palms were calloused, knuckles blackened. Sam thought of the sweaty creases in Avram's neck and the burn marks on his fingers from the pressing machine at the dress factory. Unlike Ryan, his father hadn't been happy. A son and a daughter with a future in America didn't bring him contentment. Either Avram was too haunted by the past or, having left one unhappy homeland, he could never settle into his new one. Sam wondered if he himself would ever feel settled or content here.

Ryan looked at his watch and stood to leave. They hadn't talked about Tomasio, but Sam had learned from the men in his workshop that silence didn't erase bad memories. The pain came out in other ways, drinking to the point of passing out or flying into a rage over a crooked nail. Even if describing Tomasio's death didn't help Ryan, Sam knew it was necessary for his own recovery. His eyes dared Ryan to listen as he admitted, "It still haunts me that I didn't save him."

Ryan sat down and met his gaze. "You said on the phone that the schoolhouse collapsed before you could go back inside."

"It went up like a tinder box because the dead men's sheets were doused in alcohol to stop the flu from spreading." Sam remembered the dying boy whose red hair had reminded him of Ryan. "The nurses always meant to burn the linens outside, but they never found the time."

"How'd the fire start?" Ryan ordered another pitcher. Sam was still nursing his first glass.

"I guess you could blame it on Tomasio." Ryan cocked his head and Sam recounted how Tomasio had persuaded a pretty nurse named Greta to steal the officers' cigarettes. They laughed at the memory of their friend's persuasive tongue. "He didn't want Mikovski to get any though."

"Still challenging the bastard even after boot camp?"

"He never stopped. Even when the flu almost killed us all, he kept tormenting him."

Ryan clinked his mug against Sam's. "It was the fire that killed him, not you. I know you would have saved him if you could."

"Instead I saved Mikovski."

"You what?"

Sam told Ryan how the terrified Mikovski had clutched his leg, forcing Sam to drag him outside. Tomasio, sicker than Sam but better off than Mikovski, was in the last batch of patients waiting to be evacuated. By then it was too late. Ryan slammed his glass on the table and echoed Hamble Weir's feelings. "Mikovski's the one who should have died."

"In a way he did die." Sam described standing on the beach with Mikovski the day the German fleet sank itself. "That's when the war really ended for him. The lieutenant was good at one thing, training inexperienced kids like us to stay alive. Without that role, he was just another poor kid from the slums taking orders from someone who spit on him. He went home in defeat."

Ryan swirled the suds at the bottom of his glass. "Guess you could say the bastard saved my life."

Sam was surprised to hear someone other than himself give Mikovski credit. He waited for Ryan to find the words he'd probably never uttered before.

"Remember when Mikovski made us get up in the middle of the night to practice sealing pipe leaks in the dark?"

Sam nodded. The lieutenant sometimes woke him several times before dawn, especially after a tiring day. "He was trying to break me, but it had the effect of toughening me up."

"We couldn't tell day from night when the tin fish hit us." A distant look crossed Ryan's face, his memory like a movie he was watching on screen. "We were as good as blind when the pipes burst and the ship listed. We had to see with our hands." He blinked. "I was the only crew member who'd trained under Mikovski and knew how to fix them. I saved a lot of lives, besides my own." He opened his collar to reveal a medal, but closed it before Sam got a closer look. Was Ryan modest about his heroism or mortified by the recollection? Sam knew of men who hid their awards in a box at the back of a closet.

"Funny," Sam said. "Of all us recruits, Tomasio alone had the guts to fight the Germans without Mikovski's goading. Of course, fire's a harder enemy to beat. Fickle and unpredictable. No wonder the lieutenant was scared of it." Scared of the angry fire within himself too, thought Sam, and just as powerless to put it out. No wonder it obsessed him.

"Too bad Tomasio didn't see more action. Somehow his death would have meant more."

"Guess it's up to us to make his memory count." Sam downed what was left of his beer.

"How?" Ryan asked.

"Teach your kids to stand up for themselves and never back down." Ryan nodded, but he didn't look convinced.

"Laugh when you're around them, too. That was Tomasio's best weapon."

Ryan touched the medal under his shirt and smiled. "You always were good at helping the rest of us figure things out," he told Sam. "What about you?"

Sam splayed his fingers on the table. Unlike Ryan, he had no medal to wrap them around. "I guess that's what I came back to find out."

"You need to visit Saint Anthony," said Ryan. "The patron saint for finding lost things and people." He led Sam out of the pub to a nearby church, where he lit a votive candle for Tomasio. Sam lit one too, sure God wouldn't hold it against him. To be on the safe side, though, he silently recited Kaddish, surprised at how easily the old Aramaic prayer for the dead came to his lips. Outside the men turned a handshake into an awkward hug, then Ryan headed home. "I'll teach my kid to poke fun at authority," he called over his shoulder, "as long as it ain't against me."

Sam lingered outside the church until Ryan turned the corner. He was sad to see him go, knowing it was unlikely they'd meet again. He was also relieved that their reunion was over. Looking into one another's eyes had been more painful than he'd expected. Panic surged through Sam's veins. If it was this difficult to see someone he'd known for only eight weeks, how much harder would it be to see the people he'd known all his life?

Seeking to restore a sense of calm, Sam went back inside the church to light a candle for Mikovski too. The hushed sanctuary reminded him of being in shul. He thought of Ryan hurrying home to his family. Sam didn't know if he still had a family, but perhaps he hadn't lost his community. According to Torah, the gates remain open to those who remember the past and return to God. His father's downfall was to study the past but never go further, while his uncle Gershon scoured the Talmud to succeed in the present. Sam wondered if he could use the past to help the unsettled children of immigrants build their future.

He walked to South Station and bought a one-way train ticket to New York. Either he'd die like Mikovski and the men in his workshop, or he would find a reason to live again, like Laird. Laird, Scottish for Lord. Sam Lord was ready to meet Shmuel Levinson. He didn't know which name he would choose after their encounter, but he didn't want people to light votive, or yahrzeit, candles before he was truly in his grave. He was only twenty-four, the number of hours in a day. Yom, the Hebrew word for day, also meant long age. If the Gematria, the mystic study of numbers was relevant, he had plenty of time to find himself, with or without St. Anthony's help.

chapter 54

Sam called his uncle at the office. "Onkel Gershon, it's Shmuel." It felt so strange to call himself by that name that Sam momentarily forgot how shocked his uncle would be to hear him say it.

There was a sharp intake of breath, a receiver clattering on the desk, and a silence so prolonged Sam was afraid he'd given his uncle a heart attack. Then the words, "Can this be?"

Although he'd tried to prepare for the first contact with his family, Sam was still shaken by Gershon's voice. His stomach cramped and he had to force himself to breathe. Before he'd fully recovered, he raced through the story he'd rehearsed, adding that since coming home, the Jewish Welfare Board had found him a room, including meals, at the YMHA. Gershon, usually a garrulous Talmudic debater, didn't interrupt. Either he accepted Sam's explanation, like Ryan had at first, or he was struck speechless by the sound of a ghost.

"Uncle Gershon, are you still there?" Sam asked when he was done.

There was coughing, mumbling that sounded like a prayer, and then at last Gershon spoke. "How is your mother taking this?"

Sam should have expected the question. "I haven't called anyone else in the family yet."

Gershon's voice got louder. "And when are planning on letting her know that the son she sat shiva for is alive? More important, how will you tell her so she doesn't drop dead herself?"

Sam cringed. He'd often pictured his mother missing him, but never really imagined her thinking of him as dead. He saw the lips that had kissed his bruises, told him how proud she was of him, and secretly excused him from his studies, now saying the words of the Kaddish. "I haven't figured that out yet. I thought it would help if I saw you first."

"You want me to tell my sister?"

"God, no!" Sam lowered his voice. "Please don't tell anyone. That's my responsibility."

"It's good you figured out that much."

Sam said nothing more until his uncle relented and invited Sam to talk. Gershon suggested the Mendelsons' apartment. Afraid to see his aunt and cousins, Sam proposed the basement of the Eldridge Street Synagogue, provided there wouldn't be a study session going on and his father wouldn't be there. When Gershon agreed, Sam knew Avram would be nowhere in sight.

Just as he remembered, the windowless room was unadorned, the better to focus the would-be scholars' attention on the texts. Nor were there chairs, only a long table to hold the Torah scrolls around which men stood gesticulating and arguing. With only him and Gershon in the room, the quiet was eerie. Thinking reading would be easier than talking, Sam held out the letters he'd written but never sent. Gershon, tears leaking down his cheeks, pushed them back for Sam to read aloud.

He read in a hushed voice, listening to the words of the youth he'd been when he wrote them. His world was so different now, it seemed that decades, not eight years, had passed. To Sam's surprise, Gershon's showed little curiosity about his war experiences. His attention perked up at the questions Sam had put to him: Why had Gershon given up scholarship for business in America? Was it to make money, fit in, or leave the past behind? Why had he later resumed his studies? Was it because he'd never abandoned his faith? Could Sam reconcile his love of learning with the urge to escape his father? Could he, like Gershon, make all the pieces mesh together?

Gershon waited until Sam finished before speaking. "You admire me for finding myself, but while you were writing letters, I felt like a failure for not finding you. It nearly killed me."

Sam knew his family would be upset with him for leaving, but never had he expected they would turn their anger inward. "Why blame yourself? I made it impossible for anyone to find me."

His uncle gripped the table. "I can find the most esoteric meaning in a single word of Torah. How could I fail to find you?"

Sixty-three tracts of Talmud, hundreds of years of interpretation written by thousands of sages, spilled off the shelves lining the room. "Torah yields many answers. A missing person has only *one* but Jews don't think that way." Sam smiled at his uncle.

Gershon did not smile back. "Jews read these books to make us wiser about God, but I was outsmarted by a stupid bureaucracy."

"You were outsmarted by a determined sixteen-year-old boy."

Gershon winced, then returned Sam's smile. "For some reason, that feels better." His large body relaxed and his tongue loosened. "Now, I'm outdone by women." He told Sam what a devoted mother Zipporah was and how he kvelled with pride over Ruchel's work in Washington as a women's union advocate. "My Yetta is the wisest of all. You know the tale of Rabbi Meir?"

Sam leaned forward, eager to hear the stories he'd loved as a child. The empty room filled with his uncle's voice. "Some louts in Rabbi Meir's neighbourhood were giving him trouble, and in exasperation he prayed for their deaths. His wife Beruriah said to him, 'How can you think such prayer is permitted? Instead, pray for an end to sin, that they may turn from their ways.' Then Rabbi Meir prayed on their behalf." Gershon nodded. "Like so, Yetta turns me around too."

Teshuvah, renouncing sin and turning back to God, was a mainstay of Judaism. Sam wondered if he could find his way back. "In the end, your mother outsmarted me too." Gershon's eyes bore into him. Sam nodded; he was finally ready to hear the price she'd paid for his sin.

"Rivka's grief broke my heart." Gershon placed a hand on his chest. "For a while, she lost the will to live, but eventually she found the strength to take care of others. I finally realized that she didn't feel nearly as sorry for herself as I did for her. Today your mother fights for poor immigrant women. Looking after others makes her stronger than she was before."

Hearing Rivka had recovered from his loss was a relief. Yet, Sam was also hurt, a child's reaction to discovering he wasn't the centre of his mother's life. "And taking care of Dev ...?"

"Your mother took care of Dev, and Dev took care of herself. I helped a little, but only with money. Your sister may turn out to be the wisest woman of all." Gershon told Sam that Dev was living on her own and halfway through college, planning to become a medical researcher. He wrote down her address and telephone number, handed it to Sam, and raised his eyebrows.

Sam nodded that yes, he'd get hold of Dev, and was grateful that Gershon didn't press him about when or how. Or whether he'd do so before or after seeing his mother.

"So," Gershon said, "that brings you up to date on everyone in the family."

Except Avram, Sam thought, not surprised that his uncle had failed to mention his father.

"What will you do now?" Gershon asked. "Seeing you, I can begin to forgive myself. Your mother will be shocked, but she'll grant you forgiveness. As for Him," Gershon pointed up, "the prayer book says, 'We do not ask that our sins be forgiven in the sense that their effects may be cancelled. That is impossible. All we can ask for is purer insight, fuller strength. For this we repent, atone, and receive God's grace.' The question is whether you can forgive yourself."

"I'm just beginning to realize what I need to be forgiven for," said Sam.

"You hurt your mother ... your parents," Gershon said. "But your intentions were good. You went to fight for your country."

"What if that's a lie I told everyone, including myself? Suppose the real reason I left was to escape my father's insistence that I become a rabbi?"

"To choose work other than what your parents have in mind is not such a sin, provided the work is honourable. My father wanted me to marry a poor girl and be a shopkeeper."

"I didn't just change my name and age, Onkel Gershon. I didn't keep kosher, I worked on Shabbas, and I pretended I wasn't a Jew after it was no longer necessary. I came back because something was missing from my life. I want to return to my faith, but I don't know if I'll be allowed. My sins, whatever they are, may be too great and they've gone on too long."

"Remember what the Chasidic Rabbi Bunam said to his followers: 'Our transgression is not that we commit sins—temptation is strong and our strength is slight. No, our transgression is that at every instant when we can turn to God, we do not.' Why not turn right now?"

"How do I know God will hear me?"

"One more story," Gershon said. "Rabbi Baruch's grandson was playing hide-and-seek. He waited for his playmate to find him, but after a long time realized his friend wasn't looking. Eyes brimming with tears, he came to his grandfather. Rabbi Baruch wept too and he said, 'God says the same thing. I hide but no one seeks Me.'"

"And if I did seek God? I wouldn't even know what questions to ask Him."

"Does it matter? Just to ask a question, any question, is a religious act. Without questions, the answers dry up and wither."

"Increase your knowledge, or you will decrease it." These words arose from a place deep inside Sam.

"That's from the Mishnah. See, you do remember." Gershon tapped Sam's temple.

Joy flooded him. Not only did whole passages start to come back to Sam, he was having fun trading them with Gershon. A candle of hope flickered inside him.

"God says, 'Though you be far from Me, I will draw near and heal you, if only you come toward Me.'" Gershon quoted this Midrash on repentance and return.

Sam recited Isaiah. "My hands reach out to the penitent. I reject none who give me their hearts."

Gershon opened a prayer book. "Therefore we read, 'Peace, peace be to all, far and near.' This can mean peace among the nations, but inner peace too I think. Yes?"

Sam took a deep breath. The candle within him burned brighter. It had been too long since he'd automatically felt he was a member of a community. For eight years, he'd worked hard at fitting in among strangers. With his own people, he simply had to be in order to belong.

Gershon sighed. "Welcome home, Shmuel. Come to Torah study on Wednesday night."

It startled Sam to hear someone else call him Shmuel. His identity as Sam was so deeply embedded. The small flame of resolve and confidence sputtered.

Mistaking the look of fear on his nephew's face, Gershon reassured him. "Don't worry. No one will recognize you. Your hair is longer, your skin is tougher. You've grown muscles."

"My father would know me however much I changed."

"Avram won't be there. He goes to the Sunday night study group, when Dev cooks dinner for the rest of the family, including your mother, at her apartment."

"Dev cooks?" Sam thought with a start that his little sister had probably changed as much as, if not more than, him. What would it be like to see her? How would she react to seeing him? He told Gershon he'd think about joining the Wednesday study group. Debating him was nothing like his boyhood sessions with Avram. There was an openness and freedom, a search for possible meanings, instead of the one right answer. Could he, Sam, begin to see his whole life this way?

Outside the synagogue, as stars awoke in the sky, Gershon offered Sam a last quote, from Psalms. "In the time we spend brooding, we could be stringing pearls for the joy of heaven." The two men embraced. "Call your mother," Gershon said, slipping subway fare and change for a pay phone into Sam's pocket. Sam grasped them until the cold metal turned warm between his fingers.

chapter 55

Sam wasn't ready to call his mother, or any other member of the family, yet he had to get closer to who he'd been as a child before he could find himself as an adult. He compromised by phoning his old friend Bernie, who was surprisingly calm when he heard Sam's voice.

"Did your father tell you I'd be calling?" asked Sam, who'd gotten the number from him.

"No." Bernie chuckled. "I'm a rabbi now. I believe in miracles."

Sam couldn't get over this twist in their fates. As a boy, Bernie had been a competent, if not inquisitive, Torah student. Sam tried to imagine what kind of rabbi he'd become. He took a train to the Bronx where they sat in the sanctuary of Adath Israel, not far from Yankee Stadium.

"Don't call it a shul," Bernie had warned. "My congregants, most of whom started on the Lower East Side, prefer the English word temple." Its crushed velvet seats, mahogany railings, and silver embroidered Torah covers were as far from Eldridge Street as America was from Europe.

Bernie gave Sam a tour. The congregation was a quarter-century old, but this permanent home was recent. "I was hired fresh out of seminary, a young rabbi for a new generation." Bernie spoke with pride of his rapid rise in the hierarchy, never pausing to ask Sam about his life. Rather than being relieved that he didn't have to account for his absence, Sam was annoyed. He was learning that opening up about his past was the way to discover where he wanted to go next.

He interrupted Bernie's monologue. "What's Yaakov doing now?"

"Plumber, I think. We lost touch."

"When you moved to the Bronx?"

"Earlier. Yaakov works with his hands. My people work with their heads." Bernie sniffed. "The guy never was very bright. Dimmer than me, a bare bulb compared to you."

Sam grimaced. "That's not a very rabbinic thing to say."

"I'm not a typical rabbi. I spend more time raising money than spiritual awareness." Bernie showed Sam blueprints for a school they'd soon break ground for. It had a white marble exterior, stained glass windows, and ten classrooms. The study halls had low tables and chairs so boys could sit, not stand, to pore over Torah scrolls. Dotted lines were drawn around an eleventh classroom. "For girls, once I convince the congregation it's kosher. Sometimes I go too far, even for them."

Sam remembered Dev secretly listening from the front room as he and his father debated Torah in the kitchen. She would have loved studying the arcane language in the old texts.

Bernie fingered the tzitzit on his gold embroidered tallit. "Avram may come to regret giving this to me. I'm afraid he disapproves of my liberal ideas."

"My father gave that to you?"

"You don't recognize it? He planned to give it to you after you were ordained."

Sam had never seen it before. His father had hidden it well in their tiny apartment. Why had Avram given it to Bernie? Should Sam be grateful that he was off the hook, or resentful that his father had replaced him? Avram's gift felt like an act of post-mortem revenge. Sam, shot through with pain, averted his eyes and changed the subject to Bernie's wife. He remembered his sister's best friend Leah as being Orthodox, and asked how she felt about Bernie straying from tradition.

For the first time that day, a small frown shadowed Bernie's face. "She goes along with it because she's my wife, but she has her ways of letting me know she's not happy. For example, I've urged her to help me convince parents that schooling their daughters is a good thing."

"And?"

"She'd rather stay home and take care of our daughter. And son. Plus a third on the way."

Sam shuddered. "Three children in five years. Maybe she's just tired."

Bernie laughed "The irony is that when Leah gets really annoyed at my nudging, she quips that Dev would have made a better rebbetzin after all."

Sam filled in the untold story. Bernie and Dev must have dated and been serious enough to talk marriage. The idea made him uncomfortable. How had Avram felt about it?

Bernie continued. "Your sister is too modern, even for me. Frankly

I'm glad all Leah wants is to take care of me and the kids. Still I love hearing Dev talk about her studies. Sometimes I think we're better friends than she and Leah ever were."

"Does my sister still use slang?"

Bernie grinned. "Not as much. After all, she's a serious student of science now."

Sam smiled back. "I'm glad. Her expressions could drive a person crazy." Then he frowned. "Although it's also a shame. The way she talked was sort of endearing."

"Don't worry. She still uses big vocabulary words, especially technical ones."

Sam felt mollified, a Dev word. He asked how often Bernie saw her. He couldn't picture two people he'd known well as children having a serious adult discussion. He tried to imagine himself talking to this older, more mature Dev and came up equally blank. What if he'd stayed away too long and she'd changed so much that they were doomed to remain strangers? Sam was different, but in his mind, everyone else was frozen in time.

"Dev's busy, 'assiduous' according to her, with school, but sometimes she comes for Shabbas dinner and plays aunt to our kids. The older one calls her Tantee Devee. She takes them to the park to collect stuff: leaves, berries, dead insects." Bernie laughed. "Leah throws them out as soon as Dev is gone. Dev looks for them the next time she visits and I think she's gets angry at Leah for being such a compulsive house cleaner." Bernie's chest swelled under the tallit. "Or she's mad at Leah for marrying me, after all."

"Were you angry at me for leaving without confiding in you and Yaakov?" Sam had given up waiting for Bernie to raise the subject.

"I was angry at myself for not seeing it coming."

Like my uncle, Sam thought, Bernie had turned his anger and blame inward. Was it too much to hope that his father might do the same?

"You should come to Shabbas dinner too," Bernie said. "And then go with me to services."

Sam was puzzled. "Don't you mean the reverse?"

"The modern way is to eat at home, then go as a family to temple. Men and women still sit on opposite sides, but now there's a coed middle section where most of the younger couples sit."

Sam explained that he couldn't see Bernie's family until he'd contacted his own. He swore his friend to secrecy. "Don't mention it to Leah either. She might tell Dev."

"Then just come to services. Leah stays home with the children, and if Dev comes to dinner, she goes straight home to study." Bernie grinned. "Biology, not Torah."

Sam extended his hand, but Bernie wrapped the tallit around them both in a bear hug. He handed Sam a fund-raising pamphlet and a silk yarmulke, embroidered with the temple's name. Having abandoned his faith, Sam had no right to judge others, but it seemed Bernie had replaced the worship of God with a reverence for money. If Sam had never left home, and become a rabbi after all, would the mission to serve today's Jews make him succumb to the same temptations? Sam thought not. He slipped the yarmulke into his pocket.

"Welcome home Shmuel ... Sam. Which do you want be called?"

Sam ... Shmuel ... took a final look at the Torah scroll nestled in its shiny wooden ark at the front of the ornate and cavernous sanctuary. "I haven't decided yet," he said.

chapter 56

Sam stood outside Dev's apartment, not far from where Onkel and Yetta lived. The stoop was swept clean; flower boxes outside the windows anticipated the return of spring. Sam waited, hoping Dev would spot him through the lace curtains before he climbed the stairs. Although he could have called first, he'd decided their reunion should be face to face. Anything less was cowardly, and he had to practice courage before seeing his father. A woman on the first floor eyed him suspiciously. He couldn't put off the meeting with his sister any longer.

Pulling his thin jacket close, Sam walked up the carpeted stairs. At Dev's landing, a spicy aroma drifted into the hallway. Twice he raised a hand to the pewter doorknocker before rapping. His head was still bowed, listening for signs of life, when suddenly there stood Dev, pencil tucked into her hair. Oriental rugs, strewn on the floor behind her, had dampened the sound of her steps.

Sam froze. So did Dev. Her alarm turned into puzzlement, disbelief, then joy. She hurtled into his arms, nearly knocking him down, before yanking him inside and slamming the door. "God in heaven, is it really you?" Hands covering her mouth, Dev laughed and screamed. She leaped around him like a dog released from its pen after weeks of confinement. She touched his shoulders, tapped his knuckles, and encircled his waist as far as her arms would extend, in a long hug. Then she collapsed on the couch, patted the cushion beside her for Sam to sit, and bawled.

It was the most emotional reaction to Sam's homecoming so far. That was a reflection of Dev's personality, but also a sign he was getting closer to the people at his own emotional centre. A tide of feelings— love, guilt, panic— flooded Sam's body until he was afraid he would drown. The ends of his nerves tingled as if on fire. He was navigating blind.

Sam didn't know if Dev would buy the explanation he'd used with Ryan and Gershon, but he was too overwhelmed to try anything else. Navy discipline kicked in; he repeated what he'd already practiced.

As Dev's sobs diminished, Sam narrated his story, hoping her shock would keep her from asking questions he couldn't answer. It seemed to work.

When Dev at last caught her breath, she looked at him in frank appraisal, curious to see how he'd changed. "You're not an anaemic yeshiva boy anymore," she said as she moved her hand along the muscles in his arm. "Brachioradialis, deltoid. You've grown at least a foot too."

This acknowledgment that he'd become a full-blown man restored a bit of Sam's confidence. But if he looked different, he couldn't say the same about Dev. She was a twenty-year-old version of her twelve-year-old self, dark and built solid like their father. In fact, except for the curls they'd both inherited from Rivka, Sam could have been facing Avram. An acid foretaste filled his mouth. He tousled his sister's wild hair, hoping the playful gesture would tamp down his anxiety and hide it from her. He wanted to reassert himself as the big brother.

Dev reached up and ran both hands through his hair too. Years of walking the beaches at Scapa Flow had bleached and coarsened it. Her forefinger stopped at the strawberry mark below his right ear. "I used to wonder why you wore payess, even though we weren't that religious. It wasn't until the boys in my eighth-grade class became self-conscious about their appearance that I realized you were trying to hide this. Is that why you wear your hair so long now?"

Sam removed her hand, but didn't blush as he might have long ago. "No one paid attention to how I wore it in Scotland. I suppose I should trim it now that I'm home."

"Will you grow payess again?"

"Goodness, no. I could never go back to what I was."

"Then will you leave your hair long enough to hide the strawberry mark or let it show?"

"I haven't thought about it," Sam admitted, but maybe the time for honesty had come. Not to flaunt it with pride, but not to cover with shame either. In the war, no one cared who had visible moles or scars. They were just men prepared to sacrifice their lives for one another.

"You need to eat if you don't want those new muscles to atrophy." Dev hoisted Sam off the couch and led him into the kitchen. Walking through her apartment, he was struck by its neatness, nothing like her messy corner in the front room when they were growing up. Books were stacked by subject on the shelves and the polished desk held note-books and an enamelled pen. The kitchen was neat and well stocked too. A pot bubbling on the stove was responsible for the tangy aroma he'd smelled in the hallway. Dev served him tea and homemade honey nut cake.

"Mama's recipe?" Sam hadn't eaten it in years, but he could swear it tasted different.

"I add grated orange rind and candied nuts to the batter."

"It's good, better than Mama's."

Dev blushed with pleasure. "Wait until you try these." She removed a cloth napkin from a hand-painted plate of chocolate-covered cookies.

Sam bit through the crust into a layer of spongy filling and a wafer of sweet dough. "You made these too?" He ate a second one.

"Mallomars!" Dev hooted, pulling the crinkly wrapper from the cupboard. "Store bought, but kosher, I promise. Even Bernie and Leah let their children eat them."

Sam wondered whether he should confess to no longer keeping kosher, but decided there was time to deliver such smaller shocks after she'd adjusted to the big one of his turning up alive.

"Tell me about the war," Dev said, leaning back in her chair.

"There's not a lot to tell. I didn't see much action."

"What were the other men on your ship like?"

"Young and scared, like me. Boot camp hardened us. Later on, battling storms and sighting subs became routine."

"Weren't you afraid of the enemy? We heard awful things about the Germans."

Sam swirled his tea leaves. "I was more afraid of a sadistic person in our own ranks."

"What was he like?"

"Tough on the surface, but in his own way, as scared as the rest of us underneath."

Dev sprang a curl near her temple and frowned. "I don't under-stand."

"Were you ever afraid you wouldn't get into college, that the one thing you wanted would be denied you?"

Dev nodded.

"He achieved his dream, but then it was taken away from him. Most likely forever, unless there's another war."

"Shmuel, don't even think such a horrible thought."

"Don't worry. It's the last thing I'd want, even to help a friend, let alone a man I dislike."

"Did you make any friends in the war?"

"Two." Sam pulled the shirt collar away from his throat. The kitchen felt warm, although the only nearby heat came from the low flame under the simmering pot.

Dev's eyes sparkled. "Will you see them now that you're back? Can I meet them?"

"I already saw one. He lives in Boston."

"And the other?"

Sam shook his head.

Dev drew a sharp breath. "Is that why you didn't come home when the war ended?"

"Enough questions for today. I'm back now. There's time to tell you more later." Sam held out his cup and plate, hoping to distract her.

"One more question that can't wait," Dev said, handing Sam more tea and another slice of cake. "Why did you leave without telling me? I thought we confided everything to each other."

Sam wasn't going to get off that easy after all. He tried teasing. "You were only twelve. A sixteen-year-old boy doesn't tell his little sister everything."

"Don't treat me like a child." Dev was accusatory, but not petulant. "I'm an adult now."

After hearing others blame themselves, Sam was jolted when Dev blamed him. Fearing it foretold the reaction he'd get from Avram, Sam felt the burning sensation rise again in his throat.

"I was afraid of saying anything that might get back to Papa."

"Were you worried that if you told me, I'd tip him off?" Dev's nostrils flared. "Did you think I would spill the beans as a way to get on his good side? To win out over you?"

Nothing like that had crossed his mind. "How could you believe I'd think that of you?"

"Back then, maybe I would have. I wanted Papa's love so badly and much as I loved you, I envied the attention you got." Now Dev sounded more angry at herself than at Sam.

He swallowed hard. He'd never given much thought to the pain Avram caused Dev. "We both wanted his love, only I couldn't face becoming a rabbi to earn it, so I ran."

"I didn't even have a way to earn it until Bernie proposed, and then I sacrificed it to go my own way. I had to leave home too, but I still worry that Papa will find a way to stop me."

"He's not an easy man to break away from. It would be easier if he were cruel, but he wants what he believes is best for us. What he never had himself. It's like he's the poor little child, and we're the parents telling him 'no.' We pay for our freedom with our guilt."

Dev's face softened. She nodded sympathetically. "I think that's why Mama has trouble saying 'no' to him too. Although sometimes she does. Like about my going to college."

"Mama never made us earn her love." Sam looked at Rivka's photo beside the stove. "Still, I never understood her. She defended women's rights but she never stood up to Papa."

Dev spun the platter of Mallomars. "It used to make me angry too, but now I can see her side. I have a chance to go to school and support myself. What could Mama do if she left Papa or if he threw her out? Suppose making a good home for him *is* her dream, who are we to judge?"

Sam studied his sister. She hadn't changed much on the outside, but inside she was a new person. Less self-centred, more thoughtful, kinder. He felt bad that he hadn't been there to guide her. Yet he couldn't deny that she'd done fine on her own. That hurt worse.

"You've grown up, Dev. When I left, you were always itching to pick a fight with Mama, or anyone and everything else."

Dev smiled wryly "I still need to rebel now and then."

Sam cocked his head.

"I eat trayf. Pork buns and shrimp egg rolls from Chinatown."

Sam clapped a hand over his mouth and her face fell until he winked. "Me too," he said, and told her about the unkosher food he ate during his time in the Navy.

"You had to eat that stuff or you would have starved." Dev grimaced. "I eat it by choice."

"I don't have to eat trayf anymore either. Like you, I choose to eat it now."

Dev looked up from under her thick, dark lashes. "It tastes good, doesn't it?"

Sam agreed. Why pretend he'd eaten trayf for his health or to fit in? The truth was that he liked it. He and Dev absolved each other, swearing a pact not to tell Rivka, let alone Avram. They were children again, united in their opposition, not strangers after all. And yet, the knot that bound them was weaker. The frayed rope could never be repaired. Even if Sam wanted to, he knew Dev wouldn't. All those years he'd been floundering, she'd moved full speed ahead. His little sister had out-raced him and Sam alone would mourn the seas they hadn't sailed together.

"How will you let Papa know you're back?" Dev rested her chin on her hand and frowned. "Do you want to practice what you'll say to him with me?"

"No. I have to work this out on my own," Sam said. And soon, he thought. Postponing it was a burden. Looking around Dev's orderly apartment, he was struck by the reversal in their lives too. She'd craved their father's love, but was now resolved to live without it. He'd chosen to live without it and was now hoping to win it back. Dev's life had a purpose. His was uncertain.

"It will be easier if you begin with Mama," Dev said. "Come to dinner Sunday night. I'll tell her to get here before Onkel Gershon's family." When Sam hesitated, she added, "Don't get the heebie jeebies. Papa never comes and I'll stay close in case Mama screams or faints."

This time Sam accepted Dev's offer. Walking back to his room, he thought of this new sister, how she'd kept her exuberance and curiosity while maturing into a mediator who could see both sides of a conflict. She could play the part of the older sibling now. He trusted her to help him reconcile with his mother. Trust was the first step in repairing the rift with his father too, but to confront Avram, Sam had to trust in himself alone.

chapter 57

Seeing his mother was both harder and easier than Sam expected. Harder because he hadn't felt so guilty since Tomasio's death, which he could at least partly blame on illness or accident. Easier because Rivka didn't faint or scream accusations. In fact, no sound came out of her, although she shook so hard that Dev slipped a chair underneath her for fear she'd fall.

Rivka stared into Sam's eyes as he spoke. By now, the story of his absence sounded hollow to own ears. Only after she'd gulped two glasses of water did his mother cry.

"Are you too angry to forgive me?" Sam choked out the words.

"I'm not angry at you for leaving," she said, "or letting me think you were dead. I'm angry that I missed seeing you grow from a boy into a man. It's a mother's right."

"I'm sorry, Mama." Sam knelt beside her. "How can I give you back what I took away?"

"You can't, but God willing, I'll have the rest of my life to see you become a mensch."

"That's what I came home to try to do," Sam said. His mother, more than his sister, would let him make amends. The older you were and the more limited your future, the less willing you were to write off the past. Sam grieved over Rivka's wrinkled brow, knowing he was both responsible and powerless to reverse time. Yet he also stirred with hope. His life lay ahead. Avram had turned into an old man while he was still young. Sam would not make that mistake.

It was his mother who suggested where and when Sam should meet his father. "Wait for him after Torah study, next Sunday night, at the synagogue. He's calmest then. The sessions take him back to his childhood in the shtetl, and he forgets the long days of sweating at the factory."

Sam was doubtful. "I don't know if catching him when he's thinking about the past is such a good idea. What if seeing me reminds him that he left Lemberg for nothing?"

Rivka wiped her eyes. "There's never a good time, but facing your father after he's been talking about something he knows, and that for him never changes, is a better time than others."

"When does the study session end?" Sam's nerves buzzed like they had as a boy during Friday night dinner, knowing Avram would quiz him on the Torah as soon as the meal ended.

"Between nine and eleven," Rivka said with a chuckle. "Depending on how long it takes your father to convince a quorum that his interpretation is right. He won't allow it to break up before then."

"I'll get there at nine and wait," said Sam.

So there he was, at 10:30 the next Sunday night, pacing in the vestibule of the Eldridge Street Synagogue. At last he heard footsteps mounting the stairs. A dozen men walked out the front door, some glancing at his long hair and Navy pea coat with curiosity, but none questioning his right to be there. A man Sam recognized as an old neighbour appeared, asking someone behind him, "Why did God choose Abraham, not Noah, to be the first Jew? Wasn't Noah also called a righteous man?" Sam realized they were discussing Lech L'Cha, the Torah portion in which God tells Abraham to leave his father's house and go to a new land that God will show him.

Behind the neighbour came Avram, speaking impatiently. Sam felt the urge to flee, yet he was riveted, staring at the face that had aged while the body still held itself stiff and erect. "Because Abraham understood there was one true God and that He alone ..." The book Avram held clattered to the floor. The neighbour paled at seeing what he thought was a ghost and stumbled outside, leaving Sam and his father gaping at each other. Avram picked up the fallen prayer book and kissed the cover, a sign of respect. Trembling, he eyed a nearby bench, but remained standing.

"You're dead," Avram said. "I sat shiva when you left."

Sam gulped. Had his father dismissed his life that quickly? "According to Jewish law, halakah says that without a body or eyewitness, a family should never give up hope."

"Even your mother gave up hope."

"Not until three years later, when Onkel Gershon found out I'd probably died at sea." Sam bit his tongue. Avram would know that he must have talked to his mother or his uncle.

"So I'm the last person in the family to know you're still alive?"

Sam nodded.

"Your mother I can understand, but Gershon ..." Again Avram's gruff voice trailed off.

Sam shivered. The vestibule's heat had leaked out when his father's study group opened the outer door. Sam walked into the sanctuary, dark save for the Ner Tamid hanging above the Ark and illuminating the shul's oldest Torah scroll. He sat in the second row, wondering whether Avram would follow him or leave like the others. After two minutes, the Eternal Light flickered under the shadow cast by his father's entry. Avram took a seat at the far end of the pew.

"I saved you for last," Sam said, "knowing you'd be the hardest to talk to. I haven't completely figured out for myself why I left, so I'm not sure if I can explain it to you."

Avram sat in profile, but Sam could see his eyebrows bunched in concentration. "Try."

Sam gripped the oily seat back in front of him. "I knew you wanted more than anything for me to be a rabbi, but it wasn't right for me. Studying Talmud I loved, but not arguing over minute points of law. When you grew up in the shtetl, where one day was the same as the next, the old laws still made sense. Here things change all the time. I couldn't tell a congregation how to lead their own lives, when I was so confused about mine."

"Life in America is not so different from life in the shtetl. Poor there, poor here. Both places, Jews and Catholics want nothing to do with one another unless it's to exchange money."

"Separation is not so easy in America. In Lemberg, peasants had the country, you had the village. Their farms, your shops. Here on the street, boys fight for every inch of territory. I didn't know how to fight, only how to be smart in school. I got picked on. In the shtetl, scholarship was a mark of pride. Here it was a liability. I just wanted to fit in, to be tough like the other kids."

"God demands we be tough obeying His laws, not imitating those who disobey them." Avram's shoulders twisted, as if wrestling with himself. "Why didn't you tell me how you felt?"

"I tried, but I couldn't make you listen. So I ran away. I told myself I was going to fight for my country." Sam spoke quickly to rid himself of the words. "To be honest, I was escaping you."

Now Avram turned an ashen face toward his son. In the light that was never extinguished, Sam saw his father's frayed shirt collar and the sweat-carved creases in his neck. A blood vessel throbbed in Avram's temple while Sam's blood pulsed through the strawberry mark beneath his ear. He'd never told his father how self-conscious it made him, or how he was bullied because of it. Was there any subject, other than Torah, that wasn't taboo for them to discuss?

"So why did you come back? Unless you changed your mind?" A ray of hope.

"No."

Avram rested a thumb and forefinger on his closed eyes. "Then what's the point?"

Sam took a deep breath. "In the Navy I discovered my voice as a teacher. When the war ended, I taught ruined men to use their hands, but I wasn't reaching their souls. They were lost." Avram's head was bent, listening. Sam continued. "They lacked even the will to get off their tiny island. Immigrants found the courage to leave, but they struggle in the new world, confused about what to keep and what to change."

"They keep nothing and change everything. Isn't this what you just told me? That change, all the time change, made growing up here bad?"

"I didn't say it was bad. Only that it was different from the shtetl, which made it hard for you to understand what I was going through."

Avram sniffed. "You think you can do something for these lost souls, as you call them?"

Sam slid down the bench, narrowing the distance between them. "I keep going back to an idea I had in boot camp to open a school, a cheder, where I'd teach boys to apply ancient lessons from the Talmud to life in America today. A marriage of the spiritual and the practical."

"I still don't understand," Avram said. "Give me a for instance. Dietary laws?"

"There's room for some degree of choice."

Avram scoffed. "What? Pork? Shell fish? Meat with milk?"

"If it was that or starve, yes."

"No Talmudic passage justifies such an exception."

"Jews two thousand years ago weren't faced with these decisions. But Talmud allows eating on fast days in order to save a life. I would apply the same reasoning here."

Avram threw out another challenge. "What about working on Shabbas?"

"Yes, if it is necessary to get a job. And feed your children."

"I didn't work on Saturday and still I managed to feed you and Dev."

"Things are different now than when you arrived here. Business is booming since the war ended. If workers refuse to come in on Saturdays, they won't get hired or they get fired."

"Wearing leather on Yom Kippur? Hanging teffilin from your tzitzit? Saying a hundred prayers of thanksgiving every day?" Avram peppered Sam with Jewish laws, without giving him the time to answer "I don't know yet" or "That's why I need to study" between questions.

Sam was ready to admit defeat and slink away as he'd done years ago, when the memory of Mikovski's impossible demands made him defiant. He turned the tables on Avram. "An eye for an eye, a tooth for a tooth. Do you honour this commandment, Papa?"

"One must obey the law in a civilized country. You can exact retribution symbolically."

"So you agree that some laws are not meant to be taken literally?"

Avram was silent. Sam allowed himself a glimmer of satisfaction as his father squirmed.

"And would you have Dev stoned to death because she disobeyed you and went to college instead of marrying Bernie?"

Avram raised his eyebrows.

"See, Papa. Some questions are not so easy to answer. I still think Torah holds the truth and Talmud offers solutions, but they are buried in the past. The words must be examined and interpreted for today. That's what I hope to do with the pupils in my cheder."

"You would become a rabbi to do this?" Avram's voice was again hopeful.

"I would go to seminary to learn and become a teacher, but not necessarily be ordained."

Sam inched another foot closer to his father but when Avram pulled back, he stopped. "I don't want to be the kind of absolute authority that being a rabbi conveys. I want to be a teacher who learns as much from his students as they do from him, an egalitarian teacher."

"I never heard of such a thing."

Sam smiled. "It's a Dev word."

Avram stiffened at the second mention of his daughter.

"Don't worry, I won't be like Bernie, abandoning tradition to raise money. I can manage on my savings from the Navy and the workshop." Sam said this to reassure his father, once more realizing too late that he'd confessed to seeing his friend, not just other family members, before seeking out his father. He braced himself for another wave of anger.

Instead, Avram asked quietly, "You know that Bernie ... studied with me?"

"I know you kind of adopted him after I left." Sam paused. "I might have done the same."

Avram considered the idea before shaking his head and returning to Sam's plans. "How is merely studying at the seminary different than what I and my neighbours do when we meet every week? You may learn a little more, but in the end you'd still be a labourer, like me." Sam opened his mouth to protest, but Avram talked over him. "You wouldn't even be better than Gershon, who for all his wealth, still kowtows to others for money and power. Only a rabbi earns the full respect of his community. If you're not ordained, I might as well have stayed in Lemberg."

Sam was about to give up until, seeing the Torah illuminated on the reader's table, he had an idea. He mounted the bima, opened the scroll, and spoke to Avram in the pew below. "In this week's portion, God tells Abraham to leave his father's house and go to a new place. Leaving for a new place is a way of life for Jews."

Avram leaned forward as he'd done when impressing a point in Sam's mind as a boy. "God has a destination in mind, 'the place that I will show you,' He says, meaning *the* land. When the Jews leave Egypt after four-hundred and thirty years of slavery, it is to return to that same land."

Shmuel, the child, would have accepted his father's explanation. A grownup Sam argued. "For two thousand years, since the second temple was destroyed, Jews have been exiled to many lands. The Diaspora is central to our identity."

"True, but the title of this portion, 'Lech L'cha' means 'Take and Go.' You can't speak of the second part without honouring the first. Jews are a people of exile, but always we must take with us our past. The laws—the commandments of Torah—travel with us wherever we go."

"Not when we leave Egypt. We don't even have the commandments yet. We receive them later, at Sinai, after wandering in the desert for two months. Only then does God deem us ready."

Avram shook his head. "The rabbis teach that there is no earlier or later in Torah. The moment we read the last word, we roll the scroll back to the beginning and start again. Whatever happens has always been so. God's ways are fixed, whatever the time, wherever the place."

"You could just as well interpret the rabbinic principle to mean that we must live in the present while respecting the past, not that the past should follow us unchanged into the present."

"Torah is a circle, not a line. Past and present are one and the same."

"Past and present are a never-ending cycle, not a fixed point. The Mishnah has volumes interpreting every law. Doesn't this teach us that each time we read Torah, we are bound to learn something new?" Sam lifted the yad and read God's promise urging Abraham to set forth. "I shall make of you a great nation." He held out the pointer to Avram, who mounted the bima to accept it. Together, they finished chanting the verse: "And your name shall be a blessing."

Sam considered the line. God intended Abraham's name to be a blessing through his son and those who followed, until his offspring were "as numerous as the stars in the heavens and the grains of sand on the shore." To be fruitful and multiply on that scale, Sam knew, people had to prosper in the land where they betook themselves. Would Avram, named for the Jews' patriarch, allow the fulfilment of that promise to happen here, in a faraway land, with his own son?

The scroll of his own history unwound in Sam's mind. If he'd talked to Avram one more time and not run away, would he have listened? Had tonight's Talmudic arguments persuaded Avram that Sam's school could fulfil a son's dreams without dishonouring a father's?

Avram's face was unreadable. Sam would have to leave again to find the answer. He was his own man now. Avram would survive, or perish, on his own too. Buttoning his coat, Sam went through the icy vestibule and was opening the door to the chill night air when he imagined footsteps behind him. He paused, but heard only silence. Walking outside alone, Sam pictured Avram still reading Torah, lit by the eternal, never changing light.

chapter 58

Sam stood in front of the Jewish Theological Seminary in University Heights, just as eight years earlier he'd trembled outside the Navy recruiting station on the Lower East Side. Now, instead of facing the nondescript entrance to a sooty skyscraper, he marvelled at the immaculate three-story Gothic building with graceful stone arches. Back then he'd stared up at wispy clouds, hoping in vain for a message from God. Today he blinked at one of the last clear days of fall, a few tenacious oak leaves still clinging to the massive trees. The only wispy things were the beards of the skinny young men opening the heavy wooden door, so unlike the burly recruits who long ago preceded Sam into a cold, cavernous room, ready to go to war. These youths were here to go to college, earn teaching certificates, and in some cases, be ordained as rabbis. Sam squinted into the unblemished sky, wishing his mind were as clear the weather.

Eight weeks had elapsed between his boarding the boat in Scotland and standing at these seminary gates, the same length of time as boot camp. Now he was contemplating becoming a student again, a schoolboy. Schoolman. He'd have to ask Dev if such a word existed.

Watching the students who would be his classmates, Sam felt out of place, half again their age and bulk. They ignored him, intent on their own conversations. The same thing had happened two weeks ago, when he cut his hair and shaved. He'd walked around Manhattan, steeling himself against stares and ridicule, but no one noticed his strawberry mark. Now that he saw it every day in the mirror, it appeared paler and smaller to him too.

Snatches of lively debate crackled in the air. Did a certain interpretation of halakah conform to what the rabbis said? How about a professor's argument against wearing artificial fabrics? Sam wondered what kind of teacher he would make. How would students respond to his attempts to challenge convention without abandoning it, to stay the course while exploring diverging paths? He didn't want to be like Bernie, ploughing heedlessly ahead, nor Avram, mired in the past.

He pictured accompanying his students on a journey, searching and discovering together. It was, as he told Avram, an egalitarian vision, suited to a country built on equality. Yet of the two people he'd learned the most from, his father and Mikovski, one had taught him using guilt and the other fear. He rejected both, but didn't know if his ideal of intellectual and spiritual equals could work.

Two students, one bareheaded like Sam, the other in a skull cap, approached with flyers in their hands. "Sir?" they asked. Sam was taken aback. They already saw him as a teacher.

"Please, call me Sam. Or Shmuel." Asked if he had a preference, he answered, "Whichever name you feel comfortable with."

"Shmuel," continued the one in the yarmulke. "Sam," said the other. They all laughed.

The young men invited him to a debate their freshman class was hosting on whether it was permissible to use the telephone on Shabbas. It began in an hour, and they were competing to recruit audience members who supported their respective sides.

Sam tried to remember the thirty-nine categories of work Jews were forbidden to perform on the Sabbath, such as planting, cooking, and slaughtering animals. Each category was further broken down into acceptable and unacceptable activities. He used telephones so rarely that he'd never given the question much thought, but it was fitting in a world where they were becoming increasingly commonplace. Sam said he wasn't even sure which category of work applied.

"Building," the students said in unison. Beyond that, they disagreed vociferously. "You can't use the telephone for the same reason you can't flip a light switch," said the hatted one. "We're forbidden from building a permanent structure. Completing an electrical connection completes and thus builds a circuit. Making and receiving a call is no different."

"Wrong," said the other. "A telephone call builds a relationship. Nowhere are we forbidden to do this on Shabbas. Just the opposite. We're commanded to connect with God and the Jewish people."

Sam, recalling the Talmud, addressed the first student. "We are permitted to build if the intent is temporary. Thus, for example, we can close a door, completing the locking mechanism, because the implication is that it will be reopened."

The young man objected. "If there's even a small possibility it won't be opened again, it is better to risk being robbed than to risk violating the commandment." He was adamant until Sam raised a sceptical eyebrow. Then he seemed to waver, considering the extremity of his position.

So Sam turned to the other student. "If we are forbidden from building anything that is or could be permanent, shouldn't that apply to human connections too? For example, we are proscribed from opening an umbrella, which creates a tent. Although temporary, it has the potential to stay up forever. How much more permanent, then, a telephone connection with a family member or friend? Or even a business associate?"

"Talking about business on Shabbas? That's work. Of course it's not allowed."

Sam conceded the point, but pursued his line of questioning. "Are we not also prohibited from smoothing, erasing, and extinguishing a fire? Suppose, during this Shabbas call, the parties ended a disagreement that had ruptured family ties or threatened to end a friendship? Would you permit telephone calls but have the rabbis generate a list of approved and unapproved topics? And would the callers be obliged to hang up if they strayed over the line? Who's to decide?"

A heated discussion ensued over what might be permitted or forbidden. Sam didn't know the answer, and the students began to doubt their own positions, even switching sides at one point.

As the three of them argued, they walked toward the seminary door. A young man held it open and Sam, without thinking, followed the bustling knot of people inside. Sunlight streamed in through the tall windows, illuminating shiny mosaics with scenes from Genesis. The destruction of the flood was pictured beside a land flowing with milk and honey. A sea of students flowed toward the study hall where the debate would take place.

Sam was swept forward with the tide.

acknowledgements

When I made the leap from writing nonfiction to fiction, many mentors and supporters cushioned the landing and kept me moving forward. I am fortunate to have not one, but two long-time writers groups who provide encouragement, inspiration, and thoughtful feedback. Also levity and good company, which the otherwise solitary writer needs. From my "Saturday" group, thanks to Keith Hood, Amy Gustine, Jeanne Sirotkin Haines, Danielle Lavaque-Manty, Lori Eaten, Sonja Srinivasan, Paul Many, Cathy Mellett, Marni Hochman, Kevin Breen, and Deepak Singh, and others over the years. My everlasting gratitude goes to the "Sunday" group who stayed with me from the first draft through the final version of *On the Shore*. Clasped hands go to Danielle (again), Janet Gilsdorf, Marty Calvert, Cynthia Jalinski, Jane Johnson, and Margaret Nesse.

Family and friends are the cheerleaders who urge me on after every setback (most writers can paper the walls of a mansion with rejection slips) and make me feel worthy of each success. The greatest thanks goes to my daughter Rebecca Epstein, who is and always will be my best creative inspiration. Jerry Gardner is a one-man chorus of encouragement. Other kith and kin who have reinforced the value of gluing my butt to the chair to keep writing are my brother Joel Savishinsky, late aunt Charlotte Bettinger, cousins Joy Bader and Pam Alson, and friends Terry Alexander and Lynn Liben. To the rest of you, too numerous to mention, please know how much I treasure your support.

Finally, my thanks and appreciation to Vine Leaves Press, beginning with Peter Snell on the acquisitions team, who was the manuscript's first fan, and Jessica Bell who accepted the book and dressed it in style before it went out the door. Editor Dawn Ius was enthusiastic, intelligent, curious, and thorough. Best of all, she taught me important lessons about craft. There's a line in the book, which I attributed to an Irish grandmother, but actually came from my Yiddish grandmother. Whenever my bubbe learned something new, she would say, "I'm glad I didn't die yesterday or I wouldn't have known that." To all my readers, I hope you feel that way when you finish *On The Shore*.

vine leaves press

Enjoyed this book?
Go to *vineleavespress.com* to find more.